RON EISELE

1917

Brotherhood of the Sky

Also by Ron Eisele

1917 Inherit the Blue
1917 Brotherhood of the Sky
1918 Blue Skies Aloft
The Black Albatros
Colette
1918 The Unforgiving Sky
Artois Gold

Keep up to date with all the latest book titles by
visiting Ron Eisele's Amazon biography page at
Amazon.co.uk. If you would like to find out more,
please follow Ron's Twitter account @ron_eisele

1917 Brotherhood of the Sky

This edition published 2020

Copyright Ron Eisele 2020

Cover design and book formatting by Lyndon Smith.

Contents

1. LOST AND FOUND

It was late afternoon on Sunday, the sixteenth of December 1917. A dull grey sky cast its watery light across 323 Squadron's aerodrome near Avesnes-le-Comte, a village northwest of Arras. Seated alone at his office desk, Major Freddy Wright leaned back in his chair and carefully re-read a letter he had just completed. The ink was still wet on the final paragraph.

'Your son had despatched his sixth enemy aeroplane in flames when I saw his own machine going down. The weather was very misty below and the fighting was intense. Another enemy machine came from behind and above and shot him down. Lieutenant Frank D'Arcy was, I think, one of the most dashing air fighters I have ever come across. His career with 323 Squadron has been brilliant. To all of us his loss and that of his observer Sergeant Fiske has been a terrible blow; your son set a wonderful example to the newer fellows. He was one of the keenest pilots I have ever met, and there never was a braver.'

Satisfied with this, his third draft, he signed off:

'With heartfelt sympathy

Major F. H. Wright

Commanding Officer, 323 Squadron'.

Freddy had to pause twice during his composition, overwhelmed with emotion. No matter how many similar letters of condolence he had written the effect was the same. In the quiet of his wooden hut, with only the gentle ticking of a wall clock for company, he could well imagine the recipient reading his inadequate words.

There was a sharp knock on the old, rustic timber door.

"Enter!"

323 Squadron's care-worn Adjutant, Captain Hugh Boyard, stepped over the threshold. His arrival accompanied by a strong odour of tar-lotion, a treatment he hoped would stem the loss of his once wavy brown hair.

"Patrol orders for tomorrow just in. Thought you'd like to see them before they're posted in the Mess."

"Very well, let's have a look." Freddy sighed with resignation. "Ypres-Comines Canal again I assume?"

"Afraid so." Boyard passed the papers across before warming his hands together over a small stove heater. "To Frank's parents I suppose?" He nodded toward the freshly sealed envelope on Freddy's desk.

"Yes, poor fellow. Rotten luck so close to Christmas. I've written another for Billy Fiske's family."

"Their things are all safely packed, saw to it myself." Boyard hesitated before picking up the two letters. "I'll get these sent off first thing in the morning."

"Please. Hopefully they'll arrive before those damned impersonal telegrams."

Freddy examined the fresh orders from Wing H.Q. at Saint-Pol-sur-Ternoise with dismay. "Offensive Patrol. Take-off at dawn, seven-o-clock. Thank Heaven there's only eight hours of daylight!" He glanced at the map pinned to his wall. "Fifty five miles to Ypres, fifty five back. Forecast is for an east wind at ten thousand feet tomorrow. The cold wind brings some benefit I suppose."

"Still no news about Carter and Pechell. Should have heard something by now." Boyard studied the scratched glass crystal of his military issue wristwatch. "Missing for three hours. Last seen our side, Plugstreet Wood, so there's hope." He shook his head in exasperation. "Damn I hate not knowing." Despite the stove's warmth, Boyard's teeth chattered with cold. "I've got

Sergeant Bonnestall manning the office telephone. Told him to report to us immediately anything comes through."

"Well, until then we'll just have to be patient and hope for the best." Freddy locked his desk drawer, replaced the cap on his fountain pen and slowly rose from his barrel-back leather chair "Dinner's in less than an hour Hugh. I've just about had enough for today. You all wrapped up here?"

"Yes."

"Right then, let's get ourselves over to the Mess. I want every officer present, not moping in their billets."

Heading west, eight thousand feet above Comines, Lieutenant 'Seb' Carter of 323 Squadron listened intently to the struggling Rolls-Royce Falcon III engine. With over two hundred hours experience piloting the two-seat Bristol Fighter F2b his ears had become attuned to every nuance. He could tell by sound alone if the mixture was too rich, a plug had cut out or a rocker arm broken. He focused his weary eyes on the haphazard arrangement of cockpit instruments. Petrol quantity was lower than it should be. He adjusted the fuel tank air pressure system and manipulated the controls, suspecting both main and reserve had been holed during their recent encounter with a Fokker Dr1. Loss of pressure was not in itself critical as gravity would provide an adequate feed to the engine, provided he avoided full power and a steep nose up attitude. It was a delicate balancing act, Carter needed to concentrate on maintaining as high a speed as possible.

Five minutes earlier Carter and his observer, Second Lieutenant Percy Pechell, had passed through a vicious curtain of anti-aircraft fire or 'Archie' nine thousand feet above the lines between Menin and Halluin. The air was agitated by the passage of shells whose wakes shook their fragile machine. It was one of those occasions where the difference between life and death was no more than pure luck. At the peak of the barrage Carter had responded to a slap on his right shoulder by shifting around in his cockpit to face Pechell. His observer was pointing out an aerodrome marked on his map near a town named La Gorgue. Repositioning himself, Carter noticed a jagged piece of shrapnel had cut through the upper wing mid-section and embedded itself in the cockpit's upper sloping longeron. He eyed the jagged shard with detached interest. If he hadn't moved he'd have been dead. His attitude to the high altitude bursts of shellfire never changed. Just fly through, nothing else you could do about it.

After two and a half hours of a long and arduous patrol Pechell was more than usually tired. Damp, pounding air penetrated his layers of clothing, slowly stealing away what remained of his bodily warmth. There was no protection in the rear seat. His back, shoulders and arms had been constantly pummeled by the freezing, whipping wind. Strapped tightly over his head was a fur lined brown leather flying hood. It had an aperture barely sufficient for the seal of his tinted goggles to attach to his face, yet even that was no match for the penetrating, driven air. His fingers, stiff and frigid, had ceased to bend properly. Thrusting his left hand into the pocket of his flight coat, he withdrew a small felt covered cylinder filled with a slow burning smoldering material. After passing his 'winter warmer' several times from one bared hand to the other he stowed it and replaced his gloves.

Beyond the tail, the eastern sky was awash with grey, hazy light. Interrupting his constant scan of the sky, Pechell looked down over the starboard side of their ailing Brisfit. Far below, beyond the rippling fabric, rust flaked exhaust and quivering control cables, he could see the dramatic effect of constant shelling east of Armentières. Across the flat landscape of north-eastern France, amid broken banks of streams and the winding River Lys, the terrain was nothing more than one big, disgusting mire. Splintered trees, demolished farms and dead horses were scattered amid craters filled with ice and dull green water. In places, the blackened skeletons of burnt out aeroplanes with buckled wings lay where they had fallen from the sky. Amid this desolation were darks specs, some moving, some still. Occasionally, puffs of black smoke would appear on the ground before slowly dissipating. To the north, Hollebeke was no more than a brick coloured stain on the wilderness.

The extreme desolation began to seep into Pechell's very soul. He shuddered at the thought of men living and fighting amid such chaos. Bitter cold at night, nowhere near a fire, it was hardly surprising the army had become demoralized, like so many others they could see no end to the war.

The Brisfit maintained a steady descent above Warneton-Sud and the Lys. Pechell had already secured his Mk.II Lewis gun and safely stowed his precious photographic plates in preparation for landing. Suddenly their engine faltered and the revolutions dropped alarmingly. From an indicated one hundred and twenty miles an hour Carter sensed the immediate deceleration associated with the two-seater's high drag airframe. Manipulating the joystick and rudder controls he lowered the nose sharply to maintain a safe airspeed, then throttled back and adjusted the radiator setting to steady the coolant temperature.

Seated in the observer's rearward facing cockpit, Pechell's stomach clenched in reaction to the sudden plummet. He instinctively grabbed the Scarff gun ring for support. There was little he could do to help and he knew better than to disturb his pilot unnecessarily. Settling down, he kept as much of his upper body below the coaming as possible to reduce drag and minimize airflow turbulence over the tail surface.

Carter was busy managing their faltering engine and maintaining sufficient altitude to reach La Gorgue. Approaching from the north-east, he flew by the feel of his joystick, the rudder bar under his feet and the wind on his face as he positioned the Brisfit for landing. Tired and insufferably cold, he adjusted his silk scarf to avoid the ever-present threat of frostbite. Despite muskrat fur-lined leather gauntlets, his fingertips were frozen and stung painfully as he moved his right hand away from the joystick to close the radiator shutter control. The chinstrap of his flying cap was continuously buffeted by slipstream. He pulled the brim down so that it was just below the edge of the slowly setting sun. Although restricting his general lookout, it improved the view ahead considerably. Accumulated oil, dust and cordite had smeared his goggles and the crazed windscreen glass did not help matters. Despite the glare and a layer of rapidly forming ground fog, two miles from the aerodrome he could clearly see the dark grey 'Union Jack' crisscross of cinder runways ahead amid the green and mud brown stretch of level ground.

With his eyes in line with the upper wing, Carter's view forward was excellent. He advanced the engine timing ready for landing. Flying at a steady sixty miles an hour he adjusted the radiator shutters once again to keep the Brisfit's struggling engine at an operating temperature of eighty degrees Celsius. Less than a mile from touchdown and at a thousand feet altitude he checked the security of his lap-belt while deftly correcting for each gust of bumpy, low level turbulence that rocked the wings.

The Brisfit's long shadow flickered across the ruined remains of Estaires and the old road leading east to Merville. Clearing the crests of tall Poplar trees that lined both banks of the Lys with barely feet to spare, Carter input small adjustments to the sensitive elevator and slowly raised the aeroplane's nose. He was aiming for the longest of three intersecting runways directly ahead. Crossing the threshold at fifty-five miles an hour, the undercarriage wheels and tail-skid touched down simultaneously in a classic 'three-point' landing. After a small bounce the Brisfit began to decelerate. Carter maintained a straight run by holding the stick fully back, applying weight on the tailskid as it etched a long, shallow furrow in the rolled cinder landing strip.

Pechell gave sigh of relief, but Carter was too experienced to be lulled into a false sense of security. Their approach to La Gorgue had, by necessity, been out of the prevailing breeze. As the unwieldy Brisfit swung off course, he instinctively combined quick movements on the rudder with a brief bursts of power to avoid a groundloop. The earthbound aeroplane responded, running straight back on line.

Compensating for the precessional swing of the propeller Carter maintained directional control as breathless ground crew sprinted across the apron to greet the new arrival. Helping hands took hold of each lower wingtip and guided the Brisfit and her exhausted crew the final yards to the nearest hangar. As they rolled out to a standstill Carter opened the radiator shutters to prevent overheating, retarded the timing and reduced engine speed. With the chocks in place he could finally think about relaxing. He allowed the engine to run for a minute while the temperature stabilised. After depleting what little remained of fuel tank air pressure, he turned off the selector and switches. The sudden silence was almost physical. Carter unbuckled his leather flight cap and slowly slid it back across his oil matted hair. He sat for a moment and listened to the gentle ticking of the powerful V-12 engine as it cooled. Pechell reached forward and slapped him firmly on the shoulders. Carter turned round and the two men shook hands. Neither could speak, their faces were too frozen to enunciate words properly. The next problem they faced was getting out of the aeroplane unassisted with feet, arms and legs numb from the cold.

Carter clambered out of his cockpit first. Holding onto the padded coaming with both hands, he slid slowly down the port fuselage side. The toe of his left boot dragged against the already scuffed fabric while his right foot sought out the stirrup. He dropped the last few feet and crunched down onto the cinders before reaching up to receive the maps and precious film plates being handed down by Pechell. Having safely delivered his cargo, Pechell climbed out of his cockpit and sat for a moment astride his Lewis gun ring before sliding to the ground with as much dignity as he could muster.

La Gorgue had been the home of 321 Squadron since the sixth of October 1917. Situated on abandoned farmland less than a mile east of Merville village, the aerodrome was bordered by two converging waterways. To the south lay the River Lawe and to the north the winding Lys Canal. The two water courses merged in the east, beyond the main farmhouse and a cluster of rural outbuildings. Clusters of drab, conical tents had been erected along the aerodrome's south-east perimeter. Seven corrugated iron hangars faced south across acres of open earthy loam farmland on which three cinder runways had been established.

Across the Canal's sloping reed-grown banks, rows of tall denuded Poplar trees cast their long, late afternoon shadows. As the December sun slowly dissolved into a misty horizon, it created a tangle of rainbows in oily puddles that lay motionless between deeply rutted tracks and isolated thickets of lifeless thorns. After three years of war, Beaupré Farm's arable land had become barren and desolate, while the old russet farmhouse provided facilities for squadron administration. Outside its' brick walls, amid dozens of parked Crossley tenders, a crowd of khaki clad soldiers busied themselves loading and unloading guns and other war paraphernalia. Their exhaled breath ascended in visible puffs to join the darkening sky.

Seated at his desk, acting Major Benjamin 'Bungee' Smith, 321's Commanding Officer, listened intently as Carter continued his report. He was a well-built man with a weather beaten face, deep-set grey eyes and unruly dark brown hair. His small, dimly lit office was cluttered with paperwork, filing cabinets and souvenirs from numerous air battles. The unventilated air was heavy with smoke from Bond Street cigarettes and the sweet aroma of Fuller's chocolate peppermint creams. Bungee's Adjutant, the one-handed Captain Medley Sant, sat at the far end of the desk, pen poised. Having landed less than ten minutes earlier Carter tried to disregard his painfully inflamed legs, feet, arms and hands. He'd always been susceptible to chilblains. The itching was almost unbearable.

"Carry on then, let's have the rest of it." Bungee encouraged.

Carter shifted uncomfortably in his chair. "The entire affair started off badly, two oiled plugs so we left late. East wind blowing, the machine climbed slowly. Went over the lines at nine thousand feet. Archie thick as fog, but nothing very close. We climbed to eleven and a half then the engine revs got stuck. Throttled down a bit then opened her up and climbed to twelve thousand. Just after three-thirty we'd photographed an enemy encampment at Breskins, south of Thourout, then Pechell indicated he wanted to go east as he'd spotted something he wanted to investigate on the road north of Vrijgeweed. He'd got his photographs and we were on our way back when a half hour later we were bounced by a Tripehound. Haven't seen one for weeks but there he was, came up behind and slightly below. Neither of us noticed him until the blighter started firing. I turned left straight away and Pechell brought his Lewis to bear. I just caught a glimpse of the Hun over my left shoulder, he disappeared behind us and fired again before making a big right handed sweep in the direction of Dadizeele. Whole thing lasted no more than thirty seconds. I was going to follow him but he must have hit our engine, the revs were dropping so we set course for home. Crossed the trenches between Neuve Chappelle and Bois Grenier at eight thousand feet, by that time the engine was losing speed and I knew reaching Avesnes-le-Comte would be impossible. Pechell suggested La Gorgue, so I throttled right down and followed the Lys. Never landed here before, nursed her in until I knew we were well within reach. Fortunately I could see the field quite clearly and made a pretty decent landing. Low sun was damnably tricky though."

Bungee laughed dismissively. "Always land with my eyes closed myself, don't find the sun an issue at all."

"It's hardly a laughing matter." Carter retorted soberly. "Nearly ran off the runway into one of those damn drainage gullies."

"Don't I know it." Sant acknowledged ruefully. "The place is a shocker. We arrived here from Vélu in early October, shortly after 35 Squadron moved up north to La Lovie. They're the ones who laid down the cinder runways, without them La Gorgue's nothing more than an overgrown bog and earthed up potato rows."

"Whoever decided to send a Camel squadron here needs his brains tested." Bungee interjected. "To the north you've got the Lys Canal lined with a mass of tall woody Poplars, to the south, rows of hangars backed by a road, the River Lawe and a railway line. In our first week here five of our machines ran off the cinder tracks while landing, three on take-off. Every one ended up with their tails in the air, broken props and damaged engines."

"So how've you managed?" Carter enquired.

"We use the old Merville aerodrome field, it's a couple of hundred yards west of here on the other side of the Lys. The place has been vacant since 16 Squadron moved out."

"Wish I'd known about that earlier." Carter fumbled for a packet of cigarettes from deep within a pocket of his flying overalls. "Anyway, I was near out of fuel. Came down as close to the centre cinder square as I could just in case we drifted." As Bungee offered him a cigar, Carter added as an afterthought. "I expect on a clear day you can see this place from miles away."

"That's true." Sant acknowledged as he leaned across the desk, offering Carter a monogrammed silver lighter in his steady right hand. "Which is pretty rotten as far as camouflage goes."

Immediately Carter inhaled, the strong tobacco smoke went straight to his head. After hours at altitude he experienced a sudden wave of overwhelming fatigue.

"We won't be able to get back to Avesnes tonight, that's for sure."

Sant gathered his paperwork together then stood up and stretched his back. "I'll arrange overnight accommodation for you both. Afraid we're a bit short of space, the billet huts are full so you'll have to share a room in the old field hospital here at Beaupré Farm. Sorry it's not much, but a lot better than having to trudge all the way into Estaires for a bed."

Bungee glanced at his wristwatch. "We take breakfast and luncheon here. Dinner's seven-thirty sharp in the Merville Farm Mess. There's an iron bridge across the Canal." He leaned back in his chair, raised both legs and rested them carelessly on the desk. His shiny, nut brown leather cavalry boots crushed a pile of official paperwork. "You'll enjoy your stay, we've got our own miniature world here. Chaps from every corner of the Empire, Canadians, New Zealanders, South Africans, one or two English and an Irishman or two. We're a mixed crowd and a very chipper lot, especially the Canadians, free-living kind of fellows."

Sant was already heading toward the office door. "I'll get your people on the telephone Carter. Give them the news you're both safe."

Back at Avesnes-le-Comte, a fresh dusting of drifting snow had settled across the frozen ground surrounding 323 Squadron's Mess hut. The inside was illuminated by the soft, flickering light of a dozen or so trench oil lanterns. The Mess was strangely quiet, only the voices of the pilots calling their hands at cards and the chink of bets dropping into the saucer on the table. The squadron had lost four men in two days after six weeks without a single fatality and no-one was in the mood for small-talk. Freddy Wright leant heavily on the bar, a double measure of whisky and ice before him. Condensation was beading the outside of the glass as he absentmindedly flicked through a well-thumbed copy the 'Sketch'. A young Lieutenant by the name of Oscar Olsen approached. Freddy knew Olsen well, a tousled haired youth of nineteen years who had abandoned his university studies to join the RFC as soon as his age permitted. A likeable chap and an excellent pilot, he was inclined to be overly aggressive. Freddy was protective of him and took a particular interest in his welfare.

"Any news about Carter boss?"

"Sorry Olsen, nothing."

"Oh heavens." Olsen's downcast expression betrayed his anxiety. "Not Carter and Pechell as well as D'Arcy and Fiske." There was a fleeting glimmer of hope in his eyes. "I did hear two artillery fellows report seeing them cross the lines under control. It's a damned shame if they've gone though. We really need them!"

"So do their families back home." Freddy spoke his thoughts aloud. He was aware of the gloom that descended across the entire Mess. In a far corner, the lads closest to D'Arcy and Fiske had settled down to a gloomy booze-up. The men's morale was understandably low. He beckoned everyone to join him. "Well, come on then you chaps, what're you all going to have?"

It had just passed seven-fifteen when an urgent knock on the Mess door was answered by one of the attendant stewards. Outside stood Sergeant Bonnestall, his grim features accentuated by the overhead porch lantern. There followed a brief exchange of words. The steward strode purposely toward Freddy across the suddenly silent room. "Pardon me Sir, Sergeant Bonnestall presents his compliments and says there's an urgent telephone call in your office."

"Right." Freddy downed his drink and slowly lowered the empty glass on the bar. After a meaningful glance at Boyard he exited the Mess. Bonnestall stepped aside allowing his C.O. to pass through the narrow doorway unhindered. "Good or bad Bonnestall?" Freddy closed the door behind him and braced himself for the Sergeant's reply.

"Can't say Sir. The Captain wanted to speak with you personally." In the bitter winter air, Bonnestall's exhaled breath formed a cloud of vapour that ascended into the dark, clouded night sky.

Tufts of crisp, frozen long grass crunched under Freddy's feet as he paced purposefully to his office. Passing the wireless hut, the muffled voices from the Officer's Mess became fainter. By the time he reached his destination only the steady, distant hum of the squadron's power generator masked the night's rural silence. Bonnestall opened the door and allowed his Squadron Commander to enter unimpeded. Under the harsh light of a single, unshaded pendant light bulb Freddy sat on one corner of his desk and lifted the cold metal telephone receiver to his ear. He inhaled deeply before announcing.

"Major Wright here."

For a moment he could hear nothing but the crackle of interference down the line. Then a disembodied voice.

"Captain Sant here, 321 Squadron, you'll be pleased to know we've got your chaps Carter and Pechell. They're fine."

Freddy smiled broadly and covered the telephone mouthpiece with his free hand. "Bonnestall, get back over to the Mess, tell them Lieutenants Carter and Pechell are safe would you?"

Bonnestall's back straightened immediately. He saluted sharply. "Yes Sir!"

A short while after Bonnestall's departure, Freddy was jotting down further details when he heard an uproar of cheers carry across the chill night air. He smiled and suddenly remembered how hungry he was. The squadron would dine well tonight.

Fifteen minutes later Freddy hurried back to the throng. The temperature outside had already dropped several degrees and he regretted leaving his tunic in the Mess. Boyard was first to greet him on his arrival.

"Well?" Boyard enquired anxiously.

"The boys came down safely at 321, La Gorgue. Had a few words with their C.O. Bungee Smith, seems their machine's damaged and likely take around 24 hours to repair. I said they should stay put for now and fly it back on Tuesday."

"That's a weight off the old shoulders." Boyard relaxed and inclined his head towards the gathered smiling faces. "As you can see it's bucked the fellows up no end."

As if on cue, the senior Mess steward struck the dinner gong. Freddy and Boyard made their way to their usual seats at the head of the table.

"Haven't had much to do with 321, what's their C.O. like by the way? This 'Bungee' fellow?" Boyard asked as they drew up their chairs amid a clatter of wooden seat legs on the bare timber floor.

Freddy chuckled amiably. "Old Bungee? Everyone admires him immensely, but he can be a bloody nuisance at times."

"Really?" Boyard encouraged.

"Trouble is he's overconfident, always has been." Freddy confided. "He's a born leader but totally insensitive most of the time, very little imagination too, makes his life easier I suppose. Probably why he takes on so many risks." Freddy watched appreciatively as the steward carefully poured a generous quantity of 1914 Château Margaux Bordeaux into his wine glass. "Mind you, I've never seen Bungee depressed, always puts on a show of good spirits. An excellent squadron man with a very strong, irrepressible character. Whatever he says or does commands the chap's attention. He's got a wonderful collection of lads too. Since they swapped their old Strutters for Camels they're right on their toes, morale is very high. You'd be hard put to find such a jolly crowd. Great camaraderie."

"Well, you know what they say about the Sopwith Camel." Boyard remarked as he tucked a corner of his napkin into his collar. "It'll get you either a wooden cross, the Red Cross, or a Victoria Cross."

Freddy leaned back to allow the steward to place a steaming hot bowl of carrot and onion soup before him.

"Ah, hot grub. Tuck in Boyard!"

+----

Carter opened the billet door and cast his eyes disapprovingly around their temporary accommodation at Beaupré Farm. The room was sparsely furnished. It contained two wooden chairs, a large open fireplace with no grate, a wooden table about two foot six square covered with white American cloth and two cot beds made up entirely of army blankets. Hanging from a hook on the bare-brick wall was Pechell's full length flight coat, every crease in the brown leather exaggerated by accumulated dirt, oil and cordite. Next to it hung the holster of his Mark II Smith and Wesson revolver. Having disrobed from his flying gear and washed, Pechell was already recumbent on his bed reading the previous day's edition of 'The Times.'

"Turn the old lantern up a bit Carter, getting dark in here." Pechell's weathered face appeared over the top of his well-thumbed newspaper.

Carter fumbled with the unfamiliar French 'belle lampe à petrole.' A legacy from the pre-war civilian owners. The room filled immediately with a soft flickering light.

It had been several months since the autumn when 321 Squadron changed their outdated two seat Sopwith one-and-a-half Strutters for single seat Camels. With no further need for observers Pechell applied for flight training, but his reputation had not gone unnoticed. Before his request could be processed he was poached by Major Freddy Wright and transferred to 323 Squadron to team up with Carter as his regular observer/gunner. The two men subsequently became firm friends.

"You all done with debrief then?" Pechell casually enquired.

Carter unfastened his boots, sat on the end of his allocated mattress and briskly rubbed his inflamed legs. "Just about everything I could remember. You?"

"Gave the notes and photographic plates to Sant."

"Anything worthwhile going on back home then?" Carter inclined his head towards Pechell's discarded broadsheet.

"Just the usual; headlines about an armistice with the Bolsheviks. The suffragettes making a bloody fuss as usual."

Carter smiled enigmatically. "While we're out here doing the fighting so that they can bomb Westminster Abbey and go around spouting their half-baked ideas."

"Not a supporter of universal suffrage then?"

"I'm for all types of opinion old boy. All they want and saying what they want, provided they don't irritate other people and disturb the peace." Carter paused for a moment, recalling his meeting in Bungee's office. "Medley Sant gave me the impression of being a singular sort of chap. Couldn't help notice he's got the M.C. and D.S.O."

Pechell swung round and sat up on the side of his bed. "He was a star turn with 321. I went up as his observer a couple of times back in the spring. A jolly good pilot with pin-sharp eyesight."

"Did you get any Huns together?"

"No, well not officially anyway. It wasn't for the want of trying though." Pechell smiled at the recollection. "My regular driver was Bertie Alderton. Both of us had this great rivalry with the rest over victories. It was Bungee's idea, he put up a weekend's leave in Amiens as a prize for the most Huns downed by August."

"Must have been an interesting time." Carter observed dryly.

"Oh, it was very competitive, but there was always a sense of friendliness and at least some support among the other chaps, despite the fact everyone knew he was going to be the top scorer."

"Who won?"

"We got five between us. Bungee received the official confirmation and announced our victory in the briefing room." Pechell massaged his tired eyes with the palms of both hands, then blinked in an attempt to re-focus. "Stationed at Léchelle at the time. I remember we were both so elated, then we looked around and there were the others. It was a pretty poignant moment I can tell you, they'd all tried just as hard as us. Every one of them came over and shook our hands until we were the only two men in the hut."

"What about Sant?"

Pechell shrugged. "Shot down and injured on twenty-seventh July near Polygon Wood. His observer was killed. By then every enemy machine could completely out-manoeuver our Strutters. They could beat us climbing, turning and in outright speed. Sant spent eight weeks away in hospital, that's when he lost his hand."

"He was grounded?"

Pechell nodded. "His left arm was just about paralysed. Being told he couldn't fly was the worst thing that could have happened to him. The squadron has a strong sense camaraderie though, once the chaps found out they felt sorry for the old bugger. Bungee made sure 321 got him back on strength once he'd recovered. Of course, by then I'd moved over to 323."

"So he became Adjutant?"

"Yes, made a good job of it too by all accounts. He's a top man to deal with headquarters and look after squadron affairs. Doesn't have to worry about flying anymore, so it's a great advantage to the men having him watch their backs." Pechell reclined back on his bed. "From what I've seen 321 are a better squadron for him doing what he's doing. Mind you, he's still mad as hell he's not fighting."

At seven in the evening Carter and Pechell left their room at Beaupré Farm looking forward to a hearty dinner and convivial company in the Merville Mess. The crystalline crunch of fresh snow accompanied every step as they crossed the fifty foot span iron bridge across the Lys to the north bank. Thereon a trail of oil lamps guided them the short distance across the field to their destination. On the way Carter pondered the many friendly greetings Pechell had received after they landed.

"I expect it feels good to be back among the old team. Notice many differences since you left?"

"Not really. Squadron's still full of the old enthusiastic, motivated, dedicated fellows. Don't think that's changed much."

"Come on." Carter chided good naturedly. "Couldn't have all been harmony and good fellowship. There must have been a few rifts?"

"Oh, there were some jealousies among the lads, particularly over claims and flight allocations. Several times Bungee had to call someone or another into his office for a fairly harsh discussion to straighten things out."

"How did they take it?" Carter stepped aside to avoid a frosted puddle embedded in the hardened earth.

"You need to remember, although Bungee's the be all and end all to the boys, he knows everything about everyone, where the skeletons are hidden. Essentially he told them he's the one running the outfit and, sorry, that's the way it's going to be."

"And the result?"

"They grumbled, but they knew eventually they'd be treated fairly."

The final ten yards of concrete path leading to Merville Farm glistened like white quartz. The door opened and Bungee reached out from within with a welcoming hand.

"Come on in you fellows." He encouraged. "No need to stand on ceremony. Good to see you again Pechell!"

"Your Mess is certainly in better shape than ours." Carter observed casually as he ducked below the low doorframe and glanced around the busy room. There must have been over forty officers present.

"Illusion old chap." Bungee admitted. "Usually a squadron binge begins at dusk and continues until the lads taking part are insensible. The boys have something of a bad reputation I'm afraid. Heavy sessions sometimes result in the smashing up of a Mess or local café. Not last night though, had the Brass at Wing H.Q. call in together with some red-tabbed Third Army staff from Albert so we had to be formal. Tonight it's business as usual."

"Well, I'm glad we didn't drop by yesterday then. Those fellows can really put a dampener on things." Carter observed ruefully.

Bungee laughed. "Oh we had a few diversions. One of our chaps tried to work the 'funnel trick' on a visiting American General; mistook his one star for the badge of a Lieutenant and filled his riding breeches with water!"

"That's right." Sant, standing close by, grimaced at the recollection. "The Army and Navy still regard our discipline as rather peculiar. I reminded our guests that young men give the impression of lightheartedness but that's the way they live. In my opinion nothing can change that and what's more, it works."

Sant accepted a cigar from an attentive steward and, attempting to strike a Lucifer with his right hand, clumsily dropped the matchbox and its entire contents on the floor.

"Damnation!"

"Here." Carter obliged with his own lighter.

"Thanks, still having a tricky time working things out with one hand." Sant sensed the awkward silence. "Dogfight back in July old boy, a dangerous moment. I was concentrating on shooting down an LVG when his little friend came along and tried the same thing on me. In the process filled my left shoulder and arm with lead. Took a while to patch me up. Came out of hospital with one glove too many."

"I hear the chaps were pleased to see you back again though." Carter rejoined, attempting to regain a sense of levity.

Sant chuckled amiably. "Soon as I walked into the Mess, first thing I saw was Bungee here seated at the bar. *'Well if it isn't old Sant back from his holiday!'* He says and slaps me heartily on the shoulder, exactly where that ruddy Albatros got me!"

"So he never tires of telling everyone he meets." Bungee responded ruefully. "Well, Carter. What the deuce made you opt for Pechell as your observer then? Short straw was it?"

"Not really." He lowered his voice. "Truth is he's the only one who could cope with my flying without throwing up."

Sant tapped his head absentmindedly before addressing Bungee.

"I forgot to tell you, we've a new fellow arriving early in the morning; replacement for Walworth. South African fellow, Second Lieutenant from 45 Squadron by the name of Percival. Useful Camel pilot by all accounts with three Huns to his credit. He's travelling up from Fienvillers overnight."

Bungee drained his drink in one swallow, slammed the empty glass down on the bar and gestured the steward for a refill.

"Put him with 'C' flight."

A concerned Pechell enquired after his old comrade.

"What's this about Walworth? What happened?"

"You haven't heard?" Bungee sighed heavily. "His Camel was badly shot up over Comines last week, Curtis his wingman bought it. They were diving on a gasbag and bounced from behind by a group of Fokkers from out the cloud. Walworth destroyed the balloon and managed to get one of the Huns before a burst hit his engine. He went into a spin, pulled out and limped back here where he managed a decent landing just before ten in the morning. He was no good afterwards, had to be sent home in a Red Cross ship. Lost his nerve. When you've lost your nerve, you've had it."

Sant placed his remaining hand on Pechell's shoulder. "Not his fault, but Walworth was a proud man. He saw it as weakness. Taken out of combat without physical injury was something he was ashamed of."

Bungee's careworn expression betrayed the burden of command. "Bad nerves challenge morale, discipline and fighting effectiveness. It spreads like a virus through the whole squadron. I can't allow it to infect my frontline fighters." He continued, as if to himself. "Walworth had been flying for nearly a year with hardly a break. Really ought to have been put on a train home for a rest and instructor duties a while back. Trouble is, out here experienced men who've served the longest are the most needed."

Pechell could not disguise his deep dismay. "I can't believe poor old Curtis has gone." He paused, shaking his head sadly. "And Walworth, I'd rather lose a leg, be wounded, anything but lose my nerve."

For Pechell, the fear of being killed wasn't as bad as the fear of being thought a coward by your comrades and the consequent ostracism that might follow.

While Bungee and Pechell had been engaged in conversation, several of the other officers had already commenced the evening's sporting activity. Lieutenants Alan Butcher and Peter Carpenter were covertly preparing the tables laid out in the dining room, sabotaging the furniture and re-arranging the seating plan. Meanwhile, squadron pianist Charles Findley was at the bar imbibing a few 'sharpeners' to get in the mood ahead of everyone else.

With a bitter cold night outside, the evening progressed in a manner typical of 321 Squadron's post-dinner binges, the kind of celebration that relieved the end of an otherwise 'dud' day. Lurid jokes and tales of sexual conquest increased exponentially in proportion to the amount of alcohol consumed. After the loyal toast the fun really began. Second Lietenant Paul Jamieson crawled underneath the dining table intent on tying Carter's shoelaces together and received a swift kick in the ribs for his efforts. He scrambled back to his place only to find his chair missing. A tousled hair young Lieutenant named Cecil Bamford shamelessly unrolled the latest Kirchner posters and pinned them to the timbered Mess walls to unanimous applause. Bertie Alderton, always ready for a fight on land or in the air, engaged in a duel with his former observer. Their weapons of choice, Pyrene fire extinguishers. Retiring to a safe distance from the combatants Carter took charge of the piano and, hammering out discordant notes, inspired the intoxicated audience to yell choruses of adapted RFC ballads.

It's a long way to 15,000,

It's a long way to roam,

It's a long way to 15,000,

With a Monosoupape Gnome.

Fokkers buzzing round you,

Uhlans down below,

It's a long, long way to 15,000,

But it's the safest place I know.

It may have been the cocktails, but Carter began to bless the good fortune which had brought him to this happy squadron.

Having exhausted their Pyrenes, a soaking wet Alderton and Pechell raised the challenge. "Come on then, who's up for a game of Mess Rugby?"

"What?" Carter left the battered, rosewood piano and pushed his way through the crush.

"If you have to ask, you've never dined properly!" Pechell jibed. "Grab hold of the nearest seat cushion Carter, see if you can score a try at the end of the room. No rules by the way."

Bungee was already assembling his team. "Clear the floor, all tables and chairs to the sides! Jackets and boots off men!" He shouted above the general mayhem. "No spurs!"

Card players had their tables overturned and the bar supporters forgot their drinks in the excitement of the moment.

"Be careful chaps, last time I did this I broke my leg." Captain John Cooper, 'C' Flight Commander, pleaded plaintively.

Carter disrobed as instructed, hoping the crowd would give their visitors fair quarter. He kicked a seat cushion into the middle of the hut. Straight away, devoid of any tactics or strategy except alcohol-fueled aggressiveness, the two sides set-to in a melee of lingering grudges and rivalries.

After five minutes Carter extracted himself from the howling press of humanity. Inspecting a livid carpet burn on his elbow he joined Sant in shouting insults from the sidelines. Moments later an anguished yelp of pain erupted from the scrummage. It was Cooper. "Bugger - I've done it again!"

The Squadron Medical Officer was sobered up and attempted to inspect the injury. Within minutes Cooper, supported on both sides, was limping away to the first aid hut.

Carter shook his head in disbelief. "How many fellows have been struck of duty after playing this game?" He asked.

The M.O. laughed dismissively. "Oh, they're pretty tame these days really, nowhere near the number of broken limbs as two years back."

In the aftermath, kit buttons, loose change and drying patches of blood were spread randomly across the rucked rug and bare board floor. Backlit by the glow of swaying oil-lanterns the seat cushion was in the same spot Carter had kicked it at the start of the game.

Breaking way from the exhausted pandemonium of youth, Findley adopted his usual position at the Mess piano and, in his own inimitable style, began to recite a few songs from the latest London shows. His performance attracted little attention at first, but after a while all present were soon listening with attentive silence to a painfully pleasant glimpse of life at home. By eleven-o-clock the celebrants had been willingly led into happy, alcohol fueled forgetfulness. Carpenter, suffering from an excess of 'vino incompetentus' tried to cover his Mess bill with a game of poker while Bungee ambled over to examine the following day's patrol orders posted on the wall of the Mess.

"Right, off to bed you lot." His booming voice silenced the room. He raised both hands to forestall the expected chorus of disapproval.

"Just in case any of you fellows haven't seen tomorrow's roster. With Cooper out I'm taking 'C' Flight up on a roving commission across the Hindenburg Line, south of Lille to Douai then down east of Cambrai." He clapped his hands together enthusiastically. "Bloody good eh? We'll have the chance to get a few Huns. The whole place is buzzing with the bastards. Tell you what, when the jobs over if we've all got enough fuel and ammunition left we'll hang around between Lieu-St.-Amand and Boistrancourt, see if Jasta four or five are up for a scrap."

One by one the various officers walked or limped off to bed. Soon only Bungee, Sant and one or two others were left. By a quarter to midnight the place was in darkness.

Back in their quarters and ready for bed, Carter and Pechell reviewed their evening.

"Bungee seems an easy going chap." Carter suggested.

"He's quite relaxed on the ground, looks the other way and lets the fellows relieve the tension of constant combat. Mind you, in the air he expects total discipline."

"Sounds like a good C.O."

"He is. Didn't see much of you after the game Carter, how did you get on with the lads tonight?"

"Fairly well, I spoke to a jolly nice chap called Alan Butcher, said he thought he'd met me somewhere, he hadn't, just his way of opening up a conversation. He and Findley were the ones I spoke most to. The rest were a little stand-offish."

Pechell pulled his bedsheets over and settled down with his head on his pillow. "Don't take it personally old chap. Some of them have been at this game for a long time. I expect they see Brisfit drivers as an alien species."

There followed a period of silence. Outside the dormer window was a starless, matt black darkness. A spider's web of ice crept across the glass. Wintry air seeped through the room's rotten door joints, leaching away every lick of warmth from the fading fireplace embers. Carter could feel the chill through his blankets. He was in no mood for sleep.

"I can't believe D'Arcy and Fiske have gone. Just awful."

Pechell responded wearily. "Try and get a good night's sleep." His bed creaked noisily as he turned over. "With that ruddy motor transport park below our window there's not much chance of a peaceful lie-in tomorrow."

It was seven-o-clock on the morning of Monday, December the seventeenth 1917. Sunrise was still an hour away. Under a clear twilight sky the ground was heavy with frost and ice crystals reflected light from a myriad of aerodrome lanterns. Lined up outside 'C' Flight's corrugated iron hangars at Merville a half dozen Sopwith Camels were being attentively prepared by their respective fitters and riggers. The half-light tranquility was suddenly broken by a raised voice.

"My machine still not fit to fly?" Bungee demanded, angrily striking out with his cane on an empty oil drum.

"Sorry Sir, we've been working on her all night." The young fitter's hands began to shake nervously.

"I should bloody well hope so!" Bungee stormed. "Get the damn spare out, I'll take that." Turning on his heel he stomped back to the briefing hut.

Flight Sergeant Collins, who'd overheard the brusque admonishment, extinguished his cigarette and strolled over for a quiet word with the pale faced young engineer. "Don't take it to heart lad. The C.O can be bloody rude and insufferable when he's in a bad mood, he'll go for anyone without reason. Just let it brush over you."

Having enjoyed a hearty breakfast at Beaupré Farm, Carter and Pechell were chatting in the corridor outside the Mess with Lieutenant Arnold Percival. 321 Squadron's newest member had arrived a few hours earlier and, after signing in, was already kitted out ready for dawn patrol.

"Eaten yet Percival?" Carter enquired.

"Oh, just the usual breakfast before a patrol, you know, mug of tea and a throw up."

"Pretty rotten being sent up so soon. I thought you'd at least be given a chance to unpack. You must be fagged out." Carter responded sympathetically.

"C.O's orders apparently, we're a man short." Percival shrugged his shoulders in resignation as together the three men walked out into the grey morning air.

"Dawn on a December morning is hardly the cheeriest time is it?" Carter turned up his collar then thrust his hands into the pockets of his leather flying coat. "Come on, we'll walk over to the Merville sheds together."

They arrived just in time to hear Bungee's brusque exchange outside the hangars.

"Bit harsh that." Percival cautiously observed.

Pechell shrugged, he'd seen it all before. "Bungee can be damned aggressive in his manner with the lower ranks. Unsociable to say the least. Never a 'please' or 'thank you'. Most of the ground crew are terrified of him."

"Do you think he puts it on?" Carter enquired.

"No, it's just his way." Pechell cast his gaze toward the slowly brightening eastern horizon. "All part of his egotism I suppose, personally I think it's that kind of attitude that keeps him going when other chaps would give up."

Still bristling with antipathy, Bungee paced purposely across the frosted grass toward them mouthing the worst profanities imaginable.

"Who the bloody hell are you?" He demanded of the new arrival.

"Second Lieutenant Percival Sir, Arnold Percival."

Bungee eyed the young airman for a few seconds. "You'll do. You can fly on my right wing this morning." He poked him firmly in the ribs with the stem of his Bulldog pipe. "And may God help

29

you if I get shot down."

Percival was both stunned and elated by his unexpected elevation. Bungee's outward behaviour changed. His rage dissipated and the affable C.O. returned.

"Call me Bungee. Come on then, you two as well, there's still enough time for another brew before the off." He encouraged. "Probably the best in the Corps. It'll help keep the cold out."

Sitting in the Reports Hut annexed to Merville Farm, Percival cupped a hot enameled mug of tea between both hands and listened intently as Bungee made a brief, formal introduction, then quickly moved on to the order of the day.

"South of Lille to Douai this morning, then east of Cambrai. Back via St.-Amand and Boistrancourt, I expect you know the layout of the sector well enough?"

"Pretty much."

"Good, you'll be flying 959 today. The old girl's had her fair share of action, took her up myself on Saturday for a run across the lines. If you manage to last 'till Thursday I'll fix you up with one of the new machines we're expecting."

Percival acknowledged Bungee's attempt at dark humour with a wry smile. "Always nice to know your new C.O has confidence in you."

Bungee smiled absently. His thoughts were on the upcoming patrol. He rummaged around inside the deep pockets of his flight coat, withdrawing two sealed letters and a heavily oil stained diary. He deposited them on the table and pushed them across to Carter. "Give these to Sant to hold onto 'till I get back eh?" As always with a flight over the lines, security was paramount. It was remarkable how much the enemy could learn from just a few personal documents.

Twenty minutes later the airmen assembled out on the aerodrome field. A silvery mist hung like a shroud over the Lys, against which the waiting Sopwiths were visible as silhouettes as still as a monochrome photograph. The hangar outlines were becoming clearer in the dawn while, under the unnatural electric glow of their lights, Percival examined his allocated Camel with disdain. Beneath the inner lower wings a fan of spent castor oil had congealed into a crust that completely obscured the fabric. There was a thick, smeared layer of lubricant on the cockpit floor. It clung to every surface with the consistency of brown tar.

Placing the toe of his left boot into the port fuselage stirrup he swung his right leg up and over the Camel's 'hump.' Astride the fuel tank, he ducked his head below the upper mainplane cutout then slid forward and down into the cockpit. Squeezing his shoulders together to clear the narrow coaming he settled into the padded wicker seat and slipped his feet under the straps on the rudder bar. His shins were hard against the carburettor air-intake pipes. The interior had the familiar smell of timber, castor oil and petrol, not to mention absolute fear and loose bowels. Instinctively he checked both the magneto switches were off then opened the main petrol tank tap. With fine adjustment and throttle levers in their correct positions, he manipulated the stick and rudder bar to check the function of all control surfaces.

The fuel tanks were pressurised and from the ground up front came the call of an air mechanic. "Switches off Sir. Petrol on, suck in."

The Camel rocked as its mahogany propeller was pulled round several turns. In the cockpit Percival could hear the sucking, gurgling noise of petrol and castor oil being drawn into the engine. He fastened his waist belt, wound his scarf around his mouth and nose and secured his helmet chinstrap. With the propeller stationary at its ten-o-clock position there came the call. "Contact please Sir."

Percival flicked both brass magneto switches to their 'on' position. "Contact!"

The Camel's propeller swung smartly over compression and the attached 130 horsepower Clerget 9B engine started faultlessly. An intermittent crackle of power ensued as the airscrew swept clouds of grey exhaust gasses back beneath the cowling and under the wings. Percival's white silk scarf whipped out horizontally over the upper rear fuselage. The bitter, driven airflow felt like a whetted knife against the exposed flesh of his face. He ran the engine up, holding the stick right back as the rigger lay over the rear fuselage to help to keep the tail down. Wary of overheating, Percival verified the motor's smooth operation. Having witnessed a fatal accident at Fienvillers, he would never attempt take-off with a misfire.

He depressed the magneto 'blip' button. With three hundred and eighty pounds of rotary engine spinning at twelve hundred revolutions per minute, the Camel's wings rocked from side to side with the torque release. Pushing forward the throttle lever he gradually open out the fine adjustment to achieve the correct mixture. Black exhaust smoke meant too much petrol, white too much oil. The engine surged in response. On Percival's command, the ground crew removed both wheel chocks. After checking the windsock he gave a burst to the engine to take the weight off the tail-skid and applied sufficient rudder to blow the tail around and turn into the west wind. The Camel's wheels rolled forward, traversing the uneven, frost-hardened ground. He taxied out across Merville's open grass field using the magneto cut-out switch as little as possible.

With the thick ends of two Vickers guns dominating the upper cockpit area and an Aldis sight between them, forward visibility on the ground was severely restricted. Percival looked out sideways to check the course was clear before turning into his line of vision. He kept the stick back while running across the grass, correcting the Camel's tendency to tail bounce. The engine began popping, sounding much like the staccato crackle of a Lewis machine gun. He cut down the fine fuel adjustment and regained optimum running. At the far end of the field he opened up, kicking plenty of left rudder to prevent a swing to the right. His speed increased and he pushed the stick forward. The tail-skid lifted off the ground, high enough to give him visibility over the engine cowling. As the pressure against the stick rose he eased it back until, after a hundred and fifty feet, the rumble of the undercarriage wheels vanished.

Flying west, parallel to the Lys at only a few miles per hour above stalling speed the Camel was noticeably tail-heavy. With a full twenty four gallon main fuel tank behind his back, a four gallon gravity tank and the weight of two, five hundred round belts of .303 ammunition on board, aileron response was characteristically slow and lethargic. On his left, the farm buildings at Crinquette Lotte passed by a hundred feet below. Inputting a slight forward movement to his joystick he retained altitude until his airspeed reached a hundred and fifteen miles per hour. Then, with the controls at a more sensitive level, he climbed steadily to two thousand feet maintaining a straight course above the town of Merville. Another lesson he'd learnt, never turn a Camel before gaining sufficient height.

Adjusting the spade handle joystick a few inches to the left, Percival moved it back toward his stomach, simultaneously applying a touch of left rudder. The control inputs sent the Camel into a seventy mile an hour spiraling left hand vertical bank. While the pale horizon raced around he eased the rudder, allowing the gyroscopic effect of his spinning Clerget rotary engine to push the aeroplane's nose skywards. Within a minute he'd ascended a further thousand feet and positioned himself above and slightly behind Bungee's right wing. Coordinating petrol and throttle to compensate for increased altitude, he could hear an immediate improvement in the engine's tone. The Camel's control response was so precise it felt like an extension to his own body. With all six Sopwiths in formation Bungee fired a green signal flare and the patrol set course east. Far ahead the ground and the sky seemed to melt into one. There was no horizon, just grey monochrome.

Subtle hues of colour were appearing with the morning light across Merville aerodrome. After watching the Camels disappear into the distance, Carter and Pechell caught sight of Sant who was standing alone in the shadows. Carter handed him the bundle of papers entrusted to him by Bungee. Sant slipped them into the pocket of his double-breasted greatcoat, leaned forward and gestured skyward with the stem of his pipe. "If I've learned anything, it's much easier to climb into an aeroplane and fly off for a fight than to sit on the ground and watch others doing it."

Carter and Pechell began to retrace their steps back across the Lys toward the hangars at La Gorgue. With nothing else to occupy their time, Carter in particular was keen to oversee the repairs to his Brisfit. They carefully traversed unfamiliar ground with only the distant lights of Merville Farm and an occasional lantern to guide their way. The frozen Lys and the land on either side was shrouded in a layer of impenetrable static mist. Above the damp vapour only the railings of the iron bridge were visible. As Carter crossed, he paused for a moment and looked toward the moored barge where he imagined he could see the dark shadows of several standing figures moving around the rough riverside embankment. In the half-light it was difficult to discern any shape or form. The sound of a locomotive, muffled by the mist, could be heard away in the distance. He felt a tug on his sleeve, Pechell was evidently anxious not to linger for any longer than necessary surrounded by the freezing miasma.

In an orderly row, south west of the cinder runways, La Gorgue's seven main corrugated iron hangars backed onto the River Lawe, a line of denuded, stick-like trees and a railway line that linked Merville to Estaires. Below the roof of each hanger a suffused yellow light glowed through partially open doors. The frosted earth and sparse vegetation crunched beneath their feet as Pechell took a hold of Carter's arm.

"That tea has run right through me. You go on ahead, I'll catch up with you later."

Illuminated by electric lights beneath the timber beamed roof of 'C Flight's' nearest hangar, Carter's Brisfit was raised up on trestles between an engineless Avro 504 K and a khaki painted Ford Model 'T' tender. Bullet holes in its fabric had been repaired with glued patches, those awaiting a final, finishing coat of pigmented dope showed clearly the lines of shot. Several punctures in non-critical areas had been overpainted with small 'iron cross' motifs to stabilise the frayed threads. A larger tear on the lower port wing had been stitched together.

Seeing Carter enter the hangar, Flight Sergeant Collins emerged from underneath the Avro's engine cowling. Wiping his hands on a discarded strip of Irish Linen he approached to make his report. After customary salutations, the two men walked together toward the Brisfit.

"We spliced in a repair to your fuselage longeron last night Sir. An enemy round clipped the main fuel tank's front seam, port side. Not much larger than a pinhole, enough to lose pressure. Same bullet chipped the centre section front strut, we've replaced that." He gestured toward an adjacent workbench on which lay a long, grey, punctured steel box. "Cooling expansion tank took a hit too, can't do anything until a replacement arrives. The Equipment Officer says mid-day."

"Assuming it arrives on time, when will she be ready Flight?"

"Mid-afternoon Sir. Apart from a few frayed internal bracing wires, that's the extent of the damage. My men have given her a thorough check over."

Standing on a footstool, Carter leaned over the Brisfit's cockpit coaming and inspected the repaired longeron carefully. His training had been thorough, he knew how to insert a repair section, rig the airframe, splice an eight strand flying wire and re-fit every component of the Rolls-Royce Falcon engine.

"Very tidy job Collins. Who's overhauling the guns?"

"Air Mechanic First Class Sullivan Sir, a good lad. Served his apprenticeship at BSA before the war".

"That's encouraging. My observer Lieutenant Pechell will no doubt wish to speak with him directly."

"My pleasure Sir. I'll also need to have a word with him about the camera. Did you know it was damaged?"

"No?"

Collins pointed out a significant dent in the Williamson 'L' Type aerial camera's light aluminium casing. Mounted externally on the fuselage alongside Pechell's cockpit, the thirty-seven pound instrument was particularly vulnerable to shrapnel.

"I know you're planning to return to your squadron Sir, but as we've plenty of spares, I've taken it apart and checked for internal problems. The plate changer, driving gears and shutter all look fine. Your remote shutter release Bowden cable was fouled so I swapped it out for a new one from spares."

When in automatic use, the camera's power came from a small propeller turned by the air stream and connected to the camera by a flexible drive shaft. Carter spun it with his index finger.

"Plenty of plate magazines Collins?"

"Yes Sir."

Reaching into the pilot's cockpit Carter retrieved a mislaid, palm-sized Sopwith bevel gauge that had become wedged in the wicker seat. He handed it to Collins.

"Here Flight, someone will be looking for this."

Collins' shoulders stiffened defensively, anticipating a reprimand.

"Easy thing to lose eh?"

"Thank you Sir."

"Right, I'll be off, let you get on with your work. Let me know if there is any delay on the replacement tank. I'll most likely be over in Beaupré Farm if you need me."

Returning to his duties, Collins' craggy face creased into a smile. *'A true gentleman that officer and no mistake'.*

The higher they flew, the colder and clearer the air. Viewed from ten thousand feet, the sun had risen above the eastern horizon and created a vertical pillar of light high up into the winter sky, its rays reflecting on countless tiny ice crystals suspended in the atmosphere. Nature's magnificent spectacle combined with the adrenalin pumping through Percival's veins to banish all remnants of fatigue. Bungee's red, yellow and blue flight leader identification streamer trailed stiffly behind his rudder as his Camel rode the air currents. Slowly rising and falling alongside, Percival and the half dozen scouts maintained tight 'V' formation. Occasional puffs of grey engine exhaust dissipated into their slipstream as, eight miles due east of Merville, the desolate town of Picantin marked the beginning of their transit across the front lines.

Percival's stomached tensed in anticipation of the inevitable barrage. Within seconds black clouds of Archie began exploding all around and the sky was quickly dotted with balls of dirty grey smoke. Some detonations were close enough for the pilots to see the vicious, flaming centres. Flashes of erupting ordnance reflected in the tinted, sage-green lenses of Percival's goggles while acrid fumes filled his nostrils. He could taste a metallic tang on the back of his palette. Occasionally small holes appeared through the wing fabric and loud whip-cracks rent the air as debris impacted the swirling propeller. He looked down along the vibrating fabric side of his Camel to where, ten thousand feet below the trailing edge of his lower wing, the guns twinkled like sequins along a meandering line from Hayem to Bacquart. He imagined, for a moment, countless upturned faces of enemy troops.

In less than three minutes the Camels were east of Escobecques and clear of the barrage. The formation turned south over the remains of Haubourdin and followed the Canal Deule to Seclin then Douai. Beneath scattered clouds the Scarpe River wound its way across the land like a narrow stream of molten lead. To the west, alongside the straight Roman road connecting Dechy and Leward, lay a scar on the landscape, formerly the Lambres brickworks.

Cambrai was unmistakable, its spoke-like roads radiating out from the hub. The ground west of the town was churned with fresh craters, broken trench lines, abandoned tanks and the rusting remains of artillery from November's major offensive. Dropping his port and starboard wings in turn, Percival rolled left to right and scanned the perfect, uninterrupted morning sky above. A short distance off his port wingtips Bungee swung the nose of his leading Camel left and right, checking the distant horizon ahead, expecting at any moment to see the approach of Jasta Four from their base at Lieu-St.-Amand, ten miles east.

With no sign of the enemy the Camels initiated a wide, one hundred and eighty degree turn above Caudry inputting as little bank as possible. A measure, it was hoped, that would minimize the chance of reflected sunlight on their wings betraying their position. After resuming a straight course, Percival could see the village of Estourmel and its ancient Boistrancourt Chateau five miles to the north-east. The estate factory, with attendant tall chimney stacks, seemed somewhat out of place with the otherwise cultivated landscape. As they flew closer he could see scattered bomb craters spotted around the Chateau grounds. Local industry was not the intended target, for beyond the ornamental gardens lay a line of sheds and hangars, the home of Jasta Five. Percival looked down beyond his dipped starboard wings. He could see at least three enemy machines parked out on the open field. He was too high to distinguish their make, but the absence of others indicated that the main force were already airborne and could appear at any moment.

After a glance toward his companions, Bungee pointed down to the aerodrome and jabbed his finger indicating his intention to attack. He pulled up and banked left into a dive, exposing the yellow ochre underside of his Camel and the large painted 'B' on the lower starboard wing. Watching his leader's ailerons Percival instinctively anticipated the movement of Bungee's aeroplane and followed, cut his engine and dipped the nose of his machine. The flight plunged earthwards through the early morning light like stooping falcons.

In accordance with Bungee's instruction Percival remained close alongside his leader. His Camel's wires and struts whistled through the rushing atmosphere. Powerful propwash drove turbulent air over and around his head, pummeling his helmet and triplex goggles. At five hundred feet the Camels pulled out from their dive and, in no uncertain manner, Bungee signaled 'every man for himself.' The sky above the aerodrome was filled with thick clouds of black smoke from erupting shells. It was impossible to avoid them. Percival carefully lined up the nearest open hangar. His assault was countered by a hurricane of machine gun fire from a row of revetments. A furiously riding motorcyclist flashed past his gunsight then the flat, grey hangar roof was a blur, only feet below his undercarriage. He pulled up, narrowly clearing the bare tree branches to the rear and banked hard right to avoid the towering factory chimney.

Several enemy machines had been hurriedly dragged from their hangars and were taxiing across the field to repulse the attack. Percival made a sharp, one hundred and eighty degree right hand turn and set course for an Albatros gaining airspeed across the coarse grass. Concentrating on his ring and bead gunsight, he fired from a distance of three hundred feet and perforated the DIII's green-tail. His salvo had no effect. At the same time a stream of deadly fire from 37mm revolving-barrel anti-aircraft guns, or 'flaming onions', streaked the sky ahead of him. Bullets zipped through the Camel's wing fabric, a veritable inferno had been unleashed.

The onslaught distracted Percival for only a couple of seconds, but it was long enough for the Albatros to climb away from the ground. Closing on his adversary he fired from a thirty yard range and watched his shots advance toward the cockpit and petrol tank. The pilot's body slumped onto the controls and the D.III's nose dipped. It dived steeply, impacted scrubland outside the aerodrome perimeter and flared a livid yellow flame. Immediately, the bombardment from below commenced with an even greater intensity. Machine gun bullets from a myriad of emplacements sprayed the sky ahead. Percival caught sight of Alderton's Camel sweeping across the field, weaving from side to side and attempting to silence as many of the guns as possible with his twin Vickers.

Fresnoy Farm, a cluster of rural cottages surrounded by the wintry skeletons of trees, lay half a mile east of the aerodrome. Percival set a new course, on the off-chance that it contained men or munitions. As he drew near he saw unmistakable flashes of machine gun fire directed at him from behind the outer stone walls. The chances of a strike were small. At five hundred feet altitude his Camel was dodging about, first on one wing tip then the other. Passing above the farmhouse he could see no troops, however, trenches surrounding the buildings were sufficient evidence that the enemy had made it a fortified post. He pulled up above the lime kilns of Bevillers and performed a split S turn. Once again he flew straight toward the main building, this time from the east, firing both his guns before passing directly above the target. Zooming up into a climbing turn he looked back down to witness a cloud of smoke and flying debris splashing down into the farm's pond.

After strafing Fresnoy Farm, Percival attacked the nearby railway station at Beauvois-en-Cambresis then returned to Boistrancourt Chateau. Following the straight, tree lined road to Cambrai, a stationary convoy of open-front trucks were heading away from the aerodrome, each with two or three men on the front seats. From a hundred and fifty yards range Percival opened fire on the leading vehicle. The driver fell sideways in his seat while his companions jumped down and ran toward the trees. Several troops leapt out of the back and onto the road. They saw Percival's Camel approaching and hesitated, some lay down, feigning injury while others sought cover under the vehicles. He soared overhead with both guns firing, it was impossible to assess the casualties.

Returning to the enemy aerodrome, Percival had lined up another ascending Albatros when Bungee flashed past. One glance at his leader's face was enough to tell he was in an excellent mood as he pushed up the nose of his Camel and set a course for home. The six Sopwiths climbed back up to eight thousand feet, every man alert for approaching hostile machines.

Adjusted by the squadron's riggers to be slightly tail-heavy at take-off with full tanks, after one and a quarter hours in the air the Camels had assumed their optimum balance. It required no effort at all to maintain a level flight. In skilled hands the Sopwith was the perfect fighting machine that responded to every movement of the stick and rudder. Percival could access all necessary controls without even looking at them. If they were to dogfight, now would be the best time.

Bungee was first to discern distant black specs against the horizon. There were nine of them, approaching from a slightly higher altitude in the north-east. At a numerical disadvantage, he determined that an interception would be more effective if they engaged the on-coming enemy from above. He dipped his wings to gain his comrade's attention, then pointed skyward. Raising the nose of his Camel, the others followed. Climbing up between clusters of white clouds they levelled out at fifteen thousand feet and waited.

The enemy were at least five miles away and two thousand feet below Bungee's formation. Percival watched them draw closer and before long identified the green tailed Albatros DVa's of

Jasta Five. They were climbing to intercept the Camels, unaware of the damage recently inflicted on their home aerodrome. Percival had fought against their best on previous occasions. While in their airspace, he hoped for an opportunity to settle accounts with one in particular. An Albatros with a checked motif on its side whose pilot, seven days earlier, had shot down and killed a good friend from 45 Squadron over Seranvillers.

The sound of six fully opened 130 horsepower Clerget 9B engines crackled across the sky as the Camel formation dived toward the black-crossed machines. Boring into the enemy formation Bungee was the first to fire, an Albatros rolled over onto its back, coolant streaming out into a trailing white cloud before the pilot had a chance to react. The moment Bungee pulled up from his attack run, the Jasta scattered. It would clearly be every man for himself.

Percival's Camel was immediately surrounded by a swarm of enemy machines. Fear left him, all he could feel was terror. His body and machine became one. Cut off from Bungee by two enemy aeroplanes he rolled right to avoid gunfire from a pursuing Zebra-striped Albatros and found himself facing another advancing D.V that swept past dangerously close overhead. He saw a red dragon emblazoned on the fuselage as the propwash shook him violently back and forth in the cockpit.

There was a mix of aeroplanes everywhere, noticeably more German than British. Amid the confusion of battle he found the checked Albatros he had been seeking and immediately latched onto its' tail. The effectiveness of his manoeuvres were apparent on the face of the man in front every time he turned his head. The poor fellow could tell his time had come. Percival's thumbs were poised over the firing paddles on his joystick handle when he heard the zip of bullets overhead. In an instant another Albatros with an Edelweiss motif flashed across from right to left, throwing him momentarily off course. He reacted immediately, pulling the stick back into his stomach and kicking right rudder. The Camel flicked over into a snap roll, losing speed, while the attacking Albatros was thrown off its attack.

Pulling up into a half loop, Percival looked up, craning his neck painfully in an effort re-engage the checked Albatros. Once inverted he planned a roll out and a diving assault on the enemy. The German pilot had, however, anticipated his move and performed an identical manoeuvre. The two combatants closed head-on. A deluge of metallic hail punched holes in the fabric of Percival's wings. Bullets splintered struts and pinged off the cowling. Ice-cold airflow pummeled his face, breathing was difficult. He could smell leaking petrol. The engine and rushing air were deafening. As the Albatros ducked underneath his Camel, he rolled and turned right to chase his adversary. Both machines entered a climbing turn. At once Percival found himself in a winning position and fired fifty rounds from his twin Vickers. His nose filled with cordite fumes and he could taste burnt castor oil on the roof of his mouth. The Albatros was in front, he could smell its exhaust as he closed in.

Locked in a waltz of death the Camel and checked Albatros circled each other in a seemingly endless spiral, both opponents trying to get into position for a deflection shot. The thin veneer of civilisation dropped away. It would be a fight to the finish. Percival tightened his turn as much as possible then applied enough top rudder to cause a stall. The Camel entered the first half of a spin in the same direction as his circling opponent and cut across him. Nudging the joystick back Percival set the Sopwith momentarily on her tail and fired thirty rounds into the Albatros as it flew past. He had no time to witness the damage inflicted on the enemy machine. His Camel entered a tail slide then an inverted skidding spiral that quickly evolved into an inverted spin.

It was as if time had frozen, Percival's senses were overloaded, unable to absorb or process the scene. For a moment he was completely disorientated and out of control. Fueled by adrenalin, his body and brain engaged survival mode. Unable to determine which direction he was turning he looked down into the cockpit and away from the blur outside. He throttled back, the engine faltered. Left was left and right was still his right he reminded himself. He looked up at the Camel's nose. It was spinning to the right. Centrifugal force and gravity combined to force him away from the controls. He realised he was pulling at the joystick, almost wrenching it out from its socket. With concentrated effort he kicked hard left rudder, waited for a second then focused all his energy on drawing the joystick right back at its maximum throw toward his stomach.

After a vertiginous two and a half thousand foot drop Percival's stricken Camel recovered from its spin. He neutralized his rudder setting and the machine started to climb sharply, approaching a stall. Easing the joystick just forward of centre he held the nose down to just below the horizon and the speed steadily increased, allowing the wings to collect lift. The windmilling propeller spun the engine back into life, but fuel and oil pressures were low. Instinctively Percival reached down with his right hand and pumped air into the tanks. Slowly the pressure began to rise. In a state of disbelief and shock he tried to understand what just happened. The fact he had survived began to really sink in. His knees began to tremble uncontrollably.

Climbing through a layer of nebulous cloud at eleven thousand feet Percival scanned the sky for his comrades, but they were nowhere to be seen. Hearing the fluttering of paper he immediately reached up to grab a hold of his map, He cursed aloud as it escaped his grasp. Dislodged from the pocket in his overalls in the tumult of conflict, it had torn away into the propeller backwash.

Alone in the sky, Percival used his compass to set a course north-west to Merville. As the minutes passed, he hoped to find a break in the low cloud way that would enable him to identify a familiar landmark. Eventually an area of ground became visible, but the roads directly below were faded into the muddy swamp by constant shellfire and had vanished completely. After what seemed an eternity, amid the clammy, sodden, grey and brown terrain, he saw a familiar pattern of two oval swamps and a winding river. He wiped his goggles with his scarf for a clearer view. Immediately to the north of the devastated town lay a straight line of abandoned railway that ran from west to east. It was Biache St.Vaast. By Percival's reckoning, his present course would take him over Vimy, half way between Arras and Lens.

Percival decided to cross the lines at Gavrelle. Keeping an image of the map in his mind, he aimed for a white mass of unbroken stratus four thousand feet below that would provide an effective screen from Archie. For a further ten long minutes he steered by compass until an unexpected break in the opaque veil allowed him a glimpse of the ground. The terrain presented a barren, wasted appearance, with absolutely no sign of life. There was no colour, just black and white with different shades of same in between. A few scattered shell holes spotted the ground while about half a mile to the east lay the walls of a wrecked farm-house. Unable to make out any recognisable feature, he considered the situation before slowly descending. At six thousand feet the swirling water vapour enveloped him. Buffeted by turbulent air he kept a steady eye on the inclinometer while his compass swung languidly from side to side.

Emerging from the grey underside Percival levelled out only to be met by a barrage of Archie. The air was agitated by the wake of exploding shells that tossed his Camel across the sky. Streams of bright red tracer bullets leapt up from the ground toward him. Aware that the enemy gunners had the exact range of the cloud base he descended another hundred or so feet below the black smoke. Circling to locate his bearings it took only seconds to recognise the Canal Basin at le Faubourg. It was clear he'd drifted too far east and was directly above the lines at Auchy. In a decidedly risky position, he opened out the engine, re-entered the cloud layer and continued a rapid ascent to seven thousand feet.

After a month based at Fienvillers, Percival's knowledge of the geography north of Lens was at best sketchy, but the Lys would be his lifesaver. Three miles west, the cloud was clearing and once he'd found the river he could easily track it across the land to Merville and La Gorgue.

A momentary pin-point of light flashed in the distant sky and caught his attention. He wiped his goggles and stared in the direction until his eyes watered. Five miles to the north-west sunlight reflected off the wings of five machines. The remaining members of 321 had already started a slow descent toward Merville. With a three thousand feet height advantage Percival put the nose of his Camel down and set course to re-join his comrades before they reached home. Minutes later he pulled alongside Bungee's Camel and assumed position in formation.

A mile west of La Gorgue, Merville's cinder runways were unmistakable. The inviting prospect of a hot bath followed by a stiff drink drew ever closer. Commencing his downwind landing leg, Percival approached at a thousand feet, parallel and offset from the landing field. Turning right ninety degrees he pitched out into the base leg and, adjusting his airspeed, continued an even turn until he was approaching the field once more from the south.

Five hundred feet from the ground he cut the magnetos by pressing his gloved thumb on the button in the joystick handle. After a couple of seconds he released it, allowing the engine to spin up. With most of his petrol gone, Percival's Camel was slightly nose-heavy. Adjusting the trim, he descended in a series of "S" turns that allowed plenty of room on the field ahead, just in case he came in too fast. He held off landing until the Sopwith settled at sixty five miles an hour. Gliding along, as close to the ground as possible, he watched the air speed fall away. Feeling the Camel sink he eased the joystick back to its maximum throw and landed on the frozen field. Congratulating himself on a perfectly executed 'three-pointer' he heard the roar of a rotary engine close behind and glanced up in time to witness Bungee's Camel pass by overhead, fifty feet off the deck. No doubt his C.O.

had misjudged his landing and opened out for another circuit.

Attentive ground crew manhandled Percival's Camel toward the workshop hangers. Exhausted, bitterly cold and shaking, he clambered out and onto the cement hard-standing. His thoughts were scrambled as if there were an electrical storm in his head. For a moment he stood and steadied himself, both hands resting on the oil-streaked fuselage fabric. He removed his goggles and gauntlets. Several bullets had penetrated behind the cockpit, exposing the fuselage top longeron and dorsal stringers. They were the same shots that had ripped his fur-lined leather flying coat. Staring incredulously at the singed and torn fabric, he realised it was only the thickness of his overalls that had stood between him and his life. An unexpected sensation surged through his body. It was the thrill of having survived mortal danger.

An air-mechanic approached him. "Welcome back Sir."

Percival slid off his leather flying cap and blinked to clear his eyes.

"Thank you. Have a look at the Rotherham air pump would you? Had to manually pump pressure on approach. Just as well I didn't need to go around."

"Right away Sir!" The airman acknowledged with a sharp salute.

At the end of the line of parked Camels Bungee had already dismounted and was pacing impatiently up and down alongside his machine. Percival listened to his C.O.'s barking commands and shook his head in astonishment. The stories he had heard were true, evidently all Bungee wanted to do was re-fuel, re-arm and get back up into the air. The old man would give anything to be in the thick of every action. Having caught sight of Percival, Bungee strode purposely toward him, his face set like stone. After what Percival had endured he was ready to give as good as he got.

"I told you to stick to my right wing!" Bungee asserted with cold authority as the two men walked out of earshot from the attendant ground crew.

"Yes you did." Percival responded with indifference bordering on insubordination. "But as you probably noticed I was unavoidably engaged elsewhere."

Bungee fixed Percival with an emotionless stare. For a full ten seconds the two men silently faced each other down, Percival was beyond caring about the consequences. Without warning Bungee's face creased into a smile and he bellowed with laughter. Slapping Percival heartily on the back he chortled. "I said you'll do and dammit I was right!"

By mid-afternoon the weather had changed for the worse and all flying had been cancelled. Having visited the La Gorgue hangars and signed off the completed repairs to his Brisfit, Carter intended to spend the rest of the day in the warmth and comfort of the Mess. Beneath a graphite sky he crossed the open field to Merville Farm. A bitter, gusting easterly wind blew sleet in wild vortices one moment and in diagonal sheets the next. It ran down his face as a thin, cold layer.

The trek took longer than he had expected, his boots slipping in the mud as he navigated a circuitous route around areas of deep slush filled puddles. A more cold and miserable place he could not imagine, even the scenery sapped his strength. The welcoming yellow lights shining through the Merville Farm windows never seemed to draw any closer as he trudged onward, step after weary step.

He thought of his wife, Mary and their two children back home in Reigate, Surrey. Those nights in front of the warm hearth fire, gathering together around the old refectory table for an evening meal, their familiar bed and everyday sounds of their house. In his mind he could hear quite plainly the front door latch, the gate to the back garden and dishes stacked on the kitchen drainer. He remembered fondly how he'd reach out at night and embrace his wife, so warm and comforting. Everything he treasured was so far away. Not for the first time he considered his entire purpose in the war and rued the events that had brought him to such a desolate, foreign land.

Looking ahead at Merville Farm, it occurred to him that too had been a family home, full of life and memories. Now they had all gone, to where no-one knew. Perhaps one day the occupants would return and with them the old ways. Memories and melancholy thoughts filled his mind until he reached the old red-brick farmhouse. He carefully mounted the threshold where the wintry temperature had cast water film into ice. The door opened and the clamour of voices within displaced any further contemplation.

The young officers inside were entertaining themselves as best they could in the cramped conditions. When the weather was dud there was nothing to do but sit in the Mess playing poker, putting on some records and drinking whisky or cocktails, waiting for it to clear. There was little ventilation and the Mess rafters were lost in a thick cloud of tobacco smoke. The usual huddles of friends had formed around the billiard table, piano and fireplace. Some of the less sociably inclined were seated and reading letters from home, absorbed in their own thoughts. Amid the steady background of conversational male voices, the strains of Poor Butterfly by the Victor Military Band crackled out from the squadron's wind-up Decca gramophone. Occasionally the clinking of bottles would be followed by a burst of laughter. Carter looked around for Pechell, a familiar face among strangers. Seeing him alone at the bar he gestured across, an invite to join him. While Pechell made his way through the crush, Carter responded to a tap on his right shoulder and turned around to find Percival, two empty glasses in one hand and a full decanter of brandy in the other.

"What-ho Carter, looks like you need warming up! I hear you'll be spending another night with us?"

"Filthy bloody weather. Never knew a place could be so bleak."
He could not help but notice Percival's healthy skin tone as he
gratefully accepted a generous measure of spirit. "Thanks. It'll
be summer for you back home. I bet you're missing every kop-
pie and veld."

Downing his second brandy of the afternoon, Percival's Dutch
Afrikaaner accent became even more pronounced.

"Not likely, what and miss all the fun?"

"Come off it, all that warmth and sunshine." Carter shook his
head in mock disbelief. "What in Heaven's name made you leave
and come up here?"

"Alright, alright. Long story short." Percival sighed. Overcome
with fatigue, he slumped down into the nearest deeply upholstered armchair seconds before Pechell could grab it for himself.

"I was nineteen when the war started, just begun a career in
mining. Joined the 1st Transvall Scottish and moved from Cape
Town to Luderitz for a stint in the South West. A year later I volunteered for the 4th South African Horse in German East Africa
where I went down with a dose of malaria. They shipped back
to Mossel Bay where some son of a Swaziland pioneer told me
about the RFC and I decided to volunteer."

"Mug!" An unsolicited opinion issued forth from the corner of
the Mess.

Percival shrugged his shoulders. "My father would agree with
that. He said airmen were a congregation of amusing madmen
with suicidal tendencies."

"But, you went anyway." Pechell encouraged.

"Naturally. Shipped to England in 1916 put through military
training at Hursley Park, off to Oxford for technical flying training then Uxbridge for practical stuff on Maurice Farmans. Four
hours' dual, then solo and got my wings. Did my hours in Avros

and Pups before moving on to Camels."

His next remarks were for Carter's benefit. "It's like flying a gyroscope old chap. If you can get through the first ten to fifteen hours you're relatively safe. Once I'd got the hang of it I spent a couple of weeks at St. Omer then booked out to 45 Squadron at St. Marie-Cappel. We'd moved to Fienvillers and were just about to re-locate when I was posted here."

"I heard you've bagged three Huns already." Pechell encouraged.

"Wasn't easy. Managed two Albatros Cs, one on the fourth September near Comines, the other just before sunset on twentieth October, same place. Sent a D.III down a week ago over Kastelhoek."

Leaning against the bar with his back toward Percival, Bungee was deep in conversation with Sant, a discussion that was abruptly terminated when the latter received a summons to return to his office. Having overheard Percival's comments Bungee turned toward the small group, a full whisky glass in his hand.

"Five actually, the D.III you downed at Boistrancourt this morning and that D.V you tussled with later. Alderton and Bamford both saw him go down about a mile north of Jasta 32's old aerodrome at Epinoy."

"You never mentioned that one Percival you old dog!" Findley chided good-naturedly.

Bungee interrupted the subsequent clamour of applause for the newcomer. "Just remember lads, a clever dogfighter is one who not only wins, but wins with ease. If you down a Hun without learning anything, it's a waste of time." He continued, addressing Percival directly. "I tell all my new chaps the same thing. Learn as much about the enemy machines as you can. That's a sure way to succeed. If you don't know the Hun's capabilities, but know you own machine well enough, your chances of winning or losing are equal. If you're ignorant of both, you'll likely only last a few hours."

Pushing his way to the fore, Alderton dragged Percival to his feet and put his right arm around his shoulders.

"Hard luck Percival. Squadron tradition. A fellow downs five Huns, he stands a rounds of drinks."

A crestfallen Percival looked around at the pressing mass of expectant faces.

"Sorry old lad." Bungee smiled sympathetically. He shouted across to the bar steward. "Mine's a double Scotch by the way!"

An hour later, alongside the gramophone, Jamieson was rummaging through two dozen records stored inside a wooden box originally for ammunition. Selecting 'Somewhere a Voice is Calling,' he wound the squeaky crank mechanism and soon the voice of John McCormack was issuing forth with the hiss, crackle and pop of an old record in play.

Amid general good natured-banter, Carter meandered across the Mess and found an unoccupied sofa opposite Carpenter who had just completed a letter home. Once seated he leant forward, the better to be heard.

"I was talking to Charley Findlay just now, told him I thought I might take a stroll along the riverbank when the weather breaks, clear my head a bit. He went all peculiar and warned me not to. Said the old moored barge was strictly off-limits, 'haunted' or some such utter tosh."

"Oh that." Carpenter responded sagely as he folded the letter, placed it in an envelope and relaxed back in his armchair. "Bloody thing's been around since October 1914 when 2 Squadron were based here. Stories about it started to circulate just before 16 Squadron moved out two years ago. The old tub's been used as a hospital and barracks, it's an abandoned hulk now and the bank's a frost hollow. No one goes near it if they can avoid it."

He exhaled a cloud of blue tobacco smoke and watched it roll upward to the raftered ceiling.

"We generally don't talk about it, no-one does. Keep well clear, even during the day."

"You've seen whatever it is?"

"Shortly after we moved in." Carpenter's voice lowered, a somber expression on his face. "And just in case you're thinking I'm barmy, a couple of the other chaps have too."

"Intriguing."

"Take my advice Carter, it's something you don't ever want to witness. There's an aura around the place; cold and hostile. If the other ranks have to go over there, they always team up in pairs."

Carter was taken aback by the sincerity of Carpenter's plea. "Well, if there is something going on there, it's hardly surprising, all the poor lost lads with no resting place."

Carpenter was silent for a moment, thoughtfully puffing on his cigarette and sipping his brandy. "Most of our chaps are buried over at La Gorgue Communal Cemetery. Bungee always makes an effort to bring them back to the squadron rather than leave them in some forgotten, distant grave. It's a depressing business nevertheless, I've been a coffin pallbearer for so many young boys." He stubbed out the remains of his smoke. "Thought I'd got used to it, then last week we lost young Stephens, an Australian from Melbourne. He made it back despite being badly shot up; crashed on the aerodrome. I was talking to him while they cut him free, he just faded away." Carpenter's eyes glazed. He was re-living Stephens' final moments.

"Carpenter?" Carter leaned forward and placed an encouraging hand on his shoulder. "You alright old chap?"

Carpenter blinked and looked around like a man rudely awoken from his slumber, as if Carter's voice had pulled him out of a completely different world and dropped him back into the present. "He was just sewn up in canvas, laid out on a plank of wood and covered with the flag. I could feel his corpse all cold and rigid as we carried him from the Crossley to the grave. Made me quite edgy. The others too. One of the lads passed out."

The door to the Mess opened abruptly, Sant entered accompanied by a rush of cold, damp air and wind-driven sleet. After removing his cap and dripping woollen greatcoat he hung them on a hook against the wall and cast his eyes around the Mess, finally settling on Carter who was still deep in conversation with Carpenter. Gesturing toward Pechell to join him, he made his way over.

"Sorry to interrupt. Carter, I've just had a call from your C.O."

"Surely the Boss doesn't expect us to fly back in this weather?" Carter protested.

"No, but it seems the photographs Pechell took east of Thourout have shown up something interesting. Wing want another reccy first thing tomorrow." His grey eyes fixed Carter with an intense stare. "Trouble is every aerodrome in the vicinity, including Avesnes-le-Comte, is waterlogged. That only leaves La Gorgue. Think you could manage a take-off from one of those damned cinder runways?"

Carter looked across to Pechell who was leaning against the Mess window, peering out as the sleet rattled in spiteful waves against the glass. He responded with a shrug of indifference. "Looks like we'll soon find out."

Stretched out full length on a nearby sofa with his head on the armrest, Percival overheard the conversation and staggered unsteadily to his feet. "You're going on recon over the lines without an escort?" He shook his head in disbelief. "No, no, that won't do. Won't do at all."

"I agree." Bungee called out to the assembled pilots. "Volunteers?"

Several hands shot up immediately.

"We've only got five serviceable machines in the hangars at La Gorgue and you'll have to use the hard runways lads." There was a discernable twinkle in his eyes. "It'll be bloody dangerous."

More hands were raised to join those already aloft. Bungee was evidently highly satisfied.

"Well Carter, it looks like you lads will have company."

2. INTO THE SUN

It was six-thirty in the morning of Tuesday, December the eighteenth. The cold air was heavy with moisture from a ground mist that had spread out from the River Lys and crossed La Gorgue aerodrome overnight. The aerodrome workshops were already showing signs of activity. In the darkness before dawn, five Sopwith Camels were being wheeled out one at a time and lined up as grey silhouettes against the hangar sheds.

Carter was called while it was still dark. The words of a French orderly broke his slumber.

"C'est l'heure, monsieur."

Stirring from his sleep he lay still for a moment gathering his senses while the orderly poured hot water into the wash basin. Pechell was already sitting on the edge of his bed, sipping at an enamel mug of coffee, smoking a cigarette and coughing. Outside Beaupré Farm, from the vehicle park below their window, a wide-awake driver was tunefully whistling the popular ` Missouri Waltz'.

Having dressed and shaved, they set out together for the Mess. Percival was waiting for them outside the door. He greeted Carter and Pechell with a cheery wave as they crossed the cobbled courtyard.

"Cook's prepared a topping breakfast. Ham and eggs, or you can have doughnuts, French pastries, white bread toast and marmalade jam."

Never at his best first thing in the morning, Carter responded with barely a grunt of acknowledgement. His head was still woolly from a disturbed night's sleep. A hurried shave with an unfamiliar razor had left his neck and chin sore.

Pechell responded for the both of them. "Marvelous, I'm famished." He cast his gaze around the bare and barren landscape. The eastern sky was already turning grey. There was a freezing chill in the air. "This is an un-Godly hour and no mistake."

Inside the Mess, oil lamps cast their mellow light across a small group of seven assembled diners. They sat beneath a fug of tobacco smoke, on both sides of a single rustic French farmhouse table.

"So what's the great urgency do you think?" Butcher enquired, ravenously swallowing a mouthful of ham and eggs. He was a man of medium build with close cropped blonde hair and thin moustache. Twenty three years old and wearing a wire rimmed monocle, he gave the outward appearance of a much older man.

Cupping a hot tin mug of tea between his hands, Pechell replied thoughtfully. "The photographs we took on Sunday suggest Royal Württemburg Jagdstaffel 28 have decamped from their base at Wynghene. Intelligence reports from local agents say they've moved ten miles north to Varssenaere. Wing wants confirmation"

"Of course". Carpenter added with a hint of sarcasm: "It'd be most unlike Wing to send anyone out on a fool's errand."

Several seasoned airmen cast their eyes to the ceiling.

"I know that crowd." Percival announced. "They're flying the new Albatros and their leader's a Hun named Emil Thuy. The bastard downed one of our Camels over the lines at Ypres end of November."

"Just get your ruddy photographs you two and with a bit of luck we'll be back and changed in time for elevenses." Alderton pleaded earnestly.

Seated at the far end of the table Bungee ladled a third teaspoonful of sugar into his tea and stirred it absentmindedly, his thoughts elsewhere. "Regardless of Jasta 28's whereabouts, Jasta

3 and 37 are still at Wynghene and both of them make regular patrols over their side of the lines, just about the time we'll be crossing. There's no way of knowing it they're grounded by the weather." He gesticulated with the handle of his spoon toward Carter, who was sitting opposite. "But that's our job. We'll keep a watch out for them. If we get into a scrap, I don't want you joining in, just get your damned photographs and leave any Huns to us, understood?"

One glance at Bungee and Carter realised any protest would be futile.

"Understood."

"Once we're safely across the lines, our Camels will stay up above and keep our eyes open while you and Pechell go down and do your job. I've checked the forecast, weather's clear until noon, heavy cloud and sleet moving in later so we'll only get one go at this."

"Best cross the front well north of Hollebeke." Butcher interjected. "There's an Archie battery east of Messines with an uncanny eye."

"We can get reasonable photographs with our lens from fifteen thousand feet, but I prefer thirteen for maximum resolution." Pechell added.

Bungee turned his attention to the rest of the assembled aviators.

"Right then. Take-off will be twenty minutes before sunrise, we'll climb to fifteen thousand feet together then set off northeast in close 'V' formation. Cross the lines at Ypres. Carter, you drop down to thirteen thousand once we're north of Roeselare, do what you have to do, then we'll head for home."

By seven-fifteen the eastern horizon had turned pink and the sky overhead had changed from grey to pale blue. It was light enough to fly. The hangar doors were drawn apart and, gathered around their aeroplanes, the airmen donned their fur-lined shoes and combinations. Once aloft there would be nobody to talk to, so naturally there was a good deal of conversation taking place as they adjusted their leather flying hoods and goggles

"Hey, you!" Carpenter shouted across jokingly to Alderton. "I hope some Hun ruins you this morning so I won't have to pay the fifty Francs you won from me last night!"

Alderton responded with an obscene gesture, suggesting Carpenter perform a physically impossible action upon himself.

An engineer came up to Butcher, saluted and reported. "Sorry you won't be able to use 905 this morning Sir, your engine's gone dud."

Fastening his flight cap in place Bungee queried. "What was that he said?" Butcher saluted, and with an exact imitation of the engineer's manner replied. "Have to use another machine Sir, my Camel's got the hump."

In the cold light of dawn fitters and riggers completed their final checks on the Bristol Fighter and wheeled it outside. Silhouetted against the hangar lights, Pechell's loaded twin Lewis guns protruded venomously over the observer's cockpit coaming as he supervised the installation of photographic plate magazines. Carter climbed aboard and slid down into the cockpit. His flying boots slipped snugly into the rudder bar stirrup. He wound his silk scarf carefully around his throat to prevent the freezing air entering his neck area and flying suit. Looking down at the floor, he ensured his heels were clear of the control wires that protruded from each side of the joystick pivot.

Reaching down with his right hand, he manually pumped up the fuel tank air pressure before priming the Brisfit's Rolls-Royce engine. After he'd set the throttle, advance and fuel, the ground team swung the propeller over compression and wound the starter magneto handle. The twelve cylinders roared into life, accompanied by puffs of grey smoke from the ends of both horizontal exhausts. The Brisfit's fabric sides quivered in the driven air. At the sound of the engine Pechell hurriedly climbed into his cockpit. He checked his guns and arranged his maps. Carter looked round inquiringly, Pechell nodded his assurance. They were ready.

Carefully opening the throttle, Carter watched the black faced engine revolutions dial as the white indicator climbed steadily around the scale. Temperature and pressure soon reached optimum levels. He fastened his lap-belt and, with a signal to the ground crew, waved away the wooden wheel chocks. Very little throttle was needed to get underway but the two-seater was difficult to steer and required the guiding assistance of ground personnel, one on each side, holding the outer leading edges of both lower wings. Their steady pace increased to a trot as Carter taxied out for over a hundred and fifty yards to the centre holding area some thirty yards square.

Positioned into wind for take-off, Carter slid the throttle fully open and advanced the ignition. Already uncomfortable about the forthcoming take-off, a steady cross-wind only served to increase his concerns. Their aeroplane felt like a living creature as it quickly accelerated. Carefully avoiding the drainage ditches either side of the narrow cinder runway they took to the air at forty-five miles per hour. Carter waited, patiently watching the airspeed indicator climb to sixty before easing the stick further back. They cleared the roof of Beaupré Farm by a hundred feet and in less than a minute were circling La Gorgue, gaining altitude.

A Brisfit's rate of ascent was approximately two hundred feet per minute slower than the Sopwith Camel. For that reason, 321 Squadron's escort waited until Carter and Pechell were airborne and clear of the aerodrome before starting their own take-off runs. Carter glanced at his watch; it was seven-twenty five and he hoped to be over enemy territory by a quarter to eight. Pechell too, was getting distinctly fed up with waiting when, three thousand feet below, he saw Bungee's machine move slowly across the runway. Second in line, Percival taxied out with two Air Mechanics holding his Camel's rear interplane struts.

Ten minutes after the last of the Camels left the ground the final aeroplane slid up and into formation alongside Bungee. The morning air was smooth, with none of the bumps that would otherwise push them out of position. At ten thousand feet the six machines maintained a steady ascent before setting course toward the lines.

From fifteen thousand feet, high in the rarefied winter atmosphere, the absence of water vapour, dust and smoke revealed a pristine blue sky. Buffeted by freezing air Carter was grateful for the heat thrown back from the engine. He looked to the east, where the rising sun was clearing away patches of low cloud and morning mists. He could clearly see battle activity along the lines east of Ypres. Serried, tangled lines of trenches amid the shell-torn country appeared as scratches connecting shell-holes. Occasionally, a large explosion emitted red tongues of flame that faded into brooding, drifting black smoke. The scarred landscape looked as if it were under water, with just the trace of crater rims breaking the surface. It was nothing more than a swamp. Towns and villages had been totally obliterated, all that remained the railway line at 'Hellfire Corner' was a long stretch of discoloured earth. 'Shrewsbury Forest' was a mangled mass of trees lying at all angles.

Flying at an indicated one hundred and five miles per hour, the Camels and Brisfit maintained formation as they flew through a barrage of Archie and into enemy airspace over Houthulst. Unperturbed by the multiple blasts, Bungee concentrated on the surrounding sky. The other pilots were equally alert, their necks in constant motion as they dipped their wings searching for enemy aeroplanes approaching from the direction of the rising sun. Below them, Belgium was a mass of intertwined enemy trenches, track's, organised shell holes, wire entanglements and other obstacles. Ever the diligent observer, Pechell scanned the terrain for signs of new excavations and movement of artillery or troops.

Butcher slid laterally out of formation and closed his knees around the joystick, preventing it from slowly moving to one side while he adjusted his goggles with his right hand. An old wound in his left elbow ached painfully, it was a legacy of his service with the 5th Army infantry. On the first day of the battle of Menin Ridge a German bayonet had severed a main nerve, partially disabling his arm. Despite his injuries he managed a successful transfer to the Royal Flying Corps as an observer with 321 Squadron. Drawing on his pre-war aviation experience as an amateur flier, he quickly became an accomplished Camel pilot and had already accrued three victories.

Fifteen thousand feet above Kortemark Butcher moved back into formation and maintained a constant position aft and starboard of the Brisfit. He achieved this by keeping his Camel's port wings next to the two-seater's tail and his spinning propeller to the right of its wingtips. Formation flying in a Camel required above average hand-eye co-ordination. The Sopwith had little inherent stability about its rolling axis and was an unstable machine in the air, but Butcher had plenty of practice. He waved across to Carter and Pechell who responded in like manner.

Five miles due south of Thourout, Carter dipped the Brisfit's nose and began a steady descent, watching his aneroid altimeter as the needle unwound to thirteen thousand feet. Looking down, he recognised the sweep of railway track west of Lichterveld town and the station. Behind him, Pechell held his map beneath the coaming to check their course. After five miles on their present heading they'd be directly above Wynghene. He outstretched his arm against the airflow to indicate the area for photography. Carter acknowledged with an exaggerated nod of his head.

Despite having the Camels of 321 Squadron providing top-cover, Carter was uneasy as he concentrated on their approach. Flying a predictable straight-line course to Wynghene they were an easy target for local Archie. When the anticipated barrage came, it was uncomfortably close. Shockwaves from each explosion rocked the Brisfit's wings and created a pitching motion that made photography a challenge. As they circled the target area Pechell depressed the camera release lever to take his first photograph. The exposed plate changed automatically and the shutter reset every four seconds by a pinion drive activated by the auxiliary propeller. By exposing a series of photographs directly over the main road traversing the aerodrome, he was able to capture images of local traffic between the barracks and hangars on one side, and the enemy Scouts lined up on the other. Satisfied with his work, he slapped Carter's shoulder and gave a firm `thumbs-up'.

It was a six minute flight north to their second objective and, despite the watchful Camel's re-assuring presence, Carter felt particularly vulnerable crossing enemy occupied terrain. Soon, the aerodrome east of Varssenaere appeared on the horizon. Surrounded by open countryside and a patchwork of fields, its facilities were dominated by a winding lake and magnificent Chateau set in open grounds. There were white patches on the grass airstrip where constant use had worn away grass and soil to expose the chalk substrate. Immediately north of the straight road leading west to Jabbeke lay a tree lines access track. Dispersed randomly around the perimeter were a number of stark white bomb craters, a legacy of previous air attacks. The morning was remarkably clear and long shadows from the low sun enhanced every detail of the hangars, field and support buildings.

Wynghene had forewarned Varssenaere of the Brisfit's approach and, thirteen thousand feet below, six enemy defenders were already taking off. Carter saw them racing across the field. He checked his cockpit clock. It was eight-thirty, the fighters would need just under a quarter hour to climb and intercept, giving them enough time to complete their task and re-join the Camels at fifteen thousand feet.

With numb fingers, Pechell adjusted his lens to take a sequence of photographs. The camera was mounted over the Brisfit's side and difficult to operate. He removed his gloves, crying out in reaction to the sudden pain. The metal casing was so cold to the touch it stole what remained of the warmth from his hands. Tears formed on the side of his face and froze instantly in the frigid blast of their propeller. Far below, individual puffs of gunsmoke appeared around the aerodrome perimeter followed seconds later by a multitude of concussive air blasts. Circling on a predictable course they were sitting ducks, but there was no alternative. The two airmen flew on, through expanding spheres of thousands of indiscriminate metal fragments.

A black Archie cloud erupted close by the Brisfit blasting jagged shrapnel into the sky. Flying directly through the choking gasses Carter was momentarily blinded until the smoke cleared. When they emerged from the cloud it was apparent their aeroplane had sustained multiple hits. He shifted around to check on Pechell who was insisting on one more circuit. He'd seen a new building development north of the aerodrome and was determined to capture a clear image for later analysis. Seconds later, dense clouds of residual smoke generated by ground artillery north of the aerodrome drifted across the field and rendered further photography a waste of time. Pechell slapped Carter's right shoulder, a signal that he'd finished and it was time to head home.

Carter used his scarf to clear a film of oil and burnt cordite from his goggles then focused his eyes on six ascending enemy defenders. Two of the machines were closing the gap significantly faster than their companions. He immediately identified the leading machines as Fokker Dr1s. With a climb rate of eleven hundred feet a minute, the triplanes were already less than two thousand feet below and would soon be in position to attack.

In an instant, the guns on the ground ceased fire to avoid hitting their own machines. Percival and Alderton had already broken away from the other Camels and were plunging to intercept the leading enemy interceptors. They swept past the Brisfit with the noise of a million sabres cleaving the air. Despite the rushing airflow and close proximity of their Falcon engine, Pechell could hear the unmistakable clatter of machine gun fire from below. Carter wanted to join in the contest but remembered Bungee's orders. Reluctantly, he turned west toward the township of Oudenburg and thence across the lines to Ypres. It was eight-forty in the morning and they had been in the air for just over an hour.

Bungee saw Percival and Alderton break and descend. He was about to join them when his attention was distracted by four converging enemy scouts five miles to the west from the direction of Ghistelles. They were at fourteen thousand feet and climbing steadily. After signalling his intention to the others, he led the remaining Camels on a course to intercept. With a closing speed in excess of two hundred miles an hour it was only a matter of seconds before the leading Albatros came into range. Bungee raked the enemy fuselage before its pilot had a chance to react. He swept past overhead into a cloud of coolant vapour from the DV's ruptured radiator. As he pulled up from his attack run Butcher swept past his port wing. He was closing the gap on an Albatros chasing Carpenter.

Butcher's right thumb was poised on the gun paddles. Milliseconds before he fired, a stream of ammunition from behind alerted him to an enemy machine on his tail. A frisson of shock combined with a coordinated reflex, he pulled back on the joystick, kicked right rudder, entered a snap-roll and slowed sufficiently to escape. Another Albatros appeared ahead, crossing from right to left. Instinctively Butcher fired a deflection shot. The Albatros rolled off as its engine burst into flames. Pieces of ripped wing fabric ignited. The fuselage broke away and the remains dropped like a stone.

As the combat above continued, two thousand feet below

Percival and Alderton were having a tough time combating the highly manoeuvrable Fokkers from Varssenaere. To compound their problems the remaining four ascending Albatri had arrived. Heavily outnumbered, Percival dived onto the closest biplane and fired a sustained round into its black-crossed tailplane, severing the elevator control wires. He wasted no time watching the DV go down and sought out his next target. Closing up to the tail of a second Albatros, Percival instinctively glanced back at the exact moment one of the triplanes dropped into position on his six-o-clock and fired. He broke right, but the German pilot was determined and skilled. Even employing all the Camel's advantages, Percival couldn't evade the enemy and was almost stalling when he entered a defensive right-hand circle. The lethally effective Fokker appeared invincible and was gaining position to fire.

With his head forced down by centrifugal force, Percival pulled back on the joystick and stalled. Kicking full right rudder he dropped the nose while the engine's gyroscopic precession twisted the Camel clockwise. Forced upward from his seat and into the freezing airflow by the sudden reversal in gravity, only his lap belt kept him inside the cockpit. Blood rushed to his head as he pushed the stick full forward then back to centre to cancel the movement. At eight thousand feet he had regained flying speed and lost his assailant, but his escape had come at a cost. The Sopwith's upper wing fabric had been shredded. He could sense by the response of his control cables that his machine had sustained severe damage.

Having seen off the remaining enemy fighters, Carpenter, Bungee and Butcher set immediate course to aid Percival and Alderton. The latter was flying from left to right, hotly pursued by an enemy triplane. Recognising his comrade's peril, Carpenter dived using his machine's speed advantage. On sighting the approaching Camel, the German pilot broke right and climbed. Carpenter followed and aligned the Dr1 in his Aldis sight.

Twin Vickers fired twenty rounds, shattering the triplane's port upper interplane strut. The upper portion of wing sheared off and the Fokker snap rolled to the left.

Bungee nosed down into the melee, his target, the remaining Fokker. At first, the enemy pilot saw a small dot approaching fast from the north-east. Small and black, it grew larger as it approached and assumed the distinctive forward profile of a Camel. Rapidly closing in on the Dr1's six-o-clock Bungee opened fire with his Vickers. The triplane immediately entered into a half loop. Inverted at the top, the German stretched his head back to keep his eyes on the Sopwith before rolling out with a diving attack. Bungee had anticipated the enemy move and climbed to intercept.

A metallic hail rattled between the wings of both combatants. Bungee heard the crack of bullets striking his Camel then, with a loud swish of air the two machines passed each other with only feet to spare. Both aeroplanes shook violently in the propwash, straining Bungee's neck as he was thrown from one side of the cockpit to the other.

Employing the Camel's unique advantage, Bungee initiated a sharp right turn and locked onto the Fokker's tail. Closing in for the kill, his thumb poised above his gun paddles, he saw the triplane turn in a one hundred and eighty degree flat half spin. Disconcerted by this exhibition of amazing agility, Bungee swerved to avoid a torrent of tracer and entered a zooming climb. He waited until the triplane exposed its six-o-clock then dived to attack, but the light and agile Fokker reversed and swept past, firing its twin Spandaus. Bungee climbed, rolled off the top and dived down again onto the Dr1 as it turned to face him head-on.

Surrounded by the complex three dimensional battle Alderton kept his wits about him, remaining calm and disciplined. He saw his C.O.'s desperate plight made worse by the arrival of an all-white Albatros. Locked in combat with the Fokker, Bungee zoom-climbed to escape, as the white D.V. gave chase. Although further away Carpenter had also seen Bungee's predicament and, together with Alderton, he moved in behind the two Germans.

The combat stretched out into an ascending chase. At twelve thousand feet the white Albatros pitched upward, looped and dropped back down behind Alderton and Carpenter. The moment it fired on Carpenter's machine Bungee pitched up and looped back from the front to assume position directly behind the white Albatros. He fired fifty rounds at close range into the enemy biplane which spun away, trailing an expanding cloud of opaque black smoke. The Fokker pilot, isolated from his comrade, broke off combat and continued a rapid climb beyond reach of the Camels.

The surviving five Albatros D.V's aborted further engagement and set off west in pursuit of Carter's Brisfit. Bungee re-grouped his patrol to give chase, but there was no sign of Percival.

Percival's Camel was in a bad shape after his engagement with the Fokker Dr1 over Varssenaere. Acutely aware of unusual sounds coming from the engine's cylinder bearings, he scanned the sky for any sign of Bungee or the other Camels. Finding himself alone, he looked down for a familiar landmark, anything that would tell him his whereabouts. Thrown around in the tumult of combat he had become hopelessly lost. After several minutes of fruitless search, he concluded that the best thing to do was to fly south-west, regain altitude and go home.

Ten minutes later Percival's attention was drawn to a momentary sparkle of light in the sky below his port wingtip, the sun's reflection on distant wings. He knew that, friend or enemy, the pilot would be unable to see him against the risen sun. Although flying a damaged machine, the urge to attack was irresistible. Opening out his 130 horsepower Clerget he rapidly closed the distance. Recognizing the black crosses and distinctive wing profile of an Albatros D.V., Percival intercepted the enemy side-on from above. He established sufficient lead for his guns and opened fire. Ammunition met the target as it flew though the line of tracer, hitting the fuel tank. The Albatros immediately rolled off, fire spreading back along the fuselage.

Reacting instinctively, Percival looked back over his right shoulder where four more enemy machines were diving on him at a steep angle. He employed the Camel's remarkable right-turn ability to frustrate their initial attack, but only three of the enemy swept past. An all-black Albatros had anticipated Percival's move and, having broken away from his companions, was on course to intercept him head-on. Maintaining a right hand turn Percival dropped the Camel's nose. Louder than the roar of his engine, he could hear the D.V's guns clattering as it hurtled past overhead.

Moments later both combatants were facing each other in another head-on assault. Percival applied right rudder, skidding his Camel's nose right to avoid his opponent's line of fire. The two on-rushing machines passed each other at a closing speed of over two hundred miles an hour. Percival saw another Albatros directly ahead. A green and white striped machine was closing in on a frontal attack while his black painted comrade turned onto the solitary Camel's tail. It was a classic 'scissors' manoeuvre. Percival fired his Vickers at the approaching D.V. and, as it flew by, pulled his Camel into a sharp right hand turn. Forced down into the cockpit by centrifugal force, he struggled to keep his head up and his hands on the controls. The Camel's weakened structure creaked in protest. Once again he was facing the all-black Albatros and despatched twenty well-aimed rounds into its fuselage before banking into another right turn. He looked up to witness a third Albatros descending on him in a steep, almost vertical dive. Facing a life or death situation Percival threw his Camel aggressively around the sky in a series of rapid and violent flying manoeuvres. His body was alternatively crushed into his seat and lifted from the cockpit. Jostled from side to side, the physical strain was beginning to wear him down.

Although the enemy fighters were unable to match the Camel's unique abilities, Percival couldn't withstand avoid multiple attacks indefinitely. His damaged wings and fuselage were further compromised by aerodynamic stress and impacting ammunition. Heavily outnumbered, his only hope was that one of the enemy would, at some point, make a mistake. After a further ten minutes of close combat the striped D.V. began a wide turn that Percival was able to intercept. He fired and saw his ammunition hit home. The enemy machine began to emit smoke. Percival was close enough to see inside the cockpit as fire emerged from under the instrument panel. The frantic pilot tried to fan the flames from his face with burning gauntlets. Within seconds, the stricken enemy rolled inverted and began to dive. Up until that moment Percival had regarded air combat as a battle between machines. For the first time he had witnessed the human cost and it appalled him. Every detail of the grotesque scene had seared into his mind.

A series of loud cracks sent a pulse of adrenalin through his body. Machine gun bullets were striking home on his tail, he could feel every impact transmit through the rudder control cables. Fixated on the burning Albatros he had allowed his attention to lapse for a few critical seconds. Swiveling his head around he saw the all-black enemy machine closing in behind. High above the desolate Belgian countryside Percival turned to face the enemy and the two combatants converged at over two hundred miles an hour. Once in range both machines opened fire simultaneously. It was a test of nerve and Percival was determined not to flinch first. Pieces of fabric were flying off the Camel. Ammunition discharged from twin Vickers' clipped the D.V's engine and pierced the fuel tank. Cut to pieces, the Albatros exploded in a livid ball of flame, Percival dropped his nose rapidly to avoid the expanding orb of burning debris.

At a hundred and thirty miles an hour in a near vertical descent, Percival's Camel began to shake violently. The vibration was so intense he thought the airframe would fall apart. Slowly recovering into level flight he saw a crimson Albatros passing south-west two thousand feet below, it was closing in on a lone Brisfit. He knew his machine was unfit for combat, but was compelled to intercept otherwise he'd never be able to live with his conscience. As he rolled out to his right and arced down to cut off the attack, he could see the serial number B1111 painted on the tail. It was Carter and Pechell's machine.

Pechell felt the Brisfit rock from side to side. It was Carter's signal. He'd seen an approaching sky-blue Albatros D.V and turned their two-seater so that Pechell could aim his twin Vickers directly at the German. The D.V closed in on their six-o-clock, jets of flame poured from the muzzles of both forward guns, then it dived underneath and pulled up to attack their vulnerable lower fuselage. Carter responded by skewing left and right across the sky. The Brisfit's knife-edge tapered tail minimized blind spots and gave Pechell a clear shot at the attacking enemy. While his observer was pre-occupied, Carter saw another, crimson Albatros approaching from their starboard side. Caught in a lethal crossfire of tracer, phosphorous trails streaked across the Brisfit's upper wings as the D.V swept overhead and climbed out of range.

Carter put the Brisfit into an aerial skid, bleeding off speed by 'fish-tailing' and forcing the blue Albatros to overshoot. For a fleeting moment, the enemy passed directly in front of his forward facing Vickers. His finger pressed the firing paddle, raking the German machine square centre. A long stream of white vapour trailed back from the D.Vs exhaust as it turned over onto its back and commenced an uncontrolled plummet to the ground.

From high above, the crimson D.V saw his comrade fall. Intent on retribution he rolled over and dived for another assault on the British machine. Closing in on their six-o-clock, he weaved from side to side, Spandaus spitting fire. Pechell replied with a salvo from his twin Lewis guns at a rate of five hundred rounds a minute. Their recoil skewed the Brisfit around. Dissuaded by Pechell's ammunition, the enemy ducked below then rolled up and over the top before diving to attack again. Carter side-slipped, giving his rear gunner an uninterrupted line of fire. Once again the Albatros was forced to roll off, climb, and dive for another attack. Out of bullets, Pechell resorted to throwing empty ammunition drums at the pursuing enemy as Carter dived almost vertically to escape.

Tracer was streaming past Pechell's head when a Sopwith Camel appeared, seemingly from out of nowhere. The enemy pilot was so fixated on his target that he had lost his peripheral vision and situational awareness. He hadn't seen Percival swing in on his tail. As twin Vickers fired from behind and underneath the Albatros, pieces of wood and fabric were riven from the D.Va's fuselage and wings. The German spiraled up, trying to work out the location of his attacker as Percival entered a right hand climbing turn and centered the Albatros in his Aldis sight. He fired and it exploded, the glare nearly blinding him. Flying debris littered the sky and pieces of broken aeroplane hit his propeller and wings. A six cylinder Mercedes D.III engine rushed past, turning slowly as it missed the Camel's wingtips by mere yards.

'That's enough. Let's go home or we'll be dead men for sure.' Percival spoke his thoughts aloud as he pulled up alongside Carter and Pechell. He knew his machine was barely airworthy and his fuel level was critically low. Both pilots saluted each other as a mark of mutual respect. They'd stay together on the return trip for as long as possible.

At first, Pechell didn't notice he'd been shot. His adrenalin was up and there had been so much confused activity it took him a while to realise what had happened. He felt as if he'd been hit hard on his left mid-upper thigh by a cricket bat. Then the pain came, like someone had pierced him with a red-hot poker and held it in. His leg was wet with blood.

The Brisfit tilted and dropped, nose down. Freefalling from nine thousand feet Pechell's body rose from his seat, his arms floating as loose objects and empty ammunition drums ejected from the cockpit. Carter wiped his goggles with the end of his scarf, looked to the side of his oil and cordite smeared windshield and was immediately exposed to the rushing airflow. At minus fifteen degrees Fahrenheit it was hard to breath. He regained control and righted the ailing machine, but could tell by the control response and restless throbbing sound of their engine they were in deep trouble. He was too focused on survival to be scared.

The Brisfit shook and rattled before veering sharply to the right, throwing both men against the cockpit coaming. The Falcon misfired then cut out completely. Immediately the force of thrust was reduced to zero and the Brisfit's high-drag airframe slowed airspeed. Carried forward by their own inertia, at a hundred and thirty miles an hour indicated air speed Carter pulled up and used their remaining momentum to gain as much altitude as possible. He had two options, either restart the damaged engine, or make a forced landing. In either event, swift action was required. He switched off the fuel and magnetos. The Rolls-Royce Falcon was finished. Maintaining a speed of fifty five miles an hour he acquired a glide attitude to keep them airborne for as long as possible.

Cross-checking his position, Carter searched for a suitable landing area amid the patchwork of wet, dark brown fields below. By the time they reached three thousand feet he made his choice. Carefully balancing the rudder and aileron he initiated a twenty degree right hand turn into wind, aiming for an area clear of vegetation.

Pechell prepared for the inevitable crash landing by removing the heavy twin Lewis guns from their Scarff mount and throwing them over the side. He cursed vociferously as he tightened his lap belt, angry at the unknown enemy pilot who had inflicted the final blow. As the ground approached, the blood drained from his face and his hands began to shake. He sat back in his seat and mentally judged the exact spot where the crash would happen, praying to escape the torture of fire. He hoped the end, if it came, would be quick and painless.

The uneven ground ripped past at tremendous speed. Pechell could make out trees, houses and streets. He had little doubt he was going to die. It was difficult to communicate over the shrieking wind, Carter's hand signals accompanied his shout back to Pechell. "Brace yourself!"

When the impact came, Carter felt as if a ton of bricks had been dropped on his shoulders. Forced down in his seat as the Brisfit smashed hard into the ground, he could hear the sound of splintering wood and tearing canvas. As they slid across the mud, riven shards of wreckage flew in all directions. The starboard wings separated from the rest of the aeroplane and the air was filed with suffocating oil mist and petrol fumes. Carter's lap belt snapped and his body was launched into the air. Hands above his head, legs flailing, he landed in a gorse bush some twenty feet away. He was stunned for several minutes, during which there was absolute silence.

"Oh, my God, I'm alive." Carter's vision was completely blurred from the impact. Struggling to his feet, he made his way back to the wreckage and removed Pechell's fur lined leather hood and goggles. Lips retracted and teeth clenched together, his observer's chin was quivering and his eyes stared wildly as if in horrified astonishment.

"Are you badly hurt?"

"My left thigh, either shot through, broken or both."

"Sorry old chap, but I'm going to have to get you out."

The fuselage had come to a stop on its side, tilted at an angle, the engine lay half buried in the ground. Extracting Pechell from the cockpit was no easy task. His seat had been thrust forward and a twisted upper longeron restricted any movement.

"Wriggle, come on!" Carter encouraged, but his observer's heavy brown leather flight coat was snagging on broken diagonal fuselage braces.

Kicking out with his good leg Pechell freed himself from a web of internal bracing wires. Fiery bursts of pain pulsated around his wound, amplifying with each dragging step as Carter supported him to a position of safety. They found refuge some hundred feet from the Brisfit behind a pile of stacked timber.

Carter unbuckled Pechell's belt and opened his coat, fully expecting the worst. There was a blood blackened hole in the upper left leg of his drill breeches. Assessing the extent of the injury he checked each limb was straight and of equal length to the other then used his clasp knife to tear open the khaki woollen fabric. Underneath was an entrance wound the size of a shilling.

"Can you move your lower leg?"

"Yes." Pechell laid back panting, biting his lip to keep from crying out.

"There's no nerve or artery damage." Carter encouraged. Elevating Pechell's wounded limb he supported it with a roughly hewn log. Removing his silk scarf he improvised a makeshift bandage. The two men looked at each other, no words were necessary.

Returning to the wreckage Carter retrieved his heavy brass Webley and Scott signal gun and a couple of spare flares. There was a strong smell of petrol, a steady stream of fuel was leaking from the main fuel tank. She'd burn well.

He returned to Pechell "We'll be safer here once she goes up."

For several minutes the two men laid back against the timber, breathing heavily and regaining their senses. At length, with his vision fully restored, Carter examined the map. "We've come down outside a town called Spriethoek, east of a crossroad and north of a rise in the ground marked as Piebald Farm".

"Less than five miles from our lines, well we almost made it."

"Pity Wing won't get their photographs."

"Bugger the bloody photographs." Pechell cursed. "We might as well burn the plates along with the old bus."

"Seems a waste after all our effort."

"Well, can you think of a way to get them back across the lines in one piece?" Pechell replied testily. "By then some other poor sods will already have been sent out to take more."

"Makes sense."

"What you can do is unscrew the camera lens, keep it with you, if you make it back it's worth salvaging. Here…" He reached inside his coat pocket and withdrew a compass. "Take this too."

"I've no intention of leaving you."

Pechell winced, his skin drawn tightly around the eyes. "You make a run for it. I'll set the old girl on fire. Odds are every Hun for miles around will head for the smoke. I'll give you as long as I can."

"I hate to leave you here alone, can't we at least try together for a few miles?"

"Sorry, won't work Carter."

Carter smiled sadly and crouched down alongside his comrade. "Just seems so ruddy unfair."

Pechell grasped Carter's right arm in a firm grip. "War is for the strong minded, don't look for morality lessons."

Both men recognised the inevitable. They shook hands sadly.

"Good luck chum, see you again after the war."

"Goodbye old lad, cheerio."

76

Carter set off west with a heavy heart, crossing several disused trench works and wire entanglements before he reached the long, straight road to Waterdamhoek. Fortunately his map was sufficiently detailed. It allowed him to recognise they key features, often given informal names by allied troops. Brigands' Corner, Desert Corner and Crusoe Cross Roads to name but a few. He reached the road at a point called 'Island Fork', but halted further progress when he saw a woman running toward him from the direction of two medium sized ponds on the other side. As she drew closer he could see she was a Belgian peasant girl, dressed in a plain white shirt and headscarf, with a dark shawl about her shoulders.

"Get off the road!" She urged. Grasping his hand she hurried him behind a disused barn.

"Put this on." She thrust an old jacket into his arms. "You must not enter Waterdamhoek, the enemy have troops there. I will show you a way to avoid them.

"Right." He hesitated, reluctant to place his fate in the hands of a stranger. The girl was terrified, that much was apparent in her wide eyes. Her breath was ragged and her hands trembled at her sides. He still had his revolver, if there was any sign of treachery he wouldn't hesitate to use it.

"Hurry, we must leave this place." She looked out at the road from behind the barn. "It is clear, stay close to me. Not far from here there is an old path. We will use that".

"Where are you taking me?" Carter asked, but the girl ignored him.

Their cross-county trek east of Waterdamhoek was hindered by numerous depressions made impassable by deep mud. Amid clinging undergrowth and high ridges Carter had become hopelessly disorientated. Detours often required slow passage through bracken and rusted barbed wire. They had both slipped and fallen on several occasions. It was wet and bitterly cold. By the time they reached a 'T' junction named 'Afghan Corner', Carter's map had become illegible from exposure to the sleet and mud. He cast it aside, relying entirely on his unknown guide as they continued north across disused earthworks, enemy tracks and an old German air pipeline.

They paused for a ten minute rest outside Moorslede, on the southerly remains of Martell Wood. The girl was still very nervous and spoke only a few words, glancing around at the slightest noise. She clenched her fists tightly, her nails digging into the palm of her hand. Watching her closely, Carter was taken aback by her gaunt eyes and the prominence of her cheekbones. Frozen and exhausted, he could feel his pulse pounding in his temples while his mind constantly repeated the events of the past few hours.

At midday they were about to move on when he heard a muffled thud in the distance. The girl jumped in alarm. Carter looked up in time to witness an angry vortex of smoke and debris rise up beyond the treetops on the horizon. It could mean only one thing. Pechell had set fire to their Brisfit. Either he'd been discovered, or was unable to withstand the pain of his wound any longer.

Pechell checked his wristwatch with difficulty. His clumsy fingers pulled back his sleeve and exposed the dial face. It was midday and he had been lying, curled up in a foetal position on the cold damp ground for almost three hours. It had started to sleet and the stabbing pain from his left leg had become a painful numbness, a deep, penetrating ache. Tired and confused, he had difficulty remembering how long he had been there. Unable to control waves of violent shivering he loaded a flare into the pistol, levelled the barrel toward the Brisfit and fired. The flare landed short, he re-loaded and fired again. This time the broken aeroplane ignited immediately. Petrol vapour erupted in a rolling, rising ball of livid red fire.

Even the searing heat from the burning Brisfit could not penetrate his layers of clothing. He was feeling increasingly tired and longed for sleep. From a distance he could hear the sound of a motor lorry, then a squeal of brakes accompanied by voices and barking dogs. Pechell had no illusion of what was to come and braced himself for capture and imprisonment. Even that prospect was less daunting than his present discomfort. A group of shadows appeared above the crest of a nearby mound, voices were calling out. They weren't regular soldiers but by all appearances, officers. One of their company approached and saluted.

"Good afternoon. I am Oberleutnant Hermann Kohze, Commandant of Jasta Three."

Having acquired a working knowledge of German at college, he replied in his captor's own language: "My name is Pechell, Second Lieutenant Royal Flying Corps. Forgive me for not standing." His voice was weak, his words slurred.

Kohze's eyes settled on Pechell's tunic and Observer's badge. He looked around. "Your pilot is where"?

"No idea."

"No?" Kohze sighed. "A pity." He looked up at the threatening, grey overcast, made even more ominous by ash and smoke from the smouldering Brisfit. "It is of little consequence, he will be found soon. For now we will return to Wynghene and have your injury attended to. We have an excellent doctor."

Despite his discomfort Pechell managed a smile. Three of the officers set about removing his wet outer clothing and wrapped him in dry blankets. One of them produced a patriotically wrapped bar of 'Moser-Roth' Schokolade, snapped of a square and handed it to him.

"Here."

"Thanks." Pechell's numb, stiff fingers accepted the enemy gift. Within minutes of consuming the confection he experienced the release of sugar energy.

Assisted to his feet he could see a half-dozen German flyers poking around the Brisfit's blackened wreckage, searching for souvenirs. After a few hundred yards of stumbling progress across the mud Pechell was made as comfortable as possible, semi-recumbent inside the back of a Benz truck. Ten minutes later they set off under a leaden sky. The sleet drove spitefully against the canvas awning. Sitting next to him was a German pilot officer who appeared considerably older than his colleagues.

"You are lucky to have survived landing in such a wretched area, your pilot must be especially skilled." The Leutnant offered Pechell an unfiltered 'Eckstein's' cigarette. "My name is Carl Menckhoff. When we return to Wynghene, if you are sufficiently recovered, perhaps tonight you will be our guest in the Officer's Kasino?"

He draped a woollen blanket across Pechell's shoulders. "Myself, I have been shot down and injured many times."

"You like Schnapps?" He withdrew the stopper from an embossed green glass bottle. "Here".

"Thank you." The peppermint flavoured spirit was strong yet pleasant. It helped Pechell cope with the rolling, jarring motion of the lorry that, combined with its solid rubber tyres and smell of exhaust fumes, made him increasingly nauseous. He was determined not to succumb and lose what remained of his dignity. After six miles they entered Roeselare and the ride became a little more settled as they journeyed through the bustling town.

"So now you have fallen. In the morning you'll be collected and moved to a prisoner of war camp for officers." Menckhoff smiled amicably. "You will sleep tonight in comfortable quarters in town. Under guard naturally. I will see to it that your people are notified. Our families must not suffer unnecessarily eh?"

Despite his pain, several measures of Schnapps had partially revived Pechell's mood. "I'm surprised so many of you travelled so far just to reach me."

Menckhoff shrugged dismissively. "We've nothing else to do today, our aerodrome is waterlogged." A blast of bitter air blew open the canvas door accompanied by a swirl of sleet. "I pity your pilot out in this weather, wherever he is."

After a brief rest in the forest, Carter and his guide set off on the final leg of their journey into Moorslede. For a while their route took them east, away from the town, circling the base of a sixty

80

foot high knoll until they reached the main road into town. His guide and companion noticed his discomfort.

"Not far Mijnheer." Her exhaled breath formed a swirling cloud of vapour.

Carter could only nod in response. His throat and mouth were too dry from apprehension to speak.

"When we enter town I'll go on ahead, stay well behind me but keep me in sight at all times. If I remove my head scarf it is a signal that you must run, otherwise follow me. There is a safe house. I'll stop outside and light a cigarette before moving on. The door will be unlocked, go inside. Someone will be waiting."

When they reached the first house along the road to Moorslede the girl began to pace ahead, sidestepping around puddles and dirty slush. Following at a safe distance, Carter felt unseen eyes peering at him from every window he passed. The straight road into town was empty of traffic making him feel even more conspicuous. With the collar of his borrowed jacket turned up against the driving sleet, even his footsteps seemed louder as they traversed the street. Around every corner and behind every building he expected to be challenged by a uniformed enemy. He resisted the urge to glance behind, expecting any moment to hear a barked command to halt.

The road opened out to a stone paved square littered with fallen bricks and roof tiles. Directly ahead, on the other side of the deserted market place behind the leafless branches of two Beech trees, was a church that had escaped much of the damage inflicted on other buildings. On the right, under an overcast sky, an old single storey house was the smallest in a terrace of larger dwellings. Its tiled roof was broken and the white outer walls peppered with gunshot holes. On either side of the single front door were two sash windows. Those on the left had been blown out, the room within bare. Those on the right were intact, the dirty glass reflected light from two oil lanterns within.

The girl paused outside, lit a cigarette and then walked on toward the church. Advancing cautiously beneath the overcast sky, Carter slowly opened the door and entered. A muscle twitched involuntarily at the corner of his right eye and his right hand moved to the grip of his revolver. From a backroom came the sound of movement. A figure emerged and peered at the silhouetted figure standing in the light of the opened front door. Carter closed it carefully lest he disturb the loose, over-hanging roof tiles. The hall interior smelt musty, with the pervasive odour of stale cigar smoke.

"Who is this?" Asked the figure from within. Carter noticed the RFC wings on the stranger's ragged tunic.

"A fellow flyer." He responded.

The inquisitor advanced cautiously, there was at least three day's stubble on his chin.

"So I see". He stood stock still, a smile broke across his face.

"Carter, isn't it? 323 Squadron?"

"Carter's the name yes."

"Peterson, Cecil Peterson, you remember? 303 Squadron."

"Good Lord!" Carter thrust out his hand and shook Peterson's enthusiastically. "I hardly recognised you, you've lost a fair bit of weight old boy."

"You don't look too good yourself." Peterson replied. "Been in a smash have you?"

"Afraid so." Carter took stock of his bedraggled appearance in the hall's old trumeau mirror.

"Some bloody coincidence eh?" Peterson slapped Carter heartily on the back. "Well don't just stand there old chum, put that gun down, take the weight off and bring me up to date on how the war's going."

They entered a backroom dominated by a large, open brick hearth and a bleached oak refectory table. In front of the warming fire was a metal frame chair and round wooden stool. Carter sat down on the former, removed his boots and hung his damp socks up to dry. Peterson picked up a small potato peeler from the mantelpiece, sat on the stool and resumed the preparation of his evening meal.

"Is Major McClennan still at the helm? How's Jimmy Thompson?" Peterson was anxious for news about his old squadron.

"McClennan went on patrol with Scott Cameron later in October, never came back I'm afraid. Scott's been appointed C.O. in his place. As far as I know Thompson's still at the front."

"Only two months away and it seems like a lifetime." Peterson leant forward, bared elbows on his knees. Having peeled the last potato he dropped it into a shallow copper bowl on the dusty stone floor and wiped his forehead with the back of his right hand.

"Didn't think I'd be cooking luncheon for two." Peterson apologised. "I'm afraid it's just potatoes, bread and a few vegetables from the kitchen garden."

Carter placed his sodden boots on the front hearth and massaged his bare, blistered feet. He examined his waist, it was still bleeding from where his seat strap had been ripped away.

"Must be hard to fight a war on an empty stomach."

Peterson was used to the meagre rations. "The Belgians have had a tough time, all their imports were been cut-off by our naval blockade. It's not so bad here in the 'etappengebiet' even so, just about everything comes via the Commission for Relief in Belgium. Folk here in town have been queuing at the soup kitchen."

Recalling his hearty breakfast in the Mess back at La Gorgue, Carter suddenly felt guilty.

"I'm not particularly hungry old man. You tuck in." He said quietly.

"Nonsense, have a bowl of this stuff at least. You need to keep your strength up." Adding with a conspiratorial wink. "Who knows what lies ahead eh?"

"Come on Peterson, It's not like you to rely on the whim of fate. What's going on?"

"There's a fellow coming to meet us at dusk. I'm pretty sure we can rely on him, he's a part of an organisation I've encountered before."

"An associate of the young lady who brought me here?"

"She's his niece."

"Can he get us back to England do you think?" Carter enquired hopefully.

"We'll see." Peterson shrugged his shoulders. "In this weather our chances are slim without help. I know, I've already tried several times."

"Is that how you ended up here?" Carter asked.

"In a way. It's been one hell of a journey that began back on the fifth of October." He shifted into a more comfortable position. "I took-off from Wagnonlieu to bomb and strafe the Gotha base at St. Denis-Westrem and got shot down outside the perimeter. On the run for two days until they caught me."

"Rotten luck".

"Inevitable really, but from that very moment I planned my escape. After a session with their Army Interrogation Section they sent me to Freiberg-in-Breisgau, nice spot, more like a spa than a prison. We'd go swimming in the baths followed by regular walks in the hills behind the camp. Porridge or bacon for breakfast every morning, even joined the Tuesday evening debating society. I shared a room with two other officers overlooking the grounds. Splendid views over Freiburg."

Peterson picked up a frayed embroidered tablecloth and, carrying it to the kitchen's only window, hung it from two rusty nails to blank out light from the low sun.

"Sounds very tempting to stay there and sit out the war". Carter observed.

"Not for me old boy. Trouble was, every time I made a dash for it the Huns would rough me up as punishment. Far from a deterrent, it made me more determined. I tried everything, climbing through windows dressed as a German officer, cutting wire fences in broad daylight, jumping walls, hiding in a dirty clothes basket carted away from the camp, you name it."

"Where were you heading?"

"I had a choice, south to Switzerland or west to Holland, both about the same distance. Denmark was too far. Twice I got to the Dutch border before being caught. It was bad luck. The German police are mostly beyond military age, best suited for peace time work. There's not much to fear from the elderly village policeman or his dim-witted urban counterpart."

"What did they do to you?"

"The Huns didn't want me around, moved me from one camp to another and put me in solitary confinement where I'd just sit and glare menacingly at the brutes. Senior and junior ranks, made no difference. Soon got myself a reputation as a trouble-maker. The lads would all cheer me when I arrived back from an escape, it raised their morale." Peterson laughed. "Had the opposite effect on the Huns. The Commandants would try anything to get me posted elsewhere. Eventually they sent me to a place called Fort Nine at Ingolstadt with all the other bad pennies, about a hundred and fifty of us all told, French, Canadian, Australians, Russians, you name it. They were a mine of information and experience for an escapee. Russian greatcoats can be made into passable German uniforms for instance. As you can imagine all the fellows were keen to swap advice, what food to take, clothes, how to get things like compasses, how to light a fire without smoke, transport, where to cross the border and routes to take." Peterson poked at the hearth, releasing a wave of heat from the burning logs. "Ingolstadt was a tough place though, semi-underground casement, four rowdy appells a day and the Commandant was an unpleasant cove, a real scoundrel."

"What about the guards, what were they like?"

"A bunch of Bavarian villains and some old Landsturm veterans. I got out of there along with a Captain from the 1st Canadian Mounted Rifles. Poor fellow wasn't quite all-there, he'd been hit on the head rather badly by a shell fragment. We pulled the bars out of a toilet window, climbed down the wall, slid down the grass bank and crossed the frozen moat. We were caught, which was a bloody shame. Afterwards they moved me on to Holzminden Camp where I made another dash, climbing over the perimeter wire in broad daylight. They caught me and sent me to Bad Colberg in Saxony. The Commandant said I'd be shot if I tried to get away again. He'd done it before to other chaps so I knew this would be my last chance."

Bungee taxied up to the apron and switched off. He climbed down from his Camel and slipped off his flying helmet and goggles. Beneath the burnt cordite and castor oil his face was white with rage.

Flight Sergeant Collins was the first to address him. "Sir?"

"The air pump's buggered, air speed indicator out, friction on the engine control quadrant is loose. Had to fly with one hand on the block tube lever and she's running rough on idle."

"Right Sir."

"Get it fixed! And I want a status report on the other four machines within the hour." Bungee paced toward the line of returned Camels, Sant was hurrying to greet him.

"Well?"

"Complete and utter bloody shambles!" Bungee stormed. "Lost Carter and Pechell, they went down near Spriethoek."

"I know, just spoken to Percival, said he saw them alive on the ground."

"That's some consolation." Bungee looked up at the leaden clouds gathering in the east. "Damnable waste of men and machines."

"Percival's 959 is completely shot up, back to the depot for the old girl for salvage."

"Is he alright?"

"Yes, bit shaken up though. He's lodged claims for four D.V's two destroyed, one sent down out of control and one shared with Carter and Pechell."

A hundred yards away, a Sopwith with a broken fuselage and splintered propeller was being dragged across the ground toward the nearest hangar.

"Who was it went off the track?"

"Alderton, he was first back, his machine was pretty much shot up and low on fuel."

"How is he?"

"Cut lip and a bloody nose. He's over in the first-aid hut"

"And the rest?"

"Fine. Just glad to be back in one piece."

Bungee checked his wristwatch. It was ten-o-clock. "I'd better get 323's C.O. on the 'phone, speak to him myself, let him know the score."

"Shall I call Wing H.Q. with the news?"

"The way I feel about those desk-bound bastards right now, that's probably a good idea."

The Benz truck bounced heavily over a deep rut in the road, tossing Pechell to one side as it passed through the barrier gates of Wynghene aerodrome. The wheels skidded to a halt and the back awning immediately thrown aside to reveal a leaden sky and steady fall of snow. He was too weak and depressed by his misfortune to protest as four Jasta 3 officers manhandled him out of the truck and delivered him to the medical centre. Leutnant Menckhoff, who had taken a personal interest in Pechell's welfare, remained with him while the Doctor performed his duties. The surgery door was open and Pechell caught snippets of conversation from curious passing personnel. It seemed that Jasta 3 shared the aerodrome other units. Fortunately for him, none of which were around during the devastating allied bombing raid in mid-September. If they had, his reception would have been justifiably less friendly.

A jovial, blue eyed airman stood in the corridor outside the surgery, watching Pechell as the doctor bandaged his wound. He clicked his heels in salute, laughed and remarked "Hals- und Beinbruch!" Then left in the company of several junior officers.

"That was our Leutnant Udet." Menckhoff acknowledged his

departed comrade. "He is commandant of Jasta 37 with sixteen victories. You English have heard of him yes?"

Pechell was glad of a momentary distraction from the medic's handwork. "He sent down one of our squadron's Strutters at Pont-a-Vendin last August. I was there, saw the whole thing."

"It was a fair fight. Though your aircraft were easy prey." Menckhoff responded sympathetically.

"Indeed, back then." Pechell winced as the doctor strapped a splint to his leg.

At seven that evening, Pechell entered Jasta 3's Officer's 'Kasino'. A representative of the Staffel brought him in on a three wheeled oak and rattan wheelchair and introduced him to the assembled airmen. Despite the constant aching pain in his leg, Pechell began to relax during their candlelit supper. They bonded as flyers, discarding for a moment the restriction of national affiliation. Four glasses of wine and frequent cries of 'Pröstchen!' helped him forget the pain and misery of defeat and he began a lively conversation with Menckhoff whose knowledge of English complemented Pechell's German. Soon it was hard for him to tell whether he were in a German Kasino or a RFC Mess.

What surprised Pechell was the effectiveness of the German intelligence. They knew his squadron and where he was stationed. They knew Major Wright's name and it would not have surprised him if they knew the names of his parents too. After the meal a German flyer took his place at the piano. With several shots of Schnapps inside him Pechell declared himself a passable violinist. At which point Oberleutnant Kohze, who had been following the conversation announced that he had a violin in his quarters. It was bequeathed to him by a comrade who had been killed in a crash at Wynghene last November. Kohze summonsed his batman to retrieve it. The pianist assisted Pechell in tuning the instrument and within ten minutes they were ready to begin. In the spirit of comradeship, the duo opened their performance with the German folk song `Lieb' Heimatland, ade'. Pechell played with as much intensity of feeling as he could muster and the remainder of the evening passed in pleasurable musical entertainment. As a mark of respect to their guest, at the conclusion Pechell was permitted to play the British national anthem while every enemy flier in the room stood at respectful attention. The unique celebration at Wynghene aerodrome lasted until midnight.

In the small hours of Wednesday, December nineteenth, Pechell was escorted to a nearby billet for 'Staffelpersonnel'. A former civilian property, it consisted numerous rooms with large high vaulted ceilings. Every chamber was well presented but, being difficult to heat, the Belgian owners used it only during the summer months. Pechell was shown to a one-bed room with both windows boarded up as protection from the weather. As a final precautionary measure, he was politely relieved of his wheelchair and boots.

After ensuring Pechell was comfortable, he was left alone. He laid back on his bed and relaxed. The effect of the medication he had been given, combined with alcohol left him dizzy and disorientated. His head felt as if it were falling backwards. Confident that, throughout the evening, he had not carelessly revealed any information useful to the enemy, he slept fitfully until dawn. At seven he was woken by a gentle tap on the door. A steward brought him a tray of hot coffee. Allowed facilities for a wash and shave, he was fed breakfast before a car from the Army Interrogation Section arrived to collect him. He departed at nine, expressing thanks for the Jasta's hospitality.

In Moorslede, as twilight faded into dusk, Carter and Peterson were seated alone in the abandoned front parlour. Outside, heavy driven sleet rattled against the windows, while inside two grey cotton sheets hung on brass curtain rods to provide privacy from passers-by. In the centre of the room, a cast iron paraffin stove heater was their only source of warmth. Its glow flickered against the half paneled wood walls whose bare plaster had long since been stripped of photographs and ornaments. Only the dark shadows of their frames remained. The two airmen passed the time playing Pontoon on a warped, round cherry wood dining table.

On hearing the front door open, both men looked at each other warily. Carter put down his hand of cards and withdrew his revolver. The tramp of hobnailed trench boots across the hall's bare board floor preceded the arrival of a heavy set man in his late fifties. His grey beard stained by nicotine, he was wearing a heavy woollen double breasted `reefer' jacket and faded brown cotton jodhpurs. After entering the room he took a moment to pull back the nearest window sheet and look out across the square. Satisfied his presence had been unobserved, he drew up a rustic wood ladderback chair and sat down heavily. He lit a slim cigar then studiously eyed the two English airmen.

"My name is Adrien Bourdillon." His command of the English language was excellent. "No doubt you are the men who wish to return to England?"

"More specifically to our squadrons." Carter responded.

"Naturally". Bourdillon flicked a fresh accumulation of ash carelessly to the floor. "Lieutenant Peterson, your reputation precedes you." He fixed Carter with an intense stare. "But you, Lieutenant Carter, of you we know nothing."

"I can vouch for him Sir." Peterson responded. "I met him before, in September at a squadron get together."

Satisfied with the English pilot's credentials, the Belgian seemed more at ease. He cast his gaze to the nicotine stained ceiling and inhaled a long, relaxed draw on his cigar.

"I am informed, Lieutenant Carter, that you were shot down at Spriethoek, that your observer was captured wounded?"

"We were caught in a fight east of Wynghene actually, badly shot up, tried to make it back across the lines. Almost made it, ran out of luck I'm afraid. Can you tell me anything more about Lieutenant Pechell?"

"Your observer? It seems officers from Jasta 3 recovered him. He was last seen at their aerodrome in Wynghene."

"That's decent of the Huns."

"Decent?" Bourdillon looked at Carter with incredulity. "How much do you know about the enemy? Not much it seems."

"Sorry?" Carter was taken aback.

"Back in May two of your countrymen were forced to land with engine problems. A few locals, a farmer, a labourer and a local housekeeper saw their Sopwith glide down and land. Some soldiers encamped at a nearby farm made toward their aeroplane. The pilot was seen dragging the body of his comrade before setting fire to the machine. The Boche arrived at the scene and shot the pilot dead as he tried to surrender. German officers appeared at the site and ordered their men to cease fire. They took the observer to hospital where he died the following day."

"Bastards." Peterson was stunned at such barbarity. "Cold-blooded murder."

"The witness accounts were passed to the Red Cross." Bourdillon looked directly at Carter. "These are the men who have invaded our homeland, who move among us every day, they are the reason we are starving. You think their action that day was an aberration? They have done much worse to our people."

Chastened, Carter hesitated before continuing. Bourdillon had made his point. "Perhaps you can help? The reason we were flying today was to confirm reports Jagdstaffel 28 have moved from Wynghene to Varssenaere."

"Yes, that is true. They moved all their men, machines and equipment out on the seventh and arrived at Varssenaere on the eighth." Bourdillon leaned forward and rubbed his chapped hands together close to the stove. "As I said, Jagdstaffel 3 are still at Wynghene. They have an unusually good relationship with the locals. Many of the officers live in private houses in the village, although the troops have barracks on the aerodrome. The enemy employ a number of local workers, in fact one of them is our contact. We often exchange information in the local tavern where the pilots pass their time."

"I only made it this far with the help of your niece. I'm sorry I didn't have a chance to thank her." Carter acknowledged his debt to the nameless girl.

"The best way you can thank us is to help drive the enemy out of our homeland."

"Could you get a message back to our squadrons letting them know we're alive?" Peterson asked anxiously. "Our families too."

"Any information we have is sent using a restricted channel of communication which, for security, I shan't divulge here. We must give priority to essential intelligence. I hope you understand?"

"Quite." Peterson acknowledged. His face an expression of hurt at the Belgian's lack of trust.

"I'm sorry, you see a few months ago we were betrayed. One of our comrades at Wynghene was found with explosives. He intended to destroy the hangars on the eastern side. He was arrested, court-martialed and executed immediately. We were lucky there were no further reprisals, as I have explained, the Boche are known for their brutality."

Peterson shifted uncomfortably in his chair. "I can see your need for caution. What's the plan from here on?"

"As soon as it can be arranged you will be moved to another safe house in Bruges. It is too dangerous for you both to remain here".

"That's about thirty miles." Peterson observed for Carter's benefit.

"Once there we will try to get you both out of the country and across the Channel. If that becomes impossible we can get you into neutral Holland."

It was early evening on Tuesday, December the eighteenth. Freddy Wright looked out his office window through a curtain of slush and watched the courier leave for H.Q with the day's reports. His desk was directly in front of the casement window, taking advantage of what little natural light there was. To his left, on a trestle table, an assortment of open sided boxes were full of sorted files and correspondence. His eyes were tired and red from hours of writing and dealing with assorted administration. He'd always been susceptible to eye strain.

"Couple of chaps arriving tomorrow to replace Carter and Pechell." Boyard announced with little enthusiasm. "Lieutenant Frankie Jones and an observer, Second Lieutenant Mark Long."

"Know anything about them?" Freddy asked, his mood as dark as the weather.

"Not much, it seems Jones is from 22 Squadron at Estrée-Blanche, one LVG to his credit, Long was a pharmacist before the war, joined up in '14. He's done his air gunner training and observer's course, been flying R.E.8's."

"We'll see how they fit in I suppose. At least they've some experience, not like the new fellows straight out of training."

Boyard watched Freddy pensively toy with an empty tobacco tin on his desk.

"There's a good chance they made it, after all 321's C.O. said they were both seen alive after the crash."

Freddy nodded his head, acknowledging the hope expressed by his Adjutant. "As ever it's the not knowing. Could be weeks before we get any kind of official confirmation."

"You've written to their families?"

"Yes, the usual condolences and sympathy. Tried to keep the message positive you know. I promised to keep them informed."

Boyard changed the subject, as ever the pressing exigencies of war took precedence over personal matters.

"Tomorrow's first patrol, Fergusson's 'B' Flight is a man short, Olsen's down sick with influenza so I'll ask young Yorkie to take his place if that's all right with you?"

"Sammy Sands his observer?"

"Yes, the two of them work well together."

Official business always focused Freddy's mind. "That's fine, put their names up on the board."

3. NORTH TO FREEDOM

Eight-thirty on Thursday morning, the twentieth of December 1917. It was 'jour de marché' in the occupied Belgian town of Moorslede.

A line of ten covered wagons had been set up on the far side of the market square. With most privately owned horses requisitioned by the forces of occupation, they were pulled into final position by manpower. Outside Sint-Martinuskerk church a half-dozen hand farm-carts filled the empty spaces between open-backed bullock wagons. Civilians clad in tired clothes and worn boots gathered around drab, canvas covered stalls. Bareheaded women in shawls negotiated with vendors in the bitter December cold. Youngsters with forlorn faces and broken eyes trailed their parents. Among hundreds of dirty, smudged countenances there wasn't a single smile.

Stepping back into the shadow, away from the window, Peterson watched the bustling scene from the front room of their terraced house. Among the cries of street-traders, the loudest came from two peddlers selling milk from a dogcart close to the front door. Waiting for the arrival of Adrien Bourdillon, his attention was drawn to the appealing sight of a wagon dispensing Lambic beer from wooden casks. In the back room, Carter had yet to rise, having elected to spend an extra hour in bed. Lying still gave him some measure of relief. With a back badly strained by Tuesday's crash, his ribs ached with every movement. Attempting to get up, his stomach and hips stung painfully where his lap belt had burst. He called out for Peterson.

"Sorry old chap, would you come over give me a hand? I feel as if someone's hammered a fence post into my lower back."

"All right, but keep your voice down!" Peterson remonstrated. "We're not supposed to be here remember?"

Rising to his feet Carter struggled to get dressed. Examining two, great purple welts on his hips he observed ruefully. "When you crash three things happen in quick succession. Your aeroplane hits the ground, your body hits the aeroplane, then your internal organs hit your ribs."

"Pretty much sums it up." Peterson replied sympathetically. "Similar thing happened to me when I came down, `though my crash happened at low level. On the point of a stall I pulled back on the joystick and came down amid web of suspended telegraph cables, stopped me like a safety net. Thankfully the final impact was arrested by a wire fence."

"I feel as if I'd been roughed up by a gang of toughs."

"Try moving around a bit, hurts more when you've been inactive for a while."

After a hurried breakfast of watery gruel consisting of oatmeal, treacle, water and salt, the two pilots adjourned to the front room to await Bourdillon's arrival.

At nine, a familiar figure ambled down the Kerkstraat road and past the church He didn't make directly for their house, but paused to converse with several of the market stall holders. He was, to all appearances, a well-known character in the town. The locals knew him by name. Peterson noticed how often the stallholders kept something aside they knew he would buy. He weaved through the crowds edging through the dense flow of people then, dodging behind a heavily laden wagon, he crossed to the house. Peterson unlatched the front door anticipating his arrival. Bourdillon entered carrying a bulky cotton drawstring sack over his right shoulder. He swung it down onto the hall floor.

"Good morning. Busy out there today." Peterson observed.

Bourdillon shrugged, his face gaunt and serious. "Before the war, agriculture was very profitable. Now? Only the black marketers have money."

"Thanks for coming, sorry to drag you away from your work."

"I am unemployed. Since the blockade many steel workers like myself were laid off. Last year only six of our nation's fifty-four blast furnaces were working. This year, only one. Our industry is no more. The enemy dismantle our machinery for copper."

"I'm sorry." Peterson sympathised. "Life must be very difficult."

"I have my pride, I will not suffer the public humiliation of queuing for the soup kitchen."

He untied his sack and produced two heavy overcoats. "You'll need these for the journey." Withdrawing a red leather portefeuille from his jacket he counted out some banknotes. "German Marks, you'll need money." He handed over a bundle of crumpled, grey-blue five mark notes. "German occupation issue. Belgian bank notes disappeared from circulation last year."

"Thank you. What's the plan?"

Standing in the centre of the room so as not to be seen from outside, Bourdillon gestured toward the window and the closest of the open back bullock wagons. "The market closes at twelve. That man out there with the green beret, see him?"

"Yes."

"He will leave early. When he starts loading up, go outside and help. Speak to no-one. He will take you north through Thourout before leaving you."

"Thourout, that's about half way, right?" Carter queried.

"Yes. From Thourout there is a fifteen mile straight road all the way to Bruges. It will take you into town. Can you both ride bicycles?"

The two pilots exchanged glances. "Yes, it's been a while though."

"Good. There are two in the wagon. If the weather holds you should be in Bruges an hour before sunset. Make for the Markt plaza in the city centre. Here is a photograph, it is easy to find. At the base of the Belfort tower is an arch. Someone will make contact with you."

The three men paused their conversation at the sound of a commotion outside. Raised voices and scuffling feet preceded the overturning of a laden wagon, scattering produce across the filthy ground. Punches were thrown before the arrival of local Rijkswacht police. The protesting trader was hauled away accompanied by cries of derision from the masses.

"What the hell was all that about?" Peterson enquired.

"Profiteering traders or farmers. It's illegal, those scum are often the target of retaliatory action in the market." Bourdillon buttoned up his jacket. "I will leave you now. Remember what I told you, but mention my name to no-one, you understand?"

Carter and Peterson nodded in acknowledgement then shook hands with their departing friend. When Bourdillon had left, the two men stood alone in the hall.

"I feel uncomfortable, putting my life in the hands of people I don't even know." Carter admitted.

"You and me both, and I've got a lot more to lose than you old boy. If they catch me this time it's the firing squad."

"I've still got my gun and ammunition, if the worst happens we can fight it out."

At eleven-thirty they stepped outside into the market square and were immediately struck by the earthy smell of root vegetables combined with animals and damp brickdust. Two draft dogs played boisterously around their feet until summonsed by their owner. Both men were grateful for the anonymity provided by the crowd. Ignoring the chatter between sellers and buyers, unnoticed among the throng, Carter and Peterson strolled casually across the gritty stone paving toward the designated wagon. Once there they helped load a few remaining unsold turnips, swedes and carrots onto the cart. With a curt nod of the head, the driver barely acknowledged their presence.

It was a sturdy, three wheeled vehicle with tall sides, a broad, well sprung front bench seat that could accommodate three men easily and a tail board to secure the load. Two large cartwheels on either side were balanced by a single, smaller wheel at the front centre. As Carter climbed up onto the front of the cart, a crippling spasm hit his stomach, doubling him over in pain. His eyes squeezed closed as his face contorted. The driver, having noticed Carter's discomfort, removed a small pewter hip-flask of brandy from his pocket and passed it over. No words were exchanged, but Carter's expression of thanks conveyed more than any language could express.

They traversed mile after mile of open, flat countryside. The old Roman road had become simply a long path of mud and stones with weeds growing between them. There was a loamy scent to the air. Only the occasional farmhouse or village broke the monotonous landscape. Keeping well west of Roulers they passed through Hooglede and by one-o-clock crossed the Hazelbeek River at Haantje. Once over the bridge the driver cast a wary look around then pulled up next to a roadside Chapel and stepped down. While he ostensibly adjusted the yoke around his oxen, an elderly woman emerged from the Chapel and handed him a small bundle wrapped in a red and white checked gingham cloth. After exchanging a few words he returned to the cart and passed his passengers a package of food and flask of hot pea soup. The Belgian spoke only a few words of faltering English, but managed express his opinion that they should both eat and prepare themselves for the final leg of their journey.

Reaching Thourout at one-thirty in the afternoon, they passed through the centre of the town then travelled north-east until they reached the village of Berg-op-Zoom. Their driver turned off the road and gestured the two airmen to disembark. He gave them an old, pre-war map on which he had penciled the quickest route into the centre of Bruges.

"Keep on this road, with the railway track on your right." He pointed into the distance.

Underneath a pile of muddy hessian sacks in the cart were two battered pre-war Automoto French bicycles. The airmen dragged them down and inspected the machines carefully.

"I haven't ridden one of these since I was a lad." Carter whispered. "Tell me again, how far is it we've got to ride?"

"About fifteen miles." Peterson replied.

"Bloody hell."

Peterson checked his watch. "It's two-o-clock, which gives us under three hours to get to the Belfort before sundown."

The driver shook hands with them both. "On les aura!" For the first time his craggy face creased into a smile. He then climbed back onto his cart and turned around in a wide circle across the road, heading back toward Thouout.

Mounting up, Carter and Peterson wobbled the first hundred or so yards, re-acquainting themselves with cycling. For miles they pedalled onward across west Flanders along the straight, sleet-swept road to freedom. The wintry sun was sinking down into the west. Denuded trees on either side passed by like silent sentinels, their branches whitened by frost. Thin ice on top of puddles cracked under their wheels, the sound of loose mud beneath the tyres. This was no safe ride, no break in the monotony to engage their minds. They regarded every passing traveller with suspicion.

By the time they reached the west quarter of Bruges Carter was lagging behind some fifty feet. His coat was waterlogged and his body soaking wet. The only thing keeping him warm was the pumping of his legs against the pedals. Ahead, Peterson checked his wristwatch and waved Carter to keep up.

Carter's legs were aching painfully. He leant forward on the pedals, pushing down with his body weight. After crossing a narrow bridge they were faced with the option of three roads. Peterson unfolded their map.

"Straight ahead, here, the Rue des Marechaux." His voice lowered so as not to be overheard. "It's a straight run, almost all the way through to the Grand Place."

"Good. It's getting dark, difficult to read the street signs."

"How's your belly holding up old chum?"

"I'm alright. Not far now eh?"

"Come on then."

The cobbled streets rattled the bicycle's frame and transmitted every shock though the saddle to Carter's nether quarters. The front wheel wobbled over the smallest of bumps or pot-holes. It was the most uncomfortable ride in his life to date. Peterson slowed down and squinted at the map once more in the fading light. Having satisfied himself of their position he forked right into the Rue St. Amand.

It was four-forty-five when they entered the Grand Square. A waxing crescent moon hung low in the sky above the rooftops. With a bruised posterior and barely able to straighten, Carter stepped off his mount. His legs felt shaky and were just capable of supporting his body as he wheeled his bicycle the few remaining yards to the base of the Belfort tower.

Across the square, outside the ornate gothic post office and Provincial Court building, stood a dark figure in a long dark grey greatcoat and black fedora. He strode purposely across the cobbles to meet them.

"This way, follow me."

His hat tilted low over his forehead, the stranger wasted no time loitering. He set off down the narrow Rue de la Bride with Peterson and Carter following close behind. After a hundred yards he stopped, glanced around, then ducked right and into a narrow sloping alley.

Navigating the path's confines with two bicycles was difficult. After a short distance they came to an open courtyard, at one side a series of five, time worn stone steps led up to the front door of a medieval townhouse.

"Leave the bicycles here, come inside." The stranger unlocked the door and stepped into a hallway illuminated by the flickering light of two table mounted oil-lamps.

"Hang up your coats. There is a fire lit in the back room. You can rest there."

Access to the lounge was through low doorway. Ducking their heads the two airmen entered a spacious living area. A ladder-work of exposed, heavy timber rafters covered the entire ceiling. The floor was stone paved with a central rug and two deeply upholstered sofas that faced each other over an ornately carved antique mahogany table. A renaissance oak fireplace surround dominated the far wall, within which a fire roared. Having endured months of harsh living conditions, Peterson was overwhelmed by the opulence of his surroundings.

"Thank you Sir". Carter voiced his appreciation on behalf of the both.

"Names are not necessary, but if you wish you may call me Breydel".

Peterson caught sight of himself in the reflection of the glazed double doors that led outside to a private courtyard. He looked like a vagrant and felt ashamed of his haggard appearance.

Breydel noticed his discomfort. "I know appearance is so important to English officers. No doubt you wish to bathe? I have a change of clothes for you, but you must keep as much of your uniform as possible in case you are captured."

"Thank you Breydel." Peterson responded. "That would be most welcome."

Upstairs off the landing were two bathrooms, both identically furnished. Peterson entered the first. It was scrupulously clean, on one wall a tarnished mirror reflected the light of twin candles. He sat down on a cushioned stool and undressed.

A deep marble bath had been recently filled. Peterson stepped in and slid down into the hot water, his first in months. The heat and added salts immediately filled his body with an intense feeling of well-being as they penetrated his tired, cold limbs. Floating, suspended in the water relieved his tension and relaxed his muscles and mind. Grasping a cube of Savon de Marseille soap he washed himself thoroughly then, after thirty minutes of immersion, exited the bath and sank his feet into the wool rug. The fluffy towels were freshly laundered and had been carefully folded on a white clawfoot table. After drying himself off he shaved and dressed in the clothes provided by their host.

In the bathroom opposite, Carter was enjoying a combination of isolation, quiet, and comfort. He stepped out the bath with difficulty and examined his wounds in a full length mirror. There were great purple-black welts across his waist where his lap belt had restrained him. The discolouration had deepened during the days since his crash. His upper arms were yellow-grey and a black circle surrounded his right eye. A painful swelling had risen over his right-hand number six rib.

He dressed slowly then stepped out onto the landing to find Peterson waiting with a broad smile on his face.

"That was good eh?"

"Yes, it helped a lot." Carter lowered his voice. "Peterson old chap. I think I've torn a rib cartilage."

"What makes you think that?"

"I did a little medical training before the war, got to learn the symptoms."

"I see."

"Look, I'm telling you this because I know the risks you're taking. I don't want to let you dawn."

"Stuff and nonsense old boy. You managed all right today didn't you?"

"Yes. I suppose."

"Well then." Peterson could see Carter's concern was genuine. "Look here, we'll be fine. I'm willing to chance it."

"Thanks Peterson."

"Don't think of it. By the way, it was good of you to tell me." He placed his hand on Carter's arm. "I hope this fellow Breydel has managed to lay on some grub, I'm starved."

The first floor galleried landing overlooked the kitchen and, as the airmen approached the stairs, they could see Breydel receiving a parcel at the back door. He looked up and beckoned them.

"Come downstairs. My friend owns a local 'restaurant économiques,' they provide a basic meal at a fair price. This food is with his compliments."

By seven in the evening they had finished their meal and retired to the lounge. After several glasses of local beer, both British officers were relaxed and in good spirits despite the day's ordeal. For Carter, the soporific effect of alcohol, the burning fire and the overstuffed sofa overwhelmed his efforts to stay awake. He had fallen asleep with his head against the rolled armrest. An occasional twitch at the corner of his mouth, the only indication of his wounds.

"Do you know of a trustworthy doctor for my friend?" Peterson asked softly, so as not to wake Carter.

"Is he badly hurt?" Breydel asked, concerned.

"I don't know, he's a brave fellow and doesn't show his pain much. I'd just feel a lot happier if he was given a check over by a professional that's all."

"In the morning." Breydel yawned and stretched his arms above his head. "I will send a messenger to Hospital St.Jean. The Lieutenant will be attended too."

The RFC depot at St.Omer occupied just under a square mile of an open plain called Plateau des Bruyères. In just three years, St.Omer's former racecourse had become a sprawling industrial complex with a plethora of prefabricated, half cylindrical steel Nissen huts, sheds, workshops and Bessonneau hangars. Over a thousand personnel populated the site. It was akin to a small town whose task was the supply, modification, salvage and maintenance of front line aeroplanes.

At eight in the morning of Thursday December the twentieth, Lieutenant Barry Hall arrived at the depot gatehouse. He was a stocky, well-built young man of twenty years. On the sleeve of his left tunic forearm, above the cuff, were two distinctive narrow strips of gold Russian braid. His `wound' stripes were spaced vertically, a half inch apart.

After signing in he was instructed to present himself immediately to the Officer Commanding, Pilot's Pool. Having been given directions, he deposited his kit with the gatehouse clerk and made his way on foot toward headquarters. The nineteenth century Château des Bruyères was a red brick and stucco building with manicured grounds and stood on a hill between St. Omer and the aerodrome. Inside, among the bustling personnel, red tabbed staff officers conversed in clouds of exhaled tobacco smoke. Hall was instructed to wait in a small anteroom until summonsed. After ten minutes he was ushered upstairs to an office on the far side of the landing designated 'Officer Commanding, Pilot's Pool.' He knocked and entered.

"Lieutenant Hall Sir." He stepped forward and saluted.

Seated behind his antique French writing bureau was a heavyset man in his late twenties with brooding eyes and flecks of grey in his brown hair. He was smoking a panatela cigar.

"So you're Lieutenant Hall. I'm Captain Archie Robertson. Sit down will you?" He gestured Hall toward a vacant chair. "I've read your papers, very impressive. I see you were a Lieutenant in the 2nd Army."

"That's right Sir. The Tenth Corps actually, injured back in the summer at Messines Ridge. I applied for a transfer to the RFC."

"So it says here." Robertson flicked over a loose leaf of typewritten paper in Hall's file." How's the wound now?"

"A little twinge occasionally Sir, nothing to worry about."

"Good, your report states that you were something of a star pupil at East Boldre."

"Beaulieu and the New Forest, 16 Training Squadron. I flew Avro 504's mostly and SE5a's. Good posting but hardly an ideal aerodrome, outside the perimeter is a tract of countryside at least ten miles across with hardly any landing ground."

"You're a Surrey man I see?" Robertson was more interested in the officer sat opposite.

"Yes Sir, Cobham."

"Play sports?"

"Keen rugby player before the war Sir. Played as half-back."

"Rugby eh? I'm a cricket man myself, enjoy watching the game though." Robertson had concluded his introduction. Months earlier he would spend more time with each new arrival. Now the hundreds of faces passing through St.Omer all seemed to be the same. As was his custom he offered a few words of advice.

"Look here Hall. You'll find it's a different kind of war in the RFC. As a soldier you fight alongside your comrades and a man can rely on his friends for moral and physical support, especially during combat. An aerial warrior is isolated, with no means of communication with the ground or, apart from a few limited signals, other aeroplanes. Once battle commences it's often every man for himself."

"Yes Sir."

"Right. Now you're here, you'll be assigned to general flying duties until your posting comes through. Shouldn't be more than a few days." Robertson extinguished his cigar in a brass ash tray fashioned from the base of an expended shell. He uncapped his fountain pen and signed off a duplicate form in Hall's file. "There's a major logistics operation transporting Handley Page 0/100's from here to the RNAS Coudekerque, 14 Squadron. I want you to fly as second crewmember."

"Bombers Sir?"

"I commend you on your knowledge Lieutenant. I've no doubt we'll be flying aeroplanes like the Handley Page before long. You know 97 Squadron? Formed on the first December at Waddington?"

"It's a training squadron isn't it?"

"At the moment. In fact there have been several new squadrons formed this month. Word is that a new air corps will be announced next year dedicated to heavy bombers." Robertson knew what was coming next. To forestall any argument he continued. "Don't worry, we've plenty of SE5a's on strength for you to keep your hand in."

"Thank you Sir, but haven't the Navy plenty of airmen to ferry their own machines?"

"I've no doubt one or two could be found. Won't do any harm for you to get some experience in heavies."

"As you say Sir." Hall could not disguise the disappointment in his voice.

"Off you go then. Get your billet allocation detail from Sergeant Mullins. He's downstairs, first office on the left. Use the rest of the day to settle in. Come over to my day office first thing tomorrow after breakfast. Mullins will give you directions."

Hall departed the Château with a heavy heart. It had been a shock to discover that his first duties overseas would be flying a lumbering twin engine behemoth. The revelation had certainly put a damper on his enthusiasm. He'd set his heart on single seat fighters. The prospect of starting his aviation career as a 'bus driver' had no appeal whatsoever, indeed, had he known he probably would have remained in the Army. Hall's mood was lifted by the knowledge that, for the present at least, only the Royal Naval Air Service flew the heavy, Handley Page machines.

Returning to the gatehouse his thigh ached painfully in the cold, damp December air. He was grateful that Robertson had effectively given him the rest of the day off. Hall was determined to make the most of it. Get settled in, meet some of the chaps in the pilot's pool and maybe take a trip into town. The notion of re-acquainting himself with French hospitality, with all its' benefits, quickened his pace.

He'd hoped for a billet of his own, but as he swung open the door to the first in a row of eight Nissen huts he was greeted by a chorus of welcoming voices.

"Yours is the second bed on the left old man." A uniformed, red-headed lad stood back and made room for Hall to pass. "You won't be here long so don't get too settled in." He extended his hand. "Henry Bradshaw, Harry to my friends." Hall exchanged a firm, warm handshake. "May I introduce Lieutenant Roland 'Rowley' Dexter?"

The second officer rose to his feet. "Welcome to the Savoy." He opened his arms expansively. "Private en-suite bathrooms, constant hot and cold running water and electric lighting throughout."

Hall slung his kit-bag down onto the floor alongside the iron-framed bed. "Barry Hall, good to meet you. How long have you chaps been in here?"

"Just over a week, we arrived together last Wednesday, still waiting for our posting." Dexter noticed the braid on Hall's sleeve. "So, an Army man eh? What was it, a Blighty?"

"Yes, Tenth Corps, caught a packet at Messines Ridge."

Bradshaw let out a long, slow whistle. "Bloody hell, tell you what Rowley, we've got ourselves a ruddy hero among us."

Hall joined in the laughter. He liked them, they were his kind of fellows. "I'm from Beaulieu, 16 Training Squadron, how about you two?"

"71 Squadron." Dexter replied. "Thirty six hours solo on Avro's, four on SE5a's."

"We learned on the new Gosport System." Bradshaw added. "Rowley and I both arrived at Netheravon at the same time, went through training together."

"I've logged forty hours solo, seven on SE5a's." Hall volunteered, adding disparagingly. "Now Captain Robertson wants me to help ferry 0/100's for the Navy."

Bradshaw offered some consolation. "Well, look on the bright side Hall, it'll only be until you're posted, heavy bombers are the sole prerogative of the RNAS."

Dexter was less sanguine. "We might as well get used to it old man. You've heard the Air Force Bill was given Royal Assent last month? Like it or not, it's likely we'll all be one service by the spring." He ambled over to the central stove, opened the cast iron door and threw in a shovel load of coal. Warming his hands close to the glowing, vertical stove pipe he continued: "The whole thing will probably be a complete hash-up anyway."

"Do you get much opportunity to fly at St.Omer?" Hall asked.

"Yes, ferry duties in the main. Picking up old machines, delivering new and repaired ones. Good experience but no substitute for being in the front line. All the lads here are rather keen to get stuck into the ruck."

"I'll wager neither of you have been asked to fly nursemaid in a 0/100." Hall remarked testily as he unpacked his belongings and laid them out neatly on the thin mattress.

"No, and I don't expect we will be." Bradshaw responded. "Rowley and I expect our postings to come through within the next forty-eight hours. In the meantime we're scheduled to take a couple of new SE5a's over to Bailleul later this morning. You know, 1 Squadron, they're converting from Nieuports. It's a nice little run, only a twenty five mile hop."

Bradshaw checked the time on his wristwatch. "Tell you what Hall, we're not down to fly until eleven. Finish unpacking then Rowley and I will show you around the Depot. You can see us off."

"We'll be back by mid-day, see you in the Mess for luncheon eh?" Dexter smiled amiably.

Hall unceremoniously deposited the remainder of his kit in his locker. "All done!"

Seated by the front door of the Belgian townhouse in Bruges, Carter struggled to remove his boots. Bending down or even leaning forward was restricted by a tight, elastic compression wrap the visiting doctor had applied around his lower chest. It was late afternoon on Friday, the twenty-first of December, twenty four hours since he and Peterson arrived, exhausted after their journey from Moorslede.

"Come on old chap, let me give you a hand off with those boots." As always, Peterson was on hand to offer assistance. The medic had advised rest, with no physical exertion.

"I don't know what aches more, my ribs or my legs after fifteen miles on a bicycle." Carter responded caustically. "Bruges is crawling with Navy personnel, we were lucky not to be challenged."

"So where did Breydel take you, did you meet anyone?" Peterson asked as he accompanied Carter into the sitting-room.

"Across the square, down a side road called the Rue Flamand there's a Jesuit church where we met a fellow who owns a small vessel. He's a fisherman. Specialises in oysters and mussels apparently. Seemed a decent sort, doesn't speak a word of English though."

Carter accepted Peterson's steadying arm as he sat down on the sofa near the fire. "His deck hand can speak a little of our language. A young boy, below military age. I think he's the fellow's son. Anyway, the two of them and the lad's uncle make daily runs along the canal surrounding Bruges and out to Ostend. Usually trawl around the harbour estuary, sometimes go out further. The idea is that we take a ride on his boat then meet up with another a few miles offshore that'll take us across the Channel to Blighty." He paused to light a cigarette as Peterson placed another log onto the fire. "The chap's taking an almighty risk for us, Bruges is home to the Hun's U-boat fleet and they use the canal twenty four hours a day. Those concrete bunkers we saw outside town yesterday are their shelters. The place is plastered with barracks too."

Peterson considered Carter's report. "You remember the railway station we passed yesterday after we entered the town? Well, Breydel said there's a train that runs directly from here to Ostend. Only a couple of stops, quicker and more comfortable I'd say. What if we met our friend at Ostend and boarded his boat there?"

"And risk a few hours in a confined space sitting right next to a group of Hun sailors and officers? Not bloody likely!"

"Sorry old chap." Peterson responded. "Hadn't thought that one through."

"Besides." Carter continued. "The old salt knows the times and places to avoid. There are four towns along the canal, the final one before Ostend is called Plasschendaele, not the famous one of course. Loads of troops there so we'll need to lie low until we get through the locks at Basin de Chasse and out beyond the harbour. It's quite tricky apparently, the lock-gates are still damaged from our bombardment back in September."

Warmed by the resurgent fire, Peterson sank deeper into the

sofa's upholstery. "Tempting to stick here for the remainder of the war." He sighed. "Still, duty calls. Mustn't let the side down. When do we leave, any date set?"

"Tomorrow morning at five."

"Oh well, I suppose it's for the best. A chap could get too used to this life of luxury."

For a while the two men sat in contemplative silence. The flames in the fireplace crackled as they burned the dry wood.

"You know it will take a miracle for us to get home?" In a single sentence Carter cut through all pretense and bravado. Peterson said nothing, just nodded his head by way of reply.

It was mid-morning on Saturday the twenty-second of December. An enormous, green painted, twin engine Handley Page came to a standstill on the field at RNAS Coudekerque, a wide, grass covered acreage situated on the southern edge of the village. Seated up front in the exposed cockpit, Hall was impressed by his fellow pilot's landing skills, having avoided a number of shallow ditches that evacuated surface water into the perimeter drain.

After switching off and dismounting, the three crewmembers, pilot, observer and gunner, made their way past the hangars and around a small copse to the farmhouse. They needed to report their arrival and complete the necessary paperwork. Hall entered the office first, followed by Flight Lieutenant Symonds and Observer Lieutenant Langstone. The officer at the desk received the files of documentation they had brought along then invited them to change out of their flying gear in an adjacent crew hut while waiting their return orders.

The flight from St.Omer to Coudekerque, a village immediately south of Dunkirk, was only a short hop of some twenty or so miles. Even though their journey had been brief, all three men were anxious to stretch their legs and restore circulation. After changing, they stepped outside the hut and paused for a moment by a small, partially frozen pond in front of the farm-house. The sound of a nearby gently running stream relaxed their jaded nerves.

"Anyone?" Langstone offered a freshly opened a packet of 'Wild Woodbine' cigarettes.

"Thanks." Symonds and Hall accepted graciously. "Looks like this place has taken a bit of a battering." Hall remarked on the recently repaired shell craters scattered around the aerodrome.

Langstone exhaled a cloud of smoke. "Since September the Dunkirk Command's been attacked from land, sea and air. We had to de-centralise the aircraft depot, bloody nuisance, but it hasn't caused us as many problems as the weather."

"Why? Is it particularly bad here near the coast?" Hall enquired.

"Dreadful, especially this time of year." Symonds replied. "Since November we've had driving rain, headwinds, gales, heavy mists, fog and dense clouds to contend with. In fact we almost lost an entire bomber crew on the twelfth." He pointed to a waterlogged area of the landing ground about two hundred yards away. "See over there? Hit the ground in heavy rain, flipped over. The men were trapped underneath and it took nearly an hour to recover them. Not badly injured luckily, they were flying again within days."

Langstone interjected. "The past few weeks we've been concentrating our attacks on German aerodromes and Bruges docks. That's when weather permits."

Hall coughed into his handkerchief. His two comrades waited for him to recover.

"Woodbines a bit strong for you old chap?" Symonds chided with a smile.

"More of a pipe man myself." Hall replied. "I've had to cut down a bit recently. Chlorine gas on the Mount Sorrel to St. Eloi front, that and a bullet to the leg."

"Sorry old man." Symonds and Langstone exchanged awkward glances.

Hall had no wish to dilate further on the matter. "I heard you Navy chaps have had a few organisational changes here this month?" He deftly changed the subject.

"7A became 14 Naval Squadron back on the ninth." Symonds explained. "The pilots are fresh from training in England, we've had to familiarise them with operations in France and get them used to night flying 0/100's."

"These 0/100's, are they reliable machines?" Hall was genuinely interested.

"Yes, but they're hard work." By the tone of his voice, Langstone was apparently speaking from experience. "The maintenance crews struggle to keep any number of machines airworthy. Delays in component supplies are the biggest headache. See that 0/100 over there in front of the hangar?" He inclined his head toward the nearest timber and canvas Bessoneau. "That's 1462, she's just been fitted with a new wing and bomb doors. Took a month to get the parts. We're due to fly 3116 back to St.Omer after luncheon to have new engines fitted."

"Never seen so many 'heavies' in one place before. It's an impressive sight. Who's in command?" Hall enquired.

"Squadron Commander Brackley. You might get to meet him."

The farmhouse door swung open and the desk officer beckoned the three men inside. Once seated inside his office he announced. "There's squall coming in from the coast so there'll be no more flying today, Commander Brackley's orders. Unfortunately gentlemen, you've missed the morning tender back to St.Omer and it's the only one today."

Symonds shrugged. He was used to it. He slapped the clearly downhearted Hall on the shoulder. "Cheer up old chap, you can share my billet tonight. Langstone and I will take you into Dunkirk, show you around eh?"

Hall's mood lightened with the prospect of an afternoon and possible evening off base. He nevertheless could not neglect his responsibilities.

"Can you please get a message to Captain Robinson in the Pilot's

Pool at St.Omer? He'll be expecting me back otherwise."

"Already taken care of Hall." The officer smiled. "Just don't let these two reprobates lead you astray in the meantime."

Two bridges spanned a narrow waterway alongside the Rue de la Equerre in Bruges. Between them, tied up close to the canal wall was an ancient trawler. There was little left of her blistered paintwork, the name on her bow was unreadable, broken by patches of rust. She was about forty feet long with a single wheelhouse amidships. The windows were thick with grime. Directly behind the bridge, puffs of grey smoke drifted lazily from a tall funnel and dissipated into the soft breeze. The predawn air was filled with the scent of coal.

Peterson stepped down onto the wide wooden gunwales. The three man crew were standing on the hatch covers. It was the first time he had seen the skipper. Wrinkled beyond his years, he looked at least sixty years old, every part of him was lean muscle and leathery skin. Extending a calloused hand he welcomed both airmen aboard.

It took a further half hour for the steam boiler to reach pressure. During which time the crew loaded the stokehold with coal. A drum of bearing oil was passed over the side which the skipper took below to the engine room through a deep, dark opening forward of the wheelhouse. His face illuminated by the glare of the furnace door as it opened.

Peterson and Carter were ushered down to a cabin beneath the wheelhouse, with instructions to remain out of sight. By six they were underway and moving at four knots along the waterway. Navigating through a series of channels they reached the Bassin du Commerce. It was the main dock, filled almost to capacity with military and civilian traffic. The dock led to another, the Bassin du Flottage which in turn marked the start of the Canal d'Ostende a Bruges.

The steam engine was remarkably silent. Below decks, Peterson could feel the vibration of their whirling propeller through the cabin walls. There was little sensation of motion, the water inside Ostend harbour was perfectly calm, like a peaceful lake. It was a marked contrast to the open sea where swirling blue-grey waves lashed the side of their ship. They sailed out for half a mile before turning to port. Inside the cabin the engine rattled everything, locker doors, chains and berths. The rust-riddled hull bounced higher and higher, slapping the waves hard with each fall. At length the door opened and the youth appeared. "You can come on deck now if you wish."

Peterson was relieved to finally leave the cramped and musty confines of their quarters. Emerging on deck he staggered about on unsteady legs as the ship rocked. The morning air was thick with a briny mist. He looked around for the horizon, but it was impossible to tell where the grey sky ended and the grey sea began.

"Where are we?" He asked.

"That's the Stroombank Buoy." The lad pointed ahead. "Off Raversyde Bains, once we are out of sight of the land beacon there will be less chance of us being stopped." His uncle was manning the ship's wheel, concentrating on the sea ahead. "These are dangerous waters. On the shore between Ostende and Nieuport are heavy enemy batteries." The youth continued. "Sixteen kilometers out from Ostende are rows of surface mines. A short distance beyond is a thirty five kilometer stretch of explosive net mines. At the western end of the net is a narrow channel only my father and uncle know."

Meanwhile, Carter had joined them on deck and was leaning over the side. Overwhelmed with nausea, he tried to stop retching but it was too late. His stomach contracted violently, forcing everything up and out. His face was white, he fell back and sank to his knees. The pain in his ribs returned with a vengeance as he heaved, even though his stomach was empty. He responded to Peterson's look of concern with a dismissive hand.

They continued south-west until they were a mile or so off-shore from Middelkerke Bains. The skipper slowed the engine, allowing his brother and son to lower the dredging net. There were already over fifty small vessels in the area, all similarly engaged.

"The Nieuport canal exits west of here. It is a good place for shellfish." The lad volunteered. "We regularly trawl in this place. We must not attract suspicion."

The old man called back to his son, who translated. "Father says if we return with an empty hold questions will be asked, also he needs to earn a living!"

The gulls called out overhead, diving for whatever scraps they could take. Below the slate-coloured sky, freezing, white salt spray came crashing right over the bow. For three hours they dredged the shallows. Finally satisfied with his haul, the skipper retrieved his nets and steered north-west, moving further from the shore.

"We're four kilometers off Westende Plage." The youth announced over the sound of crashing waves. "The allied lines end on the shore west of the Yser Canal. From here it is too dangerous to sail further along the coast, there are many surface mines. My uncle will steer us out along a safe passage."

Passing Peterson a pair of marine binoculars he adjusted the focus of each lens and scanned the beach. Several enemy patrol boats were guarding the mouth of the Yser Canal outside Nieuport, a town that had been levelled to the ground in July when the British Army defended their position against a major German attack. Along the coast west of Nieuport Bains, a stretch of dunes extended all the way to La Panne and beyond. Across the sands lay coils of barbed wire behind which machine guns were posted. At the most northern point of the western front, a collapsed bunker overlooked the sea. Prevailing flood conditions precluded the excavation of trenches so, behind high sandbag walls, a shallow breastwork of fortifications ran right up to beach, petering out into the sand.

"North of the Traapeooer Buoy is where we will make our rendezvous." Peterson lowered the binoculars to follow the direction his guide was pointing. "Over there."

Once more he focused the binoculars, a fuzzy dark patch assumed the shape of a black steel cone bobbing above the waves. It was topped by a tall mast and flag.

"How far?"

"Three kilometers to the north-west." The lad replied.

Peterson handed back the binoculars. He looked up as a Gotha bomber appeared briefly overhead between the swirling winter clouds. It was heading east, returning from a night-time bombing mission over Dunkirk.

Carter was nowhere to be seen. He had returned below decks, his constant retching had exacerbated the pain of his damaged ribs.

"The Lieutenant, he is feeling bad?" The concerned boy enquired.

"I'm afraid so." Peterson replied with a shake of his head. "I think he's had enough."

Approximately twenty miles offshore from Nieuport Peterson saw a fast vessel powering toward them from astern, her sleek form knifing through the water at nineteen knots. The skipper had also seen it and, after a cursory inspection though his binoculars, turned four points broad on the starboard bow.

It was a Royal Navy motor launch, her prow emblazoned in white paint with the code 'ML30'. On her forward deck was a quick-firing, three-pounder gun. She was about eighty feet in length with a wheelhouse amidships. Suspended from davits on the quarterdeck was a nine foot long clinker dinghy.

The trawler reduced her engines sufficient to keep her heading. With the two ships pointed into the wind and tide, the launch slowed and steered a course parallel to the heading of the trawler, maintaining as small as possible angle of approach abaft of the starboard beam. At a distance of a hundred yards the launch used both engine and rudder movements to reduce the distance further. The launch Commander raised a gleaming brass megaphone and hailed the trawler's crew, advising them that they were coming alongside.

The launch's crew of eight consisted of deckhands, signalmen, motor mechanics, a cook and two officers. One of the latter directed his men to position fenders along the port side at the correct height for coming alongside. The crew stood ready with coils of mooring ropes in their hands. The moment that the two ships made parallel contact, the lines were passed respectively between them. Breast and spring ropes were made fast between the bows and sterns of both boats.

The conjoined vessels followed the swell and wave motion, rising and falling together. Before leaving, Carter gave the lad the Brisfit's compass he had been carrying with him since Tuesday.

"Here, take this. It's not much, but perhaps something to remember us by. You may find it useful."

The boy's face conveyed his appreciation. "Thank you Sir."

Assisted by two burly seamen the RFC pilots clambered across the slippery gunwales onto the pine plank deck of the motor launch. Peterson saw the sleeve of one of the officers and immediately recognised the three waved rows of gold lace with a squarish curl belonging to a Commander in the Royal Navy Volunteer Reserve. The other officer was a Lieutenant, evidenced by his two waved stripes.

Two men in civilian garb exited from a hatchway on the launch's deck and, after shaking hands with the Commander, bade him farewell before crossing to the trawler. They exchanged a few words with the Belgian skipper before disappearing from sight into the cabin.

"Who are those two fellows?" Peterson asked the Navy Lieutenant standing nearby.

"What fellows?" He replied firmly.

Peterson nodded his head in understanding, obviously they were part of a covert operation. Carter, in the meantime, was leaning against the wheelhouse in considerable pain, his right arm wrapped protectively around his lower chest.

The Commander noticed Carter's distress. "Is he injured?" He addressed Peterson directly.

"I'm afraid so Sir, chest wound during his crash landing. Might he be taken below and made comfortable?"

"By all means." The Commander caught the attention of two passing deckhands. "Auden and Caddick! Assist the Lieutenant below will you? Take him to my quarters."

The trawler skipper had his eyes on the sky, his head inclined upward as he considered the weather. He spoke a few words to his son who shouted across to the departing airmen as they stood, swaying on the deck of the motor launch.

"Father says there's a storm coming, we'll need to head back to Ostend harbour straight away. Good luck my friends."

With that, the ropes were cast adrift and the two vessels began their separate courses.

The Navy ship's twin two hundred and twenty horsepower petrol engines powered them through the waves as she pressed on, pitching and weaving across the Channel. Her bow lifted high into the sky before crashing down with a bone jarring impact. With his legs braced and life jacket on, Peterson held on tight to the base of the crucifix shaped wireless mast, fearful of slipping on a deck awash with salt water. He watched the seagulls soaring freely across the sky as wind driven droplets of sea water hit his face like tiny pieces of grit. After ten minutes the cold bite of the wind became too much for him and, with a racing heartbeat, he went below.

The launch had a twelve foot beam and there was plenty of room. Carter lay in his bunk, his head resting against a nine inch thick steel bulkhead.

"Not long now old man." Peterson encouraged as he bolstered Carter's head and shoulders with three well-stuffed pillows. "How's the sea-sickness?"

"Not so bad when I'm lying down." Carter responded, his face grey. His breath came in short gasps, as if he were struggling to get enough air. "Feels like my lungs have been wrapped in barbed wire bands." He gritted his teeth in pain as the launch pitched down with a sudden jolt. "Good job they put me in the lower bunk eh? Not too far to fall."

"Just take it easy, we're on the home run now. I tell you, it feels good to be on board a Navy ship."

Carter smiled weakly. "I never thought I'd hear that from a Flying Corps officer."

At that point the ship's Lieutenant put his head around the bulkhead door.

"I overheard the trawler skipper mention your name. Lieutenant Peterson is it?"

"That's right, Cecil Peterson, RFC and this fine fellow is Lieutenant Seb Carter."

"Sorry not to have introduced myself earlier, frightfully busy. Huckstead's the name. Welcome aboard." The three men shook hands. "We're a part of the Dover Patrol, on our way back from keeping an eye on the Belgian coast. Spend most of our time submarine hunting. Work for the Office of Naval Intelligence too."

"You know, the moment I saw your ship approaching I thought we'd actually made it." The gratitude on Peterson's face was evident.

Huckstead laughed. "Don't tempt providence old man. There's

still some distance to go and these are dangerous waters." His face broke into a broad smile. "Still, it's damned good to have you fellows here. Gave Fritz the slip eh?"

"Took me several tries." Peterson admitted. "This was my last chance, they promised me a morning out with the undertaker if I was caught again."

"No sense of fair play, always been the problem with Huns." Huckstead observed. He stood aside as a crewman entered the cabin with two enameled mugs of hot, steaming coffee.

"The skipper's name is Henderson, he'd like to have a word with you on deck when you're ready. No rush though, finish your coffee first."

"That's very welcome."

A voice from above summonsed Huckstead. "Sorry, you chaps will have to excuse me, I'm needed on the bridge. Speak to you later eh?"

Peterson raised his mug in a gesture of thanks. At that moment the ship rolled alarmingly and Carter spilt some of the contents.

"Can you manage?" Peterson offered a helping hand. "Think so, just let me sit up a bit." Carter shifted awkwardly on his elbows. He sipped at the hot beverage. "Oh that's good. I needed that."

When they had both finished their coffee Peterson climbed the narrow, steep staircase into daylight. The crew were scrambling across the teetering deck to their assigned positions. Emerging into the driving wind he reached out for a handhold and missed. Unfamiliar with the rolling motion he stumbled and his left thigh struck a pillar cleat. Biting back an expletive he limped into the wheelhouse.

Six foot wide, the bridge was enclosed on three sides with narrow, eye level windows. The rear was open and shielded from the elements by a drawn, waist high canvas awning. The ship's wheel was situated centrally below the compass and adjacent to two linked levers of the engine order telegraph. Henderson was peering forward through the salt-caked windows, steering with his hands on the uppermost wheel spokes. Standing on Henderson's left, Huckstead was speaking to the engine room, his mouth over the horn of a copper voice pipe.

Aware of Peterson's presence Henderson stood aside. "Take the wheel Huckstead." He swung closed the port bridge window, blocking clouds of sea spray. "Tricky waters these. Lieutenant Huckstead tells me he's already introduced himself. I'm Commander Henderson, Royal Navy Volunteer Reserve."

"Lieutenant Peterson, 303 Squadron Royal Flying Corps Sir. My friend below is Lieutenant Carter, 323 Squadron. I've been a prisoner of war since the first week of October." He braced himself as the launch made a sudden lurch to port. "Carter was shot down at Spriethoek last Tuesday. His observer was badly wounded and captured. We are indebted to you and our Belgian friends."

"The less you know about our 'Belgian friends' as you put it, the better. They live a very perilous life and it helps if few people are aware of their activities." Henderson remarked, his attention equally divided between Peterson and the sea. "I could see you'd both had a rough time of it by the look of you when you came aboard. How bad are Carter's injuries by the way?"

"He's been told it's a torn rib cartilage. Personally I think he's broken a few. Stout fellow though, rarely complains, but he urgently needs proper medical care."

Henderson glanced at the compass then at the sky. Stormy clouds were rolling in from the south east, blocking the winter sun. He ushered Peterson forward and drew his attention to a detailed maritime chart pinned to the forward bridge bulkhead. "See here? We're currently nine nautical miles due east of the Ruytingen Buoy." Pointing to their present position he continued. "The Navy's deployed a twenty eight mile line of explosive mines connected by a net that runs from south of the Goodwin Sands across the Channel to the Dyck lightship off

Gravelines. To avoid it we'd normally sail close to the French shore off Le Clipont and then straight across to Dover. It's a journey of about forty four miles."

"Le Clipont, that's a mile or so west of Dunkirk isn't it?" Peterson had an idea. "Is there a hospital or casualty station there for Lieutenant Carter?" He asked anxiously.

"I'm not sure. Huckstead, do you know?"

"As far as I'm aware the nearest hospitals are thirty-five general and the Duchess of Sutherland, number nine at Calais."

Peterson shook his head in dismay. "That's about a thirty mile drive. No good for Carter."

"I've just remembered. What about the Friends' Ambulance Unit at Malo-les-Bains, just east of Dunkirk?" Huckstead volunteered. "The Queen Alexandria Hospital, Quakers run the place, they've proper medical facilities. We could take Carter there."

"Sounds ideal." Peterson looked across hopefully at Henderson. "Of course it's your decision Sir."

Henderson assessed his options. "There it is then. In view of the deteriorating weather and Carter's injuries, we'll put in at Dunkirk."

After communicating the requisite recognition signals the launch reduced speed and entered Dunkirk's port. The tall Le Phare lighthouse lay off to starboard. It was low tide, exposing the steep harbour walls covered in seaweed and discoloured stone. Passing several tall-masted schooners along the Avant-Port channel they continued straight through the Port d'Echouage where drifters and ketch's sought refuge from the deteriorating weather. Two massive lock gates provided access to the Bassin du Commerce. They swung open allowing a French submarine to leave. Three of her crewmen were standing on the narrow decking forward of the conning tower as they passed close alongside. Taking her turn, the launch entered the lock and, for what seemed an eternity, they waited until the water levels had equalised allowing them entry into the Bassin.

"Not far now." Huckstead could sense Peterson's growing impatience. "Our moorings are at the far end of the Bassin du Commerce at Le quai du Leughemaërt." He pointed ahead. "We'll make fast, then Commander Henderson and myself will go ashore. He'll visit Naval HQ to make his report. While he's doing that I'll arrange ambulance transport for Lieutenant Carter and find a way to let your people know you're safe."

"Thanks." Peterson hadn't given much thought as to what he should do on arrival. He'd never been to Dunkirk before. With its myriad of streets, canals and docks, the town looked a complete maze.

Within fifteen minutes the launch had moored up alongside a floating quay. "You'd best wait here Peterson, keep an eye on Carter until I get back." Huckstead encouraged as he stepped ashore.

Peterson descended the stairs to the lower deck to find Carter soundly asleep on his bunk. He nudged his shoulder gently.

"Wake up old man. We're safely in port."

Carter stirred and opened his eyes. His mouth was dry. "Dunkirk?"

"Yes, we made it." Peterson passed him a mug of water and sat down on the end of the mattress. "Bad news is it'll be the parting of our ways. They're arranging your transfer to the Queen Alexandra Hospital. It's not far, just east of the town centre."

Carter appeared less than happy at the prospect of hospitalization. "Thanks Peterson." He swallowed the water with difficulty. "It's not where I'd choose to spend Christmas, but it's better than Pechell's current billet."

"Come on lad!" Peterson encouraged. "Just think of all those lonely VAD nurses."

"You've been away too long Peterson!" Carter raised a finger in mock admonishment. "Although if you ask the Navy lads, I'm sure they know all the best places. As for me.." He chided good-naturedly. "Just remember I'm a married man."

Peterson laughed. "Sorry old chap. I'm not making fun, it's just that your comment reminded of a visiting Chaplain, Hughes was his name, he came to our squadron back in the summer and 'excused unfaithfulness to our wives while away from home in the present circumstances'. Decent chap I thought. Not often men of the church are as worldly wise."

"You just be careful and take precautions." Carter advised sagely.

"I bet the family will be pleased to learn you're safe." Peterson imagined himself in Carter's position. "There's a good chance you'll be sent back to England to recuperate and rest."

"Funny thing." Carter considered Peterson's words. "I miss my wife and children terribly, but can't wait to get back to the old squadron and resume flying. Must have a screw loose eh?"

"Not at all. In fact I feel the same way myself if truth's to be told." Peterson sighed and checked his wristwatch. It was a quarter to three. "I've no idea what they'll do with me, I'd like to be re-assigned back to the old squadron."

"So what will you do?"

"Make some calls, pull a few strings, follow orders as usual. First thing though is a postcard via the Red Cross back to Bad Colberg camp. Tell the chaps I made it. Give `em a bit of encouragement. It'll annoy the Huns no end."

Carter reached into his tunic pocket and withdrew a small, paper wrapped parcel. "Do me a favour. Get this back to my squadron would you? It's the lens from our Brisfit's camera. Old Pechell was quite insistent."

The seaman named Auden appeared in the cabin doorway. "Beggin' your pardon Sirs, the ambulance has arrived for Lieutenant

Carter."

"Thanks Auden, we'll be up directly." Peterson acknowledged. He assisted Carter sitting up on his bunk. "Think you can make it?"

"Yes, just give me a hand getting up the stairs old chap would you?"

Once on deck, Carter assessed the daunting prospect of a walk along the floating quay to the waiting ambulance.

"Want me to get the medics?" Peterson offered.

"Not likely!" Carter's face was a picture of stony determination. "I've come this far, I'll bloody well make it the last ten yards."

Standing behind the ambulance wearing mid-blue uniforms, white aprons with a red cross and handkerchief style caps tied at the nape of the neck were two VAD nurses. Together they offered Carter assistance aboard. It was a small vehicle, coach built on the chassis of a Crossley fifteen horsepower car. He lay down on a stretcher that ran the full length of the canvas covered rear. As a nurse rolled down the screen Peterson's last sight of Carter was of him smiling and giving a firm `thumbs-up'.

Mid-way up the nearby Tour du Leughenaer a clock chimed three-thirty. Peterson and Huckstead set off together from the wharf outside the bustling Le Minck storehouse. Walking through the town they made several detours to avoid streets made impassable by bomb damaged buildings. Along La Rue de l'Eglise they passed a formation of French troops that stretched for hundreds of yards. In the distance, a regimental band was playing 'La Strasbourgeois'.

"I've notified your RFC wing headquarters. They offered their congratulations and said they'll contact your squadron and let them know where you are. In the meantime you're to sit tight and await further orders."

"Sit tight where?" Peterson asked. He'd no money, what remained of his uniform was a tattered, stained rag and his footwear falling apart.

"L'hôtel de ville de Dunkerque." Huckstead pointed toward a magnificent building a mere hundred yards ahead. Its' distinctive and ornate tower was, apart from Le Beffroi, the tallest structure in the town. "A disbursement, comfortable room, meals and a replacement uniform all laid on courtesy of the RFC." Huckstead laughed. "I hope they've got your measurements!"

"That's the problem." Peterson caught sight of his reflection in a shopfront window. "Lost so much weight, I'll need to grow back into it."

"Just one more thing." Huckstead adopted a more serious tone. "No doubt you'll be asked about your successful escape. Don't mention anything about the help you received from the Belgians. Words have a habit of reaching enemy ears. Consequences you understand."

Peterson understood. "You need have no concerns on that score, and I can speak for both Carter and myself."

"Good man."

A RNAS Lanchester armoured car passed by towing a light field gun. Pungent exhaust fumes filled the air as they arrived at the hotel's entrance. The doorman bade them welcome and ushered them up the stone steps beneath a tall brick arch that led to the salle de réception. The wood paneled interior of the lobby was lavishly decorated and dominated by a large, stone fireplace. While Huckstead spoke to the desk clerk Peterson absorbed the extravagant opulence of his surroundings. He felt a surge of emotion. After months of deprivation and hardship the relief was almost overwhelming.

"Come on through to the lounge, we can have a drink." Huckstead announced, leading the way. An explosion had destroyed part of a corridor leading to their destination and the two men had to scramble over bricks, mortar and fallen wood beams. "The hotel took a hit during a bombing raid last week apparently." He brushed an accumulation of dust from his uniform. "They're sorting a room for you on the first floor with a view of the harbour. One of the porters will come through and let us know when it's ready. In the meantime I expect you're hungry too?"

"Rather!" Peterson responded eagerly. Apart from a meagre pre-dawn breakfast he'd eaten nothing all day.

"Don't get your hopes up old man." Huckstead cautioned. "The food's nothing to write home about."

"You're talking to a man who's lived on gruel and scraps for three weeks. It's all a matter of what you're used to." Peterson replied. "For me a beef tea, mutton broth, potato pie and duff pudding would be a feast."

"Oh I think we can manage something a bit better than that!" Huckstead summonsed a waiter. "Bring us a bottle of wine, and none of your pinard 'vin blong' either, something decent."

Peterson was in his room at the L'hôtel de ville de Dunkerque. It was seven in evening of Saturday the twenty second of December 1917. Refreshed after a shave and wash, he donned borrowed breeches and his worn RFC tunic. Satisfied that his efforts had given him a more civilized appearance, he set off downstairs to the bar. Huckstead was waiting for him, surrounded by other naval officers of similar rank. On seeing Peterson arrive he broke away from the crowd.

"Up for a night on the town then old boy?" He asked.

"That's for sure. Haven't had a proper beano in months." Peterson replied. "So if I conk out drag me back."

"Come on then, we were about to head-off into town, just waiting for you. Want a sharpener before we go?" Huckstead anticipated Peterson's reply and gestured to the barman. "One Gimlet over here!"

"Gimlet?" Peterson queried.

"Navy strength gin and Rose's lime cordial. Here.." He passed across a charged crystal glass. "Complements of the Royal Navy."

Peterson swallowed the simple cocktail to a round of applause from the gathered seamen. The crowd were already moving toward the hotel's lobby. "Where are we going?" Peterson asked.

"We'll do the rounds. 'Officers Only' establishments naturally. Jean Bart Square for a start then the Place de la République. Call in at some old places and try some new ones. We usually stick together at first, as the evening wears on most of us make our own arrangements."

Outside was busy with early evening bustle. Six globe lanterns fronting the hotel radiated gas-light onto the pavement, otherwise there was very little illumination of the stone paved Rue de l'Eglise. The group set off together toward Place Jean Bart engaged in high-spirited conversation. Their exhaled breath rising in clouds of cigarette smoke and water vapour. It was a cloudless night and a bright, waxing gibbous moon reflected in the polished tram rails. Peterson stepped onto the lantern lit pavement to avoid passing traffic and examined the gothic façade of the newly rebuilt L'église Saint-Eloi. Across the road stood the original church's soot-blackened, fifteenth century Le Beffroi tower. It was undamaged and dominated the skyline. He made a mental note of his location just in case he should later find himself separated from his companions and need a landmark to find his way back to the hotel alone.

The shops along both sides of the Rue de l'Eglise were closed and shuttered. Overhead, trolleybus catenary wires sparked with each passing pantograph. As the trams moved on they left a characteristic ozone smell in the bitter winter air. The street opened out into an open, brick-paved square. In the centre was a plinth, on top of which was a statue of French naval commander and privateer Jean Bart, after whom the public area was named. Huddled together, standing on the steps around the monument's base under the soft glow of four gaslights, a group of Navy officers had gathered. When they saw Peterson's troop approach they waved across and one of their number called out.

"Huckstead! Come on, let's get somewhere warm." Handshakes were exchanged, old acquaintances renewed and introductions made. The assembly moved off toward an estaminet tucked away on the corner of Jean Bart Square. Amid the procession, Huckstead ushered Peterson forward. "Peterson, there are two fellows you should meet, Lieutenant's Symonds and Langstone of the RNAS, fellow aviators."

"My pleasure." Peterson shook hands with both in turn

"Peterson's a RFC chap, shot down in October and taken prisoner." Huckstead effused. "He's been on the run. Got back earlier today. Thought we'd give him a bit of a beano." Several others who had overheard crowded around Peterson, making further progress impossible. Murmured voices rose quickly into a crescendo of congratulatory banter and backslapping.

Langstone pulled to the fore a young Lieutenant wearing an identical, though less worn tunic. "Hey Peterson! We've got one of your fellows with us!"

Barry Hall pushed through the crowd and extended his hand. "Hall, Pilot's Pool St. Omer. Pleased to meet you."

"Peterson, 303 Squadron." Hall's handshake was firm. "St. Omer you say? I was there back in May awaiting my first posting. Tell me, is Captain Archie Robertson still there?"

"Yes, as a matter of fact I spoke to him only a couple of days back."

"Good Lord. It was only seven months ago but it seem like seven years." The group resumed their progress toward the misted windows of an estaminet named `Au Grand Morien'. "So tell me

Hall, have you been allocated a squadron yet?"

"No, and for some reason Robertson's put me on a temporary assignment accompanying these RNAS chaps ferrying 0/100's."

"But you're a Scout pilot eh?"

"That's right, seven hours on the SE5a at Beaulieu, 16 Training Squadron."

"Flew SE's with my lot too." Peterson recounted. "Until I was shot down over St. Denis-Westrem." He sensed by Hall's demeanor that he was no stranger to fighting. "Seen much action yourself?"

"In June with the 2nd Army, the Tenth Corps at Messines Ridge."

"I was stationed at St. Omer then. I read about it." He hesitated. "You poor bugger."

"A lot of men came out of it worse than me." Hall replied. "Anyway, I'm fascinated as to how you managed to escape."

Peterson placed his right arm around Hall's ample shoulders. "I'm already bored with the whole subject old man. Let's just get a couple of drinks inside us."

'Au Grand Morien' was a tidy, well presented estaminet with a large contingent of well-dressed civilian customers. It had been over four hours since Peterson's last meal and he was feeling decidedly hungry. He looked up hopefully as Huckstead approached from the direction of the crowded bar.

"Sorry Peterson, Hall. I'm afraid we're not very welcome here. They don't appreciate groups of military men."

"Who said that?" Peterson demanded, directing an angry stare at the staff behind the bar.

"No-one said anything." Langstone hurriedly intervened. "Just their attitude."

Hall made a move to remonstrate, but Huckstead placed a restraining hand on his shoulder. "Come on, don't waste your time on 'em. There's plenty of other places."

They stepped outside into the crisp, cold night air. Huckstead was right, the entire square was a hive of activity. It seemed every window was backlit by flickering lights, casting shadows of eager patrons across the pavement. Music echoed off the brick edifices. There was a peculiar odour, a blend of cooked food, cigarettes, perfume and alcoholic spirit. Occasionally a shrill female laugh would penetrate the darkness.

The nomadic group moved on, visiting various bars and restaurants. Peterson had lost count of their various stops but moderated his drinking, at least until he had eaten. By eight-o-clock the bulk of their party had dispersed, leaving only the two RFC airmen together with Huckstead, Symonds and Langstone. Peterson was walking in conversation with Hall down a narrow street. Their footsteps echoed against the walls of terraced buildings on either side.

"Where are we going?" Peterson asked.

"Café Parisienne." Symonds replied with a knowing smirk. "Every officer in the Royal Navy knows his way to its doors."

Hall nudged Peterson in the ribs with his elbow. "Been a while eh?"

"Too long." Peterson acknowledged with a discernable twinkle in his eye.

The heavy wooden doors to Café Parisienne opened revealing a restaurant, the décor and patrons diffused by tobacco smoke. The owner welcomed them inside and gestured them toward a wooden bench table with sufficient space for five. They sat and perused the menu. At length their waitress arrived to take their order. An attractive young woman, dressed in the minimum of clothing decency would permit. Hall was the last to give his choice from the limited menu. His smile was reciprocated, in doing so the girl revealed two rows of the most crooked, unwashed and decayed teeth he had ever seen. Too polite to comment he waited until she had departed before confiding his distaste to Peterson.

"Well, that one's yours."

Huckstead overheard Hall's comment. "Frightful eh? Don't worry, the food here is the best in Dunkirk. Can't say much for the wine though, bit too rough for me. I usually mix the white with citron or red with grenadine, makes it more like a port."

"Think I'll stick to the beer." Peterson volunteered.

"Fair enough." Huckstead acknowledged. "After we've eaten there's some proper entertainment laid on downstairs."

Months of a semi-starvation diet had sharpened Peterson's palette. He enjoyed every morsel, washed down with a decent French light beer. Satiated he sat back, lit a cigar, and enjoyed the mellow sensation of freedom and a full stomach.

"A man needs a decent meal. Enjoying yourself Hall?" Peterson asked.

"Tonight? Yes." Hall replied. Peterson sensed his new friend's reply was lacking in conviction.

"This hanging around at St.Omer is no good for a chap like me. I need some action." He drained his glass and gestured for a refill. "As for acting as a bus driver on 0/100's." He shook his head in despair, lowering his voice to avoid causing offence to the RNAS officers present. "I'd rather have stayed with the Tenth Corps."

Peterson felt a good deal of sympathy for the airman seated alongside. "I'm sure you'll get what you want. I can't imagine Robertson wasting the talent of a good Scout pilot." For a moment he reflected on his own prospects. "Put yourself in my place. Heaven knows what they'll do with me after all I've been through. Posted to a desk job?" He slammed down his empty glass on the table. "Not bloody likely!"

"Why the glum faces you two?" Langstone had noticed the

change of mood between the RFC officers. "Enjoy yourselves tonight. Tomorrow will take care of itself." He checked the clock on the wall and nudged Huckstead. "Come on, let's go downstairs. Floorshows about to start."

The stone staircase to the cellar was steep. Peterson was far from drunk, but nevertheless cautiously descended one step at a time. It was dimly lit, but adequate for eyes accustomed to the subdued restaurant illumination. The five officers seated themselves in an alcove with a clear view of the `stage'. A rug was laid out across the stone paved floor. Nursing a glass of brandy he had brought with him Hall noticed two of the waitresses from the restaurant, including the `tooth fairy' were also present, standing at the top of the stairs.

There were three other alcoves similarly populated with Royal Navy personnel. When the audience had settled two attractive females strode forward and began to disrobe. Peterson laughed out loud as a navy Lieutenant stepped forward, fixed a monocle to his right eye and examined the embracing performers from close quarters. As the girls writhed about with increasing intimacy Huckstead remarked. "Good grief. There's no need for that!"

His protestation was drowned out by cheers of encouragement from the other audience members, some standing for a better view. The cellar was increasingly smoky, overwhelming the pervasive scent of cheap perfume. The girl's final performance was rewarded by a round of raucous applause. Gathering their discarded clothing they departed and the lights were raised. Symonds was the first to his feet.

"Right, let's move on. Plenty to see and do."

"What did you think of that?" Peterson asked Hall.

"Not a bad show. Reminded me of Thursday night when I went out on the town with two RFC lads at St. Omer." He rolled his eyes. "Got a bit wild I'm afraid."

"Get a move on you two!" Langstone encouraged from the top of the stairs. "Peterson, after two months of enforced celibacy you must be going barmy!"

"I've known chaps go insane after a week without it!" Symonds observed with mock seriousness. "So we've clubbed together to give you a special treat tonight."

Peterson looked at Hall who shrugged. "If I were you I'd make the most of it."

"Right-ho." Peterson felt a frisson of excitement. "Lead on!"

By ten-thirty the merrymakers had visited all the watering holes in the Place de la République Square. They were returning to Jean Birt via the Boulevard Alexandre III. Huckstead was lagging some twenty feet behind the rest of the group when he was accosted by two females. They trotted toward him from opposite ends of the street, each one eager to be the first. Noticing their approach at the last moment he stepped back a pace and the two girls collided head-on, falling back into an undignified heap on the ground. He leant forward to assist them to their feet. Two surly looking characters emerged from the shadows and advanced menacingly.

"I didn't touch them!" Huckstead pleaded. The girls were laughing. Hall placed his sturdy bulk between Huckstead and the two roughs. One look at the burly RFC airman was enough. They wisely decided not to take issue and returned to the darkness.

"Must be newcomers. I'm rather surprised they picked on me." Huckstead rejoined the group, flushed with embarrassment. "The girls around here know a British officer would never disgrace his uniform by consorting with 'nightingales' in public."

Cloud had rolled in from the west and a dusting of light snow was drifting across the pavements as the officers entered the Café Restaurant des Arcades. They made their way through crowds of uniformed officers toward the bar. There were all nationalities present, French, Australian, New Zealanders, South

Africans and British. The sound of good natured conversation was interspersed with roars of hearty masculine laughter while away in a smoky corner, a woman was singing 'La Madelon' accompanied by an accordion.

Hall had little difficulty reaching the bar and his imposing presence gained the immediate attention of several barmaids. He ordered on behalf of the group.

"Five French Soixante Quinze cocktails please."

"Good Lord you can knock it back!" Peterson commented on his new friend's prodigious capacity for alcohol. That evening, by Peterson's reckoning, Hall had already consumed two Sherry and Bitters, one Benedictine, one Oyster cocktail and a Japanese cocktail.

"What in Heaven's name is a 'Soixante Quinze, by the way?"

"Similar to a Tom Collins, with Champagne replacing carbonated water." Hall smacked his lips in anticipation as their drinks were shaken vigorously and strained into chilled champagne glasses. "Said to have such a kick it feels like being shelled by a French seventy five millimeter field gun."

Peterson sipped cautiously at his glass, his eyes immediately began to water. "You're not kidding!"

"I was weaned on army rum, eighty percent proof, blows your head off if you swallow it neat." Hall dismissed Peterson's discomfort. "You wouldn't believe it, but one of our company commanders was a two bottle of whisky a day man before he was wounded and sent home. Lucky to be alive, you should have seen the stuff he drank."

"When you eventually get a squadron you'll fit in well with the lads." Peterson observed, based on his own experiences. "Strong drink and lots of it helps a chap relax and forget. Only way some fellows can get to sleep."

Symonds squeezed up to the bar next to Peterson and slapped him heartily on the back. "Right. You're all set up, we've taken care of the 'establishment' fee. Better class of girl than the run of the mill blue lamps or 'maisons tolérées'." He gestured toward the more intimate cocktail and champagne lounge. "We'll take our drinks in there."

They found a vacant table and sat. Langstone leaned across to Peterson and confided. "The usual custom is find one you like, buy her a drink and then take her upstairs." He surreptitiously slipped a prophylactic packet into Peterson's tunic pocket. "Here you are old son, can't be too careful even with the best."

Peterson's attention was soon drawn to an alluring blonde girl sitting alone at an adjacent table for two. She was dressed in a flimsy silk dress and dainty lingerie. Flaunting her charms, she beckoned him over with a pleasant smile. "Excuse me chaps." Peterson rose from his seat a little unsteadily. "I think I see a likely lady."

"Oh good choice old man!" Symonds complemented Peterson's selection. "That's Simone, you'll enjoy yourself with her. Ample skill and unlimited enthusiasm so I'm told."

"No personal experience then?" Peterson replied over his shoulder.

"Hardly! Langstone laughed as he nudged Symonds playfully. "She's far too choosy for the likes of him."

"Well, thanks awfully you lot." Peterson was truly grateful for his companion's generosity.

"Enjoy yourself." Huckstead waved a waiter over. "A bottle of Champagne for that fellow and his girl." He produced several banknotes. "Here, make it two."

Twenty minutes later Peterson and Simone were ascending the stairs together. His right arm around her slender waist and his left hand holding a chased silver Champagne ice cooler. He glanced back to where Langstone, Symonds, Huckstead and Hall were raising their charged glasses in his direction. Driven on by the promise of physical delights, he acknowledged their goodwill gesture with a smile of gratitude.

Upstairs Simone ushered Peterson into a boudoir decorated in sultry red, purple and black. Beneath a cranberry glass chandelier, soft candlelight created a gentle and warm atmosphere. Bedside table lamps complemented the ambient lighting with a pink glow. All around him, grand mirrors hung from all four walls, reflecting the flickering light and imparting a feminine aura. She led him toward a gold gilt framed bed with soft pink velvet upholstery. It was enticing, incomparably comfortable and romantic. The satin and silk bed sheets were covered with plump, sumptuous velvet cushions. On the dresser, a fresh bunch of luxurious flowers had been placed in a vase, adding their natural scent to the air.

The illusion was perfect, that of a secret, special place where only the closest of Simone's friends gained permission to enter. Having decided to allow Peterson into her private world, it was understood that she was ready to reach a new level of intimacy. It was a place to dream while awake, a place to fantasise.

Peterson undressed and donned a fluffy dressing gown. The deep piled rug felt beautifully textured against the naked skin of his feet. He sat down on a velvet boudoir chair, sipped from a glass of fine champagne and indulged in a delicious box of luxury confection placed on the dresser.

Classic French chanson emanated from a vintage record player. Peterson watched, transfixed by Simone's reflection in the various mirrors as she seductively removed her clothing and drew closer. She wound her arms around his neck and he inhaled her pleasant, dusky perfume. Pressing her warm, naked body next to his, he leaned back, supporting himself against the sinuous curves of a gilt rococo French chaise. Gently taking his hand, Simone led him to the bed. Peterson laid down, his head resting on the floral needlepoint headboard. They kissed silently. Outside, falling snow brushed softly across the draped window.

The morning light struggled through a low layer of murky cloud. It was eight in the morning of Sunday, December the twenty-third and the bells of L'église Saint-Eloi were ringing out after Sunday Mass. The dining room of the L'hôtel de ville de Dunkerque celebrated the grandeur of Baroque-era France. A "Sapin de Noël" fir tree, festooned with glass baubles, took pride of place on the floor underneath the room's central chandelier. Amid paper flowers, sweets, dried cakes, pine cones and ribbons were decorative 'Lametta'. These metal fringes draped across its branches evoked angels' hair and illuminated the greenery with silver and gold. The walls were swathed with garlands and wreaths.

There were less than a half dozen guests in the restaurant. Peterson was breakfasting alone on omelette, melon and champagne. He'd returned to the hotel in the early hours of morning, head swimming from the night's excesses and stomach rebelling against the unaccustomed food and alcohol. Six hours later the physical effects had dissipated and, comfortably seated at a table for one, he could not recall a time when his mind had been so settled and relaxed. It was as if the previous night had washed away every last vestige of the deprivation and hardship he had endured since his capture over ten weeks ago. Finishing his meal, he removed his napkin, folded the crisp, white linen and placed it carefully on the tablecloth, then leaned back and sighed with contentment.

Migrating to the lounge, Peterson noticed a vacant, antique French ormolu mahogany writing bureau. He drew up a chair and focused his mind on the composition of a letter home to his parents. With due regard to secrecy, he set down the bare details in concise a manner as possible. He closed with a sincere wish that they would all meet again before too long. With a degree of regret he sealed the envelope, a mere letter was insufficient to convey his experiences.

After leaving his letter with the clerk at reception Peterson donned his borrowed greatcoat and set off to the docks via La

Rue de l'Eglise. The remainder of the morning he spent unwinding in the steam rooms at L'établissement de bains. Relaxed and refreshed, at lunchtime he returned to his hotel and was immediately called over by the desk clerk.

"Lieutenant Peterson Sir. You have visitors waiting for you in the lounge."

"Thank you." Peterson surreptitiously checked his attire in a full-length lobby mirror. He had no idea who might be waiting, but suspected it could be a military reception. He opened the double wood-paneled doors in nervous anticipation.

Major Scott Cameron, the newly appointed Commanding Officer of 303 Squadron strode forward and grasped Peterson's right hand firmly in his. A welcoming smile disguised his dismay at Peterson's haggard physical appearance.

"Hello again old chap. How very good to see you!"

"Good to see you too Sir."

"All the fellows back at Wagnonlieu wanted to travel up and welcome you back, couldn't bring everyone or the squadron would be deserted."

"Bloody well done Peterson. I take my hat off to you." Another voice boomed.

"You remember old Bungee?" Scott introduced his companion. "Last time you two met was in our Mess. He's Major Smith now, commanding 321."

Bungee slapped Peterson's shoulder and smiled broadly. "Flew up this morning from La Gorgue to welcome you back. Had too, you and Thompson saved my neck over Polygon Wood back in July and I'll not forget that."

"Get your things together Peterson." Scott encouraged. "As soon as the transport truck arrives you're off back to Wagnonlieu. We're laying on a celebration tonight."

It was the work of a moment for Peterson to return to his room, pack his few belongings and arrive back in the lounge. Bungee and Scott were standing where he left them, the latter checking the time on his wristwatch.

"A truck will be arriving shortly. We'll drop you off at Dunkirk railway station. Here are your tickets. Bungee and I will carry on to St.Omer and fly back. Your train's scheduled to arrive in Etrun at six this evening. I've arranged to have you picked up and taken back to the squadron."

Twenty minutes later the airmen were standing in the lobby as a heavy Thornycroft 'J' type truck pulled to a halt outside. Even before it had stopped an airman in flying overalls leapt out from the back onto the ground and ran full-pelt up the hotel steps. The reception doors flew open. Standing in the opening was a breathless Lieutenant Jimmy Thompson.

"Peterson! As I live and breathe!" He rushed forward, arms outstretched. His instinct was to embrace his old friend but form prevailed and they shook hands vigorously.

"Thompson!" Peterson experienced a surge of emotion. "You came up seventy miles in a truck from Wagnonlieu just to see me?"

"No, flew up to St. Omer first, then twenty seven miles by road." Thompson glanced first at Scott, then Bungee. "Has anyone told him? Does he know about his award?"

"What award?" Peterson asked with a puzzled expression.

"The Military Cross old son." Scott announced with evident pride. "Gazetted three weeks after your single-handed raid on St. Denis-Westrem."

At six in the evening Peterson alighted from the train at Etrun station. It was snowing heavily and he stepped carefully across the platform into the warmth of the ticket office. On the road outside 303 Squadron's old five-seater Renault Type DM tourer was waiting, its' exhaust pumping out a great cloud of grey gas.

He climbed aboard, shut the door and brushed snow from his double-breasted greatcoat.

Seated behind the wheel, beneath his woollen muffler, Peterson recognised Scott's faithful soldier-servant Dobby Dobson.

"What are the roads like Dobby?" Peterson asked as he wiped the misted windscreen clear with the back of his gloves. Their single window wiper frantically swept back and forth.

"Tricky Sir. Glad your train wasn't late, wouldn't want to leave it much longer to get back." Snowflakes patted against the patched canvas hood and danced in the dim light of the twin headlamps. "Luckily I know this route like the back of my hand." Dobson engaged gear. The narrow rear wheels spun momentarily before regaining traction.

It was a short, two mile journey south from the station to Wagnonlieu aerodrome. They arrived at the perimeter gate at six-thirty. The sentries acknowledged their arrival with a salute, hastily retreating back under shelter after raising and lowing the barrier. Dobson drove the rusty Renault under cover inside the nearest wood and canvas 'Bessonneau' hangar. It was only marginally warmer inside than out. Accumulated slush fell in clumps from the mudguards as Peterson stepped down and inhaled the familiar odour of wood, dope and Irish linen. At the far end of the workshop he recognised Air Mechanic First Class Charlie Bingham among the mechanics engaged beneath the flickering electric lights. Bingham had been the most able of Peterson's designated ground crew.

"Keeping busy Bingham?" Peterson called out across the hangar.

Bingham paused from his work on a Hispano engine and looked back over his shoulder to the source of the familiar voice. He pushed up his spectacles and squinted in the distance. "Lieutenant Peterson Sir?"

"None other. Couldn't keep me away."

Bingham wiped his hands on his overalls and, with a smile of welcome, trotted toward Peterson. "It's so good to see you again Sir!" He saluted. "Corporal Saunders and I were talking about you only yesterday. We heard you gave the Huns the slip."

"It would appear so."

"I'd shake your hand Sir, but.." He held up a greasy palm. Peterson shrugged. "Think nothing of it". Regardless of the grime he grasped Bingham's hand in a firm gesture of mutual respect.

"Is Corporal Saunders here?"

"No Sir, but he did ask me to convey his best wishes.

"Peterson remembered Saunders, the last face he saw before setting off on his final, fateful mission to bomb the enemy Gotha bomber base at St. Denis-Westrem.

Dobson waited for the appropriate moment to announce. "Captain Peters has arranged your billet Sir, a nice warm hut. You're sharing with Lieutenant Thompson." He rubbed his chapped hands together. "Andrews will be your soldier-servant. I'll take your kitbag over if you want to go straight to the Mess?"

"Thank you Dobby. I will." He made for the door. "Same place?"

"Same place Sir."

Peterson strode forward toward the Mess, bent over against the penetrating cold. Along the usually dark wintry path shone hundreds of lamps illuminated by flickering candles. Snow crunched underfoot and a cutting wind created deep snowdrifts against every aerodrome structure. The ground immediately outside the Mess was lit by several electric lamps and crisscrossed with footsteps. Around a crackling bonfire several 303 Squadron officers were engaged in a vigorous snowball fight under a deluge of whirling snow. Everywhere there were men in winter garb, thick woollen jackets, mitts and scarfs.

The air was thick with snowballs made from fresh fallen flakes. A split second after a shouted warning, one hit Peterson on the back of his neck. It burst open on impact showering him in glistening crystalline fragments. Peterson ducked for cover, his head brushed long icicles hanging from the Mess porch. He stooped and picked up a handful of snow with his woollen gloves. His fingers were almost immobile with cold, but the challenge had been made and there could be no possibility of surrender. His face stretched into a grin, he took his first snowball and whipped his arm back, sending the projectile flying toward the nearest target. As it impacted a young officer he let out a whoop of delight.

After fifteen minutes of intense snow warfare a breathless Peterson entered the Mess, lips tinged blue, his body numb, raw and bruised. Thompson was first to greet him.

"So that's the greatcoat they've given you?" He remarked disparagingly as he helped Peterson divest himself of his outer garment.

"What's wrong with it?"

"Looks like the kind of thing you'd wear for six months then take it around the back of a hangar and shoot it."

Peterson's old squadron-mates Dilks, Culbertson, Charlie Coleman and Sammy Brown pushed their way through the throng of officers along with the squadron's Medical Officer, Captain Roger Watts.

"Welcome back Peterson." They each took turns to shake hands.

"Let's all get nearer the warmth Peterson. Looks like you need thawing out." Thompson led the group to a vacant table and six high-backed leather armchairs adjacent to the coal fire heater. The grate was open, revealing an intense mass of pure red fire that cast long shadows over the wood plank floor. Maurice, the head steward, presented Peterson with a mug of creamy hot chocolate covered with a generous layer of whipped cream.

"So Scott's taken over from McClennan as C.O.?" Peterson observed. The airmen looked at each other awkwardly.

"McClennan went down over Polygon Wood on October twenty

first." Thompson volunteered. "He was on patrol with Scott, they came across Jasta 10. Managed to get a Pfalz D.III before he was hit. Flamer I'm afraid. Poor sod hadn't a chance."

Peterson was genuinely shocked. Major McClennan had seemed invulnerable. A father figure in the squadron to whom every man looked up to with respect.

"Whatever induced the old chap to go on patrol?"

"You're guess is as good as mine. He'd not been himself for a while. The others who were with him on the day say he went into the fight like a tiger. He had several opportunities to break off but stuck with it. Scott said he'd never seen such aggressive flying."

It was a sudden re-acquaintance with the reality of air combat. For weeks Peterson had been pre-occupied with escaping. Pressing demands of evading the enemy had, for a time, eclipsed memories of squadron life.

"Where's Chivers?" Peterson was anxious for news about 303 Squadron's old Flight Commander.

"Gone back to Blighty". Dilks announced. "Posted to 95 Squadron at Ternhill in Shrophire at the end of October to train Cadets. A new outfit formed from 43 Training Squadron."

"Chivers an instructor? Pity the poor students!" Peterson shook his head in mock sympathy. "How's poor old Hoagy getting along?" He asked Thompson, concerned about the fate of their close comrade Second Lieutenant Stephen Hogarth. The three had met back in May at the Pilot's Pool at St.Omer and quickly established a strong bond of friendship. The subsequent tragic death of Hogarth's pregnant fiancée in a German bombing raid had been the catalyst for Peterson's single-handed attack on the enemy aerodrome at St. Denis-Westrem.

"Not good I'm afraid." Thompson knew Peterson would eventually ask and decided to break the news gently. "He was sent as your replacement. Poor fellow had changed utterly. Set on revenge, he was in a bad way. Only thing that perked him up was the news you were alive and a prisoner of war."

Peterson could read Thompson's expression. He swallowed the remainder of his hot chocolate in a single gulp and gestured Maurice for a whisky.

"He's gone hasn't he?"

"Sorry Peterson."

"How did it happen?"

"Twenty sixth of October. Scott was leading 'A' Flight toward Westrozebeke and Roulers. We came across two Gothas and a fighter escort. We set too among the escorts. Hoagy was badly shot up during the fight. He rammed one of the Gothas over Langemark. I saw the whole thing. There was nothing anyone of us could do."

Peterson shook his head slowly. There was a tremor in his voice. "At least now he's in peace." The whisky arrived and Peterson raised it to his lips. Words were inadequate. He looked into the fire in hypnotized silence as the flames curled and swayed, flicking and crackling as they burned the coal.

Scott and 303 Squadron's Adjutant, Captain Frank Peters joined the small group. They drew up a couple more armchairs. Peters held out his hands into the heat. "The fellows brought you up to date have they?"

"Yes. Thanks." Peterson sighed. He maintained a withdrawn composure, he had seen too many comrades fall in combat to be unprepared, or give outward expression of the distress that was writhing within. Given time, the crisp memories would blur along with the pain.

"It was good of you to come after me Scott, after I went down at St. Denis-Westrem."

"Thompson guessed where you'd gone. We went off with McClennan's blessing. Would have sent more but the two of us were all he could spare. We saw your machine burning on the ground west of the aerodrome, thought you'd bought it." Scott recounted soberly. "Officially Frank recorded you as missing in action but we all thought you'd gone west. You know, tailor-made suit, wooden, flying crew for the use of. We even raised a toast to your memory."

"While I was on the run." Peterson responded, wryly amused at the irony. "Hiding out in Drongen, across the river from Château Mariasteen. I saw you fly over by the way. Managed to dodge the Huns for two days, they finally caught me on the seventh October. Inevitable I suppose. A fellow needs a network of local support if he's to make a successful home run."

"Still, we're all glad you finally made it." Thompson encouraged. "Too many fine airmen are either dead or languishing in enemy camps. The new fellows lack experience."

"No change there." Peters added. "We're still short of pilot's, lost another two good men during yesterday's evening patrol south of Le Quesnoy. They ran into a bunch of Albatros D.III's."

"What's the latest on their replacements?" Scott enquired.

"We're being allocated a RNAS pilot from Mont St.Eloi. Fellow by the name of McGregor. Apparently the Navy want him to conduct an assessment of the SE5a as an alternative to their Sopwith F1 Camels. Regards the other, I'm making arrangements with Wing H.Q. over in Saint-Pol-sur-Ternoise." Peters was less than enthusiastic. "Probably be sent another `quirk' from St.Omer."

"Hang on." Peterson interjected. "I met a useful sort of chap while I was in Dunkirk, name's Lieutenant Barry Hall. Decent fellow, fought with the 2nd Army, Tenth Corps at Messines. Picked up a Blighty then joined the RFC. Keen as mustard and a good hand on SE5a's too. He's kicking his heels at St.Omer at the moment."

"Think he'd fit in?" Scott knew the importance of good fellowship for squadron morale.

"Oh yes, rather." Peterson replied without hesitation.

"Alright, on your recommendation: Frank, contact Robertson at St.Omer, see if the chap's still available." Scott cast an approving glance at Peters who made a pencil note in his pocketbook.

Peterson had been waiting for the right time to ask a question that had been weighing heavily on his mind. Up until that moment he had been reluctant to say anything as he knew the answer would likely be something he didn't want to hear.

"Frank, I hope Wing will allow me to stay with the squadron. Have you heard what they've got planned for me?"

Peters exchanged a meaningful glance with Scott. It was a matter they had already decided between them and Colonel Hallum at Wing H.Q. Peterson had to know at some point, now was as good a time as any.

"Back to Blighty old son. Home Office want to interrogate you about your experiences. After that I expect you'll be posted to training duties or a Home Defence squadron for the time being." Peters announced, trying to sound positive.

Scott could see the protestation forming on Peterson's face. He needed to know the decision was final and that no argument would prevail.

"You know that if you come down behind enemy lines again, you're a dead man. You've already made a name for yourself in the German press with your escapades. The Huns will interrogate then kill you." Scott stated bluntly.

"I'll take that chance."

"It's not your choice Peterson. We can't take the risk, you know too much." Scott was adamant.

"So that's it for me?" Peterson sighed dejectedly. "Order of the Bowler Hat, or instructor duties like Chivers."

"Afraid so old chum, at least in this arena of the war." Peters tried to offer some sympathy and consolation. "Look, you've had four months on the front line and nearly three as a prisoner of war. You've been awarded the Military Cross. Now's a good time to change step."

Downhearted, Peterson accepted there was no point in arguing.

The Queen Alexandra Hospital at Malo-les-Bains lay behind a wooden fence perimeter less than a mile from the Dunkirk seafront. The surrounding terrain bore multiple scars from bombing and shelling from sea, land and air. Within the compound, gangs of Chinese labourers were either repairing damage to rows of long, pre-fabricated timber buildings or constructing walls of sandbag barricades alongside the ward huts.

Access to the hospital entrance was via a covered, open sided gangway built on brick pillars that raised it above the slush and muddy ground. Major Freddy Wright paused and stepped aside to allow a trio of nurses enough room to pass by on his left. It was Monday morning, Christmas Eve 1917.

Having introduced himself to the Sister in charge, Freddy removed his hat and entered the ward. In his left hand he was holding a wicker basket. The ward was about a hundred feet long with walls and ceiling painted white. The floor consisted of bare, polished wooden planks. It was well lit, with windows above each bed running the full length on either side. Twenty iron framed beds with mattresses covered by crisp white cotton bed sheets and grey-blue blankets were lined up, ten to each side with wide spaces between them. In the centre, below a suspended gas light, a four-legged wooden table was laden with glass vases festooned with flowers. Six feet further along, through the slatted door of a shining, round black stove a comforting light flickered from the hot coals within. Heat radiated from its' cast iron body into the wooden building. A tall crooked chimney reached vertically up into the roof. Patients either sat up in bed or were seated alongside wearing nightgowns. A doctor in a long white coat was moving among the sick and injured servicemen accompanied by a senior nurse.

Carter was at the far end, alongside some folded screens. He attempted to get out of his chair and salute as his Major approached, but Freddy merely placed his hand on Carter's shoulder and bade him to remain still.

"Let's have none of that Carter. You stay seated." Freddy could not contain his pleasure. "Congratulations old chap. Good to have you back, and I speak for everyone at the old firm."

"Thank's Boss, it's been a tough couple of days. Really good of you to visit."

"Couldn't stop me. We got the news you were here yesterday so I came up by train from Avesnes-le-Comte last night. Frightful journey, over eighty miles. Would've flown up to Dunkirk but what with the weather being so bad, I didn't want to get stuck."

"Good decision." Carter watched the flurries of large snowflakes as they swirled outside the nearest ward window. Icicles hanging from the eaves reflected the light from within.

"Fairly busy here." Freddy observed. "Plenty of company."

"They treat us too well! Carter waved a friendly greeting at a passing medic." That's Dr. Wainwright, apparently last week he was asking the chaps ready for discharge if they wanted to stay another week or two over Christmas? You'd be surprised how many of them stayed on."

"Shame about Pechell." Freddy pulled up a nearby chair and sat down. "No official confirmation or word from the Red Cross yet. All we know is what we learned from you and the Belgians. How are the injuries?"

"Seems I've broken a couple of ribs, torn some rib cartilage. They've given me some anesthesia. Apparently I was lucky not to get a punctured lung."

"But you'll make a full recovery?"

"God willing yes, but the doctor's tell me I'll need about six weeks to recover and convalesce before I'm fit for flying duty."

"How long will they keep you in here?"

"Two weeks, at least until the new year. After then back to Blighty."

"A convalescence hospital I suppose?"

"Apparently so, no idea where though."

"Look here." Freddy confided in a quiet voice so as not to be overheard. "I might be able to pull a few strings on your behalf. I'm on good terms with a chap from the Canadian Army, a Major Irving. They've got a hospital in Woodcote, Epsom. I'll try and get you in there so you can be near to your family."

Carter smiled hopefully. "That'd be wonderful."

"Well, I'll see what I can do." Freddy patted Carter's shoulder gently. "No promises mind."

"Thanks Boss."

"Is there anything else you need?" Freddy opened a fresh pack of 'Black Cat' cigarettes and offered one to Carter.

"There's no shortage of comforts here, but there is one thing." Carter attempted to reach an ash-tray on his bedside cabinet without success. Freddy obliged.

"Just name it old son."

"Word is the mail here takes over a week to reach home. Could you find a quicker way to let my Mary know I'm safe?"

"Leave it to me. I'll visit the Padre's house on the way out. Matron told me he's been known to get a message back to families in England within twenty four hours. Anything in particular you want to say?"

"Just let her know I'm in good hands and that I'm thinking of her and the children. Tell her you've seen me and that I'll write soon."

"Right-ho." Freddy patted his tunic pockets. "That reminds me, I brought along a letter for you. It came while you were away."

Carter took hold of the creased envelope postmarked Reigate and immediately noticed Mary's handwriting. It was a bulky package containing several sheets of paper. News from home he would read and digest later.

"Will you stay for luncheon?"

"If Matron agrees. What's the food like in here?"

"Not bad, they do their best." Carter replied without enthusiasm.

Freddy opened the hamper at his feet. "Something from me and the lads." Inside were individually wrapped parcels of smoked salmon, bran bread and butter, venison, foie gras and a variety of cheeses. Wrapped in straw was a bottle of 1914 Chateau Haut Brion Rouge.

"I don't know what to say." Carter was overwhelmed by his comrade's generosity. "Thank's Boss, please tell the others how much I appreciate it."

"Oh they know." Not for the first time Freddy experienced a surge of emotion and empathy for his fellow airmen. A true brotherhood of the sky. Later that evening, after Freddy had departed, Carter relaxed in his bed. Finding a position free from pain he closed his eyes and, as his head sank deep into his pillow, listened to the lilting voices of carol singers as they visited every ward. The multitude of voices from young and old alike had a stronger effect on the patients than any medicine.

4. REVELRY OF THE DAMNED

Lieutenant Barry Hall arrived at 303 Squadron at seven in the evening of 24 December. Entering the Mess he was immediately surrounded by well-wishers and good-natured banter. Peterson was first to extend his hand in greeting.

"Hello again Hall".

"Peterson! I hear it's you I have to thank for my posting."

"Waifs and strays always welcome at 303." Peterson replied warmly, ushering Hall toward the bar. "Perfect timing too old man, we're just about to dine."

"Damn sight warmer in here than outside." Hall rubbed his hands together vigorously

"Come on over to the fireplace". Thompson stepped forward and cleared a path to the hearth, elbowing a corridor through the assembled officers. The flames flickered above a pile of winter logs. A short distance away stood the squadron's old Gaveau upright piano where Sammy was playing a selection of ballads from `The Bohemian Girl'.

"The name's Thompson old man. Have you logged your arrival with Frank Peters?" He queried. Both men were served with a brandy as Hall relaxed in a deep upholstered armchair.

"Yes, just before I came over to the Mess. Captain Peters said he'd be along shortly. Apparently I'm billeted with a fellow named Culbertson."

In conversation with Dilks, Culbertson overheard his name

mentioned.

"Hello?"

"Culbertson my dear old thing, meet your new room-mate, Lieutenant Barry Hall. First-rate fellow." Thompson provided the introduction.

"Pleased to meet you Hall" Culbertson extended a friendly hand in greeting. "So you're the chap who just arrived eh? Any sign of Saint Nick yet?"

"No, but I'm quite happy to sit here by the chimney and keep an eye out for the jolly old cove."

"Well you'd better shift up, here comes old Frank, looks like he needs thawing out too."

"No flying tomorrow, not in this weather." Peters announced having pushed his way through the throng. Fresh flakes of snow were still clinging to his breeches.

"I imagine the Huns will be grounded too." Culbertson tamped down a plug of tobacco into his pipe. "We could all do with a day off."

"It'll give you a chance to get acquainted with the lads and study the local maps." Peters advised Hall, anxious that their newest comrade should make the most of his time. "I read your army file, you're a fellow who shows initiative. That's good. It's important to have men who can think as well as execute orders."

"When do you think I'll make my first flight on operations?" Hall enquired, anxious to get stuck in.

"Soon, when the weather clears." Peters acknowledged the young pilot's enthusiasm. "For your first few patrols I want you to fly alongside Thompson. He's never lost a fellow new to the game. He'll keep an eye on you as will the others, when you're better acquainted with what's going on you'll be let loose on your own."

"What's the C.O. like, Peterson?" Hall enquired, hoping for some guidance for when Scott finally arrived.

"He's a man you can trust, takes a little more than his share of the blame and a little less than his share of the credit." Peterson reflected. "We've had eighteen airmen killed or wounded in four months, yet no-one hesitates to take on the enemy".

Culbertson handed Hall a well-thumbed copy of the squadron songbook.

"Come on chaps, time for one final chorus before dinner!" Sammy called out from behind the piano. "Culbertson you've got a good voice."

"Ha!" Peterson laughed. "He couldn't keep a tune in a bucket with a lid on!"

The Mess resounded with a host of untrained voices vigorously bawling the chorus, the loudest of which was Hall's whose singing talent had been honed in countless rugby clubs.

"I dreamt that I dwelt in marble halls

With ten willing girls at my side,

And with pleas that no Earthly man's heart could withstand,

Their undying love they all sighed.

And I dreamt that one of that feminine host

Came forth for my bed to claim.

But I also dreamt which pleased me most

The rest of them joined in the game."

Amid much back-slapping and bonhomie the group adjourned to the dining table. Maurice and his Mess team had prepared a sumptuous Réveillon dinner for the officers of oysters, lobster, roast goose with chestnuts, venison and cheeses.

"Come on 'Marble' Hall, as the new boy you can sit between me and Scott. Peters encouraged.

Christmas Eve 1917 at Queen Alexandra Hospital at Malo-les-Bains closed with a beautiful starlit night. Just before midnight a large convoy of men with minor wounds arrived, cheerful at the prospect of a bath and spending Christmas in a clean warm bed. As they processed into the hospital they were singing 'Hark the Herald Angels'. Carter lay awake, listening to their voices while looking out the window at a quiet, still, moonlit night. He could hear their voices as they echoed along the hospital corridors. To hear Christmas carols while watching the stars shining was wonderful. He'd always remember that night.

By 08.00 hours heavy snow was falling on the frozen ground and the leaden clouds at five thousand feet were full and dark. Every ward window was covered with ice-white dust and the roof creaked under a heavy load. During the night, snow had piled up in drifts against the hut's outer walls. Inside, it was a day of duty as well as Christmas celebration. A party spirit on the one hand and a fully functional wartime hospital on the other.

The morning shift breakfasted in the kitchen at six and, after a Christmas service in their Mess, were busy attending their patients. Friends and relations who had made the difficult journey across town and further beyond mingled with nurses and visitors from other wards. A few patients discharged the previous week had returned during their leave for Christmas dinner. The communal corridor was festooned with carnations and decorations. Flags hung from the rafters and pink lampshades had replaced the ward's austere opalescent white glass. Some of the more mobile patients had created decorations with assistance from the nurses. On a central table there was a manger with snow on top and a light inside. On the ward's dark blue window blinds they had created a night sky with stars and snow drops.

Presents arrived throughout Christmas day, the cause of much pleasure among the men. For Carter, the letters from his wife and photographs of his family were sufficient. In the early afternoon, the doctors volunteered to carve the patient's dinner, on completion of which, the cooks were summonsed to receive a round of general applause. After a tea of sandwiches, Carter drank the red wine brought by his squadron mates and relaxed into the crisp, ironed sheets tucked into his bed. The nape of his neck caressed by the cool, cotton pillowcase, his belly full of food, he succumbed to the call of sleep with thoughts of home and family.

The Carter's isolated Victorian cottage was situated a mile south of the Surrey town of Reigate, alongside a rural track bordered on either side by evergreen shrubs interspersed with overhanging Oak, Beech and Ash trees. A rusting wrought iron gate in the round top cedarwood picket fence provided access to the small garden. The building's ground floor walls were clad with trellis panels, to which were entwined the bare branches and long, whippy shoots of last summer's Wisteria. It was early Christmas morning and the plum pudding was being steamed in the kitchen. From the single, roll-top clay chimney pot a cloud of smoke rose slowly into the still, cold early morning air and drifted across the tiled roof. Every window was closed, preserving valuable heat within. Beneath a dove grey sky, the only sound was the call of a Bittern from a nearby vernal pool.

At the rear of the dwelling, a single storey extension had been recently constructed and it was there, beneath the frosted tiles of an overhanging porch, that Mary Carter prepared her two rosy-cheeked children for the half mile walk across Reigate Heath to attend Christmas Day service. Setting off into a biting north wind the children skipped along amid the chaotic swirls of snowflakes, crunching through wintry puddles their bodies cozy inside warm coats. For Mary, the bleak grey cloud overhead reflected perfectly her grey mood inside.

In the heart of the Surrey Hills, an eighteenth century post-mill towered above the barren winter valleys. Its four double patent sails were stationary. At the base, in a single-storey roundhouse, was the small St. Cross Chapel where hung holly, evergreens and coloured paper-chains.

Christmas day Holy Communion concluded at nine in the morning. The congregation of fifty worshippers had begun to depart along the winding chalk lanes toward home. As they filed out from the Chapel, Mary ensured her two, tired young children were securely wrapped up warm against the cold. They were the last to leave. She paused in the doorway, customarily shook the Reverend's hand and thanked him for the Service.

"Mary, a word if I may?"

"Of course Vicar."

"It won't take long, shall we return inside away from the chill?" He smiled kindly at the two smartly dressed youngsters.

Together they sat down on two ladder back chairs. Above their heads, heavy oak rafters supported the weight of the windmill. The low sun shone directly through a square window immediately above the altar. Sunbeams illuminated motes of dust suspended in the air while the children busied themselves collecting prayer books.

The Reverend cleared his throat. "I received a communication this morning from the Queen Alexandra Hospital in Dunkirk concerning your husband, Lieutenant Carter."

Mary stiffened, anticipating the worst.

"You are aware that his aeroplane was reported missing on the eighteenth?"

"Yes, his Commanding Officer wrote to me personally. He said it was likely Sebastian was captured alive."

"He's safe Mary. He managed to escape back to Belgium, although he suffered a few broken ribs."

Her right gloved hand reached up to her chest, accompanied by a sharp intake of breath. "Is he at the hospital now?"

"As of yesterday, yes. Major Wright visited him and gave him your last letter. No doubt you'll be hearing from Sebastian himself soon. I'm told that he'll likely be returning to England in a couple of weeks for convalescence. Major Wright is using his contacts to arrange somewhere local."

It was difficult for the Reverend to discern Mary's reaction, her face concealed by her chapel veil.

"Thank you Vicar." There was a slight tremor in her voice as she called out to the youngsters. "Children, come here." Having straightened the piles of prayer books they obeyed, standing before her, hands clasped behind their backs, eyes wide open in expectation.

"I have the best of news, father is safe and he's coming home."

On the way back, with the prospect of a crackling fire, the winter weather seemed less dreary and more like a wonderland.

It was Christmas morning in Wagnonlieu and the timber walls of 303 Squadron's Mess were resounding to the buzz of happy voices. Decorations hung from the rafters in a riot of colour against the dark stained wood. Unwrapped parcels from relatives and loved ones revealed a variety of gifts from home. Fortnum and Mason hampers were in abundance, packed full of the most desirable provisions. Music filled the smoky air as the old Decca gramophone crackled out 'Paddy Mc Ginty's Goat' sung by the Two Bobs. Stewards weaved through the mass of airmen and the sweet aroma of luncheon perfumed the air. The atmosphere was one of happy camaraderie. It was a time for young men away from home to celebrate being alive and experience the wonder of Christmas. At one with each other, everyday thoughts and worries were banished.

Since taking over as Commanding Officer on the thirtieth of October Major Scott Cameron had engendered a healthy atmosphere in the Mess. Discouraging the forming of cliques, often the cause of bad feelings, he encouraged its use to foster a strong esprit de corps. It was a place where the young men under his command could get to know one another beyond their daily activities, establish a bond of fellowship and learn to trust each other.

Christmas Day Eucharist began at 10.30. Wagnonlieu aerodrome's largest Bessonneau hangar had been cleared especially for the occasion. The duckboards connecting it to the various squadron buildings were covered with a layer of ice, making transit impossible for anyone who had made an early start on the liquor. Fortunately, everyone managed to keep upright without falling. Judging by the singing from the cookhouse, the chefs had a head start on everyone else.

The Reverend Neville Hughes greeted the men individually on arrival. He was well respected, having won the Military Cross at Messines Ridge for bringing back wounded troops under fire. As 303 Squadron's Chaplain, not only did he provide them with spiritual guidance and sustenance, but was a key contributor to general morale.

"Must be a busy day for you Padre." Scott remarked as he shook hands and accompanied Hughes inside.

"Not as much as last year, my parish is down to four squadrons, one here and three about thirteen miles away, including your friends at Avesnes-le-Comte."

"I hope they've taken good care of you. Are you still able to join us in the Mess for Christmas luncheon?"

"Of course!" Hughes adjusted his surplice. "So far this season everybody has been perfectly charming and cheery." He cast his gaze around the seated congregation. "Though I've noticed many of the younger boys drink more than is good for them."

The service lasted until 11.30 hours, after which Hughes accompanied Scott back to his office where they could relax and enjoy a moment of tranquility before adjourning to the Mess.

Scott liked Hughes, he was one of the few Chaplains who understood life in a front line squadron. The two men were engaged in spiritual conversation when a group of airmen passed by outside singing the lyrics to a particularly bawdy RFC ballad.

"Sorry about that Padre." Scott shook his head in embarrassment.

Hughes dismissed it with a laugh. "No need to apologize Scott. I've seen and heard it all before." He lit his cigar, sat back and exhaled slowly. "Raucous singing's one of the ways the young officers deal with surplus adrenalin. It's how it is, the boys find it hard to talk about fear or loss, so levity and euphemisms become a coping mechanism to express and play down what would otherwise be the unmentionable."

Scott had long thought the same. "That and diversions like rugby, Mess games, music, superstitions and a few drinks help them deal with the strain." He hastened to add. "Although drinking is more a result of combat stress rather than a substitute for courage."

"While the Church tries to re-inforce their spiritual life, something that will help them during periods of reflection."

"I'm glad you understand Padre. Most people outside the service don't. You see, airmen assume their combat role. When you meet squadron pilots at ease in the Mess, they adopt an appearance of nonchalance by playing billiards, reading, listening to the gramophone or playing the piano. It's their way of dissipating fear without admitting they've got the wind-up about their next mission."

"They're brave men Scott every one of them."

"Even so, it's difficult. Our selection board try to find men who can ignore or suppress their anxieties for as long as possible, but every man has his limit. Even with all the distractions it gets to the point where some are unable to master and control their nerves."

"How about you Scott? I've noticed you seldom drink or indulge in other pastimes. Don't you experience fear?"

Scott shifted uneasily in his chair. "Fear's my passenger on every flight. Earlier this year I flew the first Brisfits, dangerous business until we learnt to fly them like single-seat offensive fighters rather than heavy two-seaters. I used to get the wind-up as much as the other pilots and observers when we set off, an experience I encountered with increasing frequency when I converted to SE5a's and the fighting became more intense."

"How have you managed?"

"As I see it, you can either accept that you'll die or you don't. Me, I've seen it so many times in the air I've accepted its inevitability."

Hughes was taken aback by the steely challenge of Scott's piercing blue eyes. "Now you're being morbid Scott."

Scott shrugged his shoulders. "Not morbid, just realistic." He was obviously uncomfortable discussing the subject. "I'll take you over to the Mess and introduce you to the boys, I'm sorry I won't be able to entertain you for long though, I've some duties to attend to. Should be back about two. Hope you're open minded, things can get a bit rowdy I'm afraid."

Despite the general bonhomie, 'Marble' Hall felt anxious and slightly nervous with his surroundings. An army man, he was unfamiliar with RFC Mess etiquette. Handed a glass of brandy by a passing steward he drank the contents in one swallow. As the spirit warmed his stomach, he remembered his last Christmas meal in 1916 with the Tenth Corps near Thiepval. It consisted of a tin of bully beef discarded by the previous occupants of his gun pit. He'd dug it out of the snow, fried it up, made a hash of it and eaten it with a jack knife. The whole washed down with a drop of tea from a dixie heated on a primus.

Engaged in conversation at the bar, Peters noticed Marble's discomfort and excused himself. He walked over and did his best to put their new comrade at ease.

"All right Marble old chap?"

"In the pink Captain Peters, just a bit ginger about putting a wrong foot forward that's all."

"Don't worry young fellow, we're an easy going bunch. Just remember, never discuss politics or religion. Try not to talk shop either, chaps who have nothing to discuss except their daily routine soon become intolerable bores." Peters refilled the empty bowl of his pipe with a new plug of tobacco. Lighting the contents, he continued between puffs in quiet contentment. "It's a bit like the public school Officer Training Corps. The old concepts of courage and manliness?"

"I'm an old grammar school boy myself."

Peters nodded his approval. "Me too. You'll find a lot of the chaps here are fresh from school or university. To them the squadron is like a school, house or college. They're as loyal to their squadron as soldiers are to their regiments or sailors to their ships. We live in a tight little world of our own. It's exciting, always interesting, and at times very dangerous."

"I see, thank you Captain Peters."

"Call me Frank, and if ever you need a quiet chat, something worrying you, my door is always open. The lads often bring their problems to my office."

"Well I'll try not to burden you."

"Not at all. I'm glad to help". His voice assumed a fatherly tone. "The day the boys stop coming is the day they've either lost confidence I can help them or concluded I don't care." He slapped Marble on the shoulder before taking his leave.

Amid light-hearted banter, the officers of 303 Squadron exchanged ideas, jokes, scandals and complaints. Marble relaxed and inhaled deeply. He'd received just one package from home.

Wrapped in brown paper were a pair of mittens from his widowed aunt in Esher. He turned them over in his hands, letting his eyes roam freely over every loving home-knit stitch. This day was his holiday from reality, when bitter memories were outplaced by beaming smiles and bonhomie.

As Peters made his way across the Mess the young officers stood back to give him clear passage. Thompson came over and sat on the arm of Marble's chair. "I can see why all the chaps look up to Frank." Marble commented. Thompson nodded in agreement. "No doubt you've heard the old saying: In a profession where men die young, the oldest command the greater respect". He saw the empty glass in Marble's hand. "Come on, next drink is on me."

Thompson led Marble through the throng to the bar, where a brass bell, formed from the casing of an expended artillery shell, hung from a rusty bracket. He explained: "Ringing that lets the lads know you're offering to buy a round for all present, usually after a victory or promotion. Watch out though, it's not uncommon for 'accidents' to happen after a skin-full."

Peterson broke off his conversation with Hughes to add his own advice. "And don't try to hold your own at the bar Marble, even though Dilks and Culbertson will try to convince you otherwise. Been the downfall of many a man."

Handed a wet brandy glass by the barman it almost slipped through Marble's fingers before he grasped it with his left hand. Hughes, 'in vino veritas' after several glasses of Port, issued Marble a mock-formal admonishment. "Remember the Mess commandment my son. Thy glass of spirit is served in an un-shattered container. Thou shalt return said container in the same condition."

"And as the Mess president will confirm." Peterson interjected. "If you fail to follow this commandment, your bill will reflect the wrath of your peers." Behind the bar, Maurice cast his eyes to the ceiling.

"Where's the C.O. got too?" Marble looked around for Scott, who was noticeable by his absence.

"He'll be back shortly, over in the men's canteen helping serve Christmas lunch." Peterson answered, leaning against the bar for support. For Marble's benefit he explained. "Squadron tradition old boy. On Christmas Day the C.O. waits on the lower ranks. So do the Sergeants and NCOs. They all help dish out food in the cookhouse. Turkey and roast pork this year I hear."

"That's damn decent of them." Marble commented.

"It's typical of Scott." Peterson scanned the Mess for an empty seat, having overdone the alcohol. "Look here". He slurred. "You'll find there are no good or bad squadrons in the RFC Marble – only good and bad officers and NCOs. They make or break the unit."

Standing behind Peterson's left shoulder, Culbertson added his own observation. "Airmen watch what their leaders do. You can give 'em classes and lecture them forever, but it's their C.O.'s personal example they'll follow. Attitudes are caught not taught"

Marble nodded in understanding. He remembered Messines and a soldier lying on a stretcher out in no-man's-land. The lad was looking up at the sky when his Captain crawled out to him and said: 'It'll be all-right lad. I'll get you out of here.' That soldier had faith in his Captain and his mind was at rest. That officer was a leader in the minds and hearts of his men.

"I'll say one thing about the Skipper." Culbertson confided. "The lads trust him. Without trust a C.O. might as well go home". He noticed a vacated card table close by. "Fancy a game of Cribbage Marble?"

"All right, been a while though and I'm a bit rusty."

"So when was the last time you played?"

"Back in the early summer. Myself, two Corporals and a Sergeant were all playing cards at the bottom of the trench. There was a pile of old French banknotes and coins on the table and then this chap came along to watch us. He'd got a Mills bomb in his hand

and he was messing about with it, letting the lever come up. As you know once the lever springs, you've got about five seconds before it detonates. Anyway, this cove was larking about and all of a sudden the lever flew off. We saw it go and scattered. The Corporals went over the top while the Sergeants and I went round the corner. The blighter with the bomb didn't though. He pocketed the money and off he went. You see, he'd already taken the detonator out."

Culbertson laughed so heartily he almost fell over.

Serious drinking began at midday and when Scott returned to the Mess at two in the afternoon every man present was hammered. Laid out on the long refectory table was an amount of food that on any other day would be expected to last several more. At the sight of the delicacies Marble's mouth watered, it was a tonic. With the aroma of food igniting memories of home the airmen bowed their heads and thanked God for this bountiful meal, for each other and for the salvation he bestowed through Jesus Christ. They devoured the feast with joy, piling plates while attempting to mind their manners. As they talked, laughed, and reminisced, between mouthfuls of roast pheasant cooked over charcoal fires. Scott turned to Peters and remarked:

"I don't know how Maurice manages it. The supply lorry's been cancelled, the roads are in such a state."

"Best not ask questions old chap." Peters replied with a knowing look. "I believe he has an 'understanding' with one of the local farm widows."

Scott shook his head in an attempt to clear his mind. "That milk and rum punch in the men's canteen. Dangerous stuff!"

At four in the afternoon the officers of 303 Squadron received an invite to attend the Senior NCOs' Mess. Later, as they filed in, it was apparent to the visitors that the vigorous spirit of their own establishment had become common knowledge in the squadron. The Sergeants and Corporals had emulated the Officer's Mess behaviour. Scott wholeheartedly approved, he knew the net effect was cohesion throughout his command. A popular commander with his men, Scott was known to engage with his subordinates and keep them informed. He treated them with dignity and took a keen interest in the conditions in which they lived. As Commanding Officer, he was also responsible for discipline, but ensured punishments and grievances were dealt with properly.

At eight in the evening the combined squadron personnel assembled in a specially erected marquee for their Christmas concert. Another characteristic of his leadership, Scott encouraged the men to celebrate together. It reinforced their morale and helped make life in the camp more tolerable, especially in the middle of winter. The beer was already flowing when Flight Sergeant Norman Wilson entered and ascended the dais somewhat the worse for wear. "Before we start, lads." He announced. "I'm going to ask the C.O. to come up and drink our health."

Scott stepped forward and made a welcoming speech, keeping it short as the men naturally were impatient to see the show. His brevity was rewarded by unanimous applause. He left the improvised dais to the accompaniment of the squadron band playing 'Pack Up Your Troubles'. Shortly afterwards a singsong began, 'If You Want the Sergeant-Major' and 'There's a Long, Long Trail'. Corporal Saunders disguised himself as Harry Lauder, an act that brought the house down. Scott's batman, Dobson, gave his version of 'Way Down Upon the Swanee River', then Air Mechanic First Class Charlie Bingham performed a ventriloquist and conjuring act. The band struck up 'Tipperary' and soon all the men were singing in unison:

That's the wrong way to tickle Marie,

That's the wrong way to kiss,

Don't you know that, over here lad,

They like it better like this.

Hooray pour la France! Farewell, Angleterre!

We didn't know the way to tickle Marie,

But now we've learnt how.

Christmas evening in the Officer's Mess passed in the usual manner, supper, satirical songs based on the latest music-hall ditties, drinks, cards and banter. There was always a cheerful readiness to gather around and give voice to songs about flying. It was the airmen's way of establishing a tradition and expressing their way of life.

Outside, the moon was shining in a cloud free sky. In what was otherwise a quiet, still night, the men were singing 'Hark the Herald Angels' with gusto. To Scott it was wonderful, he'd always remember Christmas 1917.

5. REVENGE

It was mid-morning of December the twenty-sixth. Thompson was playing Culbertson in a game of snooker when Peters re-entered the busy Mess along with Scott. Both men were wearing a downcast expression.

"Now pay attention lads. Stop what you're doing and listen." The conversations immediately hushed. Silence filled the Mess, except for the sound of chairs scraping on the floor and the footsteps of Scott and Peters as they walked to the far wall and unfolded a map of front lines.

"Can everybody see?" Scott motioned to the assembled audience as he sat on the edge of a table and threw his cap onto a vacant chair. "I'll come straight to the point. It's Jasta 6 at Bouchain. Thirty miles due east. Reinhard's Staffel. We've been told to attack their base at dawn tomorrow as part of a general retaliation for the enemy raids on London and the south-east eight days ago. Wing have asked for three machines from 303 Squadron, so it's only fair to draw the names at random. Frank has already written everyone's down on pieces of paper, I'll put them in my hat and ask him to make the draw. It's our target and no other squadrons are involved in this operation. Success is down to us!"

The tension during the draw was unbearable. Thompson could feel his heart pounding heavily as Scott held up his hat and Peters took out the first piece of paper. It was Culbertson. A second piece of paper was drawn out and, as it was unfolded, Thompson already knew his name would be on it. He heard his name read out loud and his heart sank. Sammy was the third name drawn. Scott invited the three airmen to join him in the

Briefing Hut and the remaining officers to resume their activities. "And not a word to anyone." He added. "Keep this to ourselves."

Once inside, Scott instructed the airman on their mission. He stressed that, in the event of their failure to reach the enemy aerodrome at Bouchain, they should deploy their bombs on either the marshalling yards at Douai, the station, surrounding barracks, or roads in the vicinity.

The three SE5a's took off from Wagnonlieu at seven fifteen in the morning of Thursday the twenty seventh of December. It had been agreed that the best time to attack the enemy base was before sunrise. Thompson intended to surprise the German airmen just as they were preparing for their day's operations. Together with Sammy and Culbertson, they planned to pick them off one by one as they scrambled to defend their aerodrome.

It was only a short, thirty mile flight east to Bouchain. Most of their time in the air was spent gaining height over Arras before following the Scarpe River and crossing the front lines above the ruins of Roeux. They reached the target at seven forty-five, but the sight that greeted them was entirely unexpected. Bouchain aerodrome's frozen grass field was deserted. There was no sign of either personnel or machines.

Disappointed, Thompson nevertheless dropped his ordnance on the darkened hangers and outbuildings as ordered. He was turning away toward their secondary objective at Douai when, in the early morning light, he saw the silhouettes of hangars north of the nearby village of Lieu-St.Amand. Signaling his intention to the others, he set course south-east across the Scheldt River marshes and adjacent railway line to discover at least ten of Jasta 4's new Pfalz D.IIIa's on the ground. Their six-cylinder Mercedes engines were already warming up in preparation for dawn patrol.

The three SE5a's began their attack from the south. Two hundred and fifty feet off the snow covered rooftops they swept in between the village's two Chapel buildings. Groups of enemy mechanics ran in all directions to escape their deadly streams of bullets. Field grey clad troops rushed to man Archie guns as Thompson dipped the nose of his SE5a and, racing across the snow, raked the black-striped enemy machines at a hundred and thirty miles an hour. He could clearly see the startled faces of German airmen looking up at him as he flashed by a mere fifty feet from the ground,

Every muscle in Culbertson's body tensed to the staccato rattle of machine gun fire from the ground. Tracer hissed past, holes ripped into the fabric of both wings and his goggles were shattered by the glancing blow of an enemy bullet. He swore, tore them off and discarded them. Despite the accuracy of enemy guns, he knew that the three SE5a's could not leave the enemy aerodrome until they'd given a good account of themselves. He saw a Pfalz taking off and entered into a shallow dive to chase after the black-crossed enemy machine. It was barely hovering above the grass when Culbertson closed up and took aim. As the climbing Pfalz filled his Aldis sight he pressed his Vickers gun paddle. Spent cartridge cases ejected into the slipstream underneath his fuselage. Fifty rounds and the enemy aeroplane slithered sideways to starboard then cartwheeled along the ground.

Sammy noticed a Pfalz with a bright yellow tail flying at low level west of the aerodrome. There was no time to close up the range so he fired. The German pilot turned to watch Sammy's stream of bullets rush toward him. It was a fatal mistake, a moment's inattention and he crashed into a copse of trees beyond the perimeter fence.

Sammy dropped so low that he barely missed a sandbagged gun emplacement with his undercarriage. In a climbing turn for another strafe of the aerodrome he input right rudder and stood the SE5a on its wings. There was a rip of fabric and he felt a sharp tug on his right upper sleeve, the force of which twisted him around in his seat. For a moment his SE5a fell off and headed for the frozen grass field below. He eased back on the joystick and

172

soared over the remains of the burning Pfalz Culbertson had just downed.

The sky grew brighter with every passing moment. The sun was just peeking out of the eastern horizon, an orange hued spear of light that pierced through the clouds and danced over the winter landscape. It was obvious to Thompson that the opposition would soon heavily outnumber the three British machines. Too many enemy aeroplanes were taking off in different directions. It was time to withdraw.

Culbertson noticed his colleagues disengage from the raid and was climbing away to follow them when, glancing back, he saw a Pfalz with a blue tail fast approaching on his six-o-clock. He turned to face his opponent and opened fire. The enemy dived to within a hundred feet of the ground. Undeterred, Culbertson followed him and commenced a hair-raising low-level chase, dodging trees and shrubs that rushed by perilously close to his wingtips. Emptying the final drum of ammunition from his Lewis gun he saw the battered Pfalz, its rudder fluttering, slide through the air toward the ground. The harassed airman was still battling to control his crippled machine when it crashed.

In just over five minutes the trio had regrouped and climbed back to five thousand feet. By then, sunrise had filled the sky with a breathtaking display of radiant colours. Bright streaks of red, pink, and orange had replaced the dark blue and purple of twilight. Thompson, however, had no time to marvel at the scene. Scanning the sky for any sight of enemy machines he saw a cluster of six black dots rising up from the direction of Avesnes-le-Sec in the south east, most probably Fokker Dr1's of Jasta 11. Thompson knew the SE5a's were low on ammunition and in no condition for combat. Confident that the British machines could easily outrun the slower triplanes, he decided on a rapid retreat. The shortest route home would cross the front at Étaing.

Sammy was flying off Culbertson's right wing, slightly behind, when he detected an acrid odour that permeated the fabric of his silk scarf. His eyes immediately scanned the instruments, checking coolant temperature, oil pressure and engine revolutions. He unfastened his leather flying cap, the better to hear the engine. Everything appeared normal so he checked his exhaust for smoke, there was none but the stench was growing stronger, a hot, metallic taint to the air. Within seconds the smell was accompanied by a deep rumbling sound. He retarded his throttle slightly, the engine note changed but the rumbling remained constant.

They were still well within enemy held territory, midway between the villages of Palluel and Lécluse when it occurred to Sammy that the unusual sound and smell might not be his own aeroplane. He glanced to his left and immediately saw the cause. Culbertson was looking down inside his cockpit and, by the rapid movement of his shoulders, adjusting the SE5a's engine controls.

There came the sound akin to a backfire, a large chunk of engine casing erupted through its mounting structure and through the side of Culbertson's cowling. Transfixed by the unexpected sight, Sammy watched metallic debris impact the lower starboard wing leading edge stiffeners in a shower of splinters. He heard the terrible sound of ripping fabric and crunching wood as the front spar snapped and the wing folded back. As if in slow motion, the interplane struts sheared at their lower mountings and Culbertson's SE5a rolled off to starboard.

Thompson had pulled down his scarf and was shouting across to Culbertson, his words lost in the howling wind and sounds of destruction. Sammy realised that he, too, was calling out to his comrade. Together they watched, helpless, as Culbertson's stricken machine dropped five thousand feet like a falling leaf until it impacted the leaden water of Lécluse Lake south of the Sensée river.

The two remaining SE5a's landed back at Wagnonlieu just before nine thirty in the morning. Thompson and Sammy dismounted and joined the huddled officers who conversed in lowered voices. They could read the pain in each another's eyes. If only it could have been someone else, that was the unspoken thought. Thompson imagined his old friend lying dead amid the submerged wreckage of his SE5a beyond the lines. As he left the landing field, he caught sight of Charlie Bingham leaning against the end of a hangar and looking east into the sky where Culbertson had vanished. His expression one of desolation.

That evening Dilks was engaged in spirited conversation with Marble and Charlie Coleman when he noticed Sammy sitting alone in the far corner, nursing an empty brandy glass in his hands. His eyes were staring vacantly at the floor. Excusing himself, he made his way over.

"You alright Sammy?"

"Not really."

"Culbertson eh? A bloody shame. I didn't know you two were close chums."

"We weren't, not really. It's just…" He was evidently trying to find the right words. "When you lose a man you admire for his flying skills to an accident, you start to doubt your abilities."

"Oh come on Sammy!" Dilks gently chided his old comrade. "In our business men get killed, we both know that, so did he. Accidents are a risk we take for our profession. We accept that risk the first time we fly."

Sammy looked hard at Dilks, trying to discern any trace of emotion. "Yes, but its' harder when that risk has a face you know and admire."

Dilks knew exactly what Sammy meant. He placed a re-assuring hand on his shoulder. Further words were unnecessary.

Scott was in conversation with Peters. "Next time I'm going

with them." He remarked bitterly. "A Commanding Officer should lead from the air, not a bloody desk!"

Peters considered Scott's words as he packed a wad of tobacco into the bowl of his pipe. It was as much ritual as it was relaxation for him. "You know Scott, many officers work hard and produce excellent results. They're promoted to command rank because they're talented and don't need to delegate." The whoosh of his wooden match was followed by the release of vanilla scented, aromatic smoke. "Unfortunately quite a few fail in their new role because they don't have the sense or character to know when they should."

Scott respected Peters' experienced counsel. In the two months of his command it was something he had come to rely on. He looked around the Mess, searching out a familiar face.

"Has anyone seen Thompson?"

"He's over in Marble and Culbertson's billet." Coleman volunteered from nearby. "Went over about a half hour ago with a long face and a bottle of Brandy. Said he was going to pack Culbertson's belongings."

"You think I should go over and check on him Frank?" Scott enquired. "The two of them were great pals."

Peters put down his glass. "No, it's alright. I'll go. Never a good thing to let a chap grieve on his own." He checked his watch. "They'll be serving dinner in a quarter hour. I'll bring him back with me."

Peters knocked gently on the timber door to Culbertson's old billet. "Thompson?"

"Door's open Frank."

Peters stepped inside. The oil lamp was turned down and in the soft shadows Thompson was seated on Marble's mattress. Beside him was a packed kit bag of Culbertson's belongings, at his feet a luggage case of bulkier possessions. Peters saw the dejected expression on Thompson's face and felt an immediate sympathy for the young airman. "I'll get Dobson to collect his things and make the arrangements. Scott's written to his family."

Thompson poured another glass of neat spirit and downed it in a single gulp. He was in a bad way.

"What do you intend Thompson?"

Thompson shrugged his shoulders. "I'll just sit here and swallow Brandy until it chokes me, that's all I can do Frank. Just soak it up until I see two vacant chairs instead of one." He looked up at Peters with bloodshot eyes. "Then I'll start laughing because I can see the funny side of it all. You see, Culbertson's out of it and I damn soon will be, so why worry."

"That's the drink talking." Peters encouraged. "The Thompson I know would never give up on himself." He pulled Thompson to his feet. "Come on old chap, Maurice is about to serve dinner and we're required in the Mess. We'll give Culbertson a proper send-off together."

For three days 303 Squadron conducted uneventful, routine patrols. Their contact with the enemy was limited to one brief and indecisive encounter north east of Cambrai with flight of Jasta 10's Albatros DVa's. Then, on Monday the thirty first of December 1917, Scott received orders from Wing H.Q. to attack an enemy ammunition depot and adjacent railway station near the Belgian town of Merbes-le-Château. The objective was almost seventy five miles due east from Wagnonlieu and well behind enemy lines. As it was outside 303 Squadron's patrol area, Colonel Hallum gave his personal authorisation.

They took off at eleven-thirty in the morning. The weather over Wagnonlieu was appalling, with clouds at three hundred feet and driving rain. Despite reduced visibility, Scott, Thompson, Marble, Sammy, Dilks and Coleman climbed through the mists and emerged into clear, unfiltered sunlight eight thousand feet south of Arras. Eleven minutes into the mission the patrol reached ten thousand feet and set course for Merbes-le-Château.

With Scott's permission, Marble had personalised his SE5a by painting its vertical tailplane forward of the national insignia with a blue and white check. He'd also substituted the four blade propeller for a two blade version, allowing a greater rate of fire from his synchronised Vickers gun. Flying in the fresh morning air, twenty feet away from Thompson's right wing, he experienced a rush of exhilaration. Having lived in the filth, hunger and stench of the land war, Marble experienced detachment from the conflict below. Watching the sun shining across the cloud-tops, he could sense the Almighty communicating with his creation, it opened his eyes. Surveying the magnificent vista, it seemed God's touch was plainly evident.

Keeping south of the Scarpe River, they crossed the lines between the ruined towns of Monch-le Preux and Boiry-Notre-Dame. Although the dense mass of cloud below gave them a free pass from Archie, the crack and crump of gunfire on the ground was still audible over their SE5a's engines. Scott used a combination of his compass and dead reckoning to maintain a course east, anxious to avoid flying directly over Jasta 33's aerodrome at Villers-au-Tertre. After forty minutes flying they descended through the clouds and found the ceiling had increased to four thousand feet. Factoring in the prevailing east wind, Scott was pleasantly surprised to discover his navigation had been unusually accurate. They had emerged from the cloudbase only a few miles west of Jeumont and the Sambre River. He could smell the appetizing aroma of mashing grains and boiling wort rising up from the town's two breweries.

Signaling the others, Scott nosed down into a steep dive across the Belgian border and swooped over the wooded Bois d'Aubrechies. The winding Sambre flashed by off their port wings. Scott, Sammy, Dilks and Coleman followed the double-track railway lines to the station and adjacent sugar factory at Solre-sur-Sambre. At the same time, Thompson and Marble banked left along the Sambre to raid the ammunition store located in an old quarry south of Monplaisin Farm.

Near the station a concentration of troops were lined up, evidently soldiers awaiting transport to the lines. Scott's SE5a jolted as he released the two twenty five pound Cooper bombs. Loaded with explosives they detonated almost simultaneously amid a dozen parked open-backed 4.5-tonne Daimler trucks, the shockwave rocked Scott's wings. Sammy, Dilks and Coleman followed in quick succession with a mix of explosive, incendiary and anti-personnel fragmentation ordnance. By then a five hundred foot column of smoke had risen up from the station and men were dispersing in every direction. The waiting vehicles had been reduced to a flaming mass of twisted metal, wood and fabric. The grotesquely mangled bodies of their crews lay scattered around. Some had leapt out, others were thrown to the ground by the force of the multiple explosions. Before the smoke had cleared a crescendo of ground fire opened up and the sky was thick with exploding shells.

Satisfied they had successfully disorganised the entrainment of much-needed troops and equipment to the hard-pressed front line, Scott and the others departed from the vicinity. Together they climbed to provide overhead cover for Marble and Thompson whose first bombs on the ammunition store had already ignited a massive detonation. Huts leapt into the air, sheets of flame shot up a hundred feet and a dense pall of dirty grey smoke spread across the wreckage. Such destruction could only have been caused by a direct hit. Surrounding the inferno, stunned enemy troops were milling around trying to extinguish a myriad of smaller fires and recover injured comrades. Flying through thousands of swirling, drifting bright sparks, Thompson pulled his SE5a around in a steep bank, intending to disrupt the survivor's valiant efforts.

Three thousand feet above, Scott's attention was elsewhere. Scanning the sky for the enemy, he was the first to see six Pfalz D.IIIa's closing in from the east. At the same time four more appeared behind him from the south. The enemy had sprung a trap, expecting the SE5a's to make an evasive turn west. Instead, Scott, Sammy, Dilks and Coleman turned east in unison to meet the six head-on. In seconds the SE5a's bored straight into the tightly packed formation of enemy machines. Scott swerved to avoid collision with their leader, but not before he had fired a burst of twenty rounds. As he flew over the leading Pfalz it rolled off, trailing a cloud of thick black smoke. He saw another black crossed machine and raked its fuselage from nose to tail as it flashed across his sights.

Returning to their leader, three hundred feet from his target Scott's Vickers jammed. At over a hundred miles an hour he thrust his hands around the windscreen and into the ice cold wind. Grasping the cocking lever he forced it over, cleared the link jammed in the breech and fired. Scott dived past and below the leader just as another hostile machine swooped down onto his tail. The enemies twin LMG 08/15 Spandau machine guns rattled and splinters were riven from the rear cabane struts inches above Scott's head, ripping the upper wing centre section fabric to ribbons. He swerved away from the line of fire. Twisting through the sky he spotted another black crossed machine on Sammy's tail and made directly for it. Positioning for maximum advantage, Scott thumbed his Vickers' firing paddle. The SE5a shook from the recoil as twenty rounds of tracer raked the Pfalz at point blank range. He was close enough to see the enemy pilot look back, wondering where Scott had come from. Torn into shreds, the Pfalz side-slipped into a steep dive and spun down trailing a stream of white coolant vapour.

At the time of Scott's intervention, Sammy's SE5a had already been badly hit. His port engine cowling panel tore loose, peeled back and jammed against the flying wires, the drag sent his SE5a into an immediate spin. Within seconds Sammy was tumbling end over end. Thrown about in the cockpit by irresistible forces, he was struggling to regain control when his lap belt snapped. Launched from his seat, his right boot snagged underneath the control panel and he instinctively grabbed hold of a rear cabane strut. Clinging on with a death-grip he was helpless. He could feel his shoulder tendons tearing. The SE5a continued pitching and spinning toward the ground. The errant panel detached and the airframe regained an upright attitude just long enough for Sammy to lever himself back inside the cockpit. The ground looked perilously close as, with adrenalin surging through his veins, he hauled the joystick back to its maximum travel and recovered control.

Coleman was fighting like a man possessed. A Pfalz dived on his tail. He banked sharply to the right and the enemy swooped past, climbed and turned on his wing tip. Coleman saw his chance and changed course to meet the attacker while simultaneously firing both Lewis and Vickers. His bullets caught the Pfalz mid-fuselage and for a moment the German seemed to hang motionless in the air before spinning down trailing black smoke and flame.

It took three minutes for Marble and Thompson to climb four thousand feet and join the others in the fray. Marble swooped on the closest of the enemy machines and approached within two hundred feet before he was spotted. He closed in until he could sense the wake vortices of the aeroplane in front, took careful aim and fired a fifty rounds from his Vickers. The Pfalz fell gracefully off on its starboard wing and spiraled down to the ground between Bois d'Aubrechies and the river Sambre.

The general mix-up continued, during which time Scott relied on all his skill and quick wits to stay alive. Then, after five minutes of intense combat, the enemy seemingly vanished from the sky.

With a prevailing wind behind them, the journey home across the lines was comparatively quick. A few gaps in the cloud cover had opened up over the front at Vis-en-Artois and Archie took maximum advantage. Dirty yellow puffs of exploding ordnance erupted all around, rocking Marble's wings and causing his SE5a to leap and drop in abrupt jolts of turbulence. Flying on the outside of a 'V' formation, he found it increasingly difficult to maintain his relative position with the others who were swinging and dipping so much that it appeared a collision would be inevitable.

Marble kept his left hand on the throttle and his eyes on the machine to his left, trying to apply gentle control inputs while being tossed about the sky. It was much worse than the familiar bumpy encounter with cumulus clouds. His head, neck and shoulders ached from the effort and his altimeter twitched with every explosion. Unwittingly, he found himself several hundred feet above the formation. Almost immediately the gunners on the ground abandoned the other machines and concentrated their fire on him. Every time Marble swerved to avoid one detonation, another appeared directly ahead accompanied by a loud 'woof'. Little rags of fabric emerged on his wing surfaces as shrapnel tore into them. It seemed impossible to avoid a direct hit.

A sudden shockwave from a detonation below struck his aeroplane as if he'd run over a pothole. Less than a second later his SE5a was up on its wings in a forty-five degree starboard bank. Hanging sideways in the sky, Marble gripped his joystick and pushed it left as hard as he could. Even with full opposite aileron the machine kept rolling right. A feeling of despair swept over him, despite his full-force wrestling match it refused to respond for five seconds before rolling level. Suitable chastened Marble re-joined the other five SE5a's, thankful no enemy machines were loitering high above the lines to pick off wayward pilots who broke formation.

Approaching Wagnonlieu, two miles south of Dainville, Sammy's SE5a limped across the sky like a badly winged duck. His rudder controls were cut, splintered ribs were visible through the torn wing fabric and loose wires whistled in the air. Steering erratically by means of one aileron Sammy watched his fuel pressure gauge carefully. It was showing just below one pound per square inch, probably a result of a tank puncture. He vigorously applied the hand pump, not wanting the engine to starve of fuel on approach to landing. Travelling at seventy miles an hour he reduced the throttle and watched his speed drop to fifty five as he lined up with the field and crossed the perimeter hedge. He held off touch-down until the SE5a was just above stall speed before accomplishing a perfect three-pointer on the grass. With one aileron broken and flapping the aeroplane rolled out straight ahead. Fortunately, no correction was needed from the damaged rudder and steerable tail skid.

Sammy switched off and, ignoring his mechanic's enquiries, climbed out the cockpit. He was retching uncontrollably as he stepped down from his aeroplane and waved away anyone who came close. Holding onto the port forward interplane strut for support he stood, grey-faced and shaking. Saunders gave him a full minute alone before approaching.

"Sir?" He handed Sammy a small hip-flask of brandy. Sammy expressed a fragile smile of thanks. In a trembling right hand he raised the flask to his lips and sipped at the contents. "They nearly got me this time Saunders." The emotional surge was too great, he turned away ashamed of appearing weak. Saunders placed a consoling hand on Sammy's shoulder. No words were spoken.

A short distance away Thompson had landed and taxied up alongside Marble's SE5a. He switched off, unbuckled his lap belt and leapt to the ground. He ran across to Marble who was conversing with his ground crew.

"You got one on your first job! Grand show old boy!" He slapped Marble heartily on his back.

Dilks trotted over and enthused. "Did you see him? He fought like a madman. No regard for his own neck, went in there guns firing. The Huns must have thought we'd let loose a raving lunatic!"

"Good for you Marble." Scott joined the group. "Nothing puts the wind up the enemy more than facing someone unpredictable like that." He looked along the row of damaged machines "How's Sammy and Charlie, are they alright?"

Without waiting for an answer he set off to where the two remaining officers were standing alongside Sammy's machine. Saunders intercepted him and saluted.

"Lieutenant Brown's machine's a nasty mess Sir. Back to the Depot for that one. The old bus had done nearly fifty hours too."

Scott gave a curt nod of acknowledgement, his thoughts were elsewhere. He called out. "Sammy? Charlie?"

As he drew closer he could smell the spirit Sammy had just imbibed. The young airman's face was smudged by deposits of oil and burnt cordite. There were two white patches around his bloodshot eyes, protected by his goggles.

"Couldn't be better Skipper!" Coleman gave a pretence of normality. "In fact we're both ready for luncheon."

Scott saw through Coleman's façade and he was too experienced not to understand exactly what Sammy was feeling. He cast his gaze over the derelict aeroplane. "Looks like your old girl's had her day Sammy. Couple of new machines coming over from St.Omer tomorrow. I was going to have one myself, but I think you deserve it more than I do."

"Thanks Skipper." Sammy made a supreme effort to sound confident and positive.

"Don't mention it." Scott encouraged. "Come on, let's make our reports to Frank then get cleaned up. First round of drinks are on me. You all bloody well deserve it!"

It was early afternoon on Friday, the fourth of January 1918. Dilks was seated in the Mess at Wagnonlieu looking particularly downcast. In his hand was a typed note.

"What's up old man?" Marble asked, peering over his shoulder.

"My Mess bill, that's what." Dilks stuffed the sheet of paper into his tunic pocket. "I've already paid in a hundred Francs before Christmas, still owe that and a bit more. If you ask me this ruddy war has taken a singularly bad turn for the worse."

"Hah! Marble dismissed his friend's plight with a wave of his hand. "I'm stone broke too, no use asking me for money. Spent everything I had during our binge in Arras last weekend."

"It's a fine way to start the new-year." Dilks grumbled. "Out of funds and in debt." He glanced up to the Mess clock. "What time's the patrol?"

"Two-o-clock, and Thompson wants us over in the Reports Hut in fifteen minutes for a briefing so we'd better get ready."

Twelve miles north-east from Wagnonlieu, between the towns of Avion and Lievin on the allied side of the front line, lay a bridge over the La Souchez River. On the afternoon of the fourth of January a large column of First Army troops, artillery and support equipment were scheduled to cross on their way to replace the remaining members of the Canadian Corps in the trenches at Avion. Wing H.Q. had instructed 303 Squadron to despatch a patrol to provide cover against likely enemy air attack.

Promptly at two, six SE5a's left Wagnonlieu aerodrome and ascended into a clear sky. Eleven minutes later the formation crossed the Scarpe River at four thousand feet. Following the straight Lens-Arras road north between Ecurie and Roclincourt, they passed over Vimy. On the northern horizon lay the former mining town of Avion where towering white cumulus clouds had formed above imperious slag heaps and dark mountains of schist. Seconds later, a unique landscape of collieries, water towers, coal shafts and rows of grim, terraced miner's houses came into view.

North of the La Souchez River little remained of Lievin, another former coalmining and industrial town. Its ancient churches and castles lay in ruin. The entire area had been obliterated by bombardment. From the air it was impossible to discern anything resembling buildings or streets amid the rubble and occasional free-standing walls.

Thompson scanned the desolation from five thousand feet, searching for a landmark that would lead him to the location of the La Souchez River Bridge. He first recognised a mound of spoil that was marked on the map as Reservoir Hill, officially Hill 65. Immediately to the south, churned into the river marshes, were the remains of a rail network. He raised his goggles and blinked to clear his eyes. Somewhere amid the grey, monochrome ruins lay the bridge and Avion's electric generating station. He initiated a wide turn and looked again at his map. Re-focusing his eyes on the ground he found their target, a different perspective and he could see the bridge quite plainly.

The motorised section of the convoy was backed up along the Lens Road at Lievin with the bulk of troops leading the procession south along Main Street. After checking his fuel gauge Thompson was confident they had sufficient petrol for another two and a quarter hours in the air. More than enough to guard the convoy and return to Wagnonlieu. He wiped his goggles clean and examined the eastern horizon. Exploding ordnance had degraded visibility above the lines with a bank of sulphurous yellow smog. Anticipating an enemy raid he signaled Coleman, Dilks and Sammy to break away and climb to ten thousand feet. They were to provide top cover for himself, Marble and the sixth member of the Flight, Second Lieutenant Richard Babbington.

For the next forty minutes Thompson's patrol orbited Avion and Lievin while the convoy moved south of the La Souchez River. High above, Sammy's eyes stung from the intense strain of extended concentration. Coleman's wings rocked and a moment later he was stabbing a gloved index finger toward Lens in the north-east. A shock like an electric charge dispelled all

Sammy's fatigue, for rising out of the horizon were at least eleven black specks.

In preparation for combat, the three SE5a's manoeuvred themselves into a strategically advantageous position above the approaching intruders and in the sun. As the enemy drew closer it became apparent that one of them was substantially larger than the others. Coleman was the first to recognise the distinctive forward profile of twin engine Gotha D.V. heavy bomber.

While still on the German side of the lines over Harnes, the Gotha and five accompanying fighters split away and descended on Avion while the remaining five Albatros D.Va's maintained altitude. Their passage across the front was accompanied by heavy burst of ground fire from allied guns. At twelve thousand feet Sammy waited patiently until the upper Albatros formation was within striking distance then, on his signal, the three SE5a's split up. As each man targeted his own opponent Sammy singled out the leader for himself and dived on the enemy from out of the sun. With no time to align his sights on target he opened his guns and let loose a dozen rounds before another enemy machine commenced firing on him. Bullets peppered his upper mainplane and Sammy immediately broke off his attack. Engaging his new opponent he found Coleman had beaten him to it and was already on the D.Va's tail.

Dilks found himself surrounded by enemy fighters. In the middle of the chaos he glanced left and saw an Albatros closing fast from his seven-o-clock. Turning toward his attacker they crossed, cockpit to cockpit, then reversed their turns and crossed again. Both pilots were attempting to get behind the other and administer the fatal shot. Dilks strained his body with every turn, constantly turning his head to keep his eyes on the enemy. He knew that the Albatros had a better turn capability than his SE5a and would soon have the advantage. On the next turn Dilks pitched upward, relying on his machine's superior climb ability. Anticipating the next cross-over the opposing airman was confused, wondering where the SE5a had gone. Looking down from above, Dilks could see the German's head turning, searching the sky before putting his aeroplane into a dive. Dilks followed in pursuit, his SE5a was a steady gun platform. At three thousand feet altitude he closed within range and fired both his Vickers and Lewis guns simultaneously. The over-stressed lower wings of the Albatros folded back and the aeroplane plunged into a field halfway between Souchez and Givenchy.

The next thing Dilks heard was the sound of projectiles zipping past his cockpit. He looked back, the blood-red spinner of an Albatros was less than a hundred feet from his tail. He banked hard left and advanced his throttle but in doing so passed right across the German's line of fire. He could smell petrol and feel the impact of bullets as they struck his tail and rudder. His oil pressure dropped to zero and the engine seized. Dilks cursed his carelessness. A helpless target, he waited for the end. Another stream of ammunition and all would be over.

Unexpected salvation was at hand as Marble, seeing his friend's distress, swept in at oblique angle and fired a long deflection shot at the Albatros. The enemy pilot was so focused on Dilks that he momentarily lost all situational awareness. Marble's ammunition traced a straight line along the German's red and blue painted fuselage. The DVa wobbled in the air before slowly turning inverted and diving vertically into the marshland. Dilks waved his gratitude to Marble and sought out a suitable place to land.

While Marble and Babbington were engaged with the DVa's, Thompson addressed the imminent threat posed by the approaching Gotha G.V. He closed in from below and behind as the bomber's mid-gunner opened fire through the lower gun channel. Thompson reacted to the threat by manoeuvring out of range. He then climbed a thousand feet above and behind the bomber, dived on its tail and lined up a direct shot on the cockpit. With the enemy pilot centred in the Aldis sight cross-hairs he opened fire. The Gotha immediately swerved to port and began to fall. Raked by Thompson's ammunition, the bomber's two engines were failing, emitting smoke and burning fuel. Thompson followed it down, watching the injured pilot valiantly attempting to level out, turn and make for home. Fighting against the icy, hundred mile an hour wind Thompson reached up to his Lewis gun, pulled it back along its mount, replaced the ammunition drum and swung behind the stricken Gotha for a second attack. As his thumb pressed the firing paddle he saw an enemy crewmember jump overboard. Seconds later the bomber exploded, disintegrating into thousands of pieces that cascaded down over Bois de Riaumont forest north of La Souchez River.

High above, the battle continued. Two DVa's flew straight between Sammy and Coleman then banked left to come around and attack the SE5a's tails. The two British machines turned right to meet them head-on. Coleman's tracer converged on the nose of the leading enemy machine but without effect. They passed each other at a closing speed of over two hundred miles an hour. Sammy heard the sound of gunfire from directly above and looked up to see another two DVa's coming down on them with their guns blazing. In unison the SE5a's climbed as the DVa's flashed by. At the apex they performed an Immellman and, once inverted, inclined their heads to look down and evaluate the situation. The Gotha had gone, and the remaining escort fighters were retreating back to their own side of the lines.

Marble circled the east of Givenchy at five hundred feet while watching Dilks level out and touch down safely on a field parallel to the old La Coulotte Road. He could see Dilks moving in the cockpit then climb out and wave, an assurance he was well.

At no more than two hundred and fifty feet off the ground an Albatros DVa appeared over the Bois de Givenchy forest, north of the town. Dilks had not seen him, he was still standing next to his aeroplane looking up at Marble who waved a frantic warning to his comrade. The Albatros opened fire. Marble saw spurts of dust kicking up from the field, tracking ever closer to his friend. Dilks heard the guns, drew his revolver and turned around just as the bullets struck him. His body twisted and fell to the ground. For a moment Marble was stunned by the appalling sight he had just witnessed. Uncontrollable rage surged through him. The image of the enemy machine seared into his mind. Red forward fuselage, Prussian blue rear fuselage and tailplane with a white death's head motif on each side behind the cockpit. He was going to get that pilot whatever the cost.

He set course to intercept the Albatros, but before he could close up for attack another machine set upon him. The enemy fired too soon, Marble saw the tracer trail, pulled hard right and performed a snap-roll. The DVa flashed past then turned to escape back across the front line. Marble dipped his SE5a's nose and fired his Vickers. Shards of wood and strips of torn fabric were riven from the DVa's tailplane before it rolled off and spun down to crash in a ditch alongside the La Coulotte Road.

The seven remaining enemy machines were making a hasty retreat, climbing as they raced back across to their own side of the lines north of Lens. Having witnessed Dilks being gunned down in cold blood, Marble forgot his primary mission, defending the bridge crossing. He resolved to dispense his own swift justice on the enemy airman responsible and abandoned his squadron mates to pursue the DVa's alone. In the trenches, casualties occurred in an environment where the enemy was mostly invisible and the weaponry of war highly impersonal. The air war was different. For the first time, it wasn't the aeroplane Marble wanted to destroy but the man inside.

He guessed that the intruders were part of Jasta 18 at Avelin, a suspicion reinforced as they tracked their way north-east along the long, straight road between Lens and Carvin. Hopping from one cloud to another Marble maintained a position above them and in the sun. With the SE5a's speed advantage he slowly closed the separation, anticipating the right moment to strike.

He intended making a diving attack, swooping down and anni-hilating the rogue pilot before turning for home.

Approaching Phalempin at ten thousand feet the enemy re-mained unaware of Marble's stalking presence and were no doubt feeling safe. His target was holding back from his com-rades and easily identifiable. A thin trail of vapour evidence of engine damage. As they flew over the site of Jasta 30's aero-drome the DVa's commenced their descent toward Avelin and Marble made his move.

He set his diving trajectory on a course to intercept the trail-ing Albatros and made a slashing, diving attack from above and behind. Closing the range, he leaned forward in his cockpit. Manoeuvring his SE5a he centred the enemy biplane in his Aldis sight. Carefully, Marble's right thumb depressed the two trig-ger paddles. With a combined, shuddering burst of sixty rounds from each gun he saw the DVa's wings rock as its pilot reacted in utter surprise to the suddenness of Marble's attack. The other DVa's scattered in alarm.

Marble pulled out of his dive and swept above the Albatros, barely clearing the tip of its blue painted tailplane. Zooming into a climb, he began a starboard roll, becoming inverted at the apex. As he looked beyond his upper wing to the DVa below he saw the German's head turning, momentarily confused, search-ing for the whereabouts of his assailant. Marble continued his roll, bringing him back into heads up level plane. He nosed his SE5a down into a second dive. Sighting the Albatros once again, he delivered another sixty rounds from both guns directly into its centre fuselage. Splinters of wood and strips of coloured fab-ric tore loose. Licks of flame flickered from the DVa's engine and grew, fanning back toward the cockpit. The pilot attempted to keep the fire away from himself by side-slipping his machine, but to no avail. Within seconds the entire fuselage was engulfed in a searing inferno. For a moment Marble considered pouring another stream of bullets into the stricken Albatros, humanely ending the pilot's agony. His thumb was poised of the gun pad-

191

dle when he thought. 'No, let the bastard burn.' The Albatros hit the ground like an impacting meteor at a place called Heurtebises Farm east of Ennecourt. Marble calmly marked the spot with a penciled circle on his map then turned west to the allied lines.

Thompson taxied up to the hangars and rolled to a stop. Switching off his engine he glanced along the lines of returned machines and immediately noticed two were missing. Wilson was the first to arrive at his side followed by a fitter and rigger.

"Some oil fumes coming from the port valve cover Wilson."

"I'll attend to it Sir."

Scott and Peters helped him down from the cockpit.

"Anyone seen Dilks and Marble?" Thompson enquired.

"I've spoken to Coleman, he said he saw Dilks' kite on the ground near Givenchy, it looked in one piece." Peters replied hopefully.

Babbington and Sammy were in conversation nearby and, having overheard Thompson's question, walked over. "Last I saw of Marble he'd just shot down a DVa near La Coulotte." Babbington added.

"I saw him too." Sammy responded, "He nearly hit the damned water tower he was that low."

"I'll give the army post at Avion a call." Peters set off to his office. "See if they've any news about Dilks."

"Right-oh Frank." Scott peered into the eastern sky. "And tell Wilson to salvage Dilks' machine. In the meantime Thompson and I will wait for Marble." He addressed the remaining three pilot officers. "The rest of you make your reports and get cleaned up."

Standing together Thompson and Scott peered into the northern horizon as the afternoon shadows lengthened and the sunlight gradually faded. Soon it would be dusk. At a rough estimation Marble had sufficient fuel to last until half-past four. Neither of them spoke a word for a full ten minutes, each man conscious that the other was marking the time left until Marble's fuel would become exhausted.

Thompson was the first to break the stillness. "Just thinking of that girl Marble met in Arras last Saturday night."

Scott nodded. "He certainly has a way with the ladies."

"Talking of girls." Thompson continued. "I heard that there's an estaminet in La Petite Place run by three of the most beautiful damsels you'd ever see."

Scott chuckled knowingly. "Yes, Café Louise. I've been there." He slashed with his cane at the clumps thistles around his feet. Thompson whistled softly to himself, trying to distract his own thoughts.

Emerging from his office hut, Peters paced somberly along the row of parked SE5a's and stepped softly up to Scott, the pink slip of a field telegram in his right hand.

"News Frank?"

"I've just heard from thirty-three Casualty Clearing Station at Bethune." He shook his head sadly.

"Dilks or Marble?" Scott braced himself for bad news.

"Dilks. I'm sorry Scott. I know you two were old chums." He inhaled deeply. "Shot down but landed safely. Some loathsome Hun strafed him on the ground. Poor fellow died shortly after in the Field Dressing Station at Givenchy."

"Thank you." Peters could see tears welling in the eyes of his Commanding Officer. Scott made every effort to regulate his emotions, at the same time keeping his gaze firmly fixed on the sky. "Any news about Marble?" There was a slight tremble in his voice.

"Not yet Scott." Peters checked his watch. It was four fifteen.

"Give him another quarter of an hour." Scott observed.

Delayed shock hit Marble with a wave of nausea and light-headedness. His legs were trembling uncontrollably. For a while he was afraid he might pass-out. Flying west at three thousand feet the landscape rolled past below, one unrecognisable feature after another. His fuel level was low. Disorientated, he determined to land at the nearest township and discover his location. He passed over an area of marshland then open farmland interspersed with small villages. A small hamlet came up on the horizon. He approached with caution, expecting any moment a barrage of ground fire. Initiating a wide turn he circled a cluster of dwellings. Alongside a canal was a working party of field grey clad German soldiers. They paid him little attention and Marble concluded they must be prisoners of war as it was unlikely the German infantry could spare front line troops for fatigue duties.

Ahead lay an extensive grass covered common. Selecting a suitable place to land he judged the wind direction as best he could and made a successful three-point touch down on the uneven ground. The SE5a bounced unsteadily, rocking on its narrow track undercarriage. Marble peered forward either side of the inclined engine cowling, looking out for any visible obstruction that lay in his path. He held the stick hard back and worked the rudder pedals to correct every swing of the tail. Coming to a halt he fully opened the radiator shutters to prevent overheating as the engine idled.

An elderly, white bearded Frenchman dressed in labourer's cloths approached. Leaning heavily on a walking stick he was stumbling in his haste.

"Aller! Partir! Le Boche!" He frantically waved his cap in his hand.

"Where am I?" Marble replied, trying to remember his schoolboy French. "Où suis-je?"

"C'est Flers. Terre ennemie monsieur!"

Marble checked his map, "Bloody hell!" He realised the front was over thirteen miles due east. The canal he saw was the Canal de la Haute Deule.

"Merci monsieur!" Marble shouted above the roar of his engine as he opened the throttle and swung round into the wind. He had scarcely enough space to take off and his wheels almost brushed the roof tops of the neighbouring village of Planque. He was crossing an area of marshland at two hundred feet altitude when, to his left, he saw several hangars and a scattering of Pfalz D.IIIa fighters. His unexpected appearance was the cause of much alarm but Marble had no intention of loitering near the aerodrome. He set course due east against the prevailing wind, crossed the railway at Beaumont and, after climbing for fifteen minutes reached twelve thousand feet before passing over the lines at Acheville, east of Vimy.

To Marble's relief, the La Souchez River bridge remained intact. There were no other machines in the air, so he concluded the others must have already returned to Wagnonlieu. He hoped that the enemy raid was the only one, and that he had not left his comrades two men down to face a second onslaught. Either way he'd soon find out.

The minutes passed slowly and with them the chances that Marble would return. The sun's rim was already dipping below the horizon amid a setting of fleecy clouds. A red glow suffused the whole of the western sky but Scott hardly noticed the changing panorama of kaleidoscopic colours.

"Afraid it's no use waiting any longer." Scott announced sadly. "Poor beggar." He turned to Thompson and remarked irritably. "I told Sergeant Major Wilkins to get that drainage channel filled in." He pointed at a collapsed channel near the boundary. "Thompson, run along and remind him."

By the time Thompson returned from his errand, the scattered groups of waiting officers had begun to disperse and walk soberly toward the Mess. Scott paused in his stride and scanned the sky, his hearing inadequate to discern the direction of a distant aero-engine. From the open hangars several mechanics emerged and stared aloft, their ears accustomed to the distinctive sound of a 200hp Hispano-Suiza engine.

"There!" Thompson raised his arm and pointed north, toward Mont-Saint-Éloi. A muted cheer issued forth from the assembled personnel. More joined them on the field. Scott's face lit up as he gazed into the distant sky. His practiced eyes at once recognised one of his own machines. Seconds later Marble's distinctive blue checked tail became visible.

"Thank God."

Passing over the familiar Bois de Maroeuil hill, Marble began his descent following the railway line south from Etrun station. Ten minutes earlier he had exhausted the twenty eight gallons of fuel in his service tank and adjusted the fuel selector to the four gallon gravity-fed reserve. With only two miles to go, he had barely enough for another ten minutes in the air. Adding to his problems, water from his leaking radiator had frozen into a layer of ice on his windshield, restricting visibility.

Noting the direction of Wagnonlieu aerodrome's windsock Marble turned into wind, approached the field and crossed the boundary. Carefully balancing the changing rudder loads he side-slipped into a neat three-point landing. Parts of the field were still frozen, rendering the steerable tail skid less effective as he began a slow taxi. Looking forward either side of the steeply inclined engine cowling he could see the assembled onlookers gathered around the hangars. Fifty feet from the closest hangar two riggers grasped hold of his wingtips and guided Marble's SE5a to a gentle halt. He allowed the engine temperature to stabilise then, at slow idle, turned off the magnetos. After releasing the fuel tank air pressure he sat back, his head resting on the cushioned support.

Scott and Peters were the first to arrive. "Welcome back Marble." The relief on Peters' face was evident as he examined the multiple shot-holes in Marble's SE5a. "Looks like you had a rough time. What kept you?"

Marbled climbed down stiffly from the cockpit. Steadying himself against the fuselage he examined a splintered aft top longeron through a hole in the canvas. "Yes, pretty bad. That Hun who killed Dilks. I chased him back across the lines and flamed the bastard east of Ennecourt."

Stony faced, Scott ushered Marble away, out of earshot from the attendant mechanics and riggers.

"What the blazes do you mean worrying us all sick while you're carrying out your personal vendettas!" He demanded, giving vent to his feelings. "Get your machine under cover and send in your report." He stopped abruptly, turned away and walked back to his office.

Peters consoled the hapless airman. "It's alright Marble. Believe me, Scott understands. In the circumstances he would have done the same as you."

"It had to be done." Marble replied defiantly.

The Communal Cemetery at Lievin was situated on the southwest side of the town, adjacent to open countryside and at the end of a straight, unmetalled road from the ruined church. It consisted of a small, level area of land covered with a haphazard arrangement of thin, simple, rough-hewn timber crosses. The opposite side of road was lined by the gutted shells of abandoned windowless houses. On each former dwelling, a scattering of roof tiles clung precariously to the exposed beams.

Scott looked up at the slate grey sky before stepping down from the squadron's Renault. Entering the cemetery he stepped cautiously around the crest of a shell crater and paused for a moment to read the dedication on a fresh wreath that lay alongside a white painted wooden cross on the bare ground. An empty, freshly dug grave nearby was surrounded by a small lattice fence, probably to prevent the unwary from falling in during the night. Scott picked up the wreath of deep claret with hints of blue and laid it reverently on the Union Flag draped across Dilks' plain wood coffin.

Scott, Marble, Thompson, Coleman, Peters and Sammy reverentially removed their hats. Together they carefully lifted the heavy casket off the tender and onto their shoulders before transporting it thirty paces across the barren ground to the open grave. Leading the solemn procession, the Reverend Neville Hughes commenced his committal oration. After the Union Flag was removed and folded, the six bearers slowly lowered Dilks' coffin into the grave. A detachment of troops from the Squadron presented themselves, guns reversed. At the conclusion of the service they raised their rifles, fired a salute, then lowered them and, with their heads bowed, ceremonially rested their hands on the stocks.

One by one, the airmen scattered a handful of loose soil into the grave before departing. Marble was the last. As the soft earth scattered on the polished wooden casket he murmured softly. "Rest easy Dilks. I've settled your account."

6. BACK TO BLIGHTY

Cecil Peterson returned from France without fanfare and under a shroud of secrecy. His escape across Europe was, to all effect, a military secret. Under strict instruction not to divulge any details of his adventure to the press he spent the following week in London, shuttling between RFC offices located in the Hotel Cecil on The Strand. The debriefing meetings with committee officials and red-tabbed staff officers were less of an enquiry as much as a recounting of events.

It was Wednesday the sixteenth of January 1918. With his promotion to Temporary Captain back-dated to the fifth of October, Peterson had used fifteen pounds eighteen shillings of his additional pay to purchase a new uniform and trench coat. After the final fitting at Robinson and Cleaver in Regent Street, he set-off with his package securely wrapped and under his arm for his hotel room at the Charing Cross Hotel.

A thaw had arrived with the milder air. The persistent snow had turned to rain and dark clouds smudged the smog-filled sky. Although it was only a mile to his destination, he took shelter under a shopfront awning and hailed a taxi-cab. The subsequent journey through heavy afternoon traffic took almost twenty minutes. The taxi weaved its way around Piccadilly Circus through a mix of horse drawn carts, private motor vehicles and B-type London buses. Street lights flickered along grey thoroughfares. Everything appeared to be in monochrome, the buildings, transport and the clothing of passers-by. Alighting at Charing Cross, Peterson paid the fare, then pushed his way through the moving bodies and past a corner newspaper vendor's stall. The gaunt and dejected faces of his fellow countrymen melded into the mean streets. A steady stream of red-cross ambulances exited the station, carrying wounded and sick troops on the last leg of their journey home.

After checking in at the hotel's bustling reception, Peterson assembled his luggage and ascended a winding main staircase to the first floor. His room was only a short distance along a wide, arched, marble corridor. Unlocking the door, he entered and assessed his temporary accommodation. The carpet was worn, with thread-bare patches and a pattern reminiscent of the 1890's. He pulled back the drapes and peered out of a sash window overlooking Eleanor Cross and The Strand. A pall of smoke hung in the air from homefires and motor exhausts. The city dirt on the panes dulled the fading ambient light leaving Peterson with an overwhelming sense of melancholy. He turned on the ceiling lamp, unwrapped his khaki uniform and tried it on, examining every seam, stitch and fold in a full length wall mirror. His freshly polished brown leather cavalry boots lustered in the gaslight. He wanted to look his best, not so much for his Military Cross investiture at Buckingham Palace the following day, but for a special guest who was due to arrive at 16.30 on the train from Exeter.

The man who walked into the hotel lounge that late afternoon looked like an aged version of Peterson. His face had the same high cheekbones and deep blue eyes. Peterson raised a hand to wave and the older man responded in an instant. His face split into a grin, then he paced over and took Peterson's offered hand in his two, shaking and squeezing. He was Peterson's father and had made his way up to London from the family home in Trethowel, a hamlet north of St Austell.

"My dear, dear boy. It's so good to see you!"

"And to see you too father." Peterson could feel tears welling up in his eyes. "I've so missed you." Despite an overwhelming surge of emotion the young airman maintained his composure. "Have you eaten?"

"Not properly, just the luncheon I brought with me on the train up."

"I'll have your things taken to our room, drop off your coat and hat and we'll adjourn to the bar before dinner."

After so many months of absence this was the chance for father and son to make new memories. Wasting time on reminiscences wasn't on their agenda.

"To the big day tomorrow son." Peterson senior raised his cocktail glass and toasted their reunion.

"Frankly I've got the wind up about the whole thing. Don't want to make a mistake in front of the King."

"Shouldn't be too concerned old chap, I'm told the ritual is quite straightforward. Besides, the place is full of staff who'll tell you what to do."

"I hope so." Peterson junior replied earnestly. "Well, what a turn-up for a couple of old country boys like us eh?"

At ten-fifteen the following morning the hotel doorman hailed a 'Unic' taxi from the line of cabs on the forecourt and the two Petersons stepped forward.

"Where to Sir?" The driver enquired of the young Captain.

"Buckingham Palace." Peterson replied, hardly believing the words himself. "I'm attending an investiture."

Father and son climbed aboard to begin the straight, mile long ride along The Strand and around Trafalgar Square. The morning traffic was heavy and the journey took just under a quarter of an hour. As they entered The Mall, the driver turned his head and spoke over his shoulder.

"If you'll pardon me for asking Sir. Are you one of the gentlemen receiving an award today?"

"My son's receiving the Military Cross." Peterson senior replied with undisguised pride. The driver nodded in acknowledgement, his back straightened. "Well done Sir."

They arrived at the entrance to Buckingham Palace at ten-thirty. Peterson dropped his father off outside the North-centre gate and was driven in alone. After checking in with a guardsmen on duty, the taxi continued through an arched entrance to the central courtyard where the driver pulled over, stepped down and opened the passenger door. He unfolded an umbrella to shield Peterson from the falling rain.

"How much do I owe you?" Peterson's hand reached to his pocket.

The cabby smiled broadly. "No charge."

"Thank you."

"My privilege Sir. My son's an airman with the RFC too. Thirteen Squadron. He's a Lieutenant."

"I've met a few of their men, they fly the R.E.8."

"That's right Sir, he's an Observer."

"You must be proud of him."

"Oh I am that Sir, so I know how proud your own father must be of you."

Once inside the Palace Peterson ascended a wide, grand staircase then deposited his hat and rattan swagger stick in a cloak room. Keeping his gloves, he went up another flight of stairs where an elderly Footman in a frock coat enquired what award he was to receive. Peterson was then introduced to another veteran member of the Palace staff who verified his name and rank. He was told to wait on one side of a large drawing room where crystal chandeliers hung from a white and gold gilt ceiling. Portraits of royal personages decorated the walls. The bright, clean splendour was a marked contrast to the dreary London outside.

Among those gathered were approximately fifty recipients of C.M.G.'s, D.S.O.'s and M.C.'s. For ten minutes Peterson stood in solemn awe among the other uniformed servicemen. Here he was, a humble Cornishman, in Buckingham Palace on the cusp of meeting the King Emperor. He caught sight of himself in a tall Regency mirror, standing stiffly in his starched and pressed uniform that marked him out as a warrior, barely recognizable as the boy he was only a year ago. Since then he had learnt how to fly, how to shoot down a fellow airman and take a life in the line of duty.

A Lieutenant-Colonel introduced himself as Lord Stamfordham, the King's private secretary. In a brief address to the assembled officers he instructed them in the correct ceremonial ritual then, one after the other, the men walked into an adjoining room. When it was Peterson's turn, Stamfordham called out: "Receive the Military Cross Captain Cecil Peterson." Nothing more, no details of the citation. Peterson entered the Throne Room, advanced six paces, halted, turned left, bowed, then took another two paces toward the King. He stood rigid as the commander-in-chief, dressed in full army uniform, pinned the silver medal cross and its blue and white ribbon to Peterson's tunic. They shook hands. The King spoke:

"I hope you have quite recovered from the ordeal of your captivity Captain Peterson."

He kept his reply cautiously brief. "Very nearly thank you, Sir."

The King shook his hand. The ceremony was over. Peterson paced back, bowed, turned right and exited through a side door.

Fifteen minutes later, as he crossed Buckingham Palace's outer courtyard, he still felt detached from reality. The adrenalin surging through his body quickened his pace. He searched the small crowd of expectant faces waiting at the iron gates and picked out that of his father. After passing through the portal he showed him the medal from a case in his pocket. For the first time he noticed that his hands were trembling.

"Well done son." Peterson senior ushered his son aside and cast a wary glance around, he wanted to avoid any newspapermen.

"I hope we're not bothered by any of those ha'penny rag photographers. Bad form for a fellow to have his picture in one of those."

The rain had ceased and under a bright sky they set off together down The Mall.

"What was it like, meeting the King?"

"Strange, not at all what I'd expected. He seemed more a private country gentleman than King Emperor".

By the time they passed through Admiralty Arch, dark clouds were gathering threatening a return of heavy rain. Peterson senior grabbed his son's arm. "Let's hail a cab back to The Strand. I've booked luncheon for us both at Simpsons. My treat."

"Simpsons? My word!" Peterson slapped his father affectionately on the back, then added earnestly. "I just hope it's not one of those damned wartime 'meat free menu' days of the week."

Peterson senior responded to his son's concern with a dismissive shake of his head. "As if!"

'Old Matt,' Simpsons' venerable doorman opened the cab door and the two Petersons stepped out one after the other onto the pavement. They walked through the elegant arched portal and into the reception. Confirming their booking they were escorted into the antique wood-paneled ground floor dining room and seated at a table for two at the far end, beneath a tall window overlooking the Savoy Buildings walkway. The older man felt a frisson of pride as he accompanied his son to their allotted table, the gaze of elderly gentlemen diners directed toward the smart young Captain in his new uniform.

The restaurant had the ambience of a luxury London club, but to Peterson just being with his father was the treat. Once seated they were attended to directly. For half a crown each they enjoyed turtle soup, roast sirloin of beef served from a silver domed trolley and boiled syrup roll. The food was hot, tasty and plentiful. The carvers, all dressed in white tunics, moved effortlessly around the tables keeping the plates full.

"I'm being posted up north to a training squadron in Shotwick near Chester. Instructor duties apparently." Peterson shrugged indifferently. His lack of enthusiasm was evident.

"Cigar son?" His father smiled kindly and offered Peterson a Cuban 'Romeo y Julieta' cigar. "I've been saving these since before the war. Just waiting for the right time to celebrate." He lit up and relaxed back in his chair. "So you're disappointed. You want to be back in France with your squadron."

He correctly interpreted his son's unspoken reply. "How many enemy machines have you been credited with? Five I think you said." He took a sip of cognac. "You've done your bit, and been awarded the Military Cross. A man with your experience can be a great help to those new boys. Teach 'em all you know, give them an even chance and send them off with the right attitude."

"I can teach them, but what really counts is experience. The kind of thing they can only get once they're in France."

Peterson senior carefully exhaled a cloud of cigar smoke into the air and closed his eyes, reminiscing. "Something your grandfather said to me after he returned from fighting in the Transvaal. 'What counts most in war is what's difficult to count.' He knew a thing or two."

"And I remember what old Gramps said to me when I asked him about the second Boer war. 'We're not perfect, but we are the good ones.' Never forgotten that."

"Wish he were alive and with us today son, he'd be as proud of you as I am."

Peterson junior raised his glass. "Then let's both drink a toast to old Gramps."

Peterson had been allocated a temporary billet in the annex of a seventeenth century house adjacent to Shotwick's Norman church of Saint Michael. It was just after eight in the morning of Saturday the twenty-fifth January 1918. He carefully descended three slippery, worn stone steps beneath the front porch. A hundred yards distant, beyond the front garden wall and a thatched tithe barn across the lane, lay a sunken field where a frozen tidal creek lay silent in the still, early morning air. Light from the risen sun barely penetrated the ground mist that clung to the hollows.

He set off south through the village along the rutted, unmetalled lane. Patches of overnight frost lingered in the shade of garden walls and Box hedges provided the only foliage amid denuded trees. To his left a water drainage course meandered its way downhill. He passed a young woman in her early twenties, a wicker shopping basket slung over her right arm. In her right hand a posy of purple and white winter flowering pansies. She smiled demurely at him. Peterson noticed the absence of betrothal on her ring finger. He doffed his cap politely.

"Good morning Miss."

"Good morning Sir."

It was a mere exchange of greetings, but sufficient to put a spring in Peterson's step as went on his way.

Shotwick aerodrome was located on a vast expanse of flat, open land north of the Great Central Railway line and four miles northwest of Chester. At an elevation of just fifteen feet above sea level the fields were prone to flooding. The site contained a number of recently constructed buildings. Peterson had never seen such distinctive architectural edifices before. Three 'Belfast Truss' general service sheds had been built in coupled pairs north of the railway line to serve as technical structures for aeroplane maintenance and repair. Their wide, curved, corrugated iron roofs were supported by internal trusses comprising short lengths of low quality timber. It was a form of construction that could be assembled quickly by a relatively unskilled workforce and reflected the pressing exigencies of wartime. Other brick buildings at Shotwick served as offices and instructional facilities for Cadet training.

The headquarters building was staffed by men who had, in the most cases, served overseas and were no longer fit to carry on abroad. Among these venerable old veterans, the Flying Examiner carried his arm in a sling, the Wireless Officer limped along with the aid of a stick, the Equipment Officer wore a neck brace and the Adjutant performed his duties with the aid of a pair of crutches. Peterson suspected that Shotwick's payroll included substantial provision for pensions and wound gratuities. Among the officers were specialists in gunnery, wireless, bombing, photography air combat and several other fields, all of which a Cadet had to pass before qualifying for his wings. Half of the office staff, clerks and telephone operators, were members of the Women's Army Auxiliary Corps or 'Women's Legion'. It was hard work, most of the staff were working a ten to twelve hour day.

Having completed the necessary paperwork concerning his new posting the previous afternoon, Peterson presented himself to the squadron Commanding Officer and then made his way to the Senior Instructor's office hut.

The last time Peterson saw Chivers was back in the autumn at Wagnonlieu. It was immediately apparent that there had been a significant change in his old Flight Commander's manner and character.

"Hello Peterson. I heard you were coming. Good to see you again." Chivers rose from his seat.

"Just arrived. Had my introduction with the C.O. Major Hamilton. Seems a decent sort of fellow." The two men shook hands cordially. "So how did you end up here Chivers?"

"Posted to 95 Squadron in Ternhill, Shrophire on the twenty ninth October. A new outfit formed from 43 Training Squadron. No time to unpack though, the following day we moved up here to Shotwick."

Chivers sat back down and reclined in his chair. "Where have they billeted you?"

"In the village, a room overlooking the green, just up the road. Not bad at all really." Peterson drew up a chair, sat down and offered Chivers a cigarette. "How have you been keeping? Are you still in touch with the charming Mademoiselle Claire Joubert?"

Chivers said nothing, lit his cigarette and exhaled slowly. Breaking the awkward silence Peterson observed.

"I noticed a few W.A.A.C.'s over in headquarters."

"Indeed." Chivers was acclimatised to the presence of female staff, but nevertheless appreciated how newcomers might regard the novelty. "They've found themselves nice little jobs as cooks, administrators and serving staff mainly, some have been made despatch riders or rigging specialists. Caused a bit of a stir among the N.C.O.'s at first. The prospect of putting work in the hands of female staff? You can imagine. Stout fellows though, they took them in hand and within a few days the men were all smiles. I've never seen their buttons and boots so brightly polished."

"How are the girls managing?"

"They keep the office going smoothly enough, though telephones can be rather annoying and the occasional letter comes across with words spelled in new and interesting ways." Chivers gave a shrug of noble resignation. "They drive the squadron cars too. The last male driver left for the depot last week. Should have seen the look of dismay on old Hamilton's face when his Crossley Tourer staff car turned up with a chauffeuse at the wheel! No doubt thinking of his perfect gears and glossy coachwork."

"I suppose changes are inevitable." Peterson recognised the need to adapt. "What sort of machines have we got?"

"504K's mainly, with a scattering of Martynsides, Pups and Camels. We've three SE5a's too, a couple on loan from 51 Training Depot Station plus what was a non-flying airframe shipped in from No. 1 Air Depot at St Omer. It was intended for ground instruction, but some of the instructors got to work on it. The engineering chaps lent a hand and we managed to get it flying so we can keep our hands in."

"I'd like to take her up sometime."

"Just be careful if you do. She's fitted with one of those damned Brasier built 8b engines, like everyone else we can't get our hands on a new Hispano. If you take my advice, try and get as many hours in as you can on the Sopwiths. It's on the cards 95 will be shipping over to France in April flying Camels."

"That's interesting." Peterson considered Chivers' information. "I've been told quite plainly my time fighting over France is over."

"Then they'll probably give you a desk job."

"Bugger that!" Peterson exclaimed, clearly discomforted by the prospect.

A wry and bitter smile appeared on Chivers' face. "We don't have a choice, we do as we're told."

Peterson realised he'd need to work the system. Once again he deftly changed the subject.

"So, what are the Cadets like?"

"Most of them are a bunch of imbeciles, total incompetents." Chivers made no effort to disguise his contempt. "They spin-in at low level or collide in the circuit, they stall when landing, stall when taking off, overshoot and undershoot the runways. If by some miracle one of them does manage to land in one piece, chances are he'll collide with another aeroplane taxiing from the opposite direction. At full pace we're having nearly a dozen crashed a day"

"Sounds like dangerous work."

"It is. Nowhere is safe. The buggers hit boundary hedges, fences, houses, or tangle in telephone wires and smash into the hangars. They're like a bunch of eager schoolboys. The majority have got it into their heads that it's a wonderful accomplishment. The locals don't help, they go around willy-nilly hero-worshipping anyone who can fly."

"There must be a high casualty rate." Peterson suggested.

"By my estimation the attrition during training is higher than our losses at the Front." Chivers' voice conveyed a momentary trace of sympathy. It didn't last. "Too many Cadets have no business flying. Frankly I feel worse about the perfectly serviceable aeroplanes they smash."

At that moment the sound of a running aero-engine some distance away was abruptly silenced. There followed a murmur of voices from outside. Chivers stood up and crossed over to a window overlooking the aerodrome. Shielding his eyes from the setting sun he watched as, approximately two hundred yards out on the field, an Avro 504 lay inverted on the grass attended by a dozen ground crew.

"And here I was thinking we'd have an entire day without a crash. A forlorn hope! You can understand why I'm very selective when it comes to who I fly with."

That evening Peterson was relaxing in the bar of the Greyhound Inn, Shotwick. Sitting alone at a corner table he sipped from a pint of Worthington pale ale and watched the comings and goings of locals, trying to guess their rural occupations by their attire. His ruminations were interrupted by the approach of a cheerful fellow officer who extended his hand in greeting.

"Oliver Stead's the name. You must be the new chap, Peterson?"

"That's right."

"May I join you?"

"Bit short of space, let me make some room." Peterson shifted his table back, allowing his fellow officer to pull out a chair and sit down.

"Heard you're billeted in town, me too, a room over at the old Hall."

"My lodgings are next door to the church." Peterson replied. He noticed immediately that Stead was wearing the same Military Cross insignia as himself. "Formerly 303 Squadron, SE5a's. You?"

Stead leaned over the table toward Peterson and lowered his voice. "Word of advice old man, we never mention military details in public outside the aerodrome. Old Chivers has convinced Hamilton there are agents in the village passing intelligence to the enemy."

"Strange, it doesn't seem a place that outsiders would pass unnoticed." Peterson observed. "I've already had several curious looks just sitting here."

"Even so." Stead shrugged his shoulders dismissively. "Personally I doubt it. I think it's just Chivers' over-active imagination. If you ask me he seems unduly stressed and sensitive." He confided. "You know, we've been here three months now, he doesn't mix with the civilians at all."

"Not even the local girls?" Peterson asked with a measure of incredulity.

"Women?" Stead shook his head. "He likes them but doesn't trust them. It's not just because they are women, he doesn't trust anyone, that's the way he is I suppose." He laughed in a friendly way. "Anyway, I can't see Chivers marrying or having a relationship. He comes across as a loner, not the sort of man who would suit domestic life."

"I've served with him before." Peterson confessed.

"Oh, I'm sorry old man, didn't know you were old comrades.

Don't want to speak out of turn."

"Not at all." Peterson replied to allay any worry that Stead may have caused offence. "Met him briefly again today myself. I got the impression he's not quite the same man I knew."

The barman deposited two fully charged, foaming pewter tankards on their table before departing. The airmen chatted at length about the troubles in Russia and the latest Mary Pickford film 'Stella Maris' then, at ten fifteen, Stead yawned and announced he was returning to his billet.

"Play golf Peterson?"

"Passably, why?"

"I've got a spare set of clubs. Fancy a round tomorrow on our day off?"

It had been years since Peterson last played the game. He hesitated for a moment. "Where?"

"Chester Golf Links down by the River Dee. South of the railway lines. Used to play there back before the war when the aerodrome was known as Dutton's Flying School, course is a bit rough now but still serviceable. No caddies I'm afraid, not with tomorrow being Sunday."

Despite his misgivings, Peterson accepted. He needed the exercise and it would be an opportunity to get to know his new comrade better.

The two men teed off at nine on a bright and windy Sunday morning. Peterson withdrew the hand-crafted hickory shaft of a driving iron from his bag and lined up his tee-shot. He hit the rubber-wound ball with a satisfying click. It landed dead-centre of the fairway.

"Good shot!" Stead complemented his partner. "So where did you do your flight training Peterson old chap?"

"35 Reserve Squadron Northolt, 18th Wing. Posted to 303

Squadron last spring flying the SE5a." He paused and waited until Stead had taken his swing. He managed a good first shot, but it caught in a gust and landed in the rough. They picked up their bags and set-off together down the fairway.

"You said you were with 43 Squadron, flying Camels on ground strafing."

"Yes, until the end of last September. We were flying out of Lozinghem when I was wounded on patrol over the Foret de Raismes, west of Escautpont. Found it difficult to sleep after that, the shock and everything. Never considered going to the M.O. until I blacked out, dozed off at nine thousand feet over Elincourt. The nose dropped and I came round a few hundred feet above Selvigny just east of the lines. Scared me witless. As soon as I got back I reported to the M.O. He took me off flying and that was the end of my combat career."

"Too bad." Peterson remarked sympathetically.

"I was lucky. Most of the lads who shipped over to France with me a year back had already gone west." Stead located his ball and carefully assessed his next shot. "Like most of the chaps, I couldn't admit I had the wind up. You know how it is. Shocking bad taste, creates entirely the wrong atmosphere. Only rank outsiders did that. It isn't done."

"Same in my old squadron." Peterson confided. "Young, healthy men, afraid of not being able to disguise their fear." His vented his frustration with a hefty swing. "The lads face injury or death on a daily basis, fighting between the instincts of self-preservation and the squadron's social code where no one can admit to being terrified."

Stead watched Peterson's ball as it arced high toward the green.

"So, you said that you and Chivers have met before?"

"Yes. He converted from Brisfits to SE5's in April last year before being posted to my old squadron. Made Flight Commander with 303 before he left back end of October. How's the old fellow been coping since then?"

Stead chipped a satisfying short shot out of the rough with his niblick and studied the ball as it rolled to a halt on the green. He smiled sadly.

"First time I met him I was fascinated because he was different. After a while my reaction was to keep away, he was difficult to understand and I didn't want to know him, then I began to accept him for what he is and visa-versa."

Peterson shook his head. "Something's changed him. I suspect he's very vulnerable."

Stead lined up a ten foot putt. The ball made a complete circle of the hole before dropping in with a satisfying plop. "He's a damn good pilot and instructor though. I quickly found out you have to prove yourself with him. He's honest and realistic, true to his word, he'll do what he promises and I like that."

They reached the eighteenth at twelve-thirty, by which time a heavy, penetrating mist had swept in across the coast. Following the course of the River Dee, it drifted across the marshland toward the golf course. Stead turned up his collar against the damp. "Better finish this last hole sharpish Peterson, while we can still see our way back to the clubhouse."

Their game ended at one in the afternoon with Stead having won by two holes. Returning to the clubhouse locker room Peterson was feeling the strain. He had not recovered as much as he had thought, but the exercise had, he assured himself, done him a measure of good.

"There are two Cadets I think you should meet." Stead suggested as he removed his spikes and massaged his feet. "Peter Perkins and Lloyd Rosper. I've been keeping an eye on those two. You know how it is? Some chaps seem to have an inborn instinct for flying. They've been training in our SE5's. You might be able to teach them a few advanced moves."

"Who's been their instructor?" Peterson responded.

"Chivers so far and done a damn good job, but he's not the sort of chap who trains Cadets beyond what's required by the book".

"What's their attitude like?"

"Natural airmen but over confident." Stead removed his socks and examined a fresh blister on his heel with disdain. "Sort of thing that can get a fellow into trouble over in France. Fast learners though, both of them."

Peterson recalled the words of his father. *'Give them a fighting chance.'*

"All right, I'll try and show them a thing or two. I expect they'll both be up for posting shortly?"

"Yes, likely St.Omer then straight into the thick of it." Stead encouraged.

"Well then, I'd better get a move on." Peterson acknowledged the urgency. "I'll speak to Chivers first thing tomorrow morning."

Tuesday morning dawned with a clear sky. A gentle breeze barely stirred the aerodrome's windsock suspended atop a ten foot pole on the roof of Chiver's office. Inside, Peterson had finished reviewing the weather outlook and scheduling his day's activities. Chivers watched his old comrade donning his flight gear.

"You still intend to take those two novices up for a decent scrap this morning Peterson?" Chivers chided good-naturedly. "Think they're worth the extra effort?"

"Well, you and Scott thought I was. Remember?"

Chivers shrugged his shoulders. "It's your neck."

Ten minutes after sunrise, patches of low level cumulus had formed above Birkenhead to the north-west and a steady three knot wind was blowing in from the east. Peterson walked slowly around his allocated SE5a, a brightly coloured machine in variegated patterns for high visibility. He was paying particular attention to the aileron control wires. A wing drop during landing or take off in inexperienced hands could easily damage the vulnerable lower aileron horns on contact with the ground. He had no desire to attempt an in-flight recovery from a loss of aileron. Peterson was so intent on his inspection he failed to notice Stead had arrived. Standing behind him he casually remarked:

"You're a cautious man Captain Peterson."

Peterson looked up, recognising the voice. "Yes, and it's a habit I'm hoping to live with."

Stead nodded in the direction of two approaching Cadets wearing full flightgear. "I see your two fledglings are on their way over." He cast an experienced glance at the sky. "Good weather for it. Well I'm off. Been told to escort two new machines on a flight over to Dublin. Best of luck old bean."

Of the two subalterns, Peter Perkins was the youngest at eighteen years seven months. The other, named Lloyd Rosper was barely two months his elder. Peterson knew from their records that both had been born and raised in the Surrey village of Ockley and had enlisted together for the RFC on the same day. Growing up together they were great pals and attended the same school. They had both played in the local village cricket team.

"Which one are you?" Peterson demanded of the nearest Cadet.

"Second Lieutenant Perkins Sir."

"Experience? In your own words."

"My first flight was last September in a Maurice Farman. I'd had three hours and forty-six minutes under instruction before I went solo on October the tenth. Between then and now I've qualified on three other types of aeroplanes."

"How about you Rosper?"

"The same Sir, only I had four hours dual before soloing."

"I see." Peterson eyed the two young airmen carefully. "Captains Stead and Chivers tell me you've both got the makings of good SE5 combat pilots." The two lads smiled appreciatively.

"Well let's see if they're right shall we?"

Perkins and Rosper were flying south-west, ten thousand feet above the Wirral Peninsula. The open sea beyond the Mersey and Dee estuaries was unusually calm that morning. There were no waves, just surface ripples that extended far out to the horizon. Drifting smoke from hundreds of factory chimneys at Wallasey Dock were the only indication of a prevailing breeze.

Flying side by side in loose formation the two Cadets scanned the surrounding sky, dipping each pair of wingtips in turn, constantly peering east toward the risen sun for any sign of Peterson. Twenty minutes after take-off they passed over the cresting waves and shimmering coastline of Anglesey. The sun sparkled against glass windows lining Carnarvon's myriad streets. To the south-east, on the windward side of Snowdon's horseshoe peaks, cumulus cloud blanketed a magnificent winter landscape of snow. The two pilots exchanged friendly salutations then set course east toward Welshpool.

Perkins turned his head to check the airspace behind and below his tailplane. The sky was an empty, azure dome above Montgomeryshire's mountains and fertile valleys. It was as if he and Rosper were the only two airmen in the sky. Wiping his goggles with the end of his silk scarf he glanced across his instruments. Fuel, temperature, oil pressure were all fine, the engine was running flawlessly. Perkins was, nevertheless, ill at ease. At a heightened level of alertness he knew Peterson was somewhere out there, stalking them, biding his time and waiting to catch them unaware. He made yet another scan of the expansive sky from horizon to horizon.

The rattle of machine gun fire jolted through Perkins like an electric shock. Tracer and live ammunition rounds passed above his mainplane. Instinctively he banked right and dived. A harlequin coloured SE5a roared overhead, climbing. On the point of a stall, the aggressor yawed around under full rudder and commenced another high speed diving attack. Perkin's initial shock transmuted immediately into barely suppressed anger. Having been caught out by Peterson, if he wanted a scrap he'd give him one.

He advanced his throttle to the maximum, pitched his nose hard up and climbed to intercept Peterson head-on, trying to keep his gunsight on target and obtain the advantage. As the two evenly-matched aeroplanes sped past each other, Perkins drew back on his joystick and applied full rudder. His SE5a responded by pulling into a tight right-hand bank, his engine racing and clattering.

Below, Peterson closed up on Rosper's six-o-clock. Rosper climbed and stalled his SE5a, attempting to evade his attacker. In the process his goggles became dislodged. Icy wind blinded him and burned his exposed flesh. He knew in that moment, that had this been a real battle he'd be easy prey. He dived, spun and zigzagged through the sky with Peterson's guns chattering behind him. Rosper sank down into the cockpit and pulled into a tight left turn. He looked around for Peterson, the bright sun blurred his vision. By the time he had repositioned his goggles Peterson had made a one hundred and eighty degree turn and was approaching head on. He rolled and passed overhead fully inverted, casually waving at Rosper.

Locked in intense concentration, Perkins was almost weeping with frustration. Each time he made a move Peterson appeared to have read his mind and anticipated his every action with the aerial agility of a swallow. It seemed the Captain possessed supernatural powers. Rosper too, had little success. Peterson was a cat toying with two mice. Time and again, rounds of ammunition swept the sky around Perkins' SE5a. He knew that with every burst Captain Peterson was demonstrating how easy a target they were. His frustration soon gave way to humility. Perkins realised he had more to learn than he imagined.

The spirit of combat was easily re-kindled in Peterson but he needed to be careful. Controlling his aggressive instinct, he ensured none of his fire came close to the novice's aeroplanes. There was no doubt that Perkins, in particular, would be a dangerous adversary given experience and the proper training. There were times when Peterson had almost been caught out by the younger man's tactics. After fifteen minutes of mock-combat he drew up alongside Perkins and gestured 'follow me'. Rosper slipped into formation on his friend's left wing and all three turned for Shotwick.

Taxiing to a halt alongside each other, they switched off and dismounted. Peterson unbuckled and jumped down from his SE5a as ground technicians attended to his machine. Sliding off his leather helmet he set a rapid pace to the Orderly Hut, calling back over his shoulder. "You two. In here now!"

Perkins exchanged a meaningful glance with Rosper. Neither knew what to expect.

"What do you make of all that Perky?" Still visibly shaken by his first 'combat' experience, Rosper had lost all his former bravado. "Live ammunition! Peterson's a lunatic!"

"I've learnt more in the past hour than I have since joining up." Perkins replied ruefully. "This isn't a game Rosser old pal. It's bloody serious stuff."

Breathless, the two novices followed Peterson inside. He invited them to sit down as he wiped the blackboard clean.

"Well?" Peterson demanded impassively.

Perkins volunteered a reply. "Sir. I didn't see you, I looked."

"I dived on your tails twice before you even knew I was there, set you up for dead men. The third time I fired over your heads. If I had been a Hun? Need I say more?"

"No Sir." Rosper replied downheartedly.

Peterson noted the crestfallen expression on the faces of both young airmen. "This has been your first proper experience of what real air combat's like. I know you were being vigilant, but it takes a while to train your eyes to focus. You need to use all your senses, instinct too. It seems impossible now, but soon it will become second nature." He let his words sink home. "So far your training records show unparalleled success, but mark me well, if you've no experience of being outmatched you'll find yourself at a disadvantage in the front line. Overconfidence will get you killed."

Peterson chalked a series of instructional diagrams on the blackboard as he continued. "We've only a few days before you're likely off to France, time is short so pay close attention. For starters I'll show you how we make a snap-roll and an Immelmann turn. Get it into your heads. Make sure your machines are refueled and checked during luncheon then meet me back here. This afternoon we'll take-off and practice in the air until I'm satisfied. Same thing tomorrow."

That evening, at seven-thirty, Peterson was standing outside Major Desmond Hamilton's office having been summonsed via a telephone call. He knocked firmly on the wood paneled door.

"Come in Peterson." Hamilton remained seated behind his desk. "Word has reached me that you armed your machine with live rounds today and fired in the vicinity of two Cadets." He flicked over a page of a report document on his desk. "Second Lieutenants Peter Perkins and Lloyd Rosper I believe."

"Yes Sir." Peterson remained stiffly at attention. The interview reminded him of attending his old headmaster's study.

"To what end?" Hamilton enquired, peering over the rim of his half-moon spectacles.

"To acquaint them with the reality of war Sir. I've seen our lads posted to front line squadrons with little or no experience of combat manoeuvres. They are easy prey for the Huns whose training is far more thorough than ours."

"Probably because they know they're outnumbered and can't afford the same wastage." Hamilton confided. "You realise such an action is outside standard regulation and practice? That if you could have possibly caused the loss of two valuable machines and the death of two airmen?"

"I relied on my judgement and experience Sir."

Hamilton's expression remained impassive. "As a Corps we're already hemorrhaging Cadets. Did you know, on average two trainee pilots die every day and several more are seriously injured?"

"No Sir."

"You've only been here a few days Peterson so you are unaware of my attitude to training combat pilots." He inscribed a perfunctory signature on the file and closed the folder. "I'm convinced that high morale and a determination to win can only be developed by hard, tough, purposeful instruction and good leadership." He leant back in his chair and removed his glasses. "But we all have to operate within the rules. I don't intend to reprimand you. In fact, a good commander should reward initiative and aggressiveness." He shrugged his shoulders. "Just be a good chap and don't do it again. I've had occasion to remind other instructors about unorthodox methods."

"Yes Sir."

"That's all Captain. Now unless there is anything else?"

"There is one matter I'd like to discuss with you Sir"

"Go on." Hamilton rose from his chair and stretched his back. Walking around his desk he perched on a corner and offered Peterson a cigarette.

"I've heard the squadron will be moving to France, operations flying the Camel. You're aware High Command have restricted me from flying combat over enemy territory?"

"And I understand, you want to keep flying."

"Yes Sir. I'd go mad assigned to a desk job like...."

"Like me you mean?"

Peterson felt trapped. "Sir, I need to fly, if only as an instructor so be it."

Hamilton held up his hand to forestall any further comment. He knew exactly how Peterson felt.

"We can't change the rules Peterson." For a moment, Hamilton studied the earnest expression on the young Captain's face. "But perhaps there's a way around them. Leave it to me, I'll see what I can do."

There was something in his sincerity that gave Peterson a glimmer of hope. "Thank you Sir."

"Right, carry on with your duties for now Captain and try to remember what I said. That's all, dismissed."

Peterson saluted. "Thank you Sir." He departed the office and closed the door behind him. As he descended the stairs a stocky figure exited the Adjutant's office and saluted. Peterson responded. There was no doubt in his mind it was Regimental Sergeant Major Walters. A man who, from the Cadet's colourful description, was a monumental character who could turn your blood to ice water with one scream. Peterson remembered his time with 35 Reserve Squadron in Northolt. It was less than a year ago but seemingly in another, long gone world.

Stead was waiting for him outside. "How did it go with the old man?"

"Not bad. Thought I was in for a rough ride."

"Hamilton's a wise old bird. He knows the score but he's hamstrung by the same regulations that apply to us all."

"Then we need to change the regulations."

"Take my advice Peterson. Don't embark on any crusades, it's more than enough just coping with what's chucked at us every day." Stead placed a re-assuring hand on Peterson's shoulder. "Come on, I'll buy you a drink down at the Greyhound."

It was nine in the morning of Thursday, January the thirty-first. The sun had risen into a still, cloudless blue sky above Shotwick aerodrome. Perkins and Rosper were conducting pre-flight checks on their allocated SE5a's outside the hangar. Their aeroplanes had been armed with live tracer ammunition for the first time, though neither had been told why. Perkins noticed an officer in full flight gear approaching from the direction of the cookhouse. It was Peterson and he was carrying a half dozen hessian sacks, three in each hand. The two subalterns exchanged a curious glance.

Peterson arrived, rosy cheeked from the effort of walking in his heavy flying overalls. He dropped the sacks onto the dew-soaked grass, the hidden contents clattered on impact.

"Today lads, we are going to do some target practice, air gunnery. Marksmanship is of equal importance to airmanship when you're in a fighting unit." He pulled open the drawstring of one sack and passed it to Perkins who peered in at the contents. Stacked inside were at least two dozen empty tin cans of assorted sizes.

"Sir?" Perkins was incredulous.

"Take one sack each, there's just about enough room on your laps. At eleven thousand over the estuary, on my signal, you'll take turns. Dump the cans overboard then chase them down with your guns. After you've done, we'll land, collect more and have another go. There's two hundred and fifty rounds in your Vickers and I've signed you off for two Lewis cartridge drums each. One's on the gun and the others in the control panel recess."

An hour and a half later, after the exercise was completed to Peterson's satisfaction, they adjourned to the Orderly Hut for debrief. He was impressed with both Subaltern's flying performance. Of the two, Perkins in particular seemed to have a natural affinity for flying and empathy for his machine. On several occasions Peterson had been surprised by Perkins' practical co-ordination and marksmanship and, on the ground, he never took notes yet absorbed and remembered everything he was told.

The two boys sat down and looked at Peterson expectantly.

"You both did very well, considering the factors against you."

"Sir?" Perkins anticipated Peterson was referring to their inexperience.

"Training units are renowned for not having the best maintained guns. Your Vickers were loaded with hemp web belt ammunition, the kind that soaks up moisture which freezes at altitude and jams the feed. They're also prone to 'whipping' during heavy manoeuvring. That jams the feed too and clogs the receiving spool. In France, most squadrons have done away with the belt altogether. We use a clip-linked system instead where the bullet forms the hinge. The discarded metal links eject out of the left side of the receiver into a small chute into the airstream on the left side of the fuselage."

"Well, my Vickers jammed twice." Perkins remarked with a deal of frustration.

"You've been trained how to clear a blockage in gunnery school?" Peterson challenged.

"Yes Sir, but I never realised how difficult it can be in the air."

"I used a rawhide mallet clipped inside the cockpit to clout the cocking lever." Peterson had noticed the older of the two subalterns nodding in agreement with his friend. "What about you Rosper? How many jams did you get?"

"Three Sir. I managed to clear them alright, but the Lewis gun?" He shook his head in exasperation. "I've never changed a cartridge drum in the air before."

"Try loading one of those eight pound drums when you're flying *and* fighting!" Peterson acknowledged Rosper's complaint. "In France we generally fit the ammunition canisters with larger leather straps. Makes handling easier. You've been told to stow the empty drum back in the cockpit. Don't, it's a waste of time. Just chuck it out over the side so it misses the tailplane and whatever else you do, never let go of the stick, either hold it with your left hand or between your knees."

At that point came a series of loud bangs on the Briefing Hut's warped wooden door. It was sticking in its frame. A final kick and it flew open to reveal Chivers who, by his appearance, had just landed.

"Been teaching the lads aerial marksmanship Captain Peterson?"

"We've made a decent start."

Chivers pulled up a chair, sat down and carelessly swung his feet up onto the table top. "Never was a good shot myself, didn't need to be. I just got up so close to the enemy I couldn't miss. Only thing was I'd get showered with splinters." He paused. "And other things."

Peterson checked his watch against the RFC fusée dial clock on the wall. "Lunchtime lads. Off you go. Get yourselves and your machines ready for take-off at 13.30 hours. There'll be enough light for two more hour's gunnery practice."

White clouds scattered the sky above Shotwick aerodrome. A slight, high altitude mist diffused the afternoon sun. Perkins and Rosper walked across the hangar apron to where their aeroplanes had been made ready. The two airmen synchronised their watches and checked the annotated notes on each other's maps before pausing for a brief conversation with the attendant mechanics. Climbing into their respective machines the air was soon resounding to the deep, regular roar of aero-engines. The two SE5a's bounded a short distance over the grass field then shot up into the air at an alarming angle. Before long both fighters were no more than tiny specks in the distance.

Peterson watched them depart with mixed feelings. Satisfaction in the student's competency on the one hand and concern for their future on the other. Over luncheon he had received official notification of their transfer to France. He contented himself that he had given of his best to enable them to survive the dangerous first few days of combat. After that, it was down to them to learn quickly. That and a measure of luck.

His contemplation was interrupted by the sound of a rotary aero-engine. He looked across the field in time to witness an Avro 504 stall on approach to landing. It fell thirty feet, nose down onto the grass, a crunch of wood and the motor was silenced in an instant. Peterson shook his head in despair. It was the sixth crash that day. The two fortunate occupants of the Avro extricated themselves from the wreckage and stood back from the remains. One of them, clearly the instructor, was angrily berating his hapless student.

"That's old Adams." Peterson recognised Stead's voice. On hearing the smash he'd emerged from one of several large sheds used for the instruction of rigging and engine maintenance.

"Adams?"

"Yes, 'Beery' Adams. That'll put him in even more of a foul temper than usual." Stead observed ruefully. "He's a short tempered disciplinarian at the best of times. I pity the next poor 'Quirk' he takes up."

Peterson shook his head in dismay. "I'm beginning to think I'm not cut out for this training lark Stead."

"You're not alone old chap." Stead attempted to boost Peterson's sagging morale. "Just about every instructor has felt the same way at one time or another."

"You've been at this game a while Stead. I'd appreciate any advice you can give me when you've the time."

Stead pondered his response for a moment. "I recommend reading up on Smith-Barry's notes, the fellow who founded the Corps' Training School at Gosport. He's got some sound ideas. Essentially he recommends giving the Cadet a thorough briefing on what he's about to do then put him in charge and let him get on with it. The instructor only intervene as a last resort if he makes a complete balls-up. When he's done the exercise, debrief him."

"Have you got a copy I can borrow?"

Stead checked his wristwatch. "What time are your lads due back?

"I've given them two hours."

"Come along over to my office." Stead encouraged. "I'll see what I can dig out."

"Thanks."

Slightly later than planned, at a quarter to four Perkins and Rosper returned to Shotwick and landed without incident. Peterson was in the Briefing Hut, thumbing through the latest recommendations from Gostport's Training School. On the following day, Friday the first of February, he had been assigned four new Cadets who were arriving from 31 Training Squadron at Wyton in Cambridgeshire.

Chivers made his usual entrance, kicking at the crooked door until it burst open.

"Two hours dual and the silly sod nearly side slipped into the ground killing us both." He stormed. A coffee pot was simmering on the stove. Grasping it by the handle he poured a large measure of hot beverage into a chipped enameled mug. His hands were visibly shaking. "Adams almost bought it this afternoon too." Raising the mug to his lips he tripped over a low stool then kicked it flying across the hut in frustration, spilling half his drink in the process.

"I saw Perkins and Rosper were up over Welshpool. Recognised their machines. What was it? Gunnery practice again?"

Peterson sensed a challenge in Chiver's question. "Yes, they're working on some of this morning's lessons."

"You're spending too much time on advanced training with those two." Chivers remarked with barely suppressed irritation. "Why bother? They'll learn what they need once they're in France. In the meantime what about the other Cadet's? How about you sharing the workload?"

In reply, Peterson passed across Rosper and Perkins' RFC Training Transfer Cards, along with their meticulously maintained Army Book 425's. Chivers opened the off-white covers and gave the contents of their Pilot's Flying Logbooks a cursory glance. He handed them back to Peterson.

"So they're leaving for St.Omer tomorrow morning. Do you want to sign them off or shall I?"

"I'll do it." Peterson replied acerbically, withholding his unspoken thoughts.

At four in the afternoon Perkins and Rosper entered the hut still wearing their flying overalls. Peterson welcomed them back and bade them sit down at the nearest vacant desks.

"How did it go?"

Perkins wiped his eyes, carefully avoiding the oil and burnt cordite that smothered the exposed parts of his face. "Much better Sir. No jams this time. Fired a few rounds to warm my guns beforehand just as you suggested. Managed some good hits."

"And how about you Rosper?"

"The Vickers synchroniser failed Sir, so I only used my Lewis. I tried what you said about changing the canister, it was much easier, only took me a few seconds."

"Good. Just remember, when you're focused on your combat target, it's important that you don't lose your awareness of what's happening around you. If a Hun latches onto your tail break off the attack and defend yourself immediately."

The boys looked up at Peterson expectantly, absorbing every word.

"You've logged nearly forty-nine hours solo each and managed five forced landings between you. You're fast learners and I'm happy with your flying abilities but Rosper, you need to tidy up your landings." He shifted aside a file of papers and sat down on the corner of his desk. "In future, both of you whenever you can, put in as much time as possible sighting your guns and practicing with ground targets."

"Will we be doing more gunnery practice tomorrow Sir?" Rosper enquired.

"No. Your orders have come through." Peterson paused, noting the lad's barely suppressed excitement. "Tomorrow morning you'll take the train down to Dover. All the arrangements have been made, you'll board HMS Racehorse for passage to Dunkirk and then the train to St. Omer. From there you'll be posted to a front line squadron."

He allowed the two Cadets a few seconds to absorb the news. "Now you're officially qualified for service at the front you can take those white bands off your peaked caps and get your wings properly stitched to your tunics."

Perkins and Rosper shook hands. Their soiled faces creased into wide smiles. The great adventure was about to begin. Peterson remembered his own posting, a lifetime ago. He shook his head, *they'll soon learn,* he thought. *That's if they're lucky and live long enough.* He cleared his throat.

"We've taught you as much as possible in the time available. Now I'll give you some final advice. When you arrive at the front, make a mental note of all the landmarks in your sector as soon as you can. It'll help you when you are lost. Crossing the lines, don't be too put off by the ground guns or 'Archie' as we call them, their bark is worse than their bite. Stay in formation or you'll be easy meat for enemy machines hanging about upstairs."

Peterson paused, letting his words sink home. "Watch your leader in the air, if he fires his guns, he's warming them ready for combat. You do the same. If he makes a sudden move, follow him because he's seen the enemy. Chances are you won't have. Always be prepared for an enemy attack from out the sun. When you're in the ruck, you need to be able to handle your machine instinctively. There will be no time to think about flying, concentrate on your position relative to the enemy. You won't have time to transition your eyes to the gunsights so follow the lines of tracer. In a fight with a Fokker triplane remember he can out-manoeuvre you but you can out-dive and out-run him." Peterson pointed at Perkins. "And never let your engine rev over twenty-two hundred."

Perkins brow creased in concentration, he'd not forget writing off a Hispano engine the previous week.

"Every one of your squadron's aeroplanes will look the same, but they all have their own individual characteristics. When you get to the front line, the likelihood is that you will be allocated your own. Get the rigging adjusted to suit your own preferences. I was fortunate to have some first class mechanics, riggers and armourers in my squadron, but I'll tell you this, ultimately the best man to look after your aeroplane is you. Adjust and sight the guns yourself."

"Sir, how long should we expect to be at St.Omer before we're posted?" Rosper asked.

"That depends on the demand for replacement pilots." Peterson answered. "But while you're there, volunteer for as many post-maintenance test flights as you can. Experience is the key to survival and success."

While Peterson was speaking, Chivers remained seated, looking absentmindedly out the hut window and giving every indication of disinterest.

"Anything to add Captain Chivers?" Peterson prompted.

Chivers turned to face the two young airmen with an expression of something like pity. He stubbed the remains of his cigarette out and exhaled a cloud of smoke. "Once you're in France you'll need to be able to carry out arduous tasks without supervision, you'll have to keep going and stay awake when fatigue is over-powering. Obey unpleasant but necessary orders and most of all, keep fighting when the instinct of self-preservation advocates something totally different."

It was Chivers' standard, oft-repeated mantra to all Cadets, but there was something in the two lad's earnest attention that caused him to add another cautionary piece of advice.

"For what it's worth, never volunteer for an Observation Balloon attack."

"Why Sir?" Rosper had never considered balloons as a particularly challenging target.

"They're bloody dangerous that's why! Fifty feet wide and two hundred feet long bags of gas filled with highly flammable hydrogen. Winched up at dawn to around two thousand feet from the back of a flatbed truck then hauled down again at sunset. Around every winch there's a defensive perimeter containing batteries of Archie and machine guns. The shells are set to detonate at the same altitude as the balloon. You have to fly through shrapnel, explosions and bullets and shoot a long burst of incendiaries into the bloody things. Short bursts seldom work. Once you've flown through all that, even if you succeed, enemy fighters are usually lurking against the sun with the advantage of height to pounce on you."

Peterson lightened the discussion, he wanted to keep the lad's sprits up. The coming night could be the last they spent in England for a long while.

"Right, off you go boys, get washed and changed and be back here in half an hour. By then I'll have signed off all your books and papers. Enjoy yourselves this evening, if you're down at the Greyhound at seven I'll buy you both a drink but make sure you're back in your billet by ten. Early start tomorrow and you've got a big day ahead."

The seventh of March 1918. Peterson had just finished his breakfast and was walking to his office when he received a summons to report promptly to Major Desmond Hamilton's office at nine. At the appointed time he presented himself to Shotwick's Commanding Officer.

"Peterson, come in, sit down."

Hamilton waited until Peterson had settled. "Over five weeks ago you spoke to me about a transfer to a fighting unit."

"Yes Sir."

"But you have been forbidden to cross the lines in France."

"Just as you say Sir."

"Quite so. Last weekend I visited the Air Council and mentioned your interest to Major-General Godfrey Paine, the Master-General of Personnel. He was not entirely unsympathetic to your case and promised me he'd make enquiries. Yesterday afternoon a courier arrived with a despatch from the War Office."

A Deputy Administrator from the W.A.A.C. knocked and entered Hamilton's office. She handed Peterson an official notification before departing.

"Those are your transfer orders Peterson. On the fourteenth you'll leave here to join the new RFC Middle East unit in Palestine. Travel arrangements are being made. On arrival at Alexandria you're to report immediately to the Fifth Wing headquarters in Rafah. Major Paine's included a personal letter of introduction for you to the officer in charge, Lieutenant Colonel Burnett."

Peterson scanned the typewritten document. He'd hoped for a posting, but never imagined being sent so far from home.

"They're providing air support for Allenby's ground formations. It's likely you'll be flying Nieuport 17's, so for the first couple of weeks after arrival you're assigned to a conversion course at 23 Advanced Training Squadron in Aboukir."

"Nieuport 17's Sir? I thought they'd been retired from front line service?"

"Only in France. Look here Peterson, don't expect to find any of our latest machines out in Palestine, they're all designated for the Western Front."

For Peterson, the new orders meant a welcome return to combat. He could not disguise his enthusiasm.

"Thank you Sir."

Hamilton leant forward across his desk and extended his right arm. The two officers shook hands amiably, though there was a hint of regret in the older man's eyes.

"Good luck Captain Peterson. There will be many Cadets sorry to lose you."

Immediately after his meeting, Peterson returned to the hangar and donned his flying gear with renewed energy. At ten-o-clock he was taking up a Cadet by the name of Anthony Phillips. A keen rugby player, the Second Lieutenant was rarely seen without a black eye, split lip or facial abrasions. He didn't know it yet, but today was to be his final dual flight before going solo.

It was a good day for flying. The weather over Shotwick was fair with good visibility, a light breeze blew in from the west while above, wisps of high cirrocumulus were the only clouds in the sky. Waiting out on the aerodrome field, positioned for take-off, was one of the squadron's new two-seat Avro 504K trainers. The grass underneath its 110 hp Le Rhone 9Ja rotary engine was blackened by spent castor oil lubricant. Ground crew were making final checks and completing their maintenance record entries.

Phillips was already waiting by his machine when Peterson arrived. He appeared in a worse state than usual with a newly sutured wound running left to right on his chin.

"Good Lord Phillips! I didn't know there was a game on yesterday."

"There wasn't Sir." Phillips replied sheepishly.

"So what happened to you?"

"Bit of a smash last night on my way back from town after a billiards match with the locals. I came off my Triumph Model H motorcycle on that left-hand bend south of Shotwick Bridge. Head over the handlebars job, landed on my chin and opened up a second mouth!"

"Must have hurt like hell." Peterson winced in sympathy.

"Not as much as the tetanus antiserum jab the nurse gave me." Phillips attempted a weak smile.

"You sure you feel up to flying today?"

"Of course." Phillips climbed up and slid stiffly into the front cockpit of the Avro. "It'll take more than a few cuts and bruises to hold me back!"

Peterson knew instinctively that this keen young airman had the right attitude.

"Come along then young fella'm'lad." Peterson hauled himself up into the rear cockpit. "We'll make a fifty mile low-level cross country flight to Preston, you know the route. Climb to ten thousand for the return leg and try a few spin recoveries. When we get back to Shotwick I want to check out the local conditions so you'll do three circuits and practice landings."

Phillips strapped himself in. He closed the engine block tube and fine adjustment levers then manually pumped up the fuel tank pressure to two and a half pounds per square inch. Under Peterson's watchful eyes he checked the function of the Avro's flying controls. At the front of the aeroplane, mechanics turned on the oil supply. Carefully avoiding the single skid that protruded beneath the propeller, they primed each of the engine's nine cylinders with fuel. The chocks were in position. On the call of "Contact please Sir" from the ground crew, Phillips responded: "Contact!"

Carefully avoiding slipping on the oily grass, two men swung the long propeller and its attached three hundred and twenty pound Le Rhone around over compression. The rotary engine caught immediately and crackled into life. It quickly burnt through the priming charge of fuel and, just as it began to splutter, Phillips manipulated the two engine adjustment levers to maintain the correct idling momentum.

Driven air, engine exhaust and the characteristic smell of burnt castor oil whipped back across both student and instructor. In less than a minute Phillips had correctly adjusted the fuel settings and was testing the engine at full power, over a thousand revolutions per minute. Returning to slow running he blipped the ignition cut out switch then waved the ground crew to remove the chocks and stand clear. The Avro began to roll forward slowly at first then, under full power, accelerated rapidly across the field. As centrifugal force enriched the mixture in each rotating cylinder Phillips made the requisite adjustments and, at the same time, instinctively compensated for the aeroplane's characteristic left-hand swing.

During climb out Phillips kept a look out for a convenient forced-landing area. He had been taught to always prepare for an engine failure. The Avro's light weight/high drag airframe would lose airspeed rapidly after any stoppage and a low altitude stall would spoil an otherwise promising day.

Within ten minutes they had cleared the busy airspace surrounding Shotwick and were crossing the River Mersey at seven thousand feet. To the left, amid the busy docks and sprawling urban expanses of Liverpool and Birkenhead, the skyline was dominated by derricks and the two, three hundred foot tall spires of the Royal Liver Building. To the right, the horizontal truss and twin two hundred foot towers of the new transporter bridge spanned the river between Runcorn and Widnes.

Seated in the rear cockpit Peterson kept his hands and feet away from the joystick and rudder bar. Although confident in the competency of his Cadet, he nevertheless remained on high alert, ready to take over immediately should anything go awry. He had only the most basic of dual controls but they were sufficient to fly the Avro in an emergency. His instrument board consisted of an airspeed indicator, altimeter, engine revolution gauge, compass, fuel tank pressure gauge and a bank indicator. Two oil pulsators showed a steady stream of lubricant entering the engine. The fuel mixture control levers on the left moved in response to every adjustment made by the trainee up front.

The Le Rhone's propwash was freezing cold and its rasping combustion deafening. Phillips sensed the engine's power, pulling against the airframe's drag. The buffeting airflow transmitted its force from the flying surfaces, through the cables to the controls. On both sides of the front cockpit, internal diagonal bracing wires vibrated as oil stained fabric drummed against the vertical spacers.

The green and languid Lancashire countryside passed by below while the River Douglas was a glittering ribbon of light in the distance. Beyond lay the dark smudge of Manchester. The sun shone on Phillips' face, there were times on a long flight when a pilot's mind might wander. To avoid loss of concentration he occupied himself with regular scans of the Avro's critical instruments, the better to be forewarned of any impending failure. Training had taught him the expediency of always keeping an emergency landing spot in sight, just in case his engine should falter. Time and again he examined the ground for roads that were clear of traffic, trees and power lines. He checked every passing field for furrows or other obstructions that could cause the Avro to flip over during landing.

Their outward flight required only one detour. A cluster of stratocumulus had formed over St. Helens, their white tops rising like castles in the sky. Phillips gave the grey, flat bases a wide berth, avoiding flying blind in turbulent air. At four thousand feet it was easy to navigate by tracking the Lancashire and Yorkshire Railway from Warrington to Wigan. From there onward the three hundred foot tall spire of Preston's St Walburge's Church was a clearly visible landmark. Flying north of the city they continued to the Lancashire district of Chipping before turning for home.

After an hour and a half in the air the Avro returned to Shotwick and rolled to a stop. Peterson unfastened his lap belt, leant forward and slapped Phillips firmly on his right shoulder. He shouted against the engine noise and rushing air.

"Good job Phillips. Just try not to overcompensate for the machine's slow roll control in future. Those last three touch-and-goes went really well."

Phillips nodded in acknowledgement. He was reaching for the magneto switches when Peterson added: "You've had four hours dual. I think it's time you flew solo. One circuit of the aerodrome. I'll get out and watch from here. If you don't think you are ready or if you aren't feeling the best, we'll reschedule for tomorrow."

"I'm as ready as I ever will be Sir!" Phillips responded with enthusiasm.

"Off you go then. Remember, if you're not happy with your landing approach don't be embarrassed to go around and try again."

"Right-ho!" Phillips' eyes lit up with enthusiasm. He felt a curious mixture of apprehension and excitement.

Peterson stepped aside as Phillips taxied the Avro to the downwind end of the field then turned into the light prevailing breeze and gave it full power. He noticed immediately that the controls seemed much lighter without Peterson's additional one hundred and eighty five pound weight. The Avro's acceleration was faster and take off was shorter, it jumped from the field into the air and within seconds reached four hundred feet. The climb out rate was much quicker too. Although quite confident of his ability, Phillips breathed a sigh of relief, he'd done it, it wasn't so bad after all. He turned left onto the base leg and soon reached his circuit altitude of two thousand feet. Sharing the sky in an active airspace he maintained a careful watch for other machines while, at all times, keeping a landing plan in mind should the engine fail.

Phillips imagined a hundred pairs of eyes focused on him from the ground, critically watching his every move. Although flying the circuit felt routine and comfortable, he nevertheless maintained maximum concentration. With minimum control input, the Avro would deviate from its course and required constant attention to maintain balanced flight. Each time he adjusted the engine speed the altered slipstream over the tail surfaces varied his pitch and yaw control. Anticipating the changes kept his mind fully occupied.

Phillips looked down over his shoulder to where Peterson was standing, waiting, on the ground. He glanced back to the empty seat and the reality hit home. He was flying by himself! His hands trembled with nerves. A surge of pride and excitement spread through his body. Enjoying the ride and sense of freedom he laughed and let loose a loud, self-congratulatory cheer.

Preparing to land he began working his way through the familiar procedures and realised he was speaking his thoughts aloud. Lining up his height and glide on a steady final approach,

Phillips positioned the 504 for a landing directly into wind. Although Peterson was far away, his reassuring voice was still in his head. He closed the fuel supply and cut power to the engine which continued to turn in the slipstream. At fifty five miles an hour he passed over Shotwick aerodrome's boundary. Despite his previous experience, this landing was unfamiliar. The lightly laden Avro was reluctant to land and floated above the field. Phillips side-slipped to increase the descent rate. Moments before ground contact he reset the engine to full power and used the ignition cut out 'blip' button to control the revolutions. It was a measure that ensured he had sufficient power should a landing swing develop or an overshoot be necessary.

It was a successful three-point touch-down, a little bumpy but solid. Phillips kept the engine running at a low setting to allow its temperature to stabilise and used the available power to navigate clear of the field. Steering between two stationary Martynsides and a wingless Camel used for ground handling, he shut down in front of the closest hangar and climbed out onto the turf. Overcome with joy, it was the proudest moment of his young life.

Three ground crew members emerged from the hangar and set about their post-flight inspection of the Avro. "There are some broken strands on the starboard landing wires. They'll need replacing." Phillips cautioned. The lead engineer nodded his acknowledgement.

A smiling Peterson stepped forward to greet him. The two airmen exchanged congratulatory handshakes. It had been a significant day for both of them.

"Well done Phillips. Splendid job."

"Thank you Sir. That flight just about caps it all this year!" Phillips enthused.

"I'll say." The two men set off toward the Cadet's hut. "I heard you recently got married. A local girl."

"Yes, in January, her name's Jane. I found out last Saturday she's expecting."

"Good Lord Phillips!" Peterson exclaimed with a mixture of admiration and surprise. "All this calls for a drink tonight down the Greyhound. First round's on me."

After signing off Phillips' log book Peterson returned to his office and, firmly grasping the handle, slammed the warped door shut behind him. Seated at his desk, Chivers was examining a stack of open log books. He looked up as Peterson entered. "Welcome back Peterson. Heard the news about Stead?"

"No?" Peterson responded, concerned. "What happened, is he all right?"

"Few cuts and bruises, nothing serious. That damned Brasier built 8b motor went dud on him five thousand feet over Kelsall. Either the reduction gears or the propeller shaft. Anyway, he came down in one piece south of Chester. The airframe's repairable but it'll likely be put back in storage until we can scrounge a decent replacement engine from somewhere."

"Where's Stead now?"

"In his billet with a sore head, feeling sorry for himself." Chivers deposited a pile of reports into his out-tray. "So you had another meeting with Hamilton this morning?"

"I did."

"...And?"

"I'm posted to Palestine. Leaving here on the fourteenth to join 153 Squadron. Seems there's something brewing around Jericho and north of the Dead Sea. I imagine the Flying Corps are bolstering support for Allenby, you know, pushing the Ottomans back across the Jordan River."

"God-forsaken shite-hole." Chivers cursed. "Can't imagine why you're so keen. A lot of chaps would give anything to stay in

Blighty and be posted to a station like this."

"I just want to finish the job I started." Peterson responded with a nuance of disapproval.

"I suppose we'd better get ready to pack our things then." Chivers gave an enigmatic smile which was unusual, as he rarely displayed any expression of humour.

"We?" Peterson queried.

"Hamilton called me into his office while you were up with Phillips. I've had my orders too. It appears I'm joining you."

7. SUNSET, STRUTS AND SHADOWS

In the weeks since Marble joined 303 Squadron, he'd begun to accept that the death of men in the Flying Corps seemed more tragic than those he'd witnessed in the army. In the trenches, he and his comrades lived their lives in an atmosphere of sudden loss. In contrast, Wagnonlieu seemed so far away from war that death regained all the unexpected shock it brought with it in peacetime. In the past month he'd seen comrades go out in the morning from comparative civilization, white tablecloths and hearty breakfasts, full of life and good spirits and never come back.

In the late afternoon of January eighteenth Marble was absent from the Mess. Instead of partaking in the usual camaraderie he'd scheduled a visit to the squadron workshop to oversee work on his allocated SE5a. The weather was overcast and dreary with a low mist. The hangar doors had been drawn back to let in as much natural light as possible, even so, the mechanics had resorted to carrying out their duties under the glow of electric lamps. It was predictably noisy. Against a background of bawdy banter and engineering activity the squadron generators droned at full capacity, powering machine tools and illumination. There was a distinctive odour, a combination of oil, dope, petrol and grease.

Marble's SE5a was situated near to the hangar door and was one of four machines undergoing maintenance. It was manufactured in September by Farnborough's Royal Aircraft Factory and subsequently delivered to St. Omer before being allocated to 303 Squadron. After three months in the front-line its pristine fabric had become faded, patched and layered with a patina that marked every hour of service. The fuselage forward of the cockpit was scarred by frequent, hurried engine maintenance and the underside stained by oil leaks. Both the lower wings and tail were ingrained with mud and dust from rustic airfields.

A follower of aviation technology, Marble regularly read the latest Air Board Technical bulletins at night in his billet. He'd then carefully study the recommendations before instigating field modifications to his assigned machine. While flying he'd make mental notes of minor jobs he could undertake on his return. After two weeks combat flying he'd already upgraded the Hispano's eight standard pistons with high compression aluminium alloy versions and improved cooling to the rear cylinders by modifying the factory fitted cowling. Taking advice from other SE5a pilots he'd also adjusted the rigging, reducing the wing's dihedral for additional manoeuvrability.

Earlier that afternoon, on Marble's instructions, Air Mechanic First Class Charlie Bingham had removed the engine cowlings on his SE5a. With open access to the 200 hp Hispano-Suiza 8b V-8 he'd removed and truncated both exhaust pipes to improve gas extraction from the engine. Having completed the primary task, Bingham repaired a reported leak between the manifold and the cast aluminium cylinder block by tightening the securing nuts. In the meantime, Marble was seated in the cockpit, attempting to adjust his rearward vision in a convex mirror he'd recently fitted to the rearmost port cabane strut. The airframe rocked as fitters finished installing a pair of bulged fairings above the forward fuselage upper longeron on either side of the cockpit. A heavy set man, Marble needed additional elbow room. The modification included a coaming adjustment to accommodate his broad shoulders. The SE5a's head rest had previously been removed to improve his rearward vision.

Marble found a peculiar solace when absorbed in aeroplane

mechanics. The total concentration required took his mind away from the ever-present stress of war. He derived a great deal of satisfaction evaluating the improvements after a job had been completed. Above all, it inspired confidence in his machine and imbued him with a thorough knowledge of its performance. The ground crew never simplified their technical language as they would with other pilots. They knew that Marble understood the terms as well, if not better, than they. When he climbed into his SE5a it felt as comfortable and familiar as an old pair of cavalry boots.

He called over to Corporal Saunders who was standing nearby.

"Sir?"

"There's a strafing operation tomorrow and I've an idea to shorten the odds." Marble climbed down to allow mechanics access to the cockpit interior.

"When we're near the ground our machines are vulnerable to fighter attack from above. You see, the enemy have the advantage of surprise and height. I want you to tone down my upper wing roundels. The white's too conspicuous against the ground and it gives a diving Hun an excellent aiming point. All the bastard has to do is shoot between the white marks and I'm a dead man."

Saunders nodded his understanding. "What do you propose Sir?"

"How about smearing the white with a couple of handfuls of mud, just as a temporary measure for tomorrow's operation? If we're going to do strafing on a regular basis I'm going to suggest to the Skipper we overdope the top-side roundels with brown PC10."

"Good idea Sir." Saunders considered Marble's suggestion. "We'll try it. I'll mention it to some of the other lads too. If Major Cameron agrees and gives Flight Sergeant the go-ahead we'll paint all the machines." He added a note of caution. "Take my advice though Sir, don't say a word to Wing. If it's not in their book of regulations? You know what they're like."

At eight in the morning of January the nineteenth, the regular roar of a Hispano 8b was quickly followed by the deep note of a second, then another. Soon half a dozen engines were proclaiming the start of another day's work. Six SE5a's bounded across the aerodrome field and, after a few yards, Thompson's patrol was airborne. Their objective was the aerodrome and hangars of Jasta 14, an enemy unit that had recently moved from Boncourt to occupy the aerodrome at Liesse east of Laon, a distance of some eighty miles south-east of Wagnonlieu.

The weather was predictably unfavourable with low, clinging fog and a south west wind at altitude. The SE5a's climbed through fifteen hundred feet and entered the grey underside of low lying Cumulus cloud. After eight minutes of severe buffeting in the turbulent mist, the flight emerged at six thousand five hundred feet into a stunningly beautiful clear sky. Continuing up to fifteen thousand they made a slow turn to the south, catching glimpses of passing towns and villages through gaps in the cloud.

Half an hour after take-off they crossed the lines east of Sinceny. Green fields gradually grew more plentiful as the shell torn region of the trenches was left behind. Roads became more clearly defined and towns more easily identified on their maps. The formation swayed with every gust of wind. Thompson's SE5a was in perfect trim and required only gentle control inputs to fly. Marble, however, had to concentrate hard on maintaining position off Thompson's right. With its reduced wing dihedral, his SE5a would tilt and stray at the slightest turbulence. In close formation even the smallest deviations were immediately noticeable. He constantly adjusted his relative distance while referencing the horizon to maintain straight and level flight.

Twenty miles from their destination they crossed the River

Oiuse at Ribemont and started to descend. Within minutes Liesse appeared on the horizon, clearly recognisable by the towering spire of its fourteenth century Notre Damme basilica. Their arrival over Jasta 14's aerodrome came as a complete surprise to the air crew and troops on the ground who appeared like ants, scurrying from barracks and hangars to man defensive positions. A number of enemy machines were parked up outside their hangars, apparently having recently returned from patrol.

Marble's first sweeping assault exposed him to a totally new kind of combat. Flying at fifteen thousand feet there was plenty of room to manoeuver and engage an opponent, but at two hundred the ground rushed past directly below his wheels. With his attention focused on both his target and the dangerous proximity of the terrain, holding his wings level for more than a few seconds made him a predictable aim for the enemy guns. He swiftly devised a new strategy. After his attack run he'd initiate a hard pull up, climb to a thousand feet and make each subsequent strafe at a ten degree dive angle, giving him more space to maneuver from the start. It would be like flying down an invisible funnel ending at the target.

He dodged and weaved across the field, trying to avoid flying through debris thrown up by exploding targets. Closing on a row of four parked Fokker Dr1's he fired his Vickers, aiming short so that the ammunition crept up on the machines until they were in range. Spurts of dirt kicked up in a straight line across the triplanes whose wings rocked under the onslaught, but with no visible damage. Slung under the fuselage of Marble's SE5a were two twenty-pound Cooper fragmentation bombs. Soaring over the triplanes he released his first device, aiming for one of the aerodrome's temporary canvas hangars. He missed the target by thirty feet and merely blew another hole in the already crater-pocked field. The next crashed through the roof of a large workshop hut, which by every appearance had already received bad treatment that day. As the marshes east of Liesse flashed by, Marble pulled up and the ground receded. He felt like a heavy weight was pushing down on every part his body. Instinctively he contracted the muscles in his calves, thighs and shoulders. Levelling out at a thousand feet, the intense pressure ceased and he had an uncomfortable sensation of falling forward.

Time and again Thompson led his flight on low-altitude passes, directly into the enemy guns. The SE5a's faced intense ground fire from hundreds of infantry rifles and machine guns in densely packed prepared positions. Thirty-seven millimeter automatic cannons, or "flaming onions" streaked the air and larger caliber flak guns fired from the aerodrome perimeter.

Babbington fixed his attention on a group of three parked fuel tenders and, deeming them a suitable target, dropped his first Cooper bomb. There followed a deafening explosion and a blast of searing heat. One of the trucks left the ground and ascended perpendicularly into the air. The other two were overturned, the ground surrounding them torn up and an adjacent building badly damaged. He released his second on a stores shed that he judged contained ammunition. The resultant explosion proved his guess correct.

An SE5a pilot set upon one of the perimeter gun emplacements and released both bombs simultaneously. One burst close to the revetment, but not close enough to do any damage, the other failed to explode. He turned his attention to a taxiing Fokker. Ignoring all else around he drew closer, unaware that he had reached an unrecoverable altitude. Seconds later his SE5a crashed into the marshland.

When the smoke of battle had cleared Thompson could see the effect of their raid. The enemy were completely disorganised. The aerodrome was littered with abandoned guns and lorries. Horse drawn carts were surrounded by scattered cargo. Fearful for their lives, ground crew had dispersed into shelters. The physical damage was not great, but the disruption was worse.

Within eighteen minutes the remaining five British machines

had climbed to fourteen thousand feet. They were flying over Crepy at an indicated hundred and twenty miles an hour when Thompson spotted a patrol of six Fokker Dr1's. The triplanes were approximately two miles away and thirteen thousand feet above the Forest of Saint Gobain on a south easterly heading. Signaling the others of his intention to attack, Thompson pushed down the nose of his SE5a, throttled back and entered into a dive. His speed increased rapidly to almost a hundred and ninety miles an hour.

Thompson set his gunsight on a Dr1 at the tail end of the enemy formation. He opened fire from a distance of three hundred feet and kept the gun paddle depressed until he had closed to thirty yards. The Fokker's horizontal stabiliser detached from the fuselage amid a shower of splinters. For a moment the severed tail seemed to hang, suspended in mid-air before the triplane tipped forward, throwing its single occupant into space. Banking away from his victory Thompson was just in time to witness Coleman shoot the top wings off another Dr1.

Amid the general set-to Marble closed on the tail of the enemy leader, a machine with drab green wings, white tail and black and white vertical and horizontal lines on the fuselage. Before he could get near enough for accurate fire the Fokker entered into a steep, right hand banking turn. A spiralling pursuit began with both airmen attempting to gain the advantage. Extending the circle east with every orbit, the German pilot enticed Marble further and deeper into enemy held territory. He glanced at his altimeter, it was showing nine thousand feet. Surrounded by bullets and enemy wings Marble knew he'd been out-manoeuvred by the German. He climbed then dived in an effort to escape. At seven thousand he and decided that the best course of action was to make a hasty retreat back to his own side of the lines. Employing his SE5a's speed advantage he dived beyond range of the pursuing enemy. At less than a thousand he pulled out, scattering a flock of grazing sheep in the field below. From thereon Marble flew cross country, chasing the land contours to

Crepy before climbing. After ten minutes he'd soared to eleven thousand feet but by then his comrades were out of sight. Chastened and alone, he set course for home.

Late morning of the following day, the twentieth of January, Marble was returning to Wagnonlieu at fifteen thousand feet. Ostensibly on a flight test, he had crossed the front lines into enemy airspace over the Forest of Saint Gobain and then set a northerly course east of the winding River Somme. A short distance north east of St.Quentin he spotted an enemy reconnaissance aeroplane two miles north-west and a thousand feet below. The two-seat Halberstadt CL.II was flying in a circuit near the lines at Bouchavesnes, probably ranging for German artillery. Marble assessed his options. An attack would be difficult at such a distance. The enemy crew were, no doubt, on high alert and would turn for home as soon as they saw him, long before he was in range.

As he was watching the enemy, a Sopwith Camel appeared from the clouds directly above the Halberstadt and took on the challenge. The two-seater dived and swerved in an attempt to evade the Sopwith but then, during its second assault, the Camel must have been hit as it rolled off and spiralled slowly then, out of control, plummeted to the shell-holed earth. The entire encounter took less than thirty seconds. The victorious Halberstadt turned east and climbed to resume its original position.

Vengeance was uppermost in Marble's mind. Determined to attack, he quickly devised a strategy. Climbing two thousand feet he entered a uniform layer of fibrous altocumulus cloud intending to track the Halberstadt's predicted course unobserved then swoop down upon it.

Judging his timing perfectly, Marble dived through the wet, swirling mists and emerged on the underside with the enemy directly below. His attack was countered by withering return fire from the German observer. In an instant he remembered something Scott had warned him about. The slower Halberstadt was most likely bait and Marble the prey. He pulled back on the joystick and zoomed back up into the cloud just as three Pfalz D.III's emerged. It was a trap.

Marble's attitude had always been the bigger the challenge, the bigger the reward. Determined to fight on, even with odds at four to one, he flew back down through the vapour and engaged the leading Pfalz. After a few rounds from his Vickers the hostile machine hesitated, then slowly fell into a spin.

The two remaining Pfalz pilots recognised Marble's distinctive tail markings. His reputation was such they nosed down and departed. The Halberstadt too, turned and dived for home. True to form Marble set about the two-seater and, gauging the moment, plunged into a second attack. He managed twenty or so rounds before his excess closing speed necessitated a sharp turn to the right to avoid colliding with the tail of his prey. Anticipating Marble's turn the enemy rear gunner swung his Parabellum MG14 machine gun around and released a salvo of 7.92mm bullets, several of which struck Marble's SE5a. He half-rolled away and put himself out of range.

Returning a third time, Marble closed in directly below the Halberstadt's six-o-clock. The pilot banked left to allow his observer to bring his guns to bear. Marble turned right in the opposite direction, keeping below the two seater and in its blind spot. Taking advantage of the SE5a's speed and manoeuvrability he turned back under Halberstadt's tail and fired forty rounds from his Vickers into the vulnerable underside. The enemy machine caught fire immediately and, enveloped in flames, entered a vertical dive. Plummeting to the ground, it tipped end over end. Either the pilot or observer fell or jumped out. Marble watched, transfixed by the awful spectacle as the doomed man tumbled, arms and legs extended, hands clawing at the rushing air.

He checked his map and marked off the point where the Halberstadt impacted the ground, noting with satisfaction it had come down behind allied lines in a ditch alongside Leuze Wood, west of Combles.

Late afternoon on Monday the twenty-first of January, after the final patrol of the day, Marble filed his report then returned to his billet to wash and change. Once suitably presented he ambled across to the Mess.

"Congratulations Marble!" Peters welcomed him inside. "Five confirmed victories in under a month."

"Six, if you include the Hun who murdered Dilks." Thompson interjected.

"Yes, well." Peters demurred. "You know Wing, no independent witnesses and over the lines. If it were up to me of course..."

Scott laughed. "If it were Frank, every man here would be an ace."

"It's just a number." Marble brushed of the accolades as if were of little consequence. "Just glad it was them instead of me."

"Amen to that." Sammy raised his glass in salute. "By the way Marble old chap. Whether you like it or not, the next round of drinks are on you!"

"Maurice!" Marble called the head stewards' attention. "Put the next round on my Mess bill will you? Make sure they get only one each, you know what a bunch of old sots they are."

"Carry on downing Huns at this rate Marble and you'll be out of funds by February." Coleman cautioned sagely.

"Too late, already am."

The friendly banter continued until dinner time. After the meal and loyal toast Scott rose to address the assembled officers.

"Now listen chaps. I've been summoned to attend Wing HQ tomorrow at nine. Something's brewing, don't have much of an idea what, but other squadron commanders in our sector have been asked to attend as well, so my guess is it's something big. I'll let you all know what I can when I return." A murmur of subdued conversation followed Scott's announcement. "No time to speculate now, Frank's laid on transport into Arras. We're off for a beano at 'Maison Amiens' to celebrate Marble's achievements."

Their transport into Arras was a pre-war Leyland 'three-tonner' truck. The back consisted of a large wooden crate used for shipping SE5a fuselage components for assembly at the destination. One after the other the officers piled aboard, there were no seats so they made themselves as comfortable as possible on an assortment of packing cases.

"Sorry lads. It's the best Flight Sergeant Wilson could do for us at short notice." Peters apologised as he climbed aboard last.

"Who's driving?"

"Scott insisted he'd give it a go."

A clash of gears and the truck lurched forward, throwing every man to the floor.

"Hold on tight!" came Scott's voice from up-front.

In the open compartment only a fold-down canvas hood protected the driver from the elements. It was a clear, starlit, moonless night and without a heater, bitterly cold. Half a mile south along the straight track to Dainville Scott began to regret his decision to drive. The controls were heavy and the clutch pedal required all the effort he could muster to depress. Every time the Leyland encountered a rut in the road its steering wheel kicked hard against his grip. As the truck thumped and rolled through town, solid rubber tyres transmitted every shock to the uncomfortable occupants

Twin dim, acetylene headlamps illuminated the three mile drive to Arras. The Leyland rocked from side to side as Scott deftly negotiated piles of rubble that partially blocked the war-ravaged roads. Entering Petite Place Square at nine in the evening he parked the Leyland alongside the shattered stump of what was once the medieval town hall bell tower.

Peters was first over the back and unfastened the tailgate. The men assisted each other down. Around them in the square stood rows of mostly intact buildings. Their upper floors were largely deserted and derelict, but trade continued to thrive along the ground floor arcades in a few shops, bars and lodgings. Illuminated by flickering oil lanterns, a steady stream of war worn customers walked the cloisters, seeking a brief respite from the daily sacrifices of their duties.

Scott led his group of airmen to the glass paneled front door of 'Maison Amiens'. Located on one corner of the square, the estaminet was a popular venue for Flying Corps airmen. Scott entered first, then ushered Marble through the press of bodies toward a wood paneled wall stained by decades of accumulated tobacco smoke. In the candlelight, hundreds of signatures and messages had been inscribed between sepia toned posters from the 1890's and modern pin-ups.

"Come on Marble." Scott encouraged, raising his voice to be heard above the roar of voices. "There's still some space on the wall here. It's traditional to sign your name."

Marble uncapped his fountain pen and, supported by his comrades, put his signature underneath that of Frank Peters. Wasting no time, the other squadron members commandeered a vacant table adjacent to the front window. Soon the drink was flowing and the officers were indulging in their usual bacchanalian celebration of male friendship, free from the confines of Wagnonlieu camp.

With all the extravagant conduct associated with airmen on a beano, the evening passed in life-affirming revelry. Several local girls joined their table, enjoying the ribaldry as much as the young men who regressed back to how they were as boys, every one encouraging more outlandish behaviour from the others.

"Hey! Frank's got an empty glass!" Babbington called over to Scott who was standing at the bar. Within seconds a glass full of brandy was pushed into Peters' hand. His head was already spinning, but refusing a drink was an affront to the festivity, so he took a sip then furtively tipped the contents into a plant pot, rather than admit he didn't want anymore.

A cry of anguish from upstairs was immediately followed by the appearance of Sammy. He was scrambling down the staircase buttoning his tunic, while being pursued by a partially clad woman shouting at him in French. She grabbed an empty wine bottle from a table and waved it above her head in a threatening manner. Sammy pushed his way through the throng and exited the front door.

"What's all that about?" Thompson asked Coleman who had a basic understanding of French.

"Seems old Sammy enjoyed the goods without the wherewithal."

"Bloody hell!" Thompson looked aghast as the woman rushed outside after Sammy. "Come on, we'd better save the poor sod!"

There was no sign of Sammy. The woman was standing in the square waving the bottle, screaming curses and obscenities. After several minutes she gave up. Exhausted, she pulled her shawl over her head and entered the adjacent `Hotel et cafe du Commerce'.

"Sammy?" Coleman called out. "It's all right old chap. She's gone, where are you?"

"Up here!" Came a disembodied voice from nearby.

"Where?" Thompson looked around.

"On your right, over the road. I can't get down." Sammy responded in a hoarse whisper. Coleman was the first to spot him, perched precariously atop a disused lamp-post at the end of the arcade.

"How the devil did you get up there Sammy?" Thompson began to laugh at the ludicrous spectacle.

"Don't know." A downhearted Sammy confessed. "She was after me, so I shot up here like a squirrel."

They helped Sammy down from his refuge. By the time he reached the ground all three were laughing so heartily they could barely stand.

Back inside Maison Amiens the festivity continued. The attention focused on Marble, who had unwisely engaged in a drinking contest with a Lieutenant from a group of 3rd Grenadier Guards seated at the adjacent table. For an hour the two men matched each other drink for drink until the army ceded defeat. Supported by two comrades, their insensible champion was escorted outside while a triumphant Marble, swaying unsteadily on his feet, accepted the accolades of his peers.

On the chime of midnight Scott called time. The inebriated airmen finished their drinks, bade farewell to the ladies and filed out into the square with as much dignity as they could muster. Linked arm in arm they meandered unsteadily across the brick-paved open space to the Leyland and climbed aboard. Once again, Scott took the wheel. He started the engine and, trailing a cloud of acrid exhaust, they set off back to Wagnonlieu.

The return journey was interspersed by numerous stops to accommodate Marble who, being indisposed by his earlier reckless competition, was very much the worse for wear. On arrival back at the squadron he went directly to his billet carrying a jug of water and vowing: "Never again!" Throughout the remainder of the night his suffering, repentant misery and frequent visits to the latrines were audible to all.

Scott returned from Wing H.Q., Saint-Pol-sur-Ternoise at three-thirty in the afternoon of January the twenty second. He entered his office, hung up his greatcoat and sat down at his desk.

Peters heard him arrive and, a few minutes later, entered with a mug of hot coffee.

"Well, what's the latest Scott?"

"We're on the move Frank, forty miles south to Estrées-en-Chaussée on the twenty ninth. The Fifth Army are asking for more air support." He turned on his desk lamp against the fading light, unpacked his leather satchel and laid the contents out on his desk. "We're not the only ones. Freddy's crew are off to Vaux-en-Vermandois on the thirty-first and Bungee's lot are moving to Combles on the first of March."

Peters shrugged his shoulders. "At least they'll both be close at hand." Then added with a note of exasperation. "I just hope Wing know what they're doing. Moving a squadron's a logistical nightmare, not to mention all the extra paperwork."

Scott inhaled deeply and, as he frowned, deep furrows of concern formed across his forehead. After barely three months in command, the burden was apparent in his face and in his every day manner. "You know we've been seeing a build-up of enemy forces recently. Transport trains, extra troops?"

"Yes, the patrol reports bear testament to that."

"Nothing specific was mentioned, but Headquarters believe the enemy are getting ready for a big offensive in the spring." Scott rubbed his eyes and sighed. "With the end of Russian hostilities, their troops released from the east are bolstering those on the western front. If the Hun's have any sense they'll launch a substantial push in our sector before the bulk of American forces arrive."

Peters knew if Scott's forecast was accurate the RFC would be in for a tough time and heavy losses. He deposited a wad of files and envelopes onto the desk. Scott's shoulders sagged in disappointment.

"Don't worry Scott, they just need your signature."

"Good. All this administration makes my head woolly."

"Tell me about it!" Peters cast his gaze to the ceiling in a gesture of exasperation. He crossed over to the window to monitor the return of Thompson's afternoon patrol. "I seem to recall 59 Squadron were based at Estrees. They left for Courcelles-le-Comte the middle of last month with their 'Harry Tates'."

"35 Squadron are still there." Scott responded. "So we won't be on our own, for the time being at least." He joined Peters at the office window, counting off each SE5a as it landed. "I met their C.O., Major Alwyn Holt this morning over at Wing H.Q. His lot are flying FK8's on reconnaissance, photography and artillery patrols. The word is they're being reassigned to the 15th Wing attached to the Fifth Army, so unless they're going to leave Estrees too, we'll have some company for the time being."

"I make that all six back." Peters' smiled with relief.

"Me too." Scott looked up to the darkening sky. The first droplets of rain spattered against the window glass. "Weather's closing in. That'll likely be it for the day. You'd best get over to the Briefing Hut Frank and take the boy's reports."

Peters paused in the doorway on his way out. "You know, I spoke to a chap from 35 last week, a Second Lieutenant, name of Tom Urwin. He said their facilities at Estrees are quite comfortable. Péronne's got a few handy estaminets too."

Scott tossed a pile of signed documents into his out tray. "I think our lads will be happier it takes us a little further away from Avesnes-le-Sec and Richthofen's Jasta."

Following a week of intense activity Scott was finally content that every aspect of the squadron's departure had been concluded. On the afternoon of Tuesday, the twenty–ninth of January he took-off from Wagnonlieu for the last time. His engine was running flawlessly and the morning's cloud had dissipated to reveal a bright, clear blue sky. Maintaining two thousand feet altitude he flew south over a vast panorama of former fields sparsely populated by ruined buildings and a network of criss-crossed narrow, straight roads.

After an uneventful half hour in the air Scott approached 303 Squadron's new home at Estrées-en-Chaussée. Taking advantage of the unusually clear visibility, he circled the aerodrome to assess the area. The town was no more than a few derelict houses surrounded by an expanse of flat terrain. A denuded area of woodland lay to the north while in the distant south, under a dome of misty haze, lay the ruins of Athies and the River L'Omignon whose banks had been breached and its original course almost obliterated. To the west, the course of the winding river Somme was barely discernable amid the waterlogged floodplain.

Estrees aerodrome lay beyond the cross-roads east of the town and was dominated by a row of four sturdily built hangars with corrugated iron roofs. At least three dozen Crossley Tenders had parked up at the side of the northernmost hangar and the crews were busy disgorging 303 Squadron's aeroplane spares. Previous heavy traffic outside the doors had already worn away the top-soil to expose large patches of chalk. From the air, the white sub-surface was indistinguishable from lingering, scattered piles of swept snow.

Scott made a wheel landing, as light as a feather, keeping his tail off the ground until the SE5a had slowed down. There was a long taxi ahead of him to the nearest hangar. He rolled out to a standstill alongside four of 35 Squadron's F.K.8's. then followed the usual shut-down procedures. Fuel cock from gravity to carburetor, open the radiator shutters, allow the engine temperature to stabilise for a few minutes at fast idle then go to slow idle and switch off the magnetos in turn. With the engine stopped he opened the hand pressurisation pump valve and released compressed air from the fuel tank, hardly noticing the sound of escaping gas as his ears slowly adjusted to normal hearing. He lifted his goggles and slid off his leather helmet. For a moment he sat perfectly still in the cockpit listening to the eerie silence.

The slowly cooling engine began ticking and he could smell the satisfying odour of a hot, well maintained machine.

The hangar doors were open and inside were ten of 303 Squadron's SE5a's. The familiar smiling face of Flight Sergeant Norman Wilson emerged from the shadows within, a clipboard in his hand.

"Good afternoon Sir."

"Everything satisfactory Flight?" Scott enquired as he stepped down from the cockpit.

"Soon will be. Tools and spares arrived this morning in as good a shape as we packed 'em."

"Billets and cookhouse satisfactory?"

"First rate Sir."

"Good. When you get a moment, give my landing wires a check will you? Oh, and the starboard aileron cable is sticking, one of the pulleys likely needs lubrication."

"Yes Sir!"

Scott unwound his red silk scarf and tucked it into his the map pocket of his overalls. He set off, walking the hundred yards to a semi derelict, eighteenth century farmhouse where 303 Squadron had been allocated two offices on the first floor.

War had inflicted irreversible damage to the once proud family home. The shutters, thrown back from the ground floor windows, were rotting away. The front wall was streaked by mildew from the leaking lead gutter that ran along the roof. The unweeded grass outside was long and unkempt. It seemed to Scott that the spirit of the house had departed with the memories of its unknown former owners. He was about to enter when he saw Charlie Coleman standing outside.

"Looking for Frank, Skipper?"

"Yes. Inside is he?"

"He's in there all right." Coleman replied with a note of caution in his voice. He cast his eyes to the sky. "Good luck."

Scott pulled open the weathered oak front door, rotten and soft with water and neglect. He ducked beneath the frame and carefully climbed the uneven stairs, holding a bannister that was no more than rope threaded through wrought iron rods. Every step was a different height from the last. Finally reaching the landing he took several paces forward, avoiding the gaps left by missing floorboards. Peters' office was in a former bedroom on the right. Behind the partially closed door Scott could hear the sound of activity.

"Frank?"

"Come in Scott."

Scott pushed on the door, it opened halfway before jamming against a packing box. Inside the room, amid open crates and empty cabinets, Frank Peters was unloading bundles of files.

"Just don't touch anything!" Peters remarked testily.

"I won't."

"Half of this paperwork belongs to Wilson. No idea why it ended up here." Peters pushed a crate into the corner. "What a bloody mess!"

Peters' office was cold, damp and draughty. The window was a gaping hole with only a wooden shutter to prevent the wind rushing in. The ceiling had collapsed and the roof sagged alarmingly. There were no tiles or thatch to contain the heat within, instead, stretched across the otherwise exposed timber beams, a khaki canvas awning flapped languidly in the breeze.

"Are you sure there's nothing I can do to help?" Scott's offer was genuine.

"I suggest you go and look in your own office before asking me that!" Peters responded.

Unable to disguise his dismay at the dilapidation of their new headquarters, Scott crossed the landing to his room. The door was hanging at a jaunty angle on its hinges and gave way to his body weight without resistance. The inside was in no better condition that Peters'. The floorboards creaked and old cobwebs clung to the walls in dark corners, flapping in the draft. The mullioned glass in his solitary window was wavy and yellowed by time. Scott squeezed through a gap between his desk and a packing crate on his way to the hearth. There was a woodpile in the corner collected by the previous occupants. He poked at the dying embers of a fire to release a little warmth before removing his flying gear. Rubbing his tired eyes, he ran his fingertips across his forehead where deep furrowed premature creases of age lined his youthful features. Slowly he began to unpack, haphazardly hanging various personal souvenirs around the cracked and bare brick walls. Among trophies his wartime flying career, he gave pride of place to photographs of former comrades and various components from vanquished enemy aeroplanes.

Downstairs, Thompson and Coleman assessed the potential of 59 Squadron's abandoned Mess. In the centre of the former lounge a slender cast iron pole supported the sagging ceiling. On the far wall a heavy drape concealed a section of damaged brickwork. An eclectic mix of unframed photographs, prints of local landscapes and village scenes hung at jaunty angles. Suspended from the picture rails, a faded band of nineteenth century tapestry encircled the room. A soot-stained oak shelf had been nailed into place above the brick fireplace, on top of which stood two column lampstands. The previous occupants had thoughtfully provided a ready supply of rough-hewn logs and stored them in alcoves either side of the hearth. Illumination was provided by three old hurricane oil-lamps suspended from the rafters.

Thompson stepped aside as a half-dozen orderlies carried in a mix of un-matched dining furniture and canvas deck-chairs, distributing them evenly around the walls.

"Where would you like this Sir?" Scott's batman Dobson entered holding a heavy, cloth covered card table. His face was red from exertion.

"Just put it down anywhere Dobby". Thompson scratched his head.

Sammy Brown arrived unnoticed and carefully examined the billiards table. Left behind by the previous squadron it was too heavy and unwieldy to move.

Dealing with the essentials first, Maurice and his team had improvised a makeshift bar away in one corner and were busy setting out glasses and stocking up the drinks. Holding a dram of whisky in his right hand Coleman observed:

"We can fit the piano in front of those drapes."

"What about dining?" Thompson around looked around for a suitable place for their long, oak refectory dining table.

"Through there, in the annex." Coleman paced out the door width. "There should be enough space."

"It'll need a good clean out first." Thompson cast his eyes over the dust covered window-sills. There was a smell of mildew in the stale air. He noticed a bird's nest in the rafters and the floor was awash with the detritus of wildlife.

"Not much to write home about is it?" Coleman shook his head in disappointment. As he spoke, a six cylinder Beardmore engine roared overhead and the shadow of an Armstrong Whitworth FK8 flashed through gaps in the boarded up window.

"Let's start by getting some fresh air in here." Thompson pulled aggressively at the loosely nailed timbers. They came down easily, the low sun shone directly through the dusty glass and filled the annex with light. A couple of gentle shoves on the frame and the window swung open. "That's better Charlie. Don't despair, we'll soon knock this place into shape."

By way of introduction, at four in the afternoon Scott made a short walk into Estrees to visit the headquarters of 35 Squadron's commanding officer, Major Alwyn Holt. He arrived just as a motorcycle courier appeared from Saint-Pol-sur-Ternoise with orders for the following day's patrols.

Holt was evidently expecting Scott's arrival and immediately invited him into his office. "Welcome to Estrées-en-Chaussée Cameron." He extended his hand in greeting. "What do you make of your new Mess? A shocker isn't it?"

"Oh, we're working on it." Scott found it hard to sound convincingly positive. "At least our N.C.O.'s and the men have some half decent accommodation.

"Well, until you get organised, you're officers are welcome to share ours."

"That's decent of you Holt. Shouldn't take us more than twenty four hours."

"Don't mention it old man. We'll lay on a good night for the boys, sort of a welcome party. Been a bit lonely here since 59 shipped out in the middle of December."

"Do you expect to be here much longer? When we met at H.Q. you mentioned you're lads are being reassigned to the 15th Wing."

"No movement orders yet, likely we'll be staying on for a while at least."

Holt opened the sealed orders that had been placed on his desk and read the contents. Scott watched his affable expression change to one of despair.

"Problem?"

"Wing headquarters have ordered a photo-reconnaissance patrol tomorrow morning, between the towns of Catalet and Gouy. Apparently there's been reports of forward artillery movement up from Beaurevoir." He rose from his seat and crossed the office to examine a large scale trench map pinned to the wall. "The target's less than ten miles from Jasta 35 at Premont, fifteen from Jasta 5 at Boistrancourt, and twenty miles from Jasta 8 at Wassigny and Jasta 15 at Cambrai."

"I know the place." Scott shook his head in dismay. "On the Escaut River, south of Prospect Hill. Archie's fairly thick there too."

"Which all means whoever I send over is unlikely to come back." Holt walked over to his window, his back to Scott. "I'll ask for volunteers."

"I'm sorry." Scott understood the turmoil running through Holt's mind. "What do you propose?"

"It's a job for two machines." Holt was thinking aloud. "About twenty miles to target. Tomorrow's forecast's a little wind, clear sky. They'll take-off at nine, enough time for the ground mist to clear."

"I'll get our lads to fly escort." Scott proffered his squadron's services. "I'm sorry I can only muster six machines, we're still in a state of disorder, what with the move."

"Thank you, Cameron." Holt turned from the window to face Scott, a clear expression of gratitude on his face. "Our 'Big Acks' are slower than your SE's, top speed's less than a hundred at ten thousand feet. We'll need half an hour to gain altitude before crossing the lines. I propose sending them in close to service ceiling for the best chance, say twelve thousand. Should arrive over Catelet around ten-o-clock when there'll be a low sun and good shadow."

"We'll provide cover at fifteen thousand." Scott assured. "How long will your boys need over the target area?"

"Can't say for sure, depends on the conditions. Believe me Cameron, they'll take the least amount of time as necessary."

Scott examined the map. "I suggest we fly north and cross the lines together here, east of Peiziere and Villers-Guislain. Archie's fairly sparse over Honnecourt Wood and the St. Quentin

Canal."

"I agree." Holt knew the area well. "Villers Hill's a good landmark." He traced the red and blue trench lines on map. "Return across the lines further south at le Verguier. The Priel Crater stands out like a beacon."

"There it is then." Scott had no illusion about the risks. "I'll lead the escort myself. I'd better get back to my squadron and let the chaps know." He glanced at his watch. "What time do you want us over in the Mess?"

"Afternoon Patrol is due back in half an hour. I'll give them time to file their reports and change, then have word with them about tomorrow. Say six?"

"Fine with me." Scott and Holt exchanged a warm farewell handshake.

As with every RFC unit, social activity centred around the bar. After the daily tensions the officers would adjourn in the evenings and ask about their friends. The gloom and low morale following a loss, either in combat or accident, would be dissipated by a cheery "Come on chaps, what're you going to have?" It kept the lads going.

Such was the mood that evening, Tuesday, the twenty–ninth of January. 35 Squadron had lost an aeroplane to enemy action in the late afternoon along with two of their most popular comrades. Nevertheless, the remaining officers made an extra effort to welcome their new neighbours. Their Mess was in a converted Nissen hut. The dining table had been extended for the occasion and an eclectic mix of armchairs had been assembled around the spacious interior.

Marble arrived promptly at six and, after introducing himself to the gathered airmen, fell into conversation with one of 35 Squadron's observers. A likeable young Second Lieutenant from Kent by the name of Hougham. Along with his pilot, Edgar Blaxland, they were two of the four successful pilots who had volunteered for tomorrow's photo-reconnaissance.

With fully charged glasses in their hands, they adjourned to a couple of comfortable, well-padded fireside armchairs close to the stove and awaited the call for dinner.

"What's your accommodation like Hougham?"

"Oh, fairly ordinary. Wooden Nissen huts to sleep in, two officers to a hut." Hougham sipped at his drink. "So you're one of the lads who'll be watching over us tomorrow?"

"Well, nothing else to do old chap. What's all this photographic lark about anyway?"

"Usually we're looking for new trenches, trains, movement of artillery or troops. It's no ruddy lark though, as you'd soon find out if you tried it. The camera gear's slung over the side of the aeroplane, tricky to operate at the best of times and more so while you're wriggling your way through Archie bursts".

As Marble and Hougham conversed, the remaining contingent of 303 Squadron arrived through the door. Marble waved in Scott's direction. "That's our Skipper over there. He's leading our flight tomorrow".

Hougham watched Scott's casual, good-natured response to Marble's greeting. "I heard Major Cameron's downed his fair share of enemy machines".

"That's the thing about our Skipper, his tremendous shooting." Marble confided. "I've seen him in action. We'd all be in the ruck trying do down a Hun then he comes along and tears him to shreds in a matter of twenty rounds".

"That's encouraging." Hougham was unable to mask his concern. "I'm afraid we're going to need all the help we can get".

Blaxland appeared from the crowded bar. He drew up an old, moth-holed round back bedroom chair, sat down and joined them. Hougham made the introduction. "This is 'Marble' Hall.

He's one of the SE5a chaps joining us tomorrow."

Blaxland reached across to Marble and the two men shook hands. "You're Barry Hall the Rugby player, Surrey half-back, yes?"

Marble was taken aback, Blaxland could see him searching his memory and offered a prompt. "We played together at Old Deer Park, December 1913. Match against Middlesex, I was fly-half."

Realisation suddenly dawned on Marble's face. "Bully!" He laughed. "Old 'Bully' Blaxland!"

"It's a small world Hougham." Blaxland cheerily remarked to his Observer. "My word it's good to see you again Hall."

"We won sixteen to four." Marble explained for Hougham's benefit as the memories came flooding back.

"That's right!" Blaxland laughed. "Middlesex leaked a converted try and a penalty goal."

"The only blot on our copybook was in the second half when Mick Rodrigues dropped a goal."

"I'll say, the silly oaf." Blaxland's expression changed to one of sadness. "Poor old Mick. He was with the 182nd Brigade at Fromelles in July '16 when a Hun shell got him."

Marble downed his drink and for a moment there was silence between the three airmen.

"Another round? It's on me." Blaxland asked as he beckoned a passing Steward.

"That's damned decent of you Bully. Why not?" Marble rejoined without hesitation. Hougham signalled his approval with a 'thumbs-up'. Around them, the Mess was filled with an atmosphere of banter and good humour.

"It's just like old times eh Bully?"

Blaxland said nothing, and with a sad smile raised his glass in salute.

The next morning Marble woke before dawn. Having washed and dressed he made his way over to 35 Squadron's Mess for breakfast. He took with him an old photograph he'd kept of the 1913 Surrey rugby team. When he arrived, he found the tables set and his old team-mate enjoying a light pre-flight breakfast with Hougham. Marble pulled up a chair and joined them.

"Recognise the old team Bully?"

"Good Lord." Blaxland wiped his hands on his napkin before accepting the print. He instantly identified himself, a mustachioed figure standing at the far right, wearing an unusually clean horizontally striped long sleeved shirt. Marble was seated on the ground in front, cross legged in his long black shorts.

"That's Alf Banby next to me. He's a Lieutenant with the 2nd Army." Marble prompted. Blaxland nodded in recognition before taking up the narrative.

"There's Lindsay our Captain, that's Ashford, there's Dudgeon, Reed and Wells too!" His index finger traced along the faces in the back row. "Poor old Freddy Todd, he was killed on the Somme, July '16. George Reed and Harry Londen went down with the destroyer Paragon in the Dover Strait last March, torpedoed." Dispirited, he handed the photograph back to Marble. "I lost touch with the others."

"So the bastards got 'Sweeny' eh?" Marble shook his head with dismay. "He'd have made International."

"Here's an idea." Hougham noticed the sudden, downcast expression of his table companions. "Why don't you two fellows each form squadron teams for a friendly match here on the field? I'm sure we could muster enough players and scrounge some kit."

"What do you think Bully?" Marble enthused.

"Take a few weeks to knock the lads into shape. Yes, sounds like a sound project." The idea had re-kindled Blaxland's spirits.

"Count me in too." Hougham swallowed the remainder of his tea and checked his watch. "Better get a move on chaps, take-off's in a half hour."

By ten in the morning six SE5a's were at fifteen thousand feet, flying in 'diamond' formation over Beaurevoir. The surrounding sky was filled with exploding Archie shells. Three thousand feet below, two FK8's flew steadily back and forth photographing road and rail traffic between Catelet and Gouy.

Scott was on the alert for enemy aeroplanes. He was fully expecting a challenge to appear at any moment. They were close to several Jasta aerodromes and the two reconnaissance machines were prime targets. His first warning of an imminent attack was the cessation of gunfire from the ground. Seconds after the barrage lifted, he lifted his right hand to shield his eyes from the sun's intense glare and saw a patrol of Fokker Dr1's diving from eighteen thousand feet.

The SE5a's met the enemy assault head-on. Moments after the triplanes swept past Thompson turned his head and saw a triplane behind his tailplane. He broke right and went down in pursuit. The Fokker pilot anticipated his intentions, turned right and dived, but the SE5a had the speed advantage. Thompson quickly caught up to within two hundred feet of its rudder before opening fire. His Vickers jammed after a half dozen rounds. Reaching around the windscreen with his right hand into the icy wind, he grabbed hold of the cocking handle to jerk it over and clear the belt in the breech. Having freed the jam, his next burst hit the plywood top decking of the Dr1's fuselage. Its upper wing fabric tore away, exposing a splintered box spar. Thompson pulled up into a roll to avoid overtaking the enemy. The world beyond his port wingtip turned sideways and the horizon swung around. For a moment he hung suspended by the leather straps of his harness before falling back into a trail of choking fumes from the Fokker's damaged engine. The enemy pilot took no evasive action. Thompson fired twenty rounds, striking the horizontal elevator, then broke right as another Dr1 attached itself to his six-o-clock.

Overwhelmed by the close combat, Babbington climbed five hundred feet above the dogfight to gain a perspective on the swirling aeroplanes. A yellow and black triplane was loitering on the perimeter of the fight, probably a novice. He dived for a broadside attack. Crouching down into the cockpit he aligned the Fokker in his Aldis just as Sammy's SE5a unwittingly drifted across in front. Babbbington cursed as Sammy opened fire and took out the Dr1. Frustrated, he manoeuvred into attack position behind another triplane with a smoking engine as it turned southeast toward Beaurevoir. His first twenty rounds went high, the second five second burst passed below the enemy machine whose pilot, recognising his peril, was manoeuvring violently. An accurate shot was difficult to achieve. The triplane swung left and, for a moment, presented the perfect opportunity. Babbington pressed the firing paddle, his aim was true. Tracer flew straight for the Fokker's cockpit. The Dr1's ammunition box ignited and its adjacent, pressurised, twenty gallon petrol tank exploded. The entire aeroplane disappeared in an expanding ball of fire.

Shock, akin to an electric charge shot through Babbington as ammunition ripped across his port wings. An instant surge of adrenalin rushed through his veins. In a reflex action he aggressively pulled the joystick back. The SE5a's nose pitched upward and, as he kicked right rudder, the riven port wings lifted while the starboard stalled. The result was a rapid horizontal spin, a high speed roll. Babbington felt the hammer blow of a bullet entering his right thigh followed by another in his left calf. The horizon ahead was spiralling around. Before the pain reached his brain he pushed the stick forward and applied left rudder. By regaining lift to the starboard wings he attempted to straighten his aeroplane, but his timing was out. He recovered inverted. Starved of fuel, the engine cut. Another bullet buried itself deep into his lower back. The first waves of pain from his wounds paralysed his limbs. A deep, throbbing agony, the like of which he had never known. He threw his head back against the head-rest, teeth clenched. A hammer blow struck his right shoulder from behind and blood spattered the windshield. As flames swept back from his static engine he removed his smouldering gauntlets. With charred, bleeding hands he unfastened his lap belt, his overwhelming instinct to escape the inferno. Gravity pulled him from the cockpit and into the void.

Coleman had used up the last of his ammunition. Frustrated at his inability to fight, he remained within the combat zone, making successive diving attacks on the enemy machines that had, by now, turned their attention on the two 35 Squadron machines. By repeatedly swooping dangerously close to the Fokkers, he forced them to abandon their assaults on the two 'Big Acks'.

A sudden stream of ammunition tracked through the air and swept over the leading FK8's forward fuselage. The two-seater lurched violently to port. Hougham abandoned his camera, grabbed the cockpit coaming and turned around into a mist of blood being swept back with the slipstream. Blaxland was slouched forward in his seat, dead. A single bullet had split open his skull. There was a grinding sound from the engine before it seized. Surrounded by tracer trails, he returned to his gun and fired a dozen rounds at the closest triplane. Then came a sledge-hammer blow to his head, he put up his hand to his leather flying helmet and found it jagged and ripped. There was blood on his fingers. He felt faint, then blacked out. Falling through the air the FK.8 spiralled toward the ground. At five thousand feet the upward rush of air revived Hougham sufficiently for him to seize the observer's joystick and break the stricken machine's fall. The FK.8 staggered, stalled, then fell vertically two hundred feet into the grounds of an ancient Chateau at Vaux le Prêtre.

High above, the fight continued with renewed intensity. Scott was bent of revenge. Having witnessed Babbington's fall, he manoeuvred behind a Fokker that had latched itself onto Marble's distinctively marked tail. Scott closed in until he could see the enemy pilot. The German's attention was totally fixated on his prey and tracer was already impacting Marble's machine. Scott fired two dozen rounds into the Dr1's cockpit. The pilot slumped over and his triplane rolled off to port before diving.

Continually twisting and turning across the sky, Marble sighted a triplane in his Aldis sight and was about to open fire when he heard the rattle of gunfire from directly behind. An enemy round cut his flying boot, the instrument panel shattered and he was immediately engulfed in a billowing cloud of smoke and water vapour. Splinters flew off the rear spar barely inches above his head. It seemed as if the whole world had exploded around him. He instinctively ducked down and raised his hands to protect his face as the SE5a lurched sideways. Looking up, large holes had been punched through the upper wing centre section. Flickers of flame around the engine rapidly developed into a continuous stream of fire. Side-slipping to prevent the flames from blowing over the cockpit, Marble could feel the flesh on his face blistering from the heat.

There was no time to panic, it didn't occur to Marble to climb out and drop, exchanging the slow agony of minutes for almost instantaneous death. Some prescience warned him a faint hope still existed. Cutting the engine's fuel supply he closed the throttle, starving the combustion chambers and manifold of air. He switched off the magnetos and initiated a steep dive with forty five degree angle of bank. The fire began to recede. That the flames extinguished so quickly indicated the cause was not an oil fire from a blown engine.

Plummeting through the sky, with an all-round field of vision Marble could see the cloud base was uncomfortably close to the ground. He realised that, in attempting to land, he could potentially end up in a nice self-dug little hole behind enemy lines. Even if he managed to touch-down in one piece, he recalled

Peterson's experiences as a prisoner of war and had no intention of being captured. He decided to try and re-start his engine. It was risky he knew, but wartime circumstances had a nasty habit of forcing less than ideal solutions upon you.

After hand-pumping air pressure back into his fuel tank Marble performed his start-up procedures. A couple of misfires then the engine kicked into life. An inordinate amount of white smoke billowed out from the exhaust and the bearings clattered in protest. The motor was undoubtably badly damaged but, nevertheless, generated sufficient power to lift the SE5a back up to fourteen thousand feet. At that altitude the extreme cold and rarefied atmosphere did little to help the struggling Hispano. The misfires were worse and the revolutions dropped. By the time Marble crossed the lines at le Verguier, his engine was running hot and increasingly rough.

Having reached friendly territory, Marble gradually reduced height to two thousand feet. A new note crept into the engine's rumble. It was firing regularly and vigorously. Marble's mood improved immediately. Estrées-en-Chaussée lay less than four miles to the west and he began to consider a bath and a good meal on landing. In the midst of his thoughts he was recalled to immediate matters by a sudden splutter of his engine. One glance at the revolutions indicator and it was falling rapidly. Crossing the aerodrome perimeter the rushing wind abruptly replaced the Hispano's roar as he cut the throttle and side-slipped down to land.

Trailing an expanding cloud of acrid white smoke, the SE5a touched down then bounced off the field's uneven surface before settling back. Before it rolled to a halt Marble turned his machine around so that the prevailing wind dispersed engine fumes away from the cockpit. Climbing stiffy out and onto the grass he warned the approaching ground crew, then stood clear and waited until their pyrene extinguishers had eliminated any fire risk.

Returning to examine his aeroplane, a single walk around was sufficient for Marble to discover all kinds of additional damage he had been too distracted to notice in the sky. Running the flat of his hand along the dorsal structure, his fingers probed a jagged tear in the fabric surrounding the aft fuselage top longeron. Incidence wires between the port interplane struts were frayed and slack. The starboard cowling had been torn away, exposing the fire damaged ash engine mounting and forward fuselage upper longeron. Most worrying of all, the main fuel tank skin and its fixing were blackened by heat. It had been a close run thing.

Bingham directed the movement of Marble's SE5a to a safe location away from the hangars and other aeroplanes. A precaution in case the aeroplane should re-ignite.

"Think you can salvage her." Marble asked, anticipating Bingham's response.

"I'll look the old girl over this evening Sir. In all honesty I can't say for sure until then."

"I understand Corporal. Let me know the verdict will you?"

"Yes Sir."

It wasn't the first time Bingham witnessed the close affinity that sometimes existed between a pilot and his aeroplane. Not too dissimilar he thought, to a Cavalry Officer and his favourite mount.

One after another the remaining SE5a's appeared above Estrées-en-Chaussée and, after landing, taxied up to the front of 303 Squadron's hangars. Following their post-flight procedures, the pilots dismounted and assembled in small groups close to their aeroplanes.

Standing apart from the others, Marble watched a returning 35 Squadron FK8 park up at the end of the row of hangars. His eyes stung painfully from smoke and strain. Squinting, he blinked and tried to clear his vision sufficiently to discern the aeroplane's markings. Still wearing his fleece lined leather flying helmet and, with his hearing not yet recovered from the clamorous noise of his engine, he was unaware of Scott's approach.

"Are you all right Marble?" Scott's voice penetrated Marble's concentration. He slowly turned around.

"Good grief!" Scott took one look at Marble's red and blistered cheeks and winced in sympathy. "Get yourself over to the Medic's Hut and have those burns seen to."

The numbing effect of freezing slipstream on his face was beginning to wear off. The scorching pain was becoming unbearable, yet the fate of his comrades was foremost in his mind. "Did we lose anyone Skipper?"

"Poor old Babbington's gone west. The others seem all right though. Sammy's just landed. I'm off to check on him now."

Scott put his right hand on Marble's shoulder and held it there for a telling moment. "I'm sorry Marble, Blaxland and Hougham didn't make it either."

Marble experienced a sudden and unexpectedly powerful surge of emotion. Unable to contain outward expression, he briefly acknowledged Scott's report.

"I see. Well, that's it then I suppose."

His throat was closing over and it didn't do to show feelings of grief. Turning on his heels, he paced briskly away in the direction of the Red Cross station.

Half an hour later, still wearing his flying overalls, Marble departed the squadron medical hut. His face was red and painful, but he was fortunate the burns had only damaged the surface layer of skin. The Doctor had applied a layer of honey to his cheekbones, overlaid with sterile gauze. An unorthodox but effective treatment he had learned while treating Chinese non-combatant workers.

Stumping noisily and heavily into his billet, Marble sat on the end of his bed, removed his boots and began to carefully disrobe from his Sidcot Flying Suit No 5. It was a bulky, one-piece over-all consisting of three layers, a thin lining of lamb's wool, a layer of airproof silk, and an outside layer of light Burberry material. Having hung his flight-gear up adjacent to the door he poured water into his wash basin and, as he cleaned his hands, noticed a six inch long cut on his right forearm. How and when it had happened he had no idea. Dismissing it as being of no consequence he applied a generous lather of Lifebuoy carbolic soap to the wound.

The wall-mounted mirror was spotted with the patina of age. He looked at himself for a moment and saw his tired, bloodshot eyes staring back. On the table next to the basin lay the photograph he had shown to Blaxland over breakfast. Picking it up, Marble scanned the faces and tried to remember their names, but his brain was fogged.

Without warning he was overcome with dizziness, his heart was racing, his arms and legs shaking. He stepped back to his bed and laid down, trying to fight back waves of nausea. Overwhelmed with fatigue he stared at the bare wooden ceiling rafters, unaware of the passing time until, at one in the afternoon, a knock came on his billet door.

"Thought I'd better drop by and check on you." Scott announced cheerily. "Had a word with the M.O. and we both agreed you should take a few days off flying, at least until those burns have healed enough to remove the dressings."

Marble sat up and ran his fingers through his hair. "I feel terrible Skipper. Can't help thinking it's my fault Blaxland and Hougham went down. I should have been closer, defending them."

"We all did our very best, don't blame yourself." Scott consoled. "If its any consolation, I feel the same about Babbington." He made an effort to brighten up. "Look, come on over to the Mess and we'll have lunch. You're a sociable fellow Marble, mixing with the chaps will soon pick you up."

"If it's all the same Skipper, I'd rather be alone for a bit. Don't think I can face the lads from 35 Squadron at the moment. Truth is I'm ashamed to face them."

"Stuff and nonsense." Scott chided amicably. He was all to familiar with the effect of a traumatic event on a fighting man. Some reacted immediately, others weeks or months later. He understood the illogic and emotional behaviour that often resulted.

"Look here Marble. We've all been through things like this. Every one of us deals with it differently, what's important old boy, is that you go easy on yourself."

Despite his distracted thoughts, Marble smiled weakly in appreciation and extended his right arm. The two men shook hands.

"Come along then, let's get you tidied up a bit." Scott encouraged. "I heard they're serving roast beef for luncheon."

"Allright Skipper and by the way, thanks for getting that Hun off my back earlier."

"Don't mention it. I expect you to do the same for me someday. In the meantime, this evening we're back in our own Mess so you can buy me a drink!"

It was late in the evening of thirtieth January. One by one the officers of 303 Squadron departed the Mess for bed. An hour before the new day and only Scott and a couple of others were left. Wiping a layer of condensation and grime from a window Peters peered out at the row of dimly lit hangars.

"Your thoughts Frank?" Scott enquired.

"Oh, just thinking. Letting my mind wander a bit." Peters' attention turned to the starlit sky. He smiled to himself. "Scott, have you ever wondered what the future will bring?"

"Not until now." Scott rarely considered life beyond the next few days.

"Have you any ideas?"

277

"I suppose as the years go on, we'll get fewer and fewer." Scott smiled sadly. "It'll finish up with one aged and decrepit RFC pilot twitching in his seat alone at a reunion dinner."

Peters winced, the concept was just too awful to contemplate.

"Do you think folk will forget?"

Scott inhaled the slow burning tobacco through the ebonite stem of his Briarwood pipe. Savouring the richly flavoured smoke he contemplated his reply. "No, I believe what we've done in this war will become entrenched in the Nation's memory, like Trafalgar and Waterloo. Eventually we'll become a part of history. The stuff folk read in their history books."

Peters lit his final cigar of the evening and considered Scott's words. "A present sacrifice for future generations whose thanks we'll never hear."

As they prepared to leave for their billets an Orderly put his head around the Mess door. Peters was wanted on the telephone, it was Wing headquarters. Scott exchanged an ominous glace with Thompson whose face filled with foreboding. Five minutes later Peters returned, his expression conveyed the unwelcome news even before he spoke.

"Offensive Patrol, the St. Quentin Canal, tomorrow at dawn".

Printed in Great Britain
by Amazon